BATTLE LINES

Part 2 of
HYBRID: The Ethereal War

GREG BALLAN

Hadrosaur Productions, Mesilla Park, NM

Battle Lines
Hadrosaur Productions
First Edition, first printing, continuous printing on demand

First date of publication: October 2019

ISBN-10: 1-885093-88-8
ISBN-13: 978-1-885093-88-2

Battle Lines

Chapter 1: Dueling with the Devil(s)

The archdemon slammed his fist upon the stone table shattering the granite top, sending several ledgers and other documents airborne. Assorted papers fell like autumn leaves covering the tile floor.

"This is the second failure in as many attempts to eliminate the hybrid. How did the sage demon die? It reported that the seraphim guarding the hybrid child was killed and they were unprotected?"

"We don't know, Lord Molec," a nervous man whispered. "We only know that the sage was vaporized by a force that arrived through one of our own portals." The man scratched an unshaved cheek. "Could Lucifer have intervened?"

Molec leaned back in his large chair, fire spewing from his nostrils. "Doubtful. It had to be that accursed hybrid. Somehow he found a way to aid them. Erik Knight, you're becoming more of a pain in my backside than Lucifer or his minions." Molec glanced over at his stolen prize. The powerful demon shook its horned head, the effect of the Ruby Crucifix was penetrating his ectoplasmic shield. Soon the force field would decay under the incomprehensible energy's continuous bombardment and evaporate. At that point, no one save for God or the hybrid child would be able to handle the artifact. The holy relic was useful as a bargaining chip only if it could be hidden away, undetectable.

"We have several other mercenary forces coordinating an assault on Knight and his son. We're hoping that a force of several can overcome the Esper's innate power."

Molec stood, stretching powerful onyx limbs. He gathered a heavy black cloth and cautiously covered the ectoplasmic sphere. "I need to move this trinket to a more secure facility. I can no longer bear its presence."

The man watched Molec carefully wrap the stolen prize.

1

"That is the last Talithum fabric on this planet. Once it's gone we can no longer shield ourselves from the relic. The forces of Light will be able to lock on to its location and reclaim their prize."

Molec spun, demonic flame radiating off his body. "Then marshal enough forces to kill Knight and his puny offspring before that happens. The Ruby Cross is irrelevant if there's no light bearer to use it!"

The nervous human bowed. "As you command, My Lord Molec."

* * *

Dawkens' Gym. Milford, MA

Erik watched warily as EJ rolled on the mat with "Little" John. The powerful young man laughed as EJ attempted to execute a hip throw and leg sweep against his massive opponent. Erik smirked, trying to enjoy the moment but his mind kept racing back to the plane crash over France, the attack on his wife and son in their home and the ominous warning given by the mysterious cleric several days ago. The detective cursed himself for involving Charlie Gallagher, but immediately dismissed that as foolish. Gallagher had access to virtually all the information stored around the globe and was an asset he needed to utilize for answers. Erik admitted he wasn't crazy about the revelations contained within those answers but knowing the 'Why' helped rationalize the mind-numbing events of the past week and a half.

"You're brooding again."

He smiled, then half spun around to face a young woman. "Guilty as charged. I'm just trying to put all the pieces together in my head and no matter how much I try and distance myself from the emotional aspects, I can't compartmentalize it. This is just too damn big. I can't rationalize the facts and the data without drowning in a sea of emotional angst."

Alissa placed a comforting hand on his shoulder. Erik told her about the revelations Charlie Gallagher revealed earlier in the week. "I wish I had some comforting words for you, Erik. Truth be told I just don't know what to say. We both sensed something large was looming, but this is more than I ever imagined possible. How does one deal with a deity and the like?"

The moody detective frowned. "Poorly."

Alissa chuckled. "How is Shanda handling all this? I can't imagine her even considering herself the new 'Mary' in this modern holy trinity."

"She's a wreck. She texts and calls me ten times a day to make sure EJ is safe. She doesn't want him at the store because she's afraid some dark force will whisk in and snatch him up in front of her, similar to what happened at the house." Erik rubbed the stubble on his upper lip. "She wants to be with her child but she's afraid she can't protect him from the things that want to harm him. She feels inadequate as a mother and it's eating away at her piece by piece." Erik ran a hand through his long ebony locks. "And it's not doing much for me either." Erik looked directly at her, fear tinged his ice blue eyes. "I don't know if I can protect him either. I'm not afraid of anything physical or even alien, but metaphysical and theological ..." Erik bit his lower lip, both hands folded under his chin. "That may be out of my league."

"You beat the wraith, Erik. From what little I've read about demonic entities, that creature is one of the more powerful. If you start doubting yourself, then you've already lost."

"I know, I know. It's almost too much right now, I'll get my hands around it. I have to. There really isn't any other choice." Erik's fists clinched and his jaw set. "Nothing is taking my son; not while I draw breath. That much I know for sure."

Alissa nodded. "Better. I just got off the phone with Mr. Denton. He's at your house checking on the repairs."

Erik's eyebrow raised. "Martin's back from Vatican City?"

"Yes, he just arrived and hoped you were home. He'll be here in a few minutes. I can order some lunch and have it sent to your office if you two need to catch up."

Erik nodded. "Yeah, that'd be perfect. We have a lot to talk about." Erik's phone beeped. "That's Shanda, checking in again."

"Why don't you ask Jeanine at the front desk if she'll scoot down to Shanda's store and watch things for a while? That way Shanda can spend a few hours a day up here with EJ under your watchful eye. She'll feel better seeing him and I'm sure EJ misses his mother."

Erik shook his head. "That's absolutely brilliant! Jeanine ran a huge retail store before she retired. I'm sure she wouldn't mind. I'll run it by Shanda right now.

* * *

Erik was wading through a sea of papers when the knock on his office door startled him.

"Erik, thank God you're in one piece." Martin Denton strode through the door.

Erik stood to offer his friend his hand. Denton pushed the hand aside and embraced the detective.

Erik felt the same wave of emotion he experienced at St. Martha's Chapel as he patted his friend on the back. "Martin, it's damn good to see you. Thanks for calling in the cavalry when my plane went down."

Both men sat and Erik described the lethal attack on the DC3 and the attack that occurred simultaneously upon Shanda and EJ. The normally stalwart counselor's body shivered as Erik described his son's transformation into a small, yet lethal Esper hybrid.

"EJ vaporized the demonic entity along with the back half of our house and the tops of two large pine trees." Erik leaned forward. "I found a fair-sized impression in the yard, close to the trees, from what I can only assume was a body. There was a battle out in the yard, from what Shanda told me they heard. I'm sure some force of Light tried to intervene and was killed. I can only assume that the fallen angel— or whatever type of being—was retrieved once EJ disposed of the dark entity."

Denton rubbed his chin contemplating the incredible tale. "I get a sense of urgency. Things are starting to accelerate. I don't believe in coincidence, Erik. This was a preemptive strike designed to eradicate you before you could come to terms with what's going on around us. Molec wanted to catch you off guard and strike a fatal blow in an attempt to avoid an all-out confrontation. I get the sense this demonic entity doesn't want you involved in the upcoming showdown and sees you as a threat to its overall plan."

Erik sighed as he considered the final tidbit. "Martin there's more."

Denton raised an eyebrow. "Please tell me it's not worse than we already know."

Erik rolled his eyes. "Do you remember Charlie Gallagher?"

"Yeah, he's a retired spook who runs a computer company and makes money selling data from a supercomputer in a reinforced bunker three floors below his business."

Erik's eyes bulged as his head tilted, impressed with his friend's knowledge. Denton smirked. "We know about Gallagher's data mining but if we put the screw to him, he'd retaliate in ways that would bring to light some uncomfortable information. He's got some sort of logic bomb set to go off if he's pushed too far. The firm lets him play 'demigod of data' in his little sand box undisturbed and in return he doesn't poke his nose where we don't want him to. It's kind of a forced détente."

"I'm impressed, Counselor. Gallagher introduced me to an old cleric scholar and our friends in Vatican City have it wrong. This isn't all about me ... it's about EJ. The chosen Light Bearer is the son of the 'Son of Adam and the stars'. This is about my son. Molec and Lucifer want to eliminate him. I'm merely an impediment, an obstacle to be overcome, a paternal bodyguard so to speak."

Martin's jaw dropped.

"These ghouls aren't coming for me. They're coming for my son. They want him dead." A tear rolled down Erik's cheek. "My little boy, Martin. They want to kill my little boy." A sob escaped the detective and he clenched his fists choking down the emotion. "Shanda is afraid to be alone with EJ. She's afraid of being attacked again and not being able to protect her son. This is tearing her apart and it's not doing me any good. I can't bring EJ everywhere with me and we certainly can't hide for the rest of our lives."

Denton leaned forward. "Maybe you need to play your part in this war and help end it. You end the war, you end the threat against your son."

"I've thought about that too. The events of the past several

days have convinced me I don't have much of a choice, but
how do I fight a war with a bunch of evil creepy crawlies waiting to snuff my child's life out like a candle? There has to be
some middle ground, some way out of this." Erik leaned back
in his chair noisily cracking his knuckles. "I'm in the middle
of this shit, Counselor, and when you're in the middle of the
forest all you see is the trees with no way out. I need to get to
higher ground in order to find a way clear of this mess."

Martin shook his head solemnly. "Erik, my friend, sometimes the forest is too deep and there's just no way out. Sometimes you need help navigating through the thickets. Sometimes there's just no higher ground."

"What would you have me do? Surrender my child to the
church or to the devil!" Erik snapped.

"No, Erik, never! You know me better than that. I've got
your back no matter what."

Erik sighed, frustrated. "I'm sorry, Martin. You didn't deserve that tirade." He looked toward his friend. "Tell me, what
would you do? Would you hide? Would you fight? Would you
run?"

Denton took a deep breath. "There's a saying, 'The enemy
of my enemy is my friend.' Right now you could use some
friends in high places." Denton looked up at the ceiling. "I'm
not saying trust implicitly, but having allies to watch your back
isn't a bad thing right now."

Erik frowned. "Yeah, I'm inclined to agree with you. I still
don't trust them but at this point I need more people on my
side." Erik paused looking slightly uncertain. "I'm sorry, Martin. I should have asked this sooner, but..." He hesitated. "The
services for William ... did they take care of him?"

Denton smiled. "It was a beautiful service, Erik, and thank
you for asking. My son has a wonderful final resting place."

Erik nodded. "I'm glad for that. William deserved that and
more."

Denton closed his eyes and bowed his head. After a moment he looked up and sniffed. "Were you able to dig up anything on Lazarus?"

Erik shook his head. "No. Honestly, I've been wrapped up
with the whole Armageddon's Son revelation. Father Lazarus

fell off my radar screen for a while."

"I can't imagine what you're going through. But please know you're not alone. I'll help you any way I can and I know the firm has its hand in the higher conflict. I'm sure they're watching and can deploy assets if needed." Denton sighed. "At least they're fixing up your house."

Erik chuckled. "Yeah. Shanda is grateful for that. Please tell the firm I'm extremely thankful. The crew they have is top notch and they're even enduring Shanda's pestering with good humor."

Erik paused, his head tilted and eyes began to burn an eerie lightning blue. "Something's wrong, very wrong!" Erik shot out of his chair and sprinted down the narrow hallway leading to the large open dojo with Denton on his tail.

Erik's large friend, Little John, was sprawled on the mat, unconscious, blood flowing from his nose and mouth. Another instructor was on the floor, holding her ribs in agony. A tall man in a large leather coat had EJ cornered and reached for the frightened child. Alyssa grasped a 'wall hanger' decorative katana. She held the weapon overhead like a battle axe preparing to attack the stranger's exposed flank. Erik motioned her back. The fearless woman retreated but kept the weapon in a firm grip.

"Get away from him!" The enraged father roared, his voice echoing off every surface.

The man turned, distracted. EJ ran to his father, ducking under the stranger's desperate attempt to grab him, with surprising speed and agility. Erik heard the man hiss and mutter a vile curse. Then he sensed it, as with the Nosferatu—the lack of humanity and the terrifying presence of evil. The hybrid moved with desperate speed, covering the distance separating him from his son. Erik scooped up EJ and retreated several steps from the intruder. He could feel the child trembling.

"It's okay, buddy. Daddy's got you."

Erik's Esper senses shrieked danger. The stranger took a step forward and looked directly at him. Erik could feel the burning intensity as the being probed and studied him. The hybrid focused his will, shielding his mind, forcing the intruder out.

"You are Erik Knight, Esper Warrior and Champion of

Light." The being's remark was more of a statement than a question.

As the stranger spoke, he attempted to close the distance separating him from the father and son. The steps were small and barely noticeable but Erik took one step back and pivoted his body using his powerful arms to shield his son. Erik knelt slowly, never taking his eyes off the charcoal black eyes that threatened to burn through him with inhuman intensity. "EJ, you go back with Alissa and Mr. Denton. Daddy and this man have some business to discuss."

"Daddy, he's bad!" EJ whispered, terrified.

"I know son. You let Daddy worry about it." Erik kissed EJ's forehead and placed the child down, his body coiled like a serpent ready to strike if the stranger moved closer. Erik tussled his son's hair, gently prodding him back to the relative safety behind him. "Alissa, take EJ to my office. Counselor," Erik's tone was steel hard as his eyes never left the demonic stranger, "call 911 and get an ambulance for John and Robin. Tell them to send the police too. Tell them we have an unwelcome guest."

"Your police cannot detain me, human. I see you've already ascertained I, like you, am not tethered to this world." The being took a step closer, watching as Alissa led EJ away. He took another step forward.

Erik also advanced, blocking his path and line of sight.

"I've come for the child. Give him to me and you'll be allowed to live … for a while at least. Lucifer will grant you wealth, power and enough women to last you well into your old age. All you have to do is give up your claim to the child and stay out of ethereal matters." The being of darkness slowly slid off the cape-like leather jacket and tossed it on a nearby chair and slowly approached, arms raised slightly.

The being was thin, almost gaunt with pale, flesh. Black veins ran beneath the ivory skin, pulsing rapidly.

Erik took a step back and unzipped his jacket. "I'm afraid I'll have to decline Lucifer's generous offer. I'm a one woman man and wealth doesn't really appeal to me nor does the kind of power you offer." Erik pointed to the door. "Leave, now. You made your offer and I've refused." He tossed his jacket behind him preparing for what he knew would come next. "The boy is my son, and you ethereal assholes can't have him." Erik gestured toward the exit. "Get out of here before you see the less pleasant side of me."

"Arrogant fool! Humans don't give orders or threaten Bartholomew, herald of darkness!" The demon charged forward with lightning speed. Anticipating the charge, Erik used a quick Aikido motion deflecting the demon while adding the force of his own fist. Bartholomew's momentum slammed him through the wall separating the dojo from the rest of the gym. Debris cascaded into the gym area and the demon arose enraged. His eyes burned with an inhuman hate.

"You dare strike me!" A bony hand extended a finger, firing a searing beam of orange and red flame.

Coiled muscle exploded as the hybrid leapt aside. Burning pain scalded his mind as the flesh on his right shoulder charred and the hair on the side of his head burnt away. Erik came up from his defensive roll, his scalp smoking and eyes burning blue suns. Blue fire bathed the hybrid's arms. He launched twin plasma orbs at the enraged demon. The bioorganic energy slammed into milk-white demonic flesh, filling the air with a stink of burning sulfur and brimstone.

Erik charged, crashing into the demon and forcing him backward. The titanic force carried both combatants deeper into the large, open gym area. Patrons shrieked with fear and panic as the two warring beings collided with a large universal weight machine. The demon's hand sprung hideous claws and he raked them across Erik's chest, shredding his t-shirt, cleaving deep gouges into his flesh.

Erik grabbed the clawed hand in a forearm lock and forced the top of the demon's hand back with his own powerful fingers, driving the four-inch claws through Bartholomew's chest impaling the enraged demon. Erik quickly followed with an elbow strike. The blow crackled like thunder. The blow's force sent the stunned demon fifteen feet across the gym where he toppled end over end until he smashed into a weight tree.

The demon cursed in pain as he pried his own claws from his body. Four rivers of greenish yellow ichor hemorrhaged from the puncture wounds. Enraged, he picked up the 600-pound weight tree and hurled the massive object toward his opponent like a speeding missile.

Erik knew he could avoid the object but the people behind him weren't as fast or as strong. He stepped into object's path and deflected it with a Shotokan Karate shuto block. The heavy mass smashed through several display mirrors but the terrified patrons were safe. The stacked steel plates clanged as they spilled onto the hard floor. The metal framework had embedded itself in the wood, sheetrock, and plaster wall.

That nearly broke my freaking arm! Erik absently rubbed his bruised forearm, his eyes burning onto the demon that was once again preparing for battle.

The demon's voice hissed angrily. Erik's stomach churned as the demonic tenor vibrated off every surface in the gym. "I will kill you for this. Your wretched flesh will burn in the hottest pit of Hell. Give me the child and you have a chance to live or else burn for eternity in a sea of Hellfire."

Bartholomew grabbed a 45-pound plate and flung the disc toward Erik. The detective snatched the speeding object from the air and, with a burst of anger-fueled superhuman strength, bent the plate in half and tossed it on the ground. "You'll need more than words or metal Frisbees!"

The demon moved quickly, gathering up lighter plates that had had fallen on the floor and hurled them toward his nemesis with lethal precision. The hybrid grabbed an Olympic weight bar as a makeshift staff deflecting the speeding discs. Crashing metal resonated as Bartholomew hurled several more plates.

Erik spun the bar rapidly, the air whistling as the heavy bar deflected each speeding projectile. The sound of deflected plates smashing into equipment was deafening. *We're going to destroy this place and kill someone in the process if we keep this up.* Erik took two steps forward and hurled the bar like a javelin towards the demon. Bartholomew wasn't prepared for the attack and the speeding missile struck him square in his face, driving the demon back several yards. The impact made a sickening dull thud as the metal bar shattered bone and sinew. The demon dropped to the floor in a pool of shattered teeth and drool. Erik approached the creature cautiously. He could hear gym members talking behind him as curiosity overcame their fear.

"Get back! There's still danger..."

The demon's foot slammed into Erik's face careening him backwards several feet. His back slammed into a large universal machine. The machine's metal frame buckled. Erik felt a rib crack and tasted blood as the red fluid filled his mouth and nose. The demon was up and upon him before he could react. Blow after blow pummeled Erik's face and body. He had no time to erect any type of defensive posture. All he could do was endure the endless sea of concussive force. Bartholomew mocked him as each blow landed. From within, his alter ego arose. The Esper Warrior was taking hold. His body strengthened and he allowed the chemical reaction to course through his bloodstream and tissues. Erik reached up and caught the demon's fist, mildly aware that it was colored red with his blood.

Bartholomew swung his other claw in a roundhouse motion in an attempt to slit Erik's throat. The hybrid raised his other hand and deflected the strike with superhuman force. The snapping of demonic bone echoed throughout the gym. Neural impulses fired and his body began to heal. The gaping tears in his flesh throbbed as they knitted together on their own and the cartilage in his nose burned as it refused. The combatants were frozen, staring at each other with looks of undisguised contempt. Erik increased his grip on the demon's captured fist, crushing the encapsulated fingers as he willed his body even stronger, something he hadn't done in years.

The demon flinched in agony as the bones in his hand were crushed to powder.

"You'll never get my son! NEVER!" The hybrid launched a solid right cross knocking the stunned demon backward. Erik grabbed the long bar he'd used earlier and hefted it like a club. Enraged, he swung the bar like a baseball bat slamming the end against the demon's shoulder. Bartholomew's arm and shoulder shattered under the impact and the demon went sprawling across the gym floor. Erik tossed the bar aside and closed the distance. He kicked the demon, hard, in the torso, propelling him like a living football across the gym. The demon landed, bounced several times, then finally stopped in a sprawling heap by the large picture window at the front of the gym. Patrons scattered in abject fear as Erik approached his fallen adversary.

The demon struggled to stand, his jaw shattered. Bartholomew's left arm dangled, hanging at an awful angle indicating the limb had separated from the shoulder. Its right arm began to glow a hideous orange/red. Erik could see the radiant heat waves. The demon was going to launch another volley of fire! He couldn't use his own energy. Too many people had gathered in terror behind the demon. The detective charged as the demon fired. He dove and rolled to his right side, feeling the blistering heat graze his arm. Erik came out of his roll and leapt into the air executing a flying kick into the demon's midsection. The force carried the demon back, smashing it through the plate glass window out into the parking lot. Erik leapt through the window, battle-ready. Bartholomew was already gone, leaving behind a puddle of chartreuse ichor and the eerie stink of brimstone.

Chapter 2: Blood of the Innocent

Erik was in a post-combat haze. Two ambulances departed for Milford Whitinsville Hospital, each one carrying a wounded instructor. The detective's shirt was covered in his own blood and the blood of the young woman mercilessly beaten by Bartholomew. His large friend, Jeff, had a broken nose, a fractured cheek, and three fractured ribs. His other instructor, Robin, didn't fare as well; the demon had crushed her ribcage on the right side, puncturing her lung. She coughed up fountains of blood as Erik did his best to tend to her wounds. The detective wished he had the power to heal others as easily as his enhanced body could heal itself. All he could do was keep the terrified girl calm and prevent her from going into shock. Both Robin and Jeff described their attacker as having beyond-human strength and speed.

Erik studied the open gym area. The brief battle had decimated the facility. A dozen weight plates and a large stacking tree were half-embedded in the back and side wall. The wall separating the dojo from the fitness area had a hole large enough to drive a car through and two expensive universal weight machines were damaged. The gym's twenty-foot picture window had shattered into tiny fragments. The bar Erik had used to deflect the speeding projectiles was not only bent and deformed, but covered in dried green demon blood as well.

The stares of those who witnessed the battle weighed on Erik as they gaped at him in awe and fear. He wondered what the witnesses had told the police and what kind of interrogation he'd be in for when the cops finally came around to question him.

"Does the booboo hurt?" EJ's tiny fingers traced the outline of a large bruise on his father's right cheek.

Erik gently patted his son's head. "Nah, it's not so bad."

EJ smiled. "You didn't duck, Daddy."

Erik still studied the wreckage. He looked down at his son and blinked as the child's innocent remark finally registered. He laughed. "You're right. Daddy forgot to duck."

"But the scary man is gone?" EJ whispered.

Erik gently held the child close in a protective embrace. "Yes, he's gone. Daddy made sure he won't come back."

Martin cleared his throat. "Erik, I hate to disturb you, but the police need a statement. I've given them as much information as I can and I've already reached out to the firm. They'll have a crew here in an hour to start the repair work."

Erik looked up from his son's loving gaze. Martin stood next to a portly police officer. Alissa surveyed the wreckage, jaw hanging open and eyes widening.

Her jaw snapped shut and she swallowed. "I can take EJ into the back office while you deal with this..." she glanced over her shoulder "...situation."

The embattled father turned his back, partially shielding his son from view. Erik closed his eyes and held out this hand. A sound like a sharp whistle broke the eerie silence as the sentient staff settled into his grip seemingly appearing from nowhere. Erik looked at the staff, his eyes burning. "Protect my son!"

The weapon flowed like a living liquid metal wrapping around EJ's forearm. It purred a type of alien lullaby and EJ began humming along with the mysterious melody.

Alissa approached and Erik handed the child to her. She gently placed the child on the ground. Tears formed in Erik's eyes.

She touched his shoulder. "I won't let him out of my sight Erik, I promise. Deal with this and I'll take care of EJ and the other students out back."

Erik nodded. "He came for my son, Alissa, my baby boy. I was hoping, praying Charlie and his odd friend were wrong, but they weren't. The so-called demonic powers-that-be painted a bull's-eye on my child." Erik's eyes began to burn and his body began to radiate energy. "I really want to smash something right now." Rage leant an edge to his otherwise soft voice.

Alissa poked him. "Keep that rage in check, getting angry and losing your temper won't help us right now. You have every right to be scared and pissed off but bury it. There's too many prying eyes that have seen enough already." She pointed down toward EJ. The boy stared off at the walls, oblivious to their conversation. "Your son, included."

Erik closed his eyes for a brief moment and when he opened them, the burning blue fire was gone "Thanks, Alissa." He touched her shoulder. "You were willing to throw down with that monstrosity to save my son. Thank you seems pathetically pale for such action."

"We're family. You fight to protect family no matter what." Alyssa half smiled. "I'll let you and Mr. Denton deal with this mess. I'll deal with the mess in the dojo. A few students are in shock and I'll call Robin's husband and try to explain how his wife got hurt."

"Thanks again." Erik looked at his son. "Why don't you go with Auntie Alissa and see how the other students are doing? I bet they're all worried about you." EJ smiled and followed her, gently reaching up and taking her hand. Erik gestured toward the front counter where the three men could have some degree of privacy.

"We checked the entire parking lot, nearby dumpsters, and we have two officers checking parked cars, Mr. Knight. We haven't found anybody. Did you see anything to indicate what direction our suspect fled?"

Erik shook his head. "No, when I stepped through the window, he was already gone."

The officer held up a plastic evidence bag full of shattered teeth and a section of jawbone. "I don't know how far he's going to get. You certainly got a good piece of him. You literally broke his jaw off, Mr. Knight."

Erik rubbed the large bruise on his cheek and his ribcage twinged along with the four lacerations across his chest. He pointed toward the lacerations and the tears in his shirt. "I didn't exactly walk away unscathed either."

The cop frowned. "Well there's more than enough corroborating witnesses but I still would like to get some kind of rational explanation for that." He pointed toward the large weight tree sticking out of the gym wall and pointed toward the greenish yellow ichor staining the gym floor. "And perhaps that

45-pound plate that's bent in half." The officer gestured toward the gym patrons gaping awestruck at Erik. "They claim you bent the plate with your bare hands and you used a heavy metal bar like a Wiffle bat to knock our suspect around like a Nerf ball." The cop looked at Erik. "Something batshit crazy occurred here, and after the magic show you just put on with that silver stick—yeah I saw it despite you turning your back—it gives the wild tales I just heard even more credibility. All the cops have heard the stories about the Hopedale Mountain Incident and we know all the crazy stories about your part in the whole sordid affair ... despite all the efforts to hush up what happened. All the local cops know the story and the body count. What's going on Mr. Knight? Are we facing another ugly situation?"

Martin interceded. "There are some things, officer, which will have to remain a mystery at this point."

The cop frowned. "Are you his lawyer? I'm not trying to arrest him. I just have to file a report and Mr. Knight did, technically, get assaulted as did two of his staff." The officer surveyed the damage. "There's shattered mirrors, holes in walls and banged up heavy steel plates sticking out of walls, not to mention broken teeth, green slime plus blood and bone fragments." The officer looked back at Erik. "I have to do my job, Mr. Knight, and part of my job is getting the facts so we can investigate this assault. Also if there's something nasty going on, I'd like to keep the damage and the body count down to a minimum or, even better, have zero innocent causalities."

Erik sighed. "I know. I wish I had more to tell you. This guy came into my dojo looking for trouble. He injured two of my staff and tried to do the same to me. He was very skilled and very strong. I'm sure you already have a good enough physical description but I can write down his height, physical features and what he was wearing. In fact, his jacket should still be in the dojo. He took it off before the fight."

"I went through the jacket. There's no wallet, no ID, no cash or even a trace of lint in the damn pockets," Denton mumbled, growing annoyed at having to deal with a local cop.

The officer nodded, ignoring the counselor's glare. "Write out as much as you can and we'll see what we can drag up." The two other officers walked in, looked over at the portly cop, and shook their heads. "Looks like our violent friend made a clean break. We'll check the local ER." The cop held up the bag containing teeth and a partial jawbone. "It's the best place to start looking for a lead, unless you have more insight to offer."

Erik shook his head as he busily wrote on a piece of scrap paper. He handed the paper to the officer. "Here's the best I can do for you. I wish we had more but like I said, he came in here looking for trouble."

The cop frowned. "Well it looks like he found it in spades. I'll let you know if we find anything. Though I don't know how in the hell anyone walks away from the kind of beating you dished out." The cop leaned in and whispered, "I know something way beyond normal happened here, and I honestly don't know what we can do about it. If you can please try and keep these people safe and out of harm's way, I'll do what I can to find some kind of lead on this mystery man for you."

Erik shrugged. "That's always my objective. I don't want anybody getting hurt here and I'd greatly appreciate the follow up."

Erik and Martin watched the police leave. "He knows we're full of shit."

Denton grimaced. "Oh hell yeah, we were pitiful. Especially since several patrons painted you as some glorified superhuman juggernaut and we neglected to mention the being's name or why he came. Both things we know and facts I'm sure some of the witnesses inside your dojo told him."

Erik held out his hands. "What good would telling him the truth do? They'll never find Bartholomew. I can only assume he just disappeared into thin air and they certainly can't put EJ into protective custody. It's best they just stay out of this."

Denton nodded. "I agree, but what are you going to do? What's your battle plan?"

Erik sighed, pondering how to answer before looking over at his friend. "Martin, I wish the hell I had one right now."

Martin shook his head. "This wasn't Molec. It was Lucifer. The other force of darkness just played its first hand in this poker game. Evil must be in a panic at this point. I'd guess Molec currently has the upper hand in the role as the number one evil entity. It's certainly shaken things up more than Lucifer has.

The Devil's reign could be coming to an end if either Molec or the forces of Light are victorious." Denton frowned, exhaling heavily. He absently scratched the back of his head and looked over at his friend. "How does one fight a three-way war with beings that can disappear in a puff of smoke?"

The embattled detective tried to shake off the numbness threatening to overwhelm him. "I don't know, Martin. I have to find a way to protect my son not only from Molec, but from Lucifer's army as well."

Erik's cell phone chimed, breaking the somber mood. He glanced down. "Oh God, what do I tell Shanda? She must have sensed the trouble through our link."

Martin placed a gentle hand on Erik's shoulder. "You tell your wife the truth; she needs to know what's going on. Besides, you don't think EJ won't spill the beans tonight?"

Erik nodded. "I think my head's gonna explode." He turned away bringing the phone up to his ear.

* * *

The Demonic Netherworld

The thin, pale demon slowly traced the outline of its reformed jaw with slender bone-white fingertips. Bartholomew looked at his new jaw bone and teeth in a small mirror as his body continued to bathe in a boiling pool of purple liquid.

"Erik Knight is much stronger than I was led to believe! No one told me he could increase his strength at will or throw plasmatic fireballs! That accursed half-ape, half-alien could have killed me!"

YOU'RE WHINING AGAIN! A disembodied voice echoed throughout the dark chamber. NO ONE TOLD YOU TO PICK A FIGHT WITH THE HYBRID. THAT WAS YOUR OWN ARROGANCE. THE IMMORTALITY POOL HAS RESTORED YOU AND HEALED YOUR WOUNDS. YOU ARE NO WORSE FROM YOUR ENCOUNTER. The voice dropped an octave. YOU WERE MERELY TO STUDY AND OBSERVE NOT ENGAGE IN COMBAT.

Bartholomew cringed. "Knight's human sycophants interfered, the large one dare lay a hand upon me. No simian upstart may do so. I was close to the boy and saw an opportunity for us to gain the upper hand. If we could have taken him at that point, our victory would have been all but assured. I tried to capitalize upon a moment and make the best of the situation at hand." The pale demon hesitated sensing his employer's annoyance. "However, I had the opportunity to study and probe the child. He is indeed the one of prophecy. The child is destined to bear the holy artifact. The forces of Light have allowed the sacred birth to occur."

I HAVE BEEN INFORMED THAT MOLEC HAS PUT OUT A SOUL CONTRACT ON THE CHILD. I HAVE ALSO PLACED A BOUNTY ON THE CHILD WITH A HIGHER PRICE TAG. BUT THE CHILD IS WORTH MORE ALIVE AS A BARGAINING CHIP FOR RANSOM THAN A CORPSE. THAT IDIOTIC MINION WILL STIR UP A BLOODBATH IF THE CHILD IS KILLED, SENDING THE CONTEST FOR THIS WORLD INTO A FULL BLOWN ETHEREAL WAR! IN SUCH A WAR THERE ARE NO WINNERS. WE MUST GET THE CHILD FIRST! HUNDREDS OF MY SERVANTS ON EARTH, HUMAN AND DEMON, WILL LINE UP TO COLLECT SUCH A PRIZE. ONE OF MY SERVANTS SHOULD BE ABLE TO ABDUCT THE TINY HUMAN AND BRING HIM TO ME BEFORE MOLEC'S FORCES CAN KILL BOTH FATHER AND CHILD. THE THEFT OF THE CROSS HAS ESCALATED A WAR WE WERE WINNING. EARTH, AS A PRIZE, MAY BE ALL BUT LOST DUE TO MOLEC'S INTERFERENCE. THE CURSED UPSTART FORCED LIGHT'S HAND WITH HIS INCESSANT INTERFERENCE AND SCHEMING. NOW MY PLANS FOR EARTH ARE IN JEOPARDY, BARTHOLOMEW. I WANT THAT DEMON'S HEAD ON A PIKE AND I WANT EARTH AS MY RIGHTFUL PRIZE. I WAS WINNING AND I LIKED IT. I WILL WIN IN THE END.

Bartholomew tilted his head and rubbed his freshly formed jaw line. "If they can circumvent the child's father. I have done more research on the hybrid. In full warrior mode he has no equal in elemental and physical power. He is the perfect guardian. He also possesses an ethereal staff formed halfway across the galaxy, a weapon that's already served to vaporize two powerful demonic forces. Your soul bounty, along with Molec's may go uncollected."

The disembodied voice hissed mildly in annoyance. Bartholomew winced momentarily wondering if he'd crossed a line with his master.

ERIK KNIGHT CANNOT SINGLE-HANDEDLY STOP A HOARDE OF DEMONS ALL BENT ON ONE OBJECTIVE. THE LAW OF NUMBERS WORKS IN OUR FAVOR. WE MAY LOSE DOZENS, OR MORE SOLDIERS, BUT IT TAKES JUST ONE TO MAKE A KILL. THE ODDS ARE STACKED AGAINST KNIGHT AND HIS SON. IT'S JUST A MATTER OF TIME. THE HYBRID WILL BE WORN DOWN LIKE A STONE IN A RE-LENTLESS ONSLAUGHT OF WATER. EVENTUALLY THE STONE DISSOLVES. KNIGHT'S RESOLVE WILL WEAKEN AND FADE OVER TIME AS MORE AND MORE BATTLES OCCUR. HE WILL CRACK. EVEN THE HARDEST DIAMOND HAS WEAK POINTS THAT CAN BE EXPLOITED. TIME AND A CONSTANT BARRAGE WILL FRACTURE THE HYBRID'S RESOLVE. AND WHEN HE HAS BECOME DISILLUSIONED AND EXHAUSTED, HE WILL FAIL AND THE CHILD WILL BE TAKEN AND EARTH WILL BE MINE.

"Or both will be killed. Either way, it will be my fondest wish to be there when Erik Knight takes that fall. I want to bury my claws through his Human//Esper heart and roast it on a barbeque spit."

THE CHILD WILL BE MINE! NOW, AS FOR YOUR IN-DEPENDENT THINKING...

A black wisp of smoke surrounded the pale demon, crushing him. Bartholomew struggled, but the wispy tendrils held him in check, slowly squeezing the demonic life from his body. The demon felt its body go numb and surrendered to the oncoming black.

Bartholomew's eyes fluttered. He was still immersed in the regenerative pool. The mystical fluid resurrected his mangled body. His skin, however, still had the scars from the tentacles that had crushed the life from him.

THE NEXT TIME, THERE WILL BE NO POOL TO RE-TURN YOU TO THE LIVING. NEVER FORGET YOU SERVE ME AND YOU FOLLOW MY ORDERS. I DON'T NEED YOU ACTING ON YOUR ON VOALITION, DO WE UNDERSTAND

EACH OTHER, BARTHOLOMEW? A fiery demonic face materialized inches above the hapless being.

The demon raised its pale hands in supplication. "Yes, yes we do." The powerful presence faded, leaving the gaunt demon alone to ponder its second chance. "Two death beatings in under a day. I may not survive a third." He leaned back, allowing his body to absorb more of the purple fluid's life-giving sustenance.

* * *

Molec's Lair

Molec closed the heavy vault door. The archdemon checked on its prize periodically noting the protective black fabric was withering away bit by bit and the ectoplasmic container holding the Ruby Crucifix would survive no more than another week before it simply vanished under the constant bombardment of holy ethereal energy.

"The strongest known containment vessel in the universe and it cannot withstand this relic." Molec sealed the heavy door knowing that the reinforced metal alloys of the vault were like paper when it came to containing the holy relic. "As the humans would say, I've got a hot potato in my hands." Molec went back to his palatial office and found an underling anxiously awaiting him.

"Sir, there's been a development."

Molec walked behind his large desk and poured a glass of brandy. His acolyte fidgeted nervously while the archdemon sat in his large chair and took a deep sip from his glass. "What's going on, Bendu?"

"One of Lucifer's soldiers attacked Erik Knight. Knight's place of employment is in shambles. The reports we've intercepted claim a demon attempted to abduct Knight's child." Bendu paused as he flipped the page of his document. "Our agent says it was Bartholomew, and the demon was badly beaten. Police gathered jaw bone, teeth and..." Bendu looked back up, "...blood ... demon blood. It would appear Bartholomew was beaten quite soundly."

Molec laughed, spewing flame from his mouth and nose.

Bendu stepped back to avoid being burned as his master continued a deep fit of laughter. "That pompous, pale toothpick finally picked a fight he couldn't win. That one has always been overconfident just like his boss. Despite my hatred for Knight and what he represents I'll gladly give him a point for knocking Bartholomew down a few pegs." Molec turned to face a large chess board adorned with large, intricate carved dark metallic and polished marble pieces. He carefully moved several dark chess pieces toward the opposing king carved from ivory-white marble. Molec absently moved several more dark pawns around the ivory king and with a swift hand motion knocked the king over. "It's a matter of time and numbers, Mr. Bendu, just a matter of time," Molec slid more pieces on top of the fallen king, "and numbers."

Mr. Bendu nodded and continued his report. "We've also intercepted some buzz through the ethereal networks; Lucifer has also offered a soul bounty on EJ Knight. We believe his forces are gathering for an all-out assault on the hybrid warrior."

Molec's onyx-black cheeks took on a red tinge. A sea of flame erupted from his nostrils incinerating several papers and folders on his desk. "Lucifer will ransom the child for leverage, I want the child dead! Increase my reward and offer the child's weight in gold credit at the Soul Market. I don't want that prick beating me out of this opportunity. EJ Knight needs to be a corpse so there can be no second coming on this planet!"

Bendu nodded nervously. "I will relay your orders and let you know when the child has been eliminated. From what I have been told, Lucifer has no intentions of mere kidnapping."

Molec frowned. "I'm not concerned with Lucifer's plans, only my own. I want him eliminated now Mr. Bendu, before Knight can make allegiances or gather his defenses. Right now, the child is most vulnerable with only the father to protect him. Light will learn of the soul bounty and scramble forces to protect the boy."

* * *

Dawkens' Gym. Milford, MA

Erik filled out the final insurance paperwork and faxed the

forms to the firm's insurance company. Martin had placed yet another call describing the incidents at the gym. Three contractors arrived within two hours after the incident and began making estimates for the extensive repair work. The embattled detective was able to use his own sheer power to straighten the heavy metal frames of the fitness equipment and bar. Erik smirked, recalling how Counselor Denton's face paled as he repaired the savage bend in the heavy 45-pound plate. Erik flexed his arm. The large powerful bicep and triceps muscles tensed steel hard and a jolt of power rippled through his body. He looked over at EJ. The boy was in a deep sleep, clutching his stuffed bear. His son was the same, endowed with titanic power. He knew this at the moment he'd seen his son at Area 51, a silver infant with fiery blue eyes. The enraged father had torn through an alien armada and pummeled the entire bedrock protective shell at Groom Lake and tore through a ten-ton titanium alloy door to rescue Shanda and his son from Colonel Ross. Erik thought that was his last battle and nothing could ever come close to such a wild, terrifying adventure. He relaxed his arm and sighed. He couldn't have been more wrong. The weary father stared at the clock on his desk. It displayed 10:15pm.

"Shit! How the hell did it get so late?" He stuffed several papers into his top desk drawer and locked it, then gathered his keys and approached his sleeping son. Erik grabbed a nearby blanket and gently covered the child. "You've had a big day, little man. Let's get you home and tucked into a nice warm bed." He gently lifted the sleeping child and carried him.

He shut down all the lights and quietly approached the door. The workers had erected a large piece of plexiglass as a temporary replacement for the shattered window. Several sections of drywall were neatly stacked in a corner with two large pails of wall plaster. The workers had cut away all the damage and assured him the new wall board would be in place before the end of the following business day. Erik absently noted that the firm had connections with some very high quality construction contractors.

"That's another one I owe you, Counselor."

Erik stepped out into the early fall night. The moon was

full and the sound of crickets coming from the small patch of trees and shrubs was a small comfort. A slight breeze tickled his face and he absently tucked the throw blanket tighter around EJ's shoulders with his free arm. As the detective approached his truck his danger sense shrieked. The comforting breeze ceased and the sound of crickets fell silent.

"Oh shit!"

Three green lances of energy slammed into his back, knocking him forward several feet. The stunned father desperately twisted his body as the force propelled him into a parked car. Erik was able to rotate far enough that the side of his body not carrying his son took the full impact. Erik's body caved in the door of a large coupe. Two more lances of energy sped toward him! Erik pushed off the crumpled door and executed three one-armed cartwheels avoiding the burning green beams that engulfed the damaged car. The vehicle erupted in crimson flame raining burning bits of metal and plastic debris. Erik ignored the searing agony raging through his already battered body as he smelled the charred scent of seared flesh.

"The truck!" Erik ran toward his truck fumbling for his keys. Amazingly, EJ remained blissfully asleep. As Erik approached the vehicle, more eerie green streaks illuminated the night sky. Erik's danger sense warned him to leap away. The hybrid launched himself thirty feet into the air as his truck exploded into a fireball. The Sentient Staff buzzed angrily. It was still in the form of a heavy forearm bracelet on EJ's arm. "I know you're there! I'm a bit busy right now. If I fail, protect my son. Don't try to save me. Save my son!" The staff growled angrily, clearly understanding but not liking Erik's command.

Out of the darkness, five beings emerged. Man-sized and reddish brown in color, the texture of their skin reminded Erik of a gnarly, diseased tree trunk. They didn't talk, or engage him. They charged as a unit, intent only on killing the father and son.

Erik crouched, leaning forward on the balls of his feet, ready to meet their attack. He couldn't escape and he couldn't hide. He could only fight and the hybrid was willing. He leapt into the air, executing a spinning back kick. Whip-like, his leg struck the skulls of three attacking creatures. He followed up with a spinning back fist, slamming against the thick skull of another attacker. The creatures howled and hissed angrily as the desperate father continued to fight. Pain seared as claws raked over the burnt flesh of Erik's back. His enhanced metabolism kicked in and began to seal the gaping wounds.

I have to get some distance! Powerful legs tensed and Erik leapt an impossibly high forty feet into the night sky, landing yards away. He had a few precious seconds and he capitalized on them. He willed his body stronger, allowing more of the Esper DNA to dominate his being. The enhanced power crackled through his body. The demons rapidly closed the distance and prepared to attack again. Erik raised a fiery blue fist and launched a searing ball of plasma energy. The superheated air around the glowing orb crackled as thunder broke the silence. The burning orb incinerated two of the demons. Their death howls shook the night. Two cars behind the vaporized creatures exploded, decapitating a third creature. The headless corpse flailed its arms as glowing orange ichor erupted from its neck. The two remaining demons separated. Burning green lances materialized in their hands as they approached.

"Daddy?" EJ stirred and squirmed.

Erik tightened his grip on the child. "Don't move buddy. Just keep your arms around Daddy's neck and shoulders, okay?"

EJ's tiny body began to shake. "More bad things!"

Erik leapt in the air again as two energy lances passed through the air he'd just occupied. The hybrid landed on top of a large light post. Razor sharp Esper claws dug into the floodlight housing establishing a solid grip. He watched, concealed behind the large lamp fixtures, hoping the stream of bright light would conceal them from their attackers. Erik cursed silently as they turned and looked up. They knew exactly where he was hiding! He spied a luminous green glow.

"Hold on tight, buddy. Daddy has to jump again." Again, Erik tightened his grip on his child and leapt as far as his enhanced legs could propel him. He landed at the edge of the parking lot—a leap of a hundred feet. The pavement cracked and buckled beneath his feet upon landing and Erik rolled once to absorb the shock and protect EJ from the rough landing. He came up just in time to see the tall lamp post fall over, bathed with white hot sparks of electricity. The fallen post smashed a nearby car and sent another loud shockwave into the eerily quiet night.

The two remaining demons turned toward father and son. Green radiance bathed their bodies and illuminated the entire parking lot. "Hang on EJ!"*STAFF!! SHIELD, NOW!!* The Sentient Staff flowed from the child's arm and almost instantaneously formed a large disk on Erik's forearm. Erik crouched down, shielding his son and himself behind the silver disc. A wave of green energy slammed into the staff and it howled angrily as sentient organic metal deflected and refracted incalculable ethereal power.

The world was dark and silent for endless seconds. Erik slowly stood, the shield still on his left forearm while he held a terrified EJ in his right arm. The two creatures approached, each carrying an ugly edged metallic weapon that glowed with the same greenish energy.

"EJ, listen to me very carefully. I want you to stay here, but if something, or someone—anyone—comes close to you, you shout and the staff will be back here to protect you before you can blink." Erik looked directly into his son's tear-filled, terrified young eyes. "Do you understand me buddy? Stay right here and if anyone or anything tries to get near you, shout. The staff will hear you and I'll sense the danger. Daddy has to face these things now."

Tears streamed down the young boy's face and he trembled. "Okay."

The stark terror in those tiny eyes fueled Erik's fury. His own pain meant nothing, but the pain of his son was more than he could bear. Erik held up the shield. *CLAYMORE BATTLE SWORD!* The staff droned as it melted and shifted, forming a massive six-foot heavy Scottish blade. Blue plasmatic energy crackled up and down the blade's massive length. Erik held the weapon high and adopted a defensive ward as he approached the demons.

Metallic blue plasma clashed with demonic green metal in a shower of sparks and light that illuminated several hundred yards. Erik swung the large blade with lethal precision, blocking several strikes and crazed thrusts from his opponents. The larger of the two demons attempted to force him away from his son, to allow the other creature to take the child. The hybrid sensed the strategy and kept pressure on both demons pressing his attack and forcing both creatures back. He winced in pain as a hooked edge slashed against his leg, cutting a large wound in his thigh. Erik dropped the blade's tip and deflected the next strike. He slid the burning silver edge down the demonic blade, bathing them all with burning sparks of violent opposing energies and, with a flip of his wrist, cut the forearm off the attacker. The demonic weapon fell heavy against the pavement and the stunned creature held up the severed upper arm in shock and surprise. Before the demon could fall back, Erik lunged forward driving the point of his sword through the demon's throat. He flexed his arm and shoulder, slicing the blade clockwise decapitating the wounded demon.

The other demon's blade burned as it pierced Erik's left shoulder. The demon pulled the weapon back, twisting the blade to open the agonizing wound. Fighting the demonic energy that threatened to consume him, the hybrid launched a hard front kick, which shattered the demon's gnarled chin and forced it back. Erik held the massive blade in his good arm and hurled it into the demon's chest like a javelin. The sword tore through the heavy hide and the blade exploded through the stunned demon's back. The creature clutched at the weapon only to be attacked by scalding jagged arcs of energy that danced along the blade's surface. Erik held out his hand and made a slicing gesture. The blade sawed through the terrified demon, spilling blood and ichor from the growing wound. The demon screamed a death cry consumed in a scalding purple fire. The Sentient Staff flew back into Erik's hand before the demon corpse evaporated, sent back to whatever hell spawned it.

Erik limped back to EJ, loosely carrying the gore covered blade. EJ ran to his father, openly weeping in terror. Erik knelt down and caught his son in an embrace, ignoring the pain of his wounds.

"It's okay, son. It's okay. They're gone now." Erik led EJ back to the large dumpster and he sat down, leaning his back against the rusted metal hulk.

"Please don't die, Daddy."

Erik reached over to touch his son's cheek. He realized that EJ's shirt was covered with his blood. Erik took a moment and tried to heal his wounds. Normally his body would heal rapidly but these wounds seemed to resist his natural healing ability. The battered warrior focused more of his remaining energy to stop the blood hemorrhaging from the multiple gaping wounds. Erik winced as the bones in his shoulder ground against each other as they reset themselves and fused back together.

EJ flinched at the crackling sound. "Does it hurt when you heal?"

Erik looked down at his son. "Not nearly as much as getting hurt. Daddy will be fine." Erik looked over at the burnt-out hulk that was his truck. "We're going to need to call Mom and get a ride home though."

EJ's head tilted and the child hissed, his eyes burning a fiery blue. Erik's body instantly followed his son's lead, picking up on the disturbance. Something was coming, something huge. Erik's Esper side struggled to the surface, the call of the warrior preparing for another battle.

The pavement in the center of the parking lot began to shake and crack. The ground shifted as if enduring an earthquake.

"What in the Hell is going on?" Erik muttered as he struggled to his feet. He tightened his grip on the blade and instinctively pushed EJ behind him. The child clung to his father's leg, eyes still burning with Esper fire.

The center of the parking lot erupted. Streams of liquid rock and fire shot into the sky while burning rocks pelted the few remaining intact cars. At the cataclysm's epicenter, a large creature rose up phoenix-like from the fire. Its eyes were orange burning embers and massive curled horns adorned its ebony, angular head. The massive entity turned, looking directly at Erik and EJ. A voice blasted out like an air horn.

"GIVE ME THE CHILD OR YOU WILL DIE!" The creature punctuated its demand by spraying a stream of scalding fire directly toward them.

Erik turned, dove and grabbed EJ. His momentum carried them behind the large dumpster. Erik shielded EJ with his body, wincing and waiting for the burning shards of molten metal to land on his body. Metallic fragments plinked overhead. Erik looked up into a silver dome. Once again the staff had acted on its own volition protecting both father and son. Another volley of flame battered the protective blister and then another. The demonic flame couldn't pierce the Sentient Staff, but the metal wasn't able to refract all of the fire's ambient heat. Eventually EJ would be cooked alive. The staff sensed Erik's concern and a small opening appeared on the far end of the dome. Fresh cool air rushed in and Erik forced himself out of the small opening. He had to face off against the large creature before his son was baked like a stuffed turkey.

"Daddy, where are you going? Please don't leave me!"

Erik paused. He ducked another searing blast of flame scampering back under the protective blister.

"Son, do you remember how you changed in order to fight off the bad thing that was hurting Mommy earlier when Daddy was away?"

EJ nodded slightly.

"Well, now Daddy has to change too so he can fight off this really big bad guy. I can't do it in this form, like you couldn't fight the ghost as a boy. You had to change. I can change too, just like you can, and now I need to change and make the bad things stop." Another salvo shook the ground and the staff moaned in response. Erik sensed the weapon couldn't endure this kind of searing punishment forever. Erik pointed to the staff. My weapon is trying very hard to protect us but it needs my help and it needs you to be brave and stay put, Can you do that?"

EJ nodded. Erik gently kissed his son's cheek and scampered out from under the protection. The surface of the staff's protective blister glowed red hot. Erik needed to move quickly...

The titanic demon spotted him. GIVE ME THE CHILD!

Erik focused his will and charged the massive creature. "I AM THE WARRIOR!" Frail pink flesh changed to metallic organic armored plate. Erik Knight was no longer human. The Esper warrior leapt into the air hissing loudly. It slammed into the larger demon like a tank shell driving the hell beast backwards.

The Esper didn't stop; it hit the massive beast with a right cross that shook the ground with concussive force. The large behemoth flew backward, sprawled out on the large parking lot, stunned by the blow. The silver warrior leapt into the night sky disappearing for three full seconds. The demon looked up and was unable to react as the silver warrior slammed into its torso with both legs, shattering its abdominal shell, and passing clear through the creature's lower back.

The demon cried out in agony clawing at its smaller opponent in a desperate attempt to remove the organic intruder from its open torso. The hybrid raised both fists over its head and unleashed a pile drive blow that shattered the creature's armored pectoral plates and crushed the heavy bones beneath. Orange and yellow fluids bubbled out of the hideous wounds, but the large demon fought on.

It tilted forward, swinging its large arm like a whip, swatting his adversary as a man would swat an errant fly or mosquito. Erik raised an arm and met the strike with a powerful forearm block. The sound of armored metal flesh impacting with demonic rock flesh echoed off every surface and reverberated throughout the parking lot. The momentum generated by the force was enough to dislodge him from the demon's torso. He landed several feet back in the ruined parking lot, his legs covered with demonic blood and sinew.

The massive beast stood and the Esper was able to look clear through the gaping hole. *HOLY CRAP, IT'S STILL STANDING!*

The demon charged, slamming both titanic fists down in a hammer blow. The Esper Warrior easily evaded the blow that shattered pavement and sent up a spray of rock and dirt leaving a five-foot deep crater behind.

I'VE GOTTA END THIS NOW! Erik tensed powerful leg muscles and launched himself toward the demon. *NOW!* He threw his whole body into his next punch, a powerful overhand right cross. His silver fist smashed through the creature's chest and the momentum pushed his entire body through the chest cavity and clear through the back of the demon's rib cage. The hybrid rolled once, coming up into a fighting stance, arms up ready for combat. He had punched clean through the creature and come out the other side! The large demon turned slowly, now with two massive holes in its twenty-five foot body. The demon's eyes began to burn hotter and it shrieked a sound of pure agony that shattered the glass panes of every building in the shopping complex. It stumbled toward its smaller foe and raised a club-like fist ready to rain down another blow. Erik reached up and caught the large fist in a vice-like grip. With slow malicious intent, he wrenched the arm with his enhanced power, tearing the limb off the critically wounded beast. The creature staggered, as the hybrid pressed his attack. Erik tensed his powerful hand and the razor sharp claws at the ends of his fingers extended several inches. He leapt toward the stunned demon, slashing his claws across the dazed creature's neck. The beast raised its remaining hand in a futile attempt to stop the flow of ichor spraying from the open wound. After three seconds, the beast's eyes flickered and its head fell, severed onto the ruined pavement. The headless torso toppled over collapsing in a gigantic heap. Whatever force held the beast together ceased and the stone skin bubbled and liquefied, evaporating into a wispy smoke.

The hybrid took a deep breath. Battle-hardened eyes studied the ruined parking lot. The once-smooth car area resembled a war zone. There was still a threat. He could feel it. Something was watching, observing and calculating. The warrior essence knew something else was there.

I KNOW YOU'RE OUT THERE. YOU'RE NOT GETTING MY SON. THAT MUCH SHOULD BE OBVIOUS BY NOW.

The ground shook again and two larger demons climbed out of the rubble. Each one nearly thirty feet tall. *YOU'VE GOT TO BE KIDDING!*

A silky smooth voice echoed through the night. *"You cannot win, Erik Knight. You can't fight for all eternity. Even you will weaken eventually. I repeat my offer. Surrender the child now and live out your life in wealth, women and power."*

Erik tried to pinpoint the location with his laser sharp Esper senses but the voice was everywhere, even inside his head. The two massive creatures paused, waiting for his reply. Erik's armored flesh recoiled. He knew what was talking to him and he felt fear. He projected his thoughts into the night sky. *Lucifer I presume?*

"*I will have the boy, human. Even with your Esper power, you can't possibly expect to prevail against me and my hosts. I heard your boast at Vatican City, human. No pathetic creature of flesh and blood—not even one like you—can oppose me. This world will be mine. Your child will be mine.*"

The hybrid looked up to the night sky his eyes burned even brighter, casting their radiance like burning beacons. *No, no he won't. You're not getting my son but you can have this!* Erik pointed toward one of the large demons. "ANARAH ANKO-LAH!!!!!" The heavens above erupted as a titanic bolt of lightning arced down from the sky slamming into one of the unsuspecting demons. The creature was vaporized and exploded, spraying tiny bits of stony flesh around the war zone. The force of the blast stunned the other demon and blew up nearly half of the parking lot. As Erik prepared to engage the other foe, a searing beam of pure white light struck the beast. The demon shrieked in agony and simply winked out of existence.

A cascade of laughter overwhelmed the night. "*You're having a bad day, old friend. You lost this round. Go back to your foul pit while you still can!*"

The voice Erik knew to be Lucifer wasn't so cocky anymore. "*You won't win. These apes are half way to my doorstep already. I have played by HIS rules and am winning. The child should not be, you know that! You...*"

"*You know nothing, Prince of the Darkness, you made your choice eons ago when the universe was young. My patience has come to an end!*" The sky lit up with pure ivory-white lightning. The thunderclap shook the entire area. Lucifer never finished his tirade.

The hybrid probed the darkness. The sense of foreboding and evil was gone. In the distance he heard crickets. He looked up into the sky and blinked in disbelief. A being of pure white hovered over the spot where EJ hid. The being spoke to the staff in a series of droning hums and moans. The hybrid recognized the significant tenor as his weapon responded to the voice. Erik moved quickly, covering the distance with one large leap, landing a scant two feet from his concealed child.

THAT'S CLOSE ENOUGH! The hybrid projected, looking up at the white, ethereal being. Erik's eyes burned like hot blue suns. Bio organic power cracked throughout his body and he made a slight gesture with his hand. The sky rumbled and blue lighting arced throughout the sky as thunder shook the landscape.

The being of light landed gently several feet away. Large wings gently folded and disappeared behind the white entity. The ethereal being held out its arms in a peaceful gesture. *"I'm not your enemy, Erik Knight and my interest here is only to protect you and your child."* The being pointed toward the large smoking crater created by his lightning strike. *"Though you appear to have the situation in hand, for now."*

You'll forgive me if I'm skeptical. Erik's approach was cautious. His will created a massive thunderhead directly over the battleground. The smell of ozone and agitated energies dominated the night.

The ethereal being looked up alarmed. *"I assure you, I am not here to battle, but I will defend myself!"* The being took two steps back as Erik approached his son.

The hybrid studied the being of Light. Both entities glared at each other, burning blue suns staring into fiery white orbs … both anticipating.

Erik sensed no evil, just an overwhelming sense of power. He'd battled enough for one evening. *I'm going to take you at you word.* He reached out, fingers extended.

Erik's staff reformed and settled in his hand. EJ stood beside his father, looking up at him with awe.

"Daddy? Did you beat the bad guys?"

Erik looked down at his son bathing his child in the light from his eyes. *THE BAD GUYS ARE GONE NOW, SON.* Erik willed himself back to human form. EJ gasped as the child watched his father appear where a titanic silver monolith once stood. Erik hugged his son, unable to stop his own tears. "I'm so proud of you little man. You were so brave."

EJ held on to his father. "I had an accident in my pants."

Erik noticed the large wet spot on the front of his son's jeans and burst out laughing. After all the child had been through, he was worried about peeing his pants. Erik held him close. "Daddy nearly wet his pants too. It'll be our secret." Erik looked down at his nearly naked body. "At least you kept your pants on, buddy, Dad's clothes are in ashes."

Erik looked back up at the being. It was smiling. *"You are brave, little one and your father is truly worthy. All Father chose well with you."* It pointed toward Erik, *"We have much to discuss, hybrid warrior. There is much you need to know. You are in great danger, more peril than you can possibly realize. More peril than even you, with your amazing power, can counter."*

Erik stood, picking up his son. He struggled to keep his sanity, his mind screaming at the impossibility of what had just occurred and what was still happening to him and his son. "What are you? I know what the religious texts call you, but is that what you really are?" He struggled to push out the word, "An angel?"

The ethereal being laughed—a laugh an adult would make if asked an amusing question by a child. *"I am called many things on many worlds, hybrid. Your human tongue is limited and even your enhanced Esper mind could not comprehend the true nature of what we really are."*

Erik frowned. "I see modesty and humility are in short supply among ethereal beings."

The entity of light laughed again. *"I apologize if my manner seems…"* it struggled, searching for the word.

"Arrogant?" Erik offered.

"Yes, precisely, Esper, arrogant, I apologize if my words and manner seem arrogant. I am unused to dealing with mortals, even enhanced mortals such as you."

"I need to ask you a question, if that's allowed."

The being scowled. *"It isn't, but you trusted me, so I make this one exception. What is your question?"*

Erik sighed, holding his son tighter. He forced the words from his lips, despite his rising gorge. "Is what my friend Charlie Gallagher said earlier true?" Erik avoided getting into details with his son listening.

The being shifted uncomfortably, weighing the consequences of answering. It looked up, eyes blazing white. *"Yes. What you were told by your friend and the old man is accurate, but not complete. There is more happening than you are aware."*

Erik shook his head. "I'm getting that impression."

"We will talk tomorrow. There will be no more battles tonight. Your victories here will give pause to the forces of darkness, but they will regroup. Take your child home. He has been through much. Tomorrow begins a new chapter."

Erik nodded. "Tomorrow."

The being's large white wings unfurled and with one delicate motion, it took to the sky. It made a sweeping gesture, pointing toward the ruined parking lot. *"Go home and rest. The battle has yet to begin."* The ethereal being beat its wings and soon vanished, swallowed by the darkness of the night sky. Erik could hear sirens closing; someone heard the commotion from the heated combat.

"We need to move, Lil' Man. I don't have a believable tale to explain this mess."

"Daddy! Your truck!"

Erik spun around and followed EJ's pointed finger. Erik's truck stood alone amid the cacophony of ruined vehicles. The pickup truck had somehow been restored. Erik walked toward the truck. It was his, same make, model, color right down to the mud flaps and light bar. But something was missing, the detective observed. The dings and surface rust were gone—all the imperfections caused from one hundred thousand miles of use no longer marred the truck's body. The vehicle looked as if it just came off a showroom floor.

"No." Erik muttered. "It can't be. It just can't be the same ride!"

He opened the door. The dome light that hadn't worked in months activated and illuminated the cab. The newspaper he'd purchased that morning was there. The picture of Shanda was taped to an immaculate dashboard right where he'd put it a year ago. Even the Uber Café coffee cup he'd left in the cup holder was there with the dregs of melted iced coffee from early in the morning. Erik spotted a pair of pants and undergarments resting on EJ's car seat along with a set of sweatpants and a hooded jacket with the Dawkens' Fitness logo emblazoned on each garment neatly tucked on the driver's seat. Erik pulled out the clothes and they quickly changed. The keys were in the ignition and the detective suddenly realized even his multiple key chains had been duplicated perfectly.

The sirens closed in and Erik could see the flashing blue lights. "Here goes nothing!" He turned the key and the engine roared to life. He quickly secured his son and put the vehicle in gear. Erik didn't know what to expect as he carefully navigated the ruined lot. He was half afraid the truck would suddenly turn into a pumpkin and several mice, leaving them both stranded. The two-tone blue and black Silverado left the parking lot as several police units arrived to the scene of mayhem. Erik looked through his rear view mirror shaking his head in disbelief. He looked forward, studying the shiny new vehicle. It was a perfect replica of his truck right down to the aftermarket pillar gauges Shanda bought him last Christmas.

"It looks just like your truck." EJ remarked not fully understanding the implication of what was occurring.

Erik nodded as he reached over and patted his son's head. "It does indeed, son." Erik spotted a cell phone on the center console. Of course it was a perfect replica of the one destroyed. He pressed some digits and handed the device over to his son. "Tell Mom we're on our way home. I'm sure she's worried about you." The detective took a deep breath struggling to control his sanity.

Chapter 3: Soul Bounty

Erik pulled into the driveway. It was nearly midnight. Despite his hope, EJ was still awake asking him questions about all the events he'd experienced. Erik did his best to downplay the horrible things they both endured but he wasn't doing a very good job.

"Daddy, I have another question."

The child's tone had changed. It took on a desperate undertone that caused Erik to focus totally on his son. "Okay buddy, what's on your mind?"

A tear flowed down the child's cheek. "You said we were different, that we can change. We can become just like the monsters. I saw you in my head. I saw you fight. I saw you kill that big thing and then the lightning you made fall from the sky! Was that really you! Are we monsters too, Daddy?"

Erik's gut clenched.

"I don't wanna be a monster! I don't wanna have to fight bad guys. I don't want my friends at playgroup to be afraid of me and not play with me anymore."

Erik's heart ripped. "Oh son, buddy, we aren't the monsters." Tears flowed down his cheeks. "I'm sorry you had to see all those horrible things. I can't lie to you though. Yes, what you saw was really Daddy fighting to save us and fighting to stop the bad guys."

"So we're really big silver monsters on the inside." EJ choked out a sob.

Erik reached over and unbuckled the seatbelt. He gently lifted his son and held the boy tight. "We're not monsters son. We're just different." He gently guided EJ's eyes up so they looked directly at his. "Look at me. Do I look like a monster?"

"No. But..."

"No buts. Look in that mirror. Look at your face. What do you see? Do you see a boy or do you see a monster?" Erik

adjusted the truck's rear view mirror so EJ could see his reflec-
tion.

"A boy."

"Yes, you're a boy and I'm a man." He held his son. "Sometimes 'Good' has to make people that have the ability to fight
the monsters. We're not the monsters, EJ, but we have the ability to fight the monsters. That's what Daddy had to do tonight.
He had to fight the monsters. In order to do that, I had to harness special abilities. The monsters are big and strong so someone who fights the monsters has to be as well." Erik struggled
to put his feelings into words. "You like watching Spider Man,
right?"

EJ nodded.

"Well is Spider Man a regular guy or is he different?"

"He's different," the child answered innocently.

Erik pushed his point gently. "Is Spider Man a hero or a
monster?"

"Spider Man is a superhero."

"Okay, so if Spider Man isn't normal. He fights bad guys
and there aren't many people like him. Does that sound like
anybody we know?"

The message resonated with the child and his face lit up.
"We're superheroes!"

Erik did his best not to laugh. "Shhhhhhhh, we need to
keep this a family secret. You're almost four. I know this is too
much for any boy to understand. Just believe me, buddy, we
are not monsters. We're people with special abilities, like Spider
Man. It doesn't make us any better or any worse than anybody
else."

"Do other Daddies have to fight monsters and talk to flying guys with wings like you do?"

Erik shook his head. "I don't know. I think every Daddy
has his own things he has to deal with; probably not monsters
and flying people though."

The front light came on. Erik looked over and saw Shanda
standing by the front door. "Mom's waiting for us ... let's go
inside. You need to get to sleep, buddy. Tomorrow is another
day."

* * *

Erik sat in the living room as Shanda tucked EJ into their bed. The boy was telling her all the wild adventures he had with daddy and how the two of them were made to fight monsters and bad guys. Erik rolled his eyes, hoping Shanda would give him some leeway with his off-the-cuff explanations. The weary detective sipped his decaf coffee wondering how his once simple life could get blown apart in the span of just a few weeks. Shanda walked down the hallway and sat on a chair opposite him.

She tilted her head, squinting. "Monster fighters and superheroes, really?"

Erik rolled his eyes. "I had to come up with something after what he saw. It broke my heart. He asked me in the truck if we were monsters like the things that attacked us. He caught me with that and I had to tell him something to make him feel better."

Shanda nodded. "I understand. What the Hell happened? I got a sense there was trouble and some panic over our link but I couldn't reach you."

"I'm sorry. It happened so fast. We were walking out to the truck and all hell, literally, broke loose. I've never seen things like this. They were ethereal beings, some just plain huge—twenty to thirty feet tall—others the size of men but still lethal." Erik took another sip of his coffee. "And then there's the," Erik paused, "the angel. Before you roll your eyes, I don't know what else to call it. It was pure white, had wings and gave off a sense of power unlike anything I've ever encountered. Plus, with a wave of its hand it duplicated my truck right down to the picture of you and the old coffee cup I left in the cab." Erik pointed to his pants. "Not to mention the clothes we're both wearing right now. EJ, the poor kid, peed his pants in terror and my clothes were vaporized. Inside the truck were these clothes folded and crisp like they were right off a clothing rack."

Shanda walked over and sat next to him, putting her arm around his neck. "Okay, so what do we do now?" She leaned her head against his powerful shoulder.

Erik shifted, bringing his arm around her and she cuddled

up against him. "I must admit, you're taking this better than I did." The brooding detective sighed. "I have a meeting with this 'angel' tomorrow at the gym." He chuckled. "What's left of the gym ... the parking lot is a complete loss, not to mention the damage done inside. This whole thing makes my head hurt, hun."

Shanda nodded as she absently caressed his shoulder. "I wasn't the one throwing down with demons and talking with divinity but I'm struggling to keep my head screwed on right now. I hate to admit this, but I'm scared. How can we protect EJ? How do we know there's not something lurking right outside just waiting to attack and take our child?"

"The being said there'd be no more violence tonight, and I believe him. These were Lucifer's forces, and the being spoke to the Prince of Dark like they were old friends. I nearly crapped myself when I heard that dark yet silky voice ringing in my head. It was seductive and convincing. It took all of my will to drive it out." Erik's voice caught and tears rolled down his cheeks. "My son, Satan came after my son. The devil spoke to me ... to me! I wanted to puke; this is so far beyond me, beyond anything." A sob escaped him and his body tensed as he fought to control his emotions.

Shanda held him tight. "It's okay, babe. You didn't buckle. You fought and you won. You do what you do best. You keep fighting, like the warrior you are and you find the strength within to continue. You're not alone. I'm here with you. You don't have to be strong with me. You can let your guard down."

"Thanks, Angel. I know I can let my guard down with you. I'm just overwhelmed right now and exhausted. It took a lot to heal this time. Wounds from demons aren't like regular cuts or bruises. It takes a lot to heal and I'm actually, physically tired right now."

Well let's curl up here and get some sleep. EJ went out after his story and if you're sure we're safe for the night, we can crash here."

Erik inhaled her scent and just wanted to fall asleep in the warmth and safety of her arms. "Staff, watch EJ, please."

The Sentient Staff purred and launched itself down the hallway.

"That still freaks me out how it understands you." Shanda covered them with a blanket as she removed her sweater. "Why don't you be my 'angel' and wrap those big strong wings around me?"

"Oh that's cute." Erik wrapped his arms around her warm body and she snuggled against him.

"Better?" she whispered holding his arms tighter around her.

"Much." Erik and Shanda held onto each other in silence, falling asleep in each other's arms.

* * *

The sound seemed so far off in the distance. The warmth of the sun on his face, the sound of waves splashing against the shore and the seagulls were all a comfort. Shanda looked amazing in her bikini and EJ was happily building a sandcastle. This was perfect, but that sound was getting louder and louder, where was it coming from?

Erik opened his eyes. The sound of his cell phone broke morning silence ruining his pleasant dream.

"Make it stop." Shanda whispered as she wrapped his arms around her tighter.

Erik smiled. He saw the large label on the phone display. It was Alissa. As the sleep fog wore off, he realized the sun was shining and he'd overslept. The fact that he slept at all was a shock. Since his change, his body never required sleep. But last night, he was both physically and emotionally exhausted. "It's Alissa. She's probably calling about the storefronts, cars and the parking lot that were destroyed last night." Erik reached over and grabbed the phone.

"Hi Alissa." He looked over at Shanda and nodded as the panicked voice over the phone described the carnage.

"Yes, I know. I'm on my way in and I'll tell you what happened. Do me a favor and call Martin. I need to see him today as well." Erik stood up and began pacing. "If people still wanna work out, let them. The gym is still functional and they can park at the lot across the street or at the other end of the parking area that wasn't wrecked too badly." Erik nodded once or twice as the conversation continued. "Tell the cops I'm on my way. And tell Martin the sooner the better on our meeting." He hung up the phone sighing heavily and looked over at his wife. "Well the shit's hit the fan. I guess there was more damage done than I thought. The other stores in the mall complex no longer have store fronts. All the glass has been shattered and blown inside the shops. The damage done to merchandise was pretty steep according to what little Alissa overheard from some pissed-off managers and shop owners. Since I'm not there, I'm the number one suspect and the gallant boys in blue want to talk to me, again."

Erik dialed another phone number, pacing back and forth clearly upset. "Yes, Special Agent Erik Knight, codename: Superman." He looked at Shanda rolling his eyes. "That wasn't my idea," he whispered. "Martin's warped sense of humor." Erik spoke back into the phone. "ID Number ALZ dash seven, four, nine, three, six, eight, one."

Shanda shook her head. "Superheroes. My God you guys are like little boys."

Erik covered the phone with his hand, grinning. "What? Superman rocks!!!!"

The voice on the other end acknowledged the code and Erik shifted his focus back to business.

"I need a heavy cleanup crew and some cover for an incident last night at Dawkens' Gym. I was forced to engage several hostiles and the damage is quite extensive, not just to our facility, but to the neighboring establishments. The police are looking to question me and I'm confident the firm doesn't want me to have this conversation since it involves players and assets at a much higher level than normal. Please relay this up the chain as an 'Alpha Zulu' incident." Erik paused, listening to the disembodied voice.

"Understood. 'Papa Bear' is en route." Erik put the phone down, shaking his head.

"Papa Bear?" Shanda giggled. "Oh shit, tell me that's not Martin's secret spy name."

Erik grinned wickedly. "Yeah when he tagged me with Superman, I bugged the agency to change his moniker. They went for it. I guess they already got wind of the problem, which only confirms my theory that the firm is wading in the ethereal pool as well."

Shanda stood up and looked directly at him. "When you meet with this being today," she paused gathering her resolve, "I need to be there, I need to know exactly what's going on."

Erik shook his head.

"Erik, I'm not asking. I'm insisting. This isn't just about you. It's about us, our family, and our son! I can't be on the sidelines."

Erik sighed. Shanda was part of this and needed to be on hand. "You're right, babe. We're stronger as a family. Let's get EJ up and get moving. I can't wait to see what Martin and the boys at the firm are gonna come up with to explain this mess."

"What's an 'Alpha Zulu'?"

Erik grinned wickedly. "A total FUBAR from A to Z."

"'FUBAR?'"

Erik nodded. "Effed up beyond all repair."

Shanda shook her head. "Do you guys have a whole department that comes up with this stuff?"

Erik laughed. "It wouldn't surprise me." He took off his shirt and headed toward the bathroom. He noticed his wife studying him. "What's wrong?"

"Two things: One I have to fix your hair. You look ridiculous with one side long and one side burned short. Second, you have scars on your shoulder and ribs. Usually your wounds heal completely without leaving a trace."

Erik ran a fingertip over the ugly scar on his shoulder. "I was impaled by some kind of demonic blade. The wound was pretty bad and extremely painful. My shoulder was broken and I was pretty much run through. It took a lot to heal and I guess it'll take longer for the scars to fade. I'm fine, really."

Shanda walked up to him and gently pressed her lips against the healed-over wound. "Please be careful, these aren't run-of-the-mill terrorists or criminals. They're supernatural entities with power we don't understand." She pointed down the hallway where EJ still slept. "We need you alive and in one piece."

Erik nodded wrapping his arms around her. "I got it ... careful ... nothing is gonna break up our family, not aliens, not corrupt military and now not even some biblical bad asses looking to make trouble." He kissed her on the forehead.

Shanda smiled. "Let's get your hair looking somewhat normal before I wake up EJ. I'll call the store and let them know I won't be in today till later in the afternoon."

Erik tilted his head. "I wasn't given a specific time for this meeting. Hopefully we won't be waiting too long."

* * *

Dawkens' Gym and Milford Shopping Plaza. Milford, MA

Erik held EJ tight as they walked through the ruined parking lot toward the gym. The damage was even worse than he'd imagined. Two backhoes were busy dropping shovels full of rock and fill into a giant crater. Several flatbed wreckers were hauling away the burned-out husks of carbon-scored automobiles. A small crane was hoisting the ruined flood lamp and fifty-foot post. He spotted at least half a dozen police officers, four reporters, and several angry merchants. One of the store managers spotted him and pointed. Two officers turned around and walked toward him followed by six angry businessmen. Erik stopped, blocking Shanda with his free arm, then handing EJ to her. He kept his arm up, protectively.

"Babe, I don't know how ugly this is going to get. I'm getting some real bad vibes from a lot of those people. Stick very close. Let's hope we can get inside before things get ugly."

They continued walking toward the gym as the police moved to intercept them. "Excuse me, Erik Knight. You are Erik Knight?" An officer blocked their path.

Erik nodded. "I am."

"Mr. Knight, we have some questions for you regarding the incidents that occurred here last night."

Erik nodded. He looked toward Shanda and smiled. "Hon, why don't you take EJ inside while I have a chat with the police." Erik winked and Shanda nodded, never taking her eyes off the angry mob. Alissa and two burly gym staff appeared and formed up around the mother and child shielding them from the crowd.

"You did this, Knight! You destroyed our businesses!"

"They'll be cleaning glass for a month inside my store. I

lost thousands of dollars in merchandise!"

Erik took a step forward as the police formed a wall between him and the angered merchants.

"Are they right?" The closest cop looked from the mob to Erik. "Did you do this?" He gestured toward the destruction all around them.

"I suppose they have proof," Erik countered praying that Martin and the cavalry would soon arrive.

The officer shook his head. "No. The video systems in the lamp posts were all fried. Almost as if some high voltage impact overloaded all the chips and circuitry. But they all know the trouble you had yesterday and there's been talk about what you did and the damage to your establishment." The cop pointed toward the plexiglass covering the picture window. "Seems reasonable to assume you had a hand in this as well."

Erik nodded. "You're free to assume all you want officer, but a detective never makes assumptions or accusations without facts—hard facts to back him or her up."

"Is that a non-denial, denial, Mr. Knight?" The officer blocked his path, determined to keep him from leaving.

"No that's simply me giving you a solid piece of advice."

"I appreciate your concern for my career, Mr. Knight, but your little quip doesn't answer my question." The officer closed the distance separating them and pointed his index finger pushing into Erik's chest. "Answer the question. Did you have anything to do with this mess?" The cop repeatedly jabbed his finger into Erik, trying his patience.

Erik grabbed the officer's hand in an iron grip. He whispered through clenched teeth. "Poke me one more time and you'll spend the next year in a hospital drinking yogurt out of a straw." The angered detective applied a jujitsu wrist lock causing the officer to yelp in pain.

The other officers were about to act when a voice warned them off.

"That's about enough, gentlemen!"

Erik recognized Martin's 'Authority' tone. The counselor was about to take charge. Twenty men in dark suits and sunglasses, visibly armed, surrounded the area as several construction trucks arrived. Fifty men in hard hats disembarked from several crew cab pickup trucks and began unloading equipment. A burly man in denim overalls pushed his way through the crowd.

"We'll start the damage assessment and put together a materials list. We have six loads of pavement en route and we're bringing some real heavy fill substrate. The junk they're using will cough up at the first frost and ruin any pavement job."

Denton nodded. "Listen up! There was an incident here last night. The details are classified. You have my word that you'll all be made whole. The United States Government thanks you in advance for your cooperation. My people will be visiting each establishment to do a complete damage assessment. The best thing you can do is head back to your stores and shops and work with our agents and crews."

The crowd slowly dispersed, talking among themselves. Martin looked over at Erik and winked. "You called?"

Erik laughed despite all he'd been through. Martin always had his back. Erik looked back at the officer. He relaxed his grip, freeing the officer's hand. "I believe we're finished here. I've got a business that needs my attention."

The cop shook his hand. "You're not above the law, Mr. Knight, despite your connections. No one is."

Erik looked at the officer. The man made a point. Erik had used his position to avoid trouble, but the truth was unbelievable and too farfetched to believe. "You're right. I'm not above the law, but what went on here is beyond you, beyond me and would give you nightmares. You don't want to know what happened here, Officer. Believe me you don't. Just be grateful to live in ignorance and that we're fixing the problem." Erik gestured toward the damaged parking lot. "The problem you can see and the bigger problems you can't." He turned and headed into his gym.

* * *

Erik was working with a student, helping the young boy execute a side kick, when the hairs on the back of his neck stood on end. He looked up. A tall, powerful man with sandy blond hair entered the dojo. A shiver went down his spine—the angel.

They locked eyes briefly and Erik nodded. He then turned to one of his brown belts. "Kevin, can you take over for me? Timmy needs to work on his side kick, then run the class through some punch and block drills." He pointed toward a young girl on the mat. "Ginny has a test in two weeks. Run her through the first three katas. She missed it the last time, and I'm not going to let her mess up again. I've got some business I need to deal with."

Kevin bowed. Erik returned the gesture. He stepped off the mat and motioned the guest toward him. The closer the man came, the more powerful his non-human presence became. Erik was amazed that none of the parents watching felt or sensed anything as the ethereal soldier walked by them.

"Hybrid, I am here as promised." The visitor's voice was barely a whisper not the trumpeting baritone blaring in his head last evening. He appeared perfectly human.

Erik nodded, pointing toward a hallway leading back to his office. "Through there. We can talk privately in my office area."

Erik escorted the being into his office where Martin, Shanda, and Alissa were all sitting. EJ was happily playing with his Lego set. The boy looked up and smiled.

"Mommy! It's the flying man! The angel is back!" The boy stood and walked over, impulsively hugging the ethereal being.

The being looked down and gave the boy a warm smile. "It is good to see you safe, young one." He knelt down and seemed to produce a chocolate bar from thin air. He glanced over at Shanda. "May I?"

The stunned mother nodded slightly and the divine being handed EJ the candy. "Young one, I need to speak with your mother and father. Would you allow us to speak privately?"

EJ wrinkled his nose as he opened his candy. "Okay, I guess."

"EJ, why don't you go into Alissa's office and she can read you *Mike Mulligan and his Steam Shovel*." Erik looked over at Alissa. "I'm sorry. Do you mind? I'll bring you up to speed after, I promise."

Alissa stood, staring at the visitor in awe. She sensed the

divine nature of their guest and nervously ushered EJ out the door. The being nodded at her and she winced, moving quickly.

He looked over at Erik in confusion. "Am I so frightening?"

Erik shrugged. "I'm sorry. It's not every day we're hosting a divine visitor. Alissa has some Esper genetics and is very sensitive to natural and supernatural disturbances." Erik pointed toward the parents of his students. "Not like the other people you walked by, obviously."

Martin stood up, walked over to the office door, closed it, and flipped the lock. He looked over at the divine being. "Okay, EJ and Alissa are gone. Now, if you'll pardon the expression, what the Hell is going on?"

The angelic being's face soured. "I wish I had better news. We have discovered Molec has a soul bounty on your son's life. Lucifer, in discovering this, has done the same and increased the price. Upon learning this, Molec has offered the child's weight in gold to any demon able to kill the boy."

Silence dominated the room. Shanda's mouth hung open in shock. Martin shook his head in disbelief, whispering curses while Erik simply clenched his fist, sighing heavily.

"So, it's open season on my son and every demonic bounty hunter on Earth is looking for the prize." Erik's fist burned fiery blue. "Surely they must know I'm not going to let them have my son. The ugly scene last night must have made that clear."

The ethereal being shook his head sadly. "Lucifer wants the child alive as leverage in our war in hopes of gaining some advantage or possibly as a bargaining chip. Molec, on the other hand, wants the child dead so the second age of man can never happen and the will of Light can never be fulfilled. The boy's death will mean there is no second coming, Mankind will expire after Armageddon and evil will have free reign on this planet."

Martin stood up. "I don't get it." He looked down at Shanda and placed a comforting arm on her shoulder. "If the lad is in danger, why not have your forces protect the boy? You have agents in the government and entities floating around everywhere." He gestured around the room. "How hard can it be to reallocate some forces to protect EJ? If the boy is a divine profit, Armageddon's Son as your prophecy claims, why don't you guys come down from your heavenly cloud bank and do something?"

"It isn't that simple. We cannot interfere directly but we can work through others. Molec has no regard for the rules, hence he can issue a soul bounty. Lucifer is more like a politician. He is smarter and more patient. He planned very well for the acquisition of Earth and executed his strategy of domination for this planet like a master tactician. Molec is more impatient, a blunt instrument of destruction seeking the quick path and instant solution. Molec's goal is to thwart Lucifer and catapult the war for his own end. Molec wants Earth for his prize and killing the child of Light will assure that nothing will ever threaten evil's presence on this world."

Martin shook his head, frustrated. "So you can stand by and do nothing while this Molec character unleashes mayhem on the entire planet and launches an army of demons to kill an innocent boy?"

"What Molec lacks in brilliance he makes up for in cunning and tenacity. The archdemon hides like a slug in the bowels of dark places where our forces on Earth cannot find him. Believe me, we would be well rid of Molec as would Lucifer. As your species says, he is a pain in the ass. Both sides would be pleased to eliminate him."

Erik walked behind Shanda. "I don't understand your rules of engagement, but nothing's going to harm my son."

Shanda reached up and held his hand.

The angel shook his head sadly. "Hybrid, I don't mean to diminish your ability, but the forces of Molec and even Lucifer will keep coming in more and more overwhelming numbers until you are eliminated and the child either killed or taken. Your life is of no consequence to these beings. You are merely an impediment to be overcome." He gestured toward the Sentient Staff concealed beneath Erik's shirt. "Even the power of your Esper weapon combined with your myriad might cannot prevail against such overwhelming odds." The ethereal being folded his arms. "Eventually you will falter."

Erik rubbed the remnants of the bruise on his face and then the scar tissue on his shoulder.

The angel's voice softened. "I get no joy from saying this.

Eventually you will lose, whether it be from a massive ambush or a lucky blow, or blast of demonic fire."

Shanda let out a cry and forced her tears back. "There has to be something we can do. I can't just sit around and wait for your doom-filled scenario to play out."

"So the only way to end this is to take out Molec permanently." Erik's eyes began to burn. "If I keep killing his soldiers, he'll have to come face me himself, and then I can end this." He turned toward the angel. "You said I'd be beaten. You must know the truth about me, about my power."

The angel nodded. "I have been informed."

"Then you know what I'm capable of doing. You know there are NO limits to my power, no end. That's the curse I'm carrying. I may not be ethereal, but the powers I *do* have are beyond my ability to measure. I can't fly across the galaxy or pop in and out like your kind but I can more than defend my son. I won't leave EJ to hunt this demonic prick down. I'll make him come to me. I'll make him rue the day he ever decided to put a price on my son's head."

Shanda gasped. "What! What do you mean no limits?"

Erik looked down at her. "That's my cross to bear, hun. I can harness the energy around me and control the very elements of this world by sheer force of will. When I fully change, the potential is limitless. I've tried to find an end point, but I've been afraid to go beyond a certain threshold for fear of causing irreparable damage. If these demonic beings are looking for a war, I'm more than willing to shake the gates of Hell apart and rain down the corpses of their dead."

Shanda's face went pale. "Why didn't you tell me?"

"I'm sorry, but what could you have done? I didn't want you worrying. You had enough on your plate with your business and EJ. When I realized what I could do after the Observer Incident at Groom Lake, I did some experiments. The results were nearly catastrophic. After that I decided not to play with fire. I knew there was more power to be harnessed, but the consequences of unleashing it were too risky. I just wanted to be normal. I wanted us to have a normal life, for you and for our son."

"We are aware of your power, hybrid. As strong as you are,

the beings you will be fighting also have great power. Use your power, unleashed and unfettered, and hundreds, maybe thousands of lives will be lost during your battles." The angel pointed toward the ruined parking lot. "What if people were in the building last night, or the parking area when you rained down lightning upon your foes? How many would have died? The beings that will come will not hesitate to use their power and you will respond in kind to protect yourself and the child. In your zeal to draw out Molec and destroy his forces, you will endanger and likely kill hundreds of innocent human souls. You believe your power to be without end. I assure you, all power has limits. Even ethereal beings are not all powerful. Only the Father has such might. We too understand the responsibility and the weight of wielding such force, which is why we must tread lightly upon this and other worlds. A full blown Ethereal War would reduce this planet to rubble." The angel paused. "There was another world in this system that had life before mankind or even the Espers were alive. Earth was still in its infancy when we battled for control of that species. Our war erupted into a full scale confrontation between Lucifer's army and the powers of Light. Lucifer was defeated in that first unfettered Ethereal War but the planet was turned to rubble and even to this day the debris serves as a reminder to all what can happen when power goes unchecked."

Martin gasped. "The asteroid belt between Mars and Jupiter? Good lord, you're saying it was once a planet full of sentient life?"

The angel looked toward Martin, his face solemn. "Billions of souls lost in a war between forces humans could not comprehend. The planet split apart and we still battled over it. The screams of billions of souls crying out at once were drowned in a tidal wave of violence and war." The being placed a hand on Erik's shoulder. "Hybrid, that cannot happen here. That is why we cannot get directly involved. That is why you cannot engage Lucifer and Molec in a war of attrition. The cost of wielding such arcane power will be measured in the lives and blood of the innocent. There is another way. Take your child to Vatican City. The city has God's blessing and protection. The dark ethereal forces cannot violate the holy ground."

"Unless they're wearing black garments." Erik frowned as he considered the angel's words. The divine being was right, though. How many people would have died if the battle he'd fought last night was during peak business hours? What kind of damage would he cause if he unleashed a blow like the one that destroyed the bedrock at Groom Lake? Or if he unleashed a lightning bolt with the power to vaporize a city like he'd done battling during that crisis? The angel made a valid point, a point he should have considered if he wasn't so wrapped up in protection mode.

"We are aware of the Talithum garments and have now taken precautions against such unearthly magics. Your child and your bride will be safe there."

Erik nodded. "Yes, safe, right where the church wants him. Right under their thumb. I don't trust their motives."

"You can guarantee our son's safety?" Shanda stood and approached the tall lean being, her own eyes burning with intensity.

"Shanda..."

"Let him answer!" Her voice cracked like a whip.

"I cannot guarantee there will be no danger. As your husband already knows, there are human forces in the employ of Molec, but demonic entities will not be able to enter and we have more of a presence in the holy city now. Your son will be safer there than anywhere else on this planet."

Shanda looked over at her shocked husband. "Erik, what do you think? Will he be safer there than here with you?"

Erik was dumbfounded, trying to accept the possibility that his son would be safer somewhere other than by his side.

Shanda put her hands on his shoulders and looked up into his eyes. "I know you don't like it. I can read the vibe you're giving off, but this isn't an ego thing. You can't blast this town to ashes." She paused. "Well you can, but you shouldn't. I don't like this any more than you do babe, but if we can hide there and give you a chance to hunt this thing down without having to fight every ghoul that comes out of the woodwork, it's certainly worth talking about." She put her arms around him and lay her head against his shoulder. "It's the only way, Erik. You can't spend the rest of your life fighting and we certainly can't hide from the devil or from God or from this other ghoulish creature."

Erik sighed as he wrapped his arms around her, wishing he could protect his family from the storm beset upon them. "You and EJ will be safer there. We can't live like this. If I can find Molec and recover the cross, this ugliness will be over." Erik gently kissed his wife's cheek. He turned toward the ethereal being. "You're right. Vatican City is the safest place for them right now. I'm trusting you, trusting that your motives are genuine and there's no politics involved." Erik extended his hand and the angel reached forward. They clasped hands. "One other detail, I have a daughter away at school in Paris, she needs protection as well. Can you do that?"

The angel nodded as he shook Erik's hand. "You have my solemn word. It shall be done." The ethereal being reached over and gently touched Shanda's cheek wiping away a tear. "I am sorry for the pain this causes you, Mother. We will protect you and your child. You must be strong for his sake." The being leaned over and gently kissed the top of her head. He stood back and nodded one last time, then simply vanished.

Erik heard a gasp. He looked over. Martin was pale. His jaw dropped open in astonishment. Erik held his wife tight as she wept. Silence hung over the small office as each one struggled with what they'd all witnessed. The phone broke the sullen quiet, ringing endlessly. Erik ignored it, grateful when the ringing ceased.

"We'll survive this, I promise." Erik kissed the top of Shanda's head and inhaled her perfume.

Martin shook his head. "I keep thinking I'm going to wake up from this nightmare."

A knock on the door caused Erik to turn.

"Erik!" Alissa's voice cut through the thin door. "I have a Bishop O'Malley on the phone. He's asking about travel plans to Rome for you, Shanda, and EJ. Are you planning on another trip?"

Erik looked over at the counselor. "Well, they didn't waste any time, did they?"

Martin nodded. "Obviously not. They have as much to lose as you." He frowned. "Don't take this the wrong way, Erik.

They actually have more to lose—like an entire planet and every soul inhabiting it."

"I know, Counselor, I know. Hopefully God will forgive me if I just focus on my son, my wife and my daughter for a while. I've saved the world from genetically engineered monsters and from an alien invasion. I think I can be forgiven for just worrying about my family this time around and leave the heavy lifting to someone else."

Shanda sat back in a chair, her face bone white.

"Are you okay, babe?"

"Honestly, no. No I'm not. I feel like my head's going to explode. I was just kissed on the head by an angel and he called me 'Mother'. That feeling, that presence was overwhelming."

Another knock ended their discussion. "Erik, do you want to take this call?"

"I'm sorry, Alissa. Transfer it back over, please then bring EJ here. We need to talk."

* * *

Erik swung the Sentient Staff in a lethal figure eight pattern, whipping the sleek weapon in front of his body as he advanced, cat like, on the dojo mat. He changed his stance and swung the weapon with a blinding quick overhead strike followed by a sweeping semi-circular slice. The air hissed as the staff sliced through empty space. The alien weapon purred with each attack and Erik felt the bond between him and the staff increase. It sensed his moves and at times seemed to guide his hands and arms rather than be directed. A second set of lights activated, stopping the impromptu training.

"Why on Earth are you still here?" Alissa looked over at EJ sleeping with his stuffed bear on a small couch. "And why is he not home resting in his own bed?" She glanced at her watch. "Good lord, you have to be on a plane in less than nine hours."

The staff returned to its dormant state and Erik sheathed the weapon. "Yeah, I know, Shanda's been pinging telepathically for the last hour. I just needed to get through a few things."

Alissa tilted her head. "What's wrong? I know that doom-filled tone of voice you have right now."

Erik chuckled. "You know me too well. I find being that predictable to somebody annoying as all hell."

The young woman gestured toward the empty observation area. "You'll get over it."

Erik walked over and pulled the blanket up over EJ's shoulders and then sat in a nearby chair. Alissa flopped down heavily next to him.

"I have a bad feeling—that feeling I get when I know something's going to go terribly wrong. I don't know if it's just because I'm overwhelmed with all this and it's a false warning about things I'm already aware of or there's something bigger I'm not seeing and I'll get blindsided as soon as my back is turned."

Alissa nodded. "I honestly don't know what to tell you." She shrugged, wrapping her arms around her torso, trembling. "I've never encountered beings like this. I never really believed in religion, angels, God or even the devil. The sense of power is overwhelming." She looked up at Erik. "You give off a power and a psychic echo like no one on this planet. But through it all I can sense your humanity. What was in here earlier may have looked human but there was nothing human about it, nothing natural. Even the Seelak had a sense of 'physical being' about them. This entity didn't." She looked toward her friend. "I don't know what to say about your premonition. I don't have any insight to give you, Erik. There's no baseline for me to measure against."

Erik nodded, reaching over and gently brushed her shoulder. "That's okay. I didn't expect you to, but I appreciate you being a sounding board. You're an amazing woman, Alissa, and I'm grateful for your friendship." Erik shook his head. "No, you're family. If I had a sister, I'd want her to be just like you."

The young woman blushed. "Thank you. You are probably the best big brother in the world." She pointed toward the door. "Take your sister's advice now, big brother. Go home. Get rest and keep your Esper senses on full alert."

Erik leaned over and hugged her. "I will. Thank you."

Alissa smiled through tear-filled eyes. "Focus, Erik. Don't think about this. Little John will be back in a few days and so will Rebecca. We can manage things here and I'm sure the firm already knows what's going on, I expect some unsolicited assistance from them as well."

Erik nodded. "That wouldn't surprise me, but keep me apprised anyway. I'll do my best to keep you in the loop. If Brianna calls, contact me. She always calls the office phone."

The young woman gave a curt nod. "We'll take care of everything here. You have your family to protect, and a war to prevent."

* * *

Vatican City. Rome, Italy

The long limousine pulled up to the Audience Hall by Saint Martha's Palace. Erik spotted Bishop O'Malley and several other high-level clergy gathered to meet them. Shanda was visibly apprehensive and held EJ tight as the young boy was captivated by all the different sights. Martin seemed tense. The normally stalwart counselor had been very quiet on the ride over. Erik didn't know if it was due to the long plane ride or if his mentor was having some flashbacks to their experiences on the last trip and the mixed feelings of knowing his son was resting here for all eternity. The detective placed a comforting arm on Denton's shoulder. "Are you okay Martin?"

Denton smiled and nodded. "I'm sorry. I'm just a bit jet lagged is all. My back side is a bit sore from all this sitting."

Erik nodded. "Yeah, we all need a rest." He looked over at an animated EJ. "Well most of us need a rest."

They came to a stop and the driver opened the door. As they climbed from the limo, Erik spotted the Archbishop. The old man walked toward them and the officials seemed to part like pigeons allowing him to approach the new arrivals.

"Mr. Denton, Mr. Knight, welcome back to Vatican City." The old man looked over toward a nervous Shanda. "And you are Shanda Knight. Welcome."

Shanda nodded. "Thank you..." She wrung her hands. "Sir? I'm sorry. I don't know how to address you."

The Archbishop smiled. "Most people call me, 'Your Grace,' but that seems a bit formal."

Shanda did her best to smile. "Your Grace."

The Archbishop nodded. His eyes went wide as he spied EJ. He took two steps toward the boy. EJ moved forward to greet him but Shanda held him close. The Archbishop stopped abruptly and knelt. "Hello, young man, how are you?"

EJ smiled. "Hi! I'm EJ." The child looked at the Archbishop, his brow furrowed. "Why are you wearing a robe? Did you just wake up?"

Erik rolled his eyes. Martin broke out laughing and Shanda turned beet red.

The Archbishop, to his credit, nodded and smiled at the boy. "It does look like I have a bathrobe on doesn't it. But I've been up for a while."

Bishop O'Malley walked forward. "Archbishop, we have refreshments inside. I'm sure our guests are weary and would be glad for a chance to sit so we can get reacquainted."

They were escorted to a large corner room. A lavish buffet had been set up and Erik suddenly felt famished. Two young nuns entered and offered to take EJ to a separate room with food, games and several toys. Shanda refused. "He's fine here with me, but thank you for offering."

Erik leaned over. "Hon, you wanted to come here. This is protected ground. If something happens, I'll know immediately. He's just going to get bored and antsy here." He gave his wife a moment to reconsider.

Shanda sighed, then nodded. "EJ, do you want to go with the nice ladies and play with some toys?"

Erik motioned for his son and the boy came over quickly. The protective father reached inside his shirt producing his Esper weapon. "Protect EJ!"

The staff hummed an eerie baritone octave and flowed around the boy's wrist taking the shape of a heavy bracelet.

EJ held up his forearm. "It feels warm."

Erik nodded. "You'll get used to it in a few minutes." He held his son close, looking directly into his eyes. "Mom and dad need to have some adult talk with our friends here. You be on your best behavior. Okay, buddy? I'll be by to get you later."

EJ nodded and walked over to the nuns. He took their hands as they gently led him out of the room.

"Do you like Lego?" EJ asked as the door to the conference

room closed. "I like your hats!" was the last sound they heard as the boy happily walked down the hallway.

Martin snickered.

"A most robust, inquisitive child," The Archbishop complimented. "You have done well."

Shanda's eyes remained fixed on the door where EJ had gone. "Thank you."

The tension in the room grew palpable. "Agent Knight, it seems we owe you an apology. Our records regarding you and your son were flawed. I am extremely embarrassed. We are supposed to have the preeminent archive of all records. It's disturbing to discover that an underground anti-government activist has more accurate biblical data than the Vatican archives."

Erik laughed. "I assume you're referring to Charlie Gallagher."

The Archbishop inclined his head. "Yes. I believe that's the gentleman's name."

"Mr. Gallagher is very resourceful, but he is on a leash, I assure you." Denton remarked as he sliced into a side of roast beef.

"We believe our records were tampered with during the establishment of our computer systems. One of our clerics that manage our information systems is running a thorough check to make sure nothing else has been corrupted."

Bishop O'Malley leaned in. "May I ask a question?"

Erik shrugged. "Fire away, Your Excellency. We're all friends here and we're all allies. We're going to have to be open and honest with each other and trust each other. I freely confess that's a weakness in my character; trust. But I'm willing to give it freely."

O'Malley raised an eyebrow. "We appreciate that, Agent Knight and we'll do our best to be worthy of your trust." O'Malley looked at Shanda. "And you, Mrs. Knight, does your husband speak for you as well?"

"No, he doesn't," Erik jumped in. "Mrs. Knight is free to make up her own mind."

All eyes focused on Shanda, she looked over at Erik. He winked. She smiled and blew out a long breath. "In this case, I'll defer to my husband's good judgment."

O'Malley nodded and the tension in the room evaporated. "Excellent. Now let's get down to business. We have a great deal of ground to cover. What's been going on? We were only told that you would be returning and there was a disturbance of great magnitude?"

Erik poured a cup of coffee, then offered the carafe to Shanda as he began to speak. "You know about the attack on the DC3 by the gargoyle-like creatures, but my wife and son were also attacked at the same time by some kind of dark, smoky entity. It tried to kill them. I was able to send my staff through a portal and EJ was able to use the weapon and vaporize the demon—" Erik grinned "—and the entire back side of our house and two large pine trees. That was a clear attempt at killing me and my family in one simultaneous assault. The next day, an entity named Bartholomew came for EJ at my gym and insisted that I surrender him. I declined the offer and we discussed our difference of opinion by exchanging demonic fire for plasma blasts, nearly ruining my gym in the process. Later that evening, EJ and I were attacked by several more demonic forces, progressively stronger, with some beings over twenty feet in height. The entire plaza and parking lot were damaged during the battle." Erik paused as the gathered clergy gasped in shock.

O'Malley shook his head in dismay. "There are specific rules and laws that forbid such creatures traversing into this realm. Bartholomew is an agent of Lucifer. He knows the rules and has never before violated them. I can only assume that with the discovery of the chosen being of Light, Lucifer is desperate to keep his advantage."

Another cleric poured a glass of water for the Archbishop. The old man accepted it with a shaky hand. "Lucifer would not break the covenant. Bartholomew is often rash and impulsive while doing his master's bidding. I suspect your interaction was nothing more than bravado. No doubt Lucifer has punished him in some way. But as for the other acts against you, that stinks of Molec and his army. But why all these forces would attack now in tandem makes no sense. Many demons are like mindless predators, reluctant to work together and difficult to control. I am grateful you took shelter here, Agent Knight."

Erik shook his head. "I don't know if it was Molec who

organized the fight in the parking lot. Lucifer spoke directly to me, as a voice in my head. Also, I had backup during the second attack. A winged being of pure white vaporized one of my larger opponents and restored my ruined truck with a simple wave of his hand. This being and Lucifer spoke like they knew each other and had battled before. This entity extended the protective offer of Vatican City. He also told us of the price my son has on his head by both Molec and Lucifer. I'm not sure what it all means but I know it's bad. Perhaps you'll enlighten us as to just how bad?"

Bishop O'Malley scratched his head. "Can you describe the first entities that attacked you?"

Erik nodded. "Between six and seven feet tall. Their skin resembled gnarled tree bark. They were rust and brick colored. They had glowing green edged weapons and could project greenish energy." Erik rubbed his shoulder. "They were very skilled fighters and very persistent."

O'Malley rubbed his chin. "Were there five of them?"

"There were."

"The Quint Demons! They are in the employ of Molec functioning as his primary assassins for hire. I think you experienced a mixed bag of freelancers, Agent Knight. I imagine both Molec and Lucifer are equally frustrated at this point."

Denton cleared his throat. "If these demons are all mercenaries, then they'll work for the highest bidder. I guess the question is whose going to raise the stakes higher, Lucifer for possession of the boy or Molec wanting the child eradicated?"

Shanda shuddered, then looked up at Erik.

"Your thesis doesn't give me a warm fuzzy, Counselor." Erik sighed heavily.

Denton nodded. "I know. I'm sorry." He glanced over at Shanda. "But right now EJ is safe and Shanda is safe. The forces of Dark had their shot and they blew it. Had they joined their forces and organized an assault, who knows what would have happened. Our enemy's hatred of each other may work to our advantage. I'm guessing Lucifer and Molec will be fighting each other as well as fighting us. That gives our side an advantage. We just have to figure out how to capitalize on it."

The Archbishop leaned forward. "I know you have been

informed of the dangers by Light's messenger. There is little we can add to what you've been told save that a soul bounty is forbidden. It's obvious that Molec wants the boy dead, period." He looked at Erik. "He wants you dead as well, which explains the attack at your house and on the plane. It seems Lucifer would rather possess the child than kill him, which is why demons are attacking in groups and with some organization."

Erik frowned. "I don't know, those large creatures seemed pretty intent on barbecuing us both at one point. If not for the staff's protection, my son would be toast. If Lucifer wanted to kidnap EJ, he's going about it in a peculiar fashion."

"Not really." The Archbishop shook his head. "Lucifer wants the boy alive. Your life, however, is expendable. By threatening the child, the evil one forces you out in the open where you can be engaged directly and possibly destroyed. If the child has no guardian, he can be taken easily. Lucifer knows you have to be eliminated. I believe this first attack by Bartholomew was exploratory. Bartholomew has been known to be arrogant and an opportunist. He probably was hoping to impress his master with his bravado. The Dark Lord wanted to test you with the other attacks, see the extent of your power by throwing progressively more powerful foes at you and observe as you responded to each threat. This would give him time to study you, gather vital data, and look for weakness. Only after his hordes ground you down would the real attack begin." The old man fumbled with a water glass. "Lucifer, the devil, simply wants to win, and having the boy alive would feed his sizeable ego and give him a much-needed edge. Whether or not God would directly interfere at that point is unknown. I believe, and it pains me to say this, but Lucifer isn't the real threat at this point. Molec and the forces he can bring to bear are the real danger right now. Molec has zero regard for rules or life. The archdemon doesn't care about anything except causing the most damage to both sides and ruling in Lucifer's place. We've provided a temporary stopgap by hiding you here. The child is protected from all demonic attacks while in this sanctuary. We are still susceptible to human intervention as you discovered earlier." The Archbishop gave Shanda a reassuring smile. "Worry not, Mrs.

Knight we've been cleaning house over the last weeks and most of the rats and cockroaches have been purged. There are enough elite guard and other entities within our walls to keep your child and you well protected."

Martin exhaled heavily and rubbed his forehead. "I don't want to appear combative, Your Grace, but I'm not comfortable assigning human motive and human desire to beings that clearly aren't human. How do we even know what Molec or Lucifer really want? We can assume and guess based on the limited information available to us, but do you really know? Does anyone really know?"

Erik jumped in. "I understand your concern, Martin. But the divinity in my office pretty much had the same assessment. I would have to believe that he..." Erik looked over at the Archbishop. "Are there male and female divine entities? He seemed like a man."

The Archbishop actually chuckled. "They are divine, immortal beings that assume a familiar form when making appearances to man. Angels are not human and don't reproduce like mortal species. They do not have a gender, Agent Knight. And to answer your question, Mr. Denton, despite their inhumanity and immortality, the traits of greed, avarice and ambition are not limited to the human species."

Denton frowned shaking his head. "I meant no offense."

"None was taken. On the contrary, your mind is sharp and you asked a relevant, pointed question."

Erik knew his friend was tired and jet lagged. Shanda displayed signs of fatigue as well. They needed some time to recuperate and rest. "As I was saying, I'd have to believe the entity we spoke to understands the motivations of beings like itself." Erik looked over at his wife and winked. She seemed tense, constantly looking toward the door. He could sense her desire to be with her child. "Have any other of your sources come up with any kind of lead on Molec? Is there anything we can use as a starting point?"

Bishop O'Malley shook his head vehemently. "Nothing. Our people, divine and otherwise are looking feverishly, but the demon is very adept at hiding."

Erik glanced over at Martin. The detective cracked his

knuckles, balled his hand into a fist and grumbled. "We're going to have to fly back to DC. I want a few words with Speaker Collins and his staff. We need answers."

O'Malley waved his hands. "I don't think the Speaker will be very cooperative."

Erik's eyes went steel hard. "I'm sure I can convince him."

Denton laughed. "Special Agent Knight can be most persuasive, Your Excellency. His methods are a tad unorthodox but still effective."

"I suspect if we tip over enough apple carts in DC, we'll find some slugs and worms we can twist until they bleed out a few leads."

The Archbishop leaned in. "When you get to the capital pay a call to Congressman Anderson. He is one of our trusted servants. You'll find he can be of great use in helping you navigate your way through the labyrinth of DC politics. Sometimes it's better to navigate the maze with a guide than to just smash through the walls upsetting every applecart, Agent Knight."

The detective grinned. "Maybe, but that's not nearly as much fun." Erik looked over at Martin. "What do you say, Counselor, we eat some more of this great food, then grab some shut eye?"

Martin nodded. "Yeah, some sleep sounds wonderful." Denton shot O'Malley a snide look. "Not to be a rude guest, but since we're all chummy now, can I assume we'll have the courtesy of privacy in our respective quarters? I can set up another white noise box but I'd really rather not."

Bishop O'Malley blushed and gave an almost imperceptible nod. "I will personally guarantee your privacy."

Denton smiled. "Thank you."

Erik looked over at Shanda. He could sense her unease and discomfort. He leaned over and whispered in her ear. "Are you okay, babe? I'm usually the one giving off bad vibes, but I can sense your discomfort. If you're not comfortable here just say the word and we take EJ and head home on the next flight out. We're not prisoners here, you know that."

"I know. I'm sorry. I didn't think I'd be so uncomfortable. I didn't think you'd be leaving so soon after we just got here."

Erik put his arm around her. "I can spend another day or

two here to see if you get acclimated. If not, we'll be on a plane for home."

Shanda lightly kissed his cheek. "Just give us one day together before you leave and I should be fine."

"One day it is." Erik looked over at the Archbishop. "Excuse me, I'd like to make a slight adjustment to our itinerary. I'd like an extra 24 hours to stretch my limbs and be with my wife and son."

The Archbishop nodded. "I suppose we can delay another day. EJ is safe, and we can inform Congressman Anderson of your arrival and ensure the maze of bureaucracy won't require your pummeling. In the meantime, we can do our best to overwhelm your lovely bride with our hospitality."

Shanda blushed. Erik knew the Archbishop sensed her distrust and the old man was going out of his way to be accommodating. The detective appreciated that. They were allies now and he had to trust them along with his new divine partners. Erik knew the ethereal beings had their own agenda beyond his capacity to understand, but he had to focus on the here and now. Protecting EJ and Shanda was his goal. In order to do that, he had to stop Molec. This was the only viable course of action open to them.

Chapter 4: Shelter from the Storm

Molec's Lair

"I'm not interested in hearing about our failures, Mr. Akaowa. I'm only interested in success. Why is the child still breathing?" The archdemon swept his long coal-black forearm, pointing a lethal sharp claw at each human subordinate dressed in expensive Italian suits. "You all assured me Erik Knight and his child would be handled. I pay for and expect results!"

Mr. Akaowa trembled. The paper he held vibrated with each gesture of his hand. "I understand, Lord Molec. The Quint Assassins have never, ever failed. I was assured that..."

An angry fist slammed against heavy mahogany. "Are you offering excuses? I didn't ask for excuses. I asked and paid for results. I don't see results, gentlemen."

Akaowa flinched and shrank back.

"You can't blame us for the failure of your forces, Molec!"

The large demon stopped mid-rant and spun toward the skeletal demon lounging on a sofa in the far corner. "I didn't ask for your opinion, Wraith."

The wraith dared to point a pale bony finger at Molec, its voice as cold and chilly as death. "Knight killed our leader, vaporized him while barely cracking a sweat. Now you have every one of our forces out there forming alliances and blood pacts in a desperate attempt to kill this child to satisfy your Soul Bounty. You know how formidable Knight is, and you neglect to tell your forces. You're sending your followers to their doom, hoping some being gets in a lucky strike." The wraith opened a glass globe and produced a glowing orb. It held the struggling ball of light in dead hands. A faint shriek of terror whispered through the large room. The wraith bit into the globe like a ripe apple, ignoring the death shriek of the hapless soul. The humans winced as the sound echoed then faded away.

Molec leaned back, the heavy chair creaking under his immense bulk. Another human suit stepped toward the wraith. "What would you suggest we do? Even Lucifer's Golem Giants fell to Knight's power."

The wraith hissed. "One Golem fell to another power, a higher Lord of Light."

"The archangel!" Molec hissed. "We are drawing the higher lords' interest. Michael is His personal puppet. For the standard bearer of Light's army to become involved in human affairs means we need to move forward with even more urgency. The archangels cannot be allowed to interfere. They must be kept in the dark until the child is eliminated."

"How do we do this, Lord Molec?" A third suit began thumbing through several sheets of paper. "Knight, his bitch, and the child have all fled to Vatican City. Dukath, the War Angel, now guards the hybrid's female human child. Even those lesser relations at his work place are under the protective envelope of the firm and their ethereal forces."

Molec began moving several intricately carved horned demon chess pawns toward a large ivory king. "You cannot hide from me, Knight. Your child will die. It's merely a matter of time and resources. My time may be limited, but I have more than enough resources. I'll keep coming at you again and again until you wither and fall. Then I'll take the child and slit his throat in front of you and laugh while the petty, staunch Lords of Light watch in horror as I accomplish what Lucifer has failed to over many millennia." Molec swept all the pieces off the large board with one sweep of his powerful hand. "I will have this world and I will have Hell itself." The archdemon stood. "I want whatever forces we have remaining in Vatican City to avoid causing any turmoil but have them keep watch. If they have even the remotest chance at killing the child, they are to take it. I want Light's chosen one dead!"

"My Lord Molec, you must realize any human even attempting to harm the child in Vatican City will be signing his own death warrant under Angelic Law. No one would risk ethereal execution. The forces of Heaven have reinforced their security, both human and divine. An attempt on the hybrid child would be suicide."

Molec clenched his fists. "If they refuse, I'll personally hunt them down and feed their souls to the nosferatu. Which death would they find preferable?"

The human looked over at the skeletal wraith, still feasting on what was once a human soul. "I will relay your instructions at once."

Molec leaned forward "Listen to me! Speed is of the essence now. We have the cross, but it burns through its confinement. Once freed, we can neither contain nor control it. The forces of Light will come to claim their prize and we will not be able to resist the unfettered might of Light's army. But if we kill the child, we win by default. The cross is useless. We cannot keep this relic within our possession much longer. We must kill the child if our plans are to succeed!"

* * *

Vatican City, Rome.

Erik and Shanda walked arm in arm through Vatican City. EJ insisted on "playing" with the nice ladies with the funny hats. Shanda reluctantly relented, allowing the couple to spend some quiet, alone time.

They came to the area where Erik had battled the first nosferatu. The open park was still in ruins. Work crews were busily replacing glass panes and filling in the titanic crater caused by his lightning strike and the massive explosion.

"My God, Erik. This looks like a war zone that just got carpet bombed!" She looked up at him. "You did all this?"

Erik nodded as he surveyed the destruction. "Yeah, pretty much. Though when the thing exploded, it only added to the destructive force."

She stopped and looked directly into his eyes. "You said you had no limits. Was that bravado at the time or were you speaking the truth?"

Erik sighed. "As far as I know, there are no limits. At least none that I can find or dare approach. There's a certain line I'm afraid to cross, babe. I came close during the Observer War. I pounded through several layers of bedrock with one massive blow to the ground and I could have vaporized the Observer fleet in space if I wanted to. And you saw the size of their carrier ship. When I thought you were in danger, I didn't pay much heed to limits or caution. I could have destroyed the entire state if I kept going. The angel was right. To unleash that kind of power is reckless and foolish … so I do my best to keep it in check. But if I have to go to war to protect you and EJ, I'll push the boundaries to the very edge and beyond if need be."

Shanda fell into him, wrapping her arms around his torso. "Let's hope you can find Molec and end this without having to push yourself too far."

Erik nodded. "Even with all my power, babe, I still can't comprehend these ethereal beings. They move through galaxies like we move from one room to another. The rules of space and time don't seem to apply to them. We must seem like cockroaches."

Shanda put her head against his shoulder. "Maybe us, but not you. You killed some of them and that has them disturbed. They don't appear to be as formidable as their legend. You said the Seelak used Netherspace to move through distances instantaneously. Maybe our divine friends have a similar type of travel. You sent your staff half way across the world in the blink of an eye to save us from that hellspawn. Yes, they're immortal and powerful, but do they have the redeeming qualities that make human life so precious? Can they feel love, compassion and kindness?"

Erik shrugged. "I honestly don't know. But we have to trust them for now. I don't see any other choice." He wrapped his arms tightly around her. "I'm sorry for all of this. I wish I had the power to make it end now. With everything we've learned, I'm afraid we may never get back to what was once 'Normal'. How do we get it back, baby? How do we get back to normal after all this shit plays out for good or for bad?"

"I don't know, Erik. I don't know. But we go forward and make our lives again for us and for our son. We can't let this one event define us, as titanic as it seems. We have to move through it as a family."

They held each other tight, finding comfort and warmth inside love's embrace.

"Special Agent Knight?"

Erik looked up. "Damn it!"

He reluctantly let her go and turned toward the voice. A young cleric quickly approached. There was an air of urgency in the young man's stride. "Special Agent Knight, I've been instructed to escort you to the White Room. Mr. Denton, Bishop O'Malley, the Archbishop and several Vatican Councilmen are already there."

"I don't understand. My wife and I were supposed to have this day together."

"I don't know, sir. We were told to fetch you and Mr. Denton."

Erik shook his head, mildly annoyed. "Something's up." He kissed Shanda quickly. "I'm sorry, I'll get though whatever's got our holy friends on edge and meet you back at our suite."

"Don't apologize. Do what you have to do. I'd love to tour Rome, but…" She let her words hang.

"But there's probably a dozen things lurking out there just waiting for you." Erik finished her thought.

"Yeah, nothing like being a prisoner for my own safety. I feel like I'm under house arrest." She sighed. "I'll head over to the makeshift daycare and see how EJ is doing. Hopefully he's not embarrassing us with more unique observations."

Erik chuckled. "The boy has no filter. Where did he get that trait from?" Erik's eyes sparkled briefly as he teased her.

She blushed as Erik turned to go. Shanda reached for him again, rushing into his arms. "Promise me you'll fix this and make it better. As long as I've known you, you've always made it better." She looked up with tear-filled eyes. "I'm scared, I'm afraid for our son and for us."

Erik held her tight. "I swear to you, I'll do everything within my power to make things right."

She smiled. "I know you will, babe. I guess I just needed to hear you say it again."

Shanda let go, turned and walked away. Erik heard her sobbing.

"I am sorry to interrupt, but the Council is waiting. We must go."

He wiped away tears as he turned. "Lead the way."

The cleric moved quickly toward the large conference

building that contained the fortified room.

Special Agent Erik Knight got that queasy feeling as he entered the White Room. His enhanced senses quickly adjusted to the powerful illusion and he was able to define the barely visible walls and ceiling. He looked over at his old friend and could see him struggling to cope with the never-ending sea of white.

He noted again that all of the clergy had donned matching robes and it appeared that their heads were floating in air as the fabric perfectly matched the endless sea of bleached white light.

Erik sat next to Martin and silently poured himself a glass of water. He gestured toward Martin and the older man nodded, holding out his glass.

"You look perturbed."

The detective gave a curt nod. "I don't like being summoned, especially when I requested to spend this day with my wife who's apparently about to come apart thanks to all of this holy revelation."

"Clergy don't marry. They probably don't understand that type of relationship." Denton whispered behind his glass of water.

"Well I am, Counselor, and my bride is not very happy right now, which tends to make my mood rather foul."

Denton chuckled. "I understand, believe me. I remember those days all too well."

The Archbishop looked over at Erik. "Special Agent Knight, thank you for joining us. Our young cleric informs me that we interrupted a moment of intimacy with your spouse. I do apologize, but we need to agree upon a course of action. I hope you and your bride will forgive our intrusion."

Erik didn't really trust himself to speak. He was annoyed, but the Archbishop's apology was genuine "Thank you, I'll relay your apology to Shanda later on. I thought we had agreed upon a course of action. Mr. Denton and I were going to DC to turn over some stones and rattle some cages."

Bishop O'Malley nodded. "Yes, but we have gathered some further insight. Washington is abuzz in activity. The human politicians controlled by Lucifer have been much more active the past week. Several demonic agents of great influence have been to the capital city which indicates something is truly amiss." O'Malley looked at a sheet of paper then glanced over at Erik. "You may find this of interest. Bartholomew, the herald of Lucifer, was spotted outside the speaker's office yesterday afternoon. He was in conference with Collins and the senate majority leader for several hours. Our men saw the majority leader leave, but not Bartholomew. We can only assume he simply vanished." O'Malley studied the report. "It says here Bartholomew was constantly rubbing his jaw as if in discomfort."

Erik smirked. "I knocked his jaw out of his head with a barbell, Your Excellency. Apparently, he found a replacement and isn't quite accustomed to it yet."

O'Malley snickered. "Our friends discomfort warms my heart, Special Agent Knight. But having the demon in Washington is noteworthy. We can assume they're just as busy looking for Molec and the Ruby Crucifix. It pains me to admit that our dark adversaries have a head start. Molec, despite being a renegade, uses conventional demonic routes and contacts that all earthbound hellspawn can access. This means he can be tracked or spotted by any other demons. We don't have that advantage. Molec's foot soldiers are probably well known to Lucifer and his forces, the number of spies they have searching must be quite sizeable at this point. Molec has the advantage over his former master right now and has made his intentions known by taking out the bounty on your child. Lucifer has countered that action but still needs to find the artifact and the archdemon to regain his strategic advantage on Earth. The King of the Damned cannot be happy with the current turn of events."

The Archbishop leaned forward. "I strongly urge you and Mr. Denton to tread lightly. Washington is in an upheaval right now and if you two charge in wreaking havoc and mayhem, all hell will literally break loose. We don't want Lucifer or Molec to know what we're doing. And we don't want any of our agents or networks in DC compromised. Despite the tumultuous events in play we cannot have humanity aware of the level of divine involvement within human affairs."

Martin nodded while Erik shook his head.

"Free will my ass, Archbishop. Your hands are just as deep in the cookie jar as Lucifer's."

The room fell silent. Erik and the Archbishop locked eyes. The hybrid's eyes burned a fiery intense glow. "We're not supposed to be pawns for divine amusement."

"Special Agent Knight, our hand in the cookie jar isn't to steal the cookies in your clever metaphor but to prevent the dark hand of Lucifer from emptying the jar."

Erik smiled a shark-like grin that sent a shudder through the room. "Methinks thou doth protest too much, Archbishop. But now isn't the time to argue semantics or the impact of divine intervention in the affairs of man." Erik took a sip of his water. "We'll hunt down Molec, but I'll do it my way with my methods. I won't trample through the halls, but I'm not going to pussyfoot around either." Erik looked over at Martin. "The counselor and I have enough experience dealing with bureaucrats. Just point us in the right direction and we'll get the job done."

The Archbishop sat back, eyes wide, as though he'd been slapped. "These are not normal times. I urge you to let caution overrule your proclivity to wreak havoc."

Denton stepped in. "We understand the epic calamity, Your Grace, but politicians are consummate liars, especially politicians that happen to represent the interests of Satan. One can only assume that they are the best at lying and deception. When dealing with characters of low scruples, it's often necessary to encourage cooperation through some personal discomfort."

The Archbishop frowned. "Will you at least coordinate with our contact before you begin 'persuading' anybody on Lucifer's payroll? You start breaking fingers and arms straight away, Lucifer will clear out his agents and we'll have to spend even more time locating them again. The Dark Prince may even send more of his own forces to neutralize the both of you if you push too hard."

Denton laughed. "A hack politician will never leave Washington, Your Grace. Their mouths and pocketbook are glued to the taxpayer dime. I don't think we have any intention of riling up the demonic side of Washington, but the human side needs a little cage-rattling. As for Lucifer sending out the shock troops, the firm has a few toys I've recently discovered and I know my young associate here is more than capable of dealing with such problems. I don't think Lucifer or Molec are going to throw any more resources toward us and they must know the child is here, protected. If I were a betting man, Archbishop, I lay odds moving EJ here has both sides in an uproar. They're scrambling now to find a way to counter that move."

"Why do you think that, Mr. Denton.?"

Erik interrupted. "Because if we were on the opposing side, we'd be addressing ways to breach this compound."

Bishop O'Malley's face paled, nearly matching the ivory background. "You don't think they would be so bold as to attack the Holy City? We've reinforced our guard and Light's forces patrol the streets and the sky above, unseen."

Erik looked over at Denton. The old man nodded, rolling his eyes. "You said EJ was the key, the chosen one. By hiding him here and providing us shelter, you've drawn all the attention to Vatican City. The ghouls and creepy crawlies are no longer interested in me because I'm no longer the obstacle, this fortress is. This place is what stands between EJ living and dying now. You said this place was protected and assured me my family would be safe. You must have realized what would happen once we took shelter here. Lucifer's and Molec's objectives haven't changed. They just have a new obstacle to overcome." Erik pointed toward the Archbishop and Bishop O'Malley. "You."

"They cannot get here, Agent Knight, not with the forces of Light on guard and ready to do battle." The Archbishop countered adamantly.

Erik looked back over at the old man. "I hope so, for all your sakes. I'm staking the lives of my son and my wife on that. My being in Washington won't upset the applecart nearly as much as you did by providing us sanctuary."

The Archbishop nodded. "You're very astute, Special Agent Knight. I commend you and Mr. Denton. Your minds are sharp and agile, but I assure you we are more than able to dissuade and repel any advances by the forces of darkness. We will keep your family safe while you and Mr. Denton recover our stolen relic."

"We'll see if we can pick up the trail in DC," Erik replied. "I also haven't forgotten about Father Lazarus. I believe he's been dusted by those who hired him, but I'd like to be one hundred percent sure." Erik looked over at his friend. "That's a debt I'm not leaving unpaid."

Martin nodded and smiled.

Bishop O'Malley leaned forward. "Our associate in DC can probably shed light on that topic as well. Our friend is Congressman Anderson. He's a low level politician that has the knack of escaping notice. But he's the best source of information on the ethereal games played in Washington. Beyond Speaker Collins, he can point you to the other big players on the other side and who may or may not be privy to vital information and intelligence on Molec, his forces and movements."

"You have my word, Archbishop." Denton looked over at his young associate. "We'll start there and get the lay of the land before we visit the speaker or any of his staff."

"Splendid, and we will continue using our resources here to unearth any new developments and we'll keep your lovely bride and child safe and reasonably entertained."

Erik folded his arms. "I would be most grateful for that."

The friction in the room seemed to dissipate. It was clear to the Vatican officials that Erik Knight was not going to be manipulated or controlled. Despite their alliance, the detective was still assuming control. Erik looked over at Martin and nodded.

"Will you leave tomorrow?"

Erik looked over at O'Malley. "Yes. Tomorrow will be fine."

"We'll make the necessary travel arrangements and let our forces know. We don't want more gargoyles trying to shoot you out of the sky."

"Neither would I," said Erik.

* * *

Vatican Suites. 7:30PM

"He's out like a light. I've never seen him so excited to be anywhere before." Shanda sat on the large chair. Erik and Martin were discussing their trip and their afternoon meeting with the Archbishop.

"This is a big adventure to him. Thankfully, he's not focusing on what happened to us earlier." Erik drained the remains of his coffee.

"Ah the joy of youth, that blissful ignorance of innocence," Martin commented from a nearby sofa.

Shanda smiled. "I could use some bliss right about now, Martin."

"I'll call room service. They have just about everything else available." Denton pointed toward a gigantic menu on the coffee table.

"If only." She glanced over at Erik. "Did I interrupt something?"

"No, we were just comparing notes regarding this afternoon's meeting." Erik slid over on the couch and gestured. Shanda came over and sat by him. "I've scanned the area around Vatican City, Counselor. Our holy friends were correct, the skies do have eyes. I spotted at least a dozen separate ethereal beings circling directly over the city and the human security has been vastly improved since our last visit."

"So you think it can withstand an attack?"

Erik nodded. "Yeah, I'm inclined to believe God won't let anything happen to this place. I understand the rules about non-interference, but I also suspect the higher powers on either side bend that particular rule like a pretzel when it suits their need."

Denton chuckled. "You weren't exactly the pillar of cooperation earlier. I get you don't trust them, but after your big speech about us being allies and all..." He let his words hang.

Erik picked up the cue and continued. "We should be beyond that, I know, but our friends seem to want to drive the train and dictate what we do and how we do it. That's not gonna work here. They've been flat footed for decades and constantly on the losing end. Why would either one of us take advice from bureaucrats ... even ones that represent divinity? If the Ethereals want to tell me something, I'm confident our tall, blond friend will pop in unannounced and pass along the good tidings."

Denton chuckled. "Let's hope you're right." Denton looked over at Shanda. "What about you? Are you comfortable here? I know it's not really my place to ask but you both are like family to me. I still feel like I got you into this mess by asking you to investigate William's murder. Things seemed to escalate out of control shortly thereafter."

Shanda reached over and placed a comforting hand on Denton's. "Nonsense. This revelation would have happened with or without you being involved, Martin. You actually allowed us to get in front of it in a way. We would have been blindsided by all of this if Erik hadn't agreed to help you."

"She's right, Counselor. This isn't your doing. And right now you're helping me protect my son, so it's Shanda and I who are grateful."

The old man sniffed and hastily wiped away a tear. "We're family."

Shanda held up a glass of soda. "To family."

They touched glasses and drank a toast.

Denton stood. "I think we've covered all the ground that needs to be covered. I'm going to head back to my room and let you two have a quiet evening together. Don't bother getting up. I'll see myself out."

Erik watched as Martin left, closing the heavy wood door behind him. "He's a good man. I can tell he's still hurting. He should be home, grieving for his son not jetting around the globe chasing goblins, demons and corrupt politicians let alone shady Vatican leaders."

Shanda gently caressed his back. "Martin is as stubborn you are, babe. He wouldn't sit this out for anything. Like you, it's not in his nature."

Erik nodded. "If something happens to him, I'll never forgive myself."

"Martin's a big boy and we both know he can take care of himself. Don't start getting all melancholy. You need to be sharp as a razor."

"I know." Erik looked directly at her, "Are you gonna be okay here? I know you're still not comfortable."

Shanda shook her head. "I'll be fine." She looked back

toward the room where EJ was sleeping. "He'll be fine too. He's charmed the wimples off Sisters Charice and Cecelia. EJ is far more adaptable to change than his mother."

Erik laughed. "Or his father for that matter."

Shanda's face tightened. "How did they do it, Erik?"

He tilted his head. "You're pivoting again, Angel, and you totally lost me."

She blushed. "Sorry. I'm referring to Mary and Joseph. How did they deal with knowing what their son was and all the shit he'd be facing? I don't want to see my son die like Mary did. I couldn't bear that."

Tears streamed down her face and Erik held her tight.

"That won't happen. You can't think like that. I remember from the teachings that Jesus knew he had to die and that he'd rise up again. That's not in EJ's destiny. He's supposed to herald in a new age of man, not die and be reborn for mankind's sins."

Shanda nodded. "But evil was gunning for Jesus, was it not?"

Erik held her tighter. "Yeah, but Joseph couldn't punch through a mountain or vaporize demons. I can and will in order to protect our son." Erik pointed toward the sky. "There's also enough ethereal air power overhead that no demon would dare make any attempt. You were right. Coming here was the right move. God knew what he was doing when he chose you, there is no better mother on the planet."

Erik gently kissed her cheek, then her lips. Shanda fell deeper into him losing herself in his powerful embrace. Soon all the fears and problems were forgotten. All that mattered was the blending of their hearts.

Chapter 5: Dabbling in the Dark

Washington DC

"That was a particularly grueling flight." Denton moaned settling into the limousine.

Erik smiled. "Quit griping, Counselor. You get to keep the frequent flier miles. When this is all over, we can book a trip to Maui and relax on the beach with one of those funny umbrella drinks. We can watch EJ make sandcastles and go to one of those fancy pig roasts with the guys twirling fire batons."

Denton fidgeted. "I'll hold you to that." The counselor glanced at his phone. "We should be there any minute."

"I don't know why Anderson picked such an out of the way location for a meeting?" Erik looked out the window as their car passed several rundown buildings and tenements.

Martin chuckled. "I'm sure he's been told to keep us far away from DC until after our chat. If he's seen talking with us, I'm sure his cover, whatever that may be, would be severely compromised."

Erik frowned as the limousine pulled into a small diner parking lot. Erik studied the small neon sign and felt a pang of remorse. "Madame's."

Denton leaned over staring at the sign. "Sonovabitch. Go figure. What are the odds of that?"

The driver opened the door, clearly nervous. "I was told to come back in twenty minutes."

Denton nodded, slipped the man a twenty dollar bill and headed toward the glass door. He glanced back. Erik was still studying the sign. "I'm sure the food isn't as good and the coffee tastes like shit. C'mon Erik, let's get inside."

The detective sighed and followed.

Congressman Anderson looked out of place, seated at the large booth. Contrary to what Erik expected, the small diner smelled heavenly. The scent of fresh brewed coffee reminded him of the place he'd considered home for so many years.

Anderson was wisp thin, swallowed by the poorly tailored suit and mismatched tie. "Mr. Denton, Mr. Knight, welcome to my little oasis in a desert of urban blight."

Anderson shook their hands and pointed toward the food sitting on the table. "I think I got it right, vegetable beef soup and a grilled chicken breast sandwich. Mr. Denton, I know you're fond of burgers so I had a house special with steak sauce prepared for you."

Erik raised an eyebrow. "Well Congressman, you've obviously done your homework."

"Not me, Mr. Knight, my ethereal associates." Anderson pointed upward. "He sees all."

"The ultimate spy," Erik mumbled, sliding into the booth.

A waitress came over and poured coffee for each man, flirting with the Congressman and exchanging pleasantries with the two newcomers. The similarity to Erik's Madame's was alarming. The detective sipped the coffee and wasn't surprised with the mild flavor that reminded him so much of his old home.

Anderson smiled. "Try the soup. It's delicious."

Erik sampled the soup. It was identical to his friend Jeff's recipe. He bit into the grilled sandwich and experienced the same delicious flavor of unique marinade and spice Jeff used. "This can't be. It's exactly the same as Jeff's. It's not similar. It's exactly the same. Jeff said it was a secret family recipe handed down from his great grandfather."

Anderson nodded. "Bear with me a moment." He tuned and shouted, "Jeanine? My friend here wants the recipe to your chicken."

A pleasant, friendly voice responded from the kitchen. "That's a secret from my great granddaddy. You know that Michael. I'm never gonna tell."

Erik felt his flesh tingle. His eyes narrowed. "Mr. Anderson, I'm no longer amused. I'm annoyed. I don't wanna play your game anymore."

Anderson nodded. "I'm sorry, Erik. I just needed you to

understand something, to realize that you've always been surrounded by ethereal influence. Jeff, like his sister, Jeanine, are
unwitting agents of Light. Oh they don't realize it. Their role is
simply to provide a haven, a comfortable place for souls to sit,
relax and unwind. People feel safe and warm here because evil
is strongly repelled. Some humans come in and out, enjoy the
food and the ambiance, never understanding the significance.
But you, you were drawn to an oasis. You set up a business
in one and were an integral part of such a place." Anderson
pointed toward a rugged looking middle aged man with thin-
ning hair, typing away on a laptop. "Sometimes an oasis will
attract a peacekeeper, some special soul that resonates with the
unique qualities of such a place. Hal over there is a regular guy.
He works a fifty-plus-hour a week job but really wants to write
the great American novel. He comes in here more and more
to write. He says the atmosphere helps him concentrate. One
night a few months back several men tried to rob this place.
Hal stopped them. He is skilled as you are in the ways of lethal force. He took a bullet in the process but earned himself
a special place here, part of the oasis family, like you were at
Madame's in Hopedale. Oh, he can't do the things you do. He's
just a simple guy with a simple life who found some needed
tranquility. And," Anderson smiled, "Hal and Jeanine have become an item recently, furthering the bond and the light of this
establishment."

Erik sipped his coffee. "I never knew Jeff had a sister. In
all the talks we've had, he never mentioned any of his family."

"Jeff was a private man, listening to others, rarely speaking
of himself—a trait we look for."

"She wasn't at his funeral, or the wake. Does she know
he's dead?" Erik looked over at the seemingly happy cook.

"She knows, and she grieved in her own way. She took his
passing very hard."

A lump formed in Erik's throat as he remembered his departed friend. "Can I talk to her?"

Anderson nodded. "I'm sure she would love to. After all
you knew her brother better than she did. To tell you the truth,
Special Agent Knight, you and your friend were connected in a
deeper way than you ever imagined."

Erik looked back. "How many? How many of these 'Oasis' diners are there?"

Anderson drained his coffee as Martin continued to devour his burger and fries. "Just a handful across the country. When your Madame's closed, another place was selected, but has no champion, yet, I gather someone special will feel the pull and become bonded just as you were to your place, as Hal is to this place. A soul will find peace and fulfillment there as well."

"This is all interesting," Denton wiped his mouth, "and delicious, but what does it have to do with finding Molec and the Ruby Cross?"

Anderson smiled as a waitress refilled his coffee. He waited until she'd moved on to another table. "Absolutely nothing, but I just needed you to know that you're not as much of an outsider as you believe. You've always been drawn to the Light, Special Agent Knight, even if you didn't realize it. You've been a part of the greater scheme longer than you believe."

Erik nodded, watching the man at the corner booth typing away. He seemed at peace, smiling at the waitresses and the way he looked over at the woman in the kitchen. He could see the genuine love. "Don't fuck his life up."

Anderson tilted his head. "Excuse me?"

"I said don't fuck his life up. He's happy. Let him be happy and have a good life. Don't drag him into the quagmire like you dragged me."

Anderson sipped his coffee, studying the detective. "You have a genuine compassion for your fellow man. How utterly rare. Mr. Hal Foster has his own destiny, as do we all. All paths are fraught with turmoil and trials, Special Agent Knight. His path will be no different. But I assure you he will lead a long fulfilling life." Anderson gestured toward Erik's plate. "Eat up before it gets cold. You eat and I'll talk for a bit." The congressman took a breath. "The game played in the capital is brutal. The ethereal beings are controlling more and more human pawns. We've been so busy plotting and scheming against each other that our country has been weakened greatly the last decade. We've allowed Molec to rise up and threaten this world." He gestured and another stunningly beautiful waitress filled his coffee cup. Anderson relished the hot beverage and continued.

"The two main power brokers for Lucifer are Senator Paul McMahon and House Speaker Andrew Collins. McMahon holds all the power in the senate despite not being the majority leader. He decides what bills are voted on and when. He has something on Majority Leader Ryan, and we don't know what it is, but we're looking. Ryan won't even go to the bathroom without McMahon's blessing. Art Milton on the Senate Arms Subcommittee is also a demonic player. He's been possessed by a demon for the past twenty years." Anderson sipped his coffee. "It's become a symbiotic thing, and Milton is a ladies' man and goes through women like I go through coffee. The demonic influence helped him overcome a certain embarrassing male issue and now he makes the most of it and does whatever bidding he's instructed, and spends all his non-session time at several high class brothels."

Anderson slid a folder over to Erik. The detective stopped eating and browsed through the pages. "All these people are taking orders from Lucifer?"

Anderson shook his head. "No, but they all take direction from those that do. In effect, this is the network that we know of. I know there's dozens more that could be and I admit we simply don't know who or what Molec controls."

Erik folded the papers. "This is all well and good, but we need to start at the top of the food chain rather than the bottom."

Anderson tilted his head. "That could be dangerous. Lucifer won't appreciate his two major players being intimidated." Anderson smirked. "Or physically accosted. The fine balance established would be severely disturbed."

Erik shook his head. "Well then, Lucifer shouldn't have sent his goon to my dojo to kidnap my son! Congressman, do you want your cross back? Do you want to avoid the war that's brewing?"

Anderson nodded. "Of course, any sane being wants to avoid the end of our world and the end of mankind."

The detective leaned forward. "Then let me do my job the way I need to do it and stop worrying about pissing off the other side. Maybe if the forces of darkness were kept off balance they wouldn't be so damned organized and always two steps ahead of you."

Anderson sighed, tilting his head. "Touché." He took another deep drink of his coffee. "You're right, but just be careful. I'll let our people know what's coming so they can prepare."

Denton leaned forward. "And how secure is your line of communication?"

"Very secure, I assure you Mr. Denton."

Denton patted his stomach. "Okay, I appreciate the good meal, but we need to get to work. The longer we delay, the more likely it is we'll lose our element of surprise."

"I agree, Counselor." Erik extended his hand. "Thanks for the leads and the lay of the land."

Anderson took a deep breath. Erik sensed the man's discomfort. "Special Agent Knight, I'd also like to apologize to you."

"Why?"

"For my father's role in the Observer Incident."

Erik fell back in his seat. "Lt. Col. Anderson is your father."

The congressman nodded. "Yes. My father retired immediately after the final reports were filed. They tried to have him discharged but he had too many damaging secrets and contingency files stashed away. He was afraid for his life shortly afterward. Dad was trying to repent until the cancer became too much for him."

Erik sighed. "Cancer. I'm sorry. How bad is it?"

Anderson looked down at the table. "Terminal, I'm afraid. He doesn't have much time left."

Erik reached over and placed a gentle hand on the congressman's shoulder. "When you see your dad, you tell him Erik Knight bears him no ill will. Please tell him I'm grateful, as is my wife, for the help he gave her." Erik took a breath. "Your father shouldn't be carrying any guilt over the Observers. That was all his boss' doing."

Anderson looked up. He was struggling to maintain his composure. "Thank you, Erik. I know that will make him rest easier."

The two men exchanged a handshake. Erik drained his coffee once again amazed at how much it tasted like the old Madame's he knew. He looked back over at the man happily typing away and felt a pang of envy. Hal looked up at him. He smiled and nodded. Erik lifted his coffee cup in a friendly gesture as he stood to leave. "It's nice to know a place like this exists. I'm gonna have to come back here."

Anderson smiled. "Are you going to speak to Jeff's sister?"

Erik looked toward the kitchen and sighed. "Another time, when all of this is done, I'll come back here for a visit. I have some of Jeff's personal belongings that should go to his family."

Anderson nodded. "A prudent course of action. The door is always open Special Agent Knight. You are, after all, part of the oasis family. I remind you that God, like nature, abhors a vacuum. Look closer to home. You may find a refuge there."

Denton stood. "Our ride is back, Erik."

"Be careful, gentlemen. You're not just dealing with crooked politicians. You're dealing with the Devil. Up to now things haven't been going his way. He may get a bit more agitated once you start poking him in the eye with a stick."

Erik nodded toward Anderson. "He's poked my eye, Congressman, and ethereal being or supernatural boogeyman, I intend to poke back."

Anderson nodded. "I understand your rage, Erik, but just know the forces you're challenging. They don't tolerate mortal interference."

Erik stood. "There's no way to recover your relic without mortal interference. Let's just hope God and his forces will have our back when the shit hits the fan."

Anderson stood, walking the men to the door. "Good luck, gentlemen. May Light watch over you."

* * *

Martin kept staring at Erik as the limousine navigated the highway into DC. Erik finally turned toward his mentor. "What? You've been gawking at me the last fifteen minutes, Counselor. Get it off your chest."

"It's nothing really." Denton hesitated. "You were awfully generous regarding Anderson's father."

The detective stared out the window. "It didn't cost me anything, Martin and if it'll give the man some comfort in his dying days, all the better. He did help Shanda and EJ and, at this point, what good does holding a grudge do?" Erik looked over. "What does the good book say? Let he who is without sin cast the first stone, or something along that line."

Denton nodded. "Yeah, something along those lines." He paused. "You seem to be involved with these ethereal forces more than you realize. That whole oasis revelation is pretty interesting."

Erik scratched the back of his neck. "Yeah, there was something special about Jeff's place. Now I know. Again, I'm not sure we really have a free will. Maybe we're all just puppets in some grand theatre." The moody detective sighed. "I'm not a puppet and I resent having my strings pulled. It's time to cut the cord and fly solo." Erik pointed out the window. "There's DC. We need to get our game faces on. I don't expect our friends to part with their secrets willingly."

Denton nodded. "I don't know if our puppet masters see it the same way you do."

Erik and Martin approached the palatial office of the House speaker. His hybrid senses buzzed. There were several non-human biometric signals emanating from human shells. "Cripes, Counselor, half the people here have some sort of supernatural imprint. I've been to DC before and have never, ever picked up on such a presence."

Denton whispered, "I think you hit the nail on the head earlier. Molec has overturned the applecart and both sides are frantically struggling to set things right again."

Erik walked to a receptionist and flashed his agency credentials. "I need a few moments with Speaker Collins."

The woman studied him and her eyes fell on Denton. The old man flashed his senior bureau credentials. "We all know the speaker is in." He leaned forward. "It'll be a much easier day for everyone here if we're allowed a few moments of the speaker's time."

The woman tapped her keyboard accessing several data screens. "I'm sorry Special Agent Knight and Bureau Chief Denton." She looked from her screen. "You don't appear to be on the speaker's calendar. Speaker Collins is booked clear through the next two weeks. I can schedule you both later on?"

Erik shook his head. "I'm afraid that won't work for me. I'll just go in and introduce myself."

The detective walked toward the heavy door. Two burly uniformed guards approached him. Without breaking his stride, Erik casually tossed one of the men across the foyer. The large man hit the floor hard, skidding into several clerks, knocking them over like bowling pins. The second guard reached for his weapon but Erik kicked him squarely in the chest. The guard sailed back, crashing into the heavy door, collapsing the locked barrier inward.

Several panicked shouts erupted from the office, and four men with non-human biometric readings rushed forward. One being produced a glowing orange knife, the weapon simply materializing as he rushed toward the detective. The guard lunged forward in an attempt to push the blade through Erik's torso. He tilted his body, avoiding the thrust, and grabbed the man's wrist, slamming his other hand down on the elbow joint shattering the arm bones and joint. The sickening snap echoed off the heavy stone tile work. The guard gasped in pain as Erik slammed his elbow into the man's ribcage and tossed him like a sack into two of his cohorts. Erik spun to face the fourth man but Martin had his pistol drawn and held him at bay.

One of the guards he'd knocked over shot back up and attacked. The man's eyes burned an angry amber as he launched precision punches and kicks at superhuman speed. Erik blocked and countered each attack, then went on the offensive. He launched a series of left jabs faster than the enhanced human could follow. Each blow cracked like a whip. The guard stepped back as blood spilled from his nose. Erik followed with a low Thai kick taking out the guard's forward leg. The powerful kick snapped the man's femur. The crippled guard fell to the floor wincing but slowly stood, hobbling, favoring his other leg. An orange, burning knife materialized in his hand, similar to the other guard's but much larger and more formidable.

The guard leapt forward, slicing at a forty-five degree angle. Erik cartwheeled backwards avoiding the weapon. The demonic blade sliced right through the heavy door jamb and frame. Erik raised his arms. Tucked inside its sheath, his staff moaned.

"Not now, I can handle this." The staff fell silent but Erik could sense the weapon's presence and desire for combat.

The guard attacked again. Erik stepped forward into the attack raising his arm to block the guard's overhead strike. The detective launched a brutal open palm punch into the man's sternum. Several ribs cracked and splintered under the powerful blow. The guard's eyes popped and he gasped, wheezing as the breath was driven from his body. Erik stepped back. The guard dropped to the ground holding his ribcage, coughing up blood and some greenish fluid. The orange blade dissipated into nothingness.

"Stay down." Erik barked. "I don't want to hurt you anymore."

The guard looked up. His face began to change. The pale skin wrinkled and melted away revealing furrowed black flesh."

"You will lose, Lord of Light. Darkness will rule this planet." Violet fire consumed the being, flaking off ash and withering it away.

Erik looked down at the burn marks staining the floor. He shook his head. "We'll see, but you won't be around to know either way." Erik looked back over at Martin. "The door's open now, Counselor, and Speaker Collins' calendar suddenly has an opening. Shall we drop in for tea?"

Denton took two steps forward, never dropping his weapon from the fourth guards' head. "Right behind you." Denton dropped his finger on the trigger of his Colt .45 and locked the weapon's sights on the terrified guard's left eyeball. "I'm going to turn away now, but before I do I want you to start walking away from here. I strongly advise you not to do anything stupid, and no funny orange crap popping from your hands. Nod once if you fellow my meaning."

The nervous guard nodded, his hands dropped limply by his side. He slowly turned, his open hands held out as he walked away.

"Very nice." Denton took several cautious steps backward keeping his weapon locked on the retreating target. "Are our other friends secure?"

Erik nodded. "Yeah, one dead and two sleeping it off."

Several police officers rushed into the office. Denton flashed his credentials and pointed toward the unconscious demonic guards. "These two are very slippery and strong. Cuff them in steel bracelets, not the plastic restraints." The counselor turned and joined Erik, standing like a sentinel directly outside the speaker's office. "Well, let's not keep our host waiting any longer."

Erik smiled and they walked through the destroyed doorway, stepping over the unconscious guard.

Several men stared open-mouthed as Martin and Erik walked into the palatial office.

"Gentlemen, Speaker Collins is going to have to cancel this meeting." Erik pointed toward the shattered doorway and filleted door frame. "I'm sure you can show yourselves out."

Two men and one woman looked over at Collins, waiting for the speaker to say or do something. Collins, to his credit, didn't seem panicked. He made a small gesture with his right hand. "That's all right. We'll finish this discussion later this afternoon. Tell the President I'm not budging on the spending bill and if he wants his rider attached, he needs to play ball and get with the program."

The woman nodded. "I'll pass along your message, Mr. Speaker, but we have the votes to uphold a veto. You must know that."

Collins smiled a shark-like grin. "Ahhh, Ms. Vinsen, you should know by now it's never over until all the votes are counted."

"And everyone's been bribed or blackmailed." Vinsen stood gathering her briefcase and papers.

Collins dramatically put his hand over his heart. "You wound me, Madame."

The three filed out of the speaker's office clearly not happy about something. The woman glanced up at Erik. She studied the damage done by the two men. "Smack him one for me if you feel so inclined."

Erik studied the cocky man behind the desk. He looked down at the frustrated woman. "I'll take it under advisement, Ms. Vinsen."

Denton slipped his .45 into its holster and approached the table seating himself directly across from the senior congressman. "Mr. Collins, we have some questions for you regarding a particular theft of a very valuable object."

Collins' upper lip stiffened. Other than that, there was no facial expression. Erik detected a wave of discomfort despite the man's effort to remain calm. The House Speaker was not going to be rattled so easily.

"Well, I do like a dramatic entrance, Special Agent Knight, and greetings Mr. Denton. Word on the street is you're retiring."

Erik raised an eyebrow as he took a seat next to Martin. "I'd rather have made a more peaceful entrance, but your receptionist was less than hospitable, as were your guards."

Collins looked over Erik's shoulder as one of his men began to stir.

"Tell him to take a break, Mr. Speaker. There's been enough fisticuffs for one day."

Collins appeared to be weighing options. The detective knew he was considering the odds of having more of his demonic security unleashed.

"Special Agent Knight vaporized a wraith not too long ago and sent several other major demonic players back to Hell. I don't think you want this place reduced to a pile of rubble." Denton leaned forward. He too knew what was going through the speaker's mind.

Collins leaned back and addressed his guard. "Bruce, take a long lunch. See if the men outside need medical attention and have Colleen clear my calendar for the next hour or so. Also, get a crew up here to fix my door and polish the tiles where Hank met his demise."

The shaky guard nodded and disappeared.

"Okay, gentlemen, you have my attention." Collins stood and made his way toward a wet bar and began mixing a large drink. He turned back toward Erik and Martin and raised a bottle of very old Scotch. "Gentlemen?"

Both shook their heads.

"Your loss. Discussions are always better over a good drink." Collins resumed his seat. "Now what's so all-fire important that you had to kill and cripple my guards and interrupt a budget bill meeting?"

Denton leaned forward. "Erik, if I may."

Erik nodded, happy to let Martin begin.

"My son was murdered along with two other clerics in Vatican City not too long ago. During our investigation of that murder, we discovered the theft of a very special relic that holds a great deal of significance to certain elite forces that are waging a stealth war on this planet."

Collins sipped his drink, studying Denton with ice-cold eyes.

"We were able to apprehend a few bad apples during our visit in Vatican City. Several clergy are sweating out their sins in a penitence prison at the basement of Vatican City as we speak. In exchange for not being turned over to a divine judgment, they sang like canaries. Your name was on top of their song list, Mr. Speaker. You and a certain senior senator seem to be playing outside of your league with some very dark forces."

Collins' face set to stone. He took another sip of his drink, taking time to compose his response. "I don't know what you're talking about, Agent Denton. I have no dealings with the Vatican nor do I have any interest in the fairy tales spun by some delusional cleric whose only past time was probably diddling altar boys."

"Your guards reek of ethereal influence. Two of your men produced blades from thin air, Congressman." Erik sat back in his chair. "If you want to do this the hard way, I have no problem." Erik tensed his hand and a burning blue ball of plasma the size of a small pearl materialized. "You must know what I'm capable of, Mr. Collins. Today isn't the day to try my patience." Erik snapped his arm forward like a cobra strike. The micro plasma ball slammed into the wet bar. The bottles and the entire bar were enveloped in blue energy. Bit by bit they vaporized as the burning energy ate away the molecular structure vaporizing the plaster wall behind the structure as well.

Collins' face tensed. A bead of perspiration formed on his brow. "I know who you work for. I know who pulls your strings." A burning ball the size of an orange materialized in Erik's outstretched hand. The ambient heat from the energy caused both Martin and Collins to shield their faces. "A projectile of this size will vaporize the entire back wall and keep going for several yards." Erik turned the burning sphere on the House speaker. "Or it can vaporize you as well. You and your friends have a soul bounty out on my son and you've attacked my wife and ruined my home and my business as well as crippling several decent people in my employ." The plasma sphere continued to intensify. The papers on the table next to Erik burst into flame. "I'm not in the mood for games of deception or intrigue, Mr. Speaker. You either tell me what I want to know or I'll send your soul to Hell right now and you can spend eternity in some real fire. Are you willing to die right now, today? Because I'm more than willing to kill you and anyone else that's a threat to my son and my wife." The fire spread to more papers. The expensive mahogany wood began to smoke and char. Collins was visibly shaken as Erik brought the burning sphere closer to his face. "Five, four...."

Denton batted out the burning papers. He looked over at the now-terrified politician. "For Christ Sake Collins, do you really wanna die today?"

"Three, two...." Erik's arm tensed.

Collins broke. "All right, all right!" He flinched, backing away from the burning weapon. "Just make that thing go away!"

Erik relaxed and willed the agitated ions to disperse. Collins shook his head. "We didn't put the soul bounty on your son. We just want the boy detained so he can't take possession of the cross. Molec put the mark out on your kid."

Denton leaned forward. "Go on."

Collins leaned toward the counselor and whispered, "I got the call informing me that Lucifer wanted the cross." He pointed toward a phone sitting alone on a glass table. "Whenever I get ethereal instruction it's from that phone. I don't question the orders. I just do what I'm told. So when I was told to arrange the heist, I needed a mercenary that knew Vatican City and had an axe to grind against the Church."

"Lazarus," Denton snarled.

"Yes, my associates recommended Lazarus. No sane man or woman is going to go into Vatican City to steal. Even as immoral as humans have become, there are still some lines most crooks won't cross, if you'll pardon the pun." Collins took another sip of his drink. The man was sweating. "Lazarus was ideal—an excommunicated priest turned to the darkness and doomed to live outside all he held so dear while he lived. Father Lazarus was the perfect mercenary and he jumped at the chance to take some vengeance against the papal dynasty and the very church that betrayed him."

"Did you tell him to kill?" Denton's hands balled into fists.

"Hell no! Just the opposite, in fact. We wanted stealth—an in and out operation. Our agents in Vatican City staked out St. Martha's Chapel for weeks, studying the comings and goings of the staff and clerics. Nobody was supposed to be in that chamber. It was supposed to be a simple smash and grab. I acquired the stealth garb so he could get inside despite his particular affliction and get the job done, then get out unseen. What good is taking something of such value if those you robbed immediately know it's missing? Especially if your marks are the forces of Light." Collins tone was desperate.

"I didn't think stealing this thing was wise but I wasn't going to question my superiors. When Lazarus returned with the relic, he was vaporized by one of our employers for his brash, cold blooded murders. The vampire was a good thief but we couldn't risk him compromising us or indicting us in this theft. This was a huge rule violation and the implications are catastrophic to both sides. It was at that point we realized the orders we received weren't legitimate. Believe me, I expected to get incinerated right there on the spot. Our side is less forgiving and tolerant of failure. We can only figure that somehow Molec was able to influence somebody higher up in our organization. And I know everyone is being thoroughly vetted from the lowest congressional staffer to the highest ranking officials."

Erik looked over at Martin. The old man grinned, taking some solace knowing his son's killer was dead. "Your thief killed several good men. That blood is on your hands. You hired him. You bear the responsibility too."

Collins shook his head. "You can blame me all you want. I was just doing what I was ordered to do. It's what I've done and what those working for the forces of Light have done for centuries, dating back to when this country was founded."

Erik's curiosity piqued. "Explain."

Collins laughed. "Special Agent Knight, I don't have the

time to give you a history lesson but ask yourself this, how did a ragtag bunch of farmers defeat the mightiest army on the planet and gain their independence? Do you really think Washington and his pathetic army won that war without divine interference? Lucifer had blocked France's involvement initially but somehow your side was able to overturn his leverage allowing the French Navy to blockade the colonies, cutting off the British Army. Ethereals were on both sides of that conflict. The forces of Light wanted to establish America as a new country. Our side didn't. We found order under English rule and we had King George's ear. But that's a history lesson for another time."

Martin looked pale. "How can you willingly work for the devil? Can you please explain that to me? You know what Lucifer is and what happens to those who follow him? Are you that attached to power and wealth that you'd sacrifice your soul for a few decades of it?"

Collins shook his head. "There's a saying, Mr. Denton. History is written by the victors, not the vanquished. You're getting a very one-sided view of the war between Light and Dark, good and bad, or 'Evil' as we've been so successfully branded. Our side is more about freedom of choice and expression and not nearly so bound to rules and regulations as are the stiff, unrelenting Lords of Light. You believe God to be this merciful, forgiving being of eternal love and sunshine. You believe those who worship other deities will have their souls burn for eternity. True, some souls do get damnation. The rapists, murderers, molesters, the real salt of the Earth nasties do get what the Bible refers to as the sea of fire. The forces of darkness don't want those souls either, but as part of losing the war and being cast out, we have the thankless job of dealing with and housing the truly vile." Collins took another sip from his scotch. "Humans aren't the only evil in the universe, gentlemen, but I know you're already aware of that. We have to manage all kinds of nasty souls. Most make human beings look like tame little kittens and puppies. You accuse me of being evil. I've never personally killed a single being." He looked over at Erik and Martin. "Can you both make that same claim? You've both killed under orders, I assume, given the nature of your jobs."

He pointed directly at Erik. "You just killed one of my guards, I've read parts of your file, Mr. Knight. You're not all lily white and satin. I follow orders from my employer and sometimes bad things occur, but we have the tougher job. We have to house all these loons. Your side gets all the nice, peace loving, happy souls. We house the scum of the Earth. It does tend to make one jaded after several hundred years."

Erik steepled his hands on the charred conference table, his eyes burning with intensity. "Lucifer didn't want mankind to develop. He didn't want us to have dominion on this planet. You're serving an entity that wanted our species eradicated."

Collins shook his head. "That's more propaganda from your side. You don't see the big picture, Agent Knight. Earth is just a pinhead in a vast ocean. The contest is cosmic in scale and larger than our limited human brains can fathom."

Before Collins could continue, Erik cut him off with a curt gesture. "I'm not here to discuss semantics or theology. I'm here to recover what you stole and apparently had stolen from you. I'm here to assure my son's survival. Beyond that, I don't care if you hump goats and sacrifice chickens or make plans to rule every galaxy for light-years around." Erik leaned forward menacingly, his eyes burning blue embers. "I want to know everything you know about Molec, his possible contacts, where his human agents are and any other tidbits you've picked up." He reached across the table, grabbing the lapel of Collins' custom tailored suit. "And so help me God, if I find out you're holding out on me I'll come back here and burn a hole clean through you."

Collins trembled, showing abject fear for the first time. "That's the problem, I don't know much about Molec. Just that he was Lucifer's right hand during the first Ethereal War that occurred in Heaven. Molec didn't want a direct war, he wanted a stealth overthrow. After the war was lost, Molec was discontent serving under Lucifer. He did to Lucifer what Lucifer tried to do in Heaven. Molec failed, but the archdemon was able to flee and disappear. Molec has been able to hide when it serves his purpose." Collins drained his glass. "And it serves his purpose. The archdemon is powerful, clever, and a master of stealth. Not even your forces have been able to hunt him down."

Erik released the speaker from his grip. Collins sat and straightened out his jacket. "Where did you hide the relic?"

Collins shook his head. "A secure vault outside of DC. I don't know the exact location. Even we keep secrets from each other. We knew we had a hot potato and we wanted to effectively put it on ice for a while until we could figure out what to do with it. We had even gone so far as to inform the forces of Light that we had the relic and we were in the process of returning it to avoid escalating the hostility and put the genie back in the bottle!"

"Who constitutes we?" Denton pressed.

Erik flexed his fingers into a fist and cracked his knuckles. "Names."

Collins flinched. "The vault belongs to one of my colleagues, Senator Paul McMahon."

* * *

"Do you think Collins gave us everything?" Martin sipped lukewarm coffee from a paper cup.

Erik snorted. "I highly doubt it. But he gave us a lead and pretty much confirmed what we learned from O'Malley. Collins wasn't going to rat out his boss." Erik's brow furrowed. "He gave us just enough to avoid having a hole burned through him while at the same time keeping his soul from being snuffed out by Lucifer for betrayal." The moody detective smirked. "Collins is a damn good politician. He sees the bigger game, Counselor, and understands it on a level we don't and probably never will."

Denton tossed his cup into a nearby trash barrel. "I don't think I want to understand this game. I already have problems sleeping. If I know any more, they're gonna have to fit me for one of those funny white jackets and book me a padded cell."

"They can book a room for me right next to you." Erik pointed toward a large building. "McMahon's in a meeting there. Let's go make his day more complicated."

"Do you think Collins tipped him off?"

Erik grinned. "I have no doubt."

Erik and Martin entered the conference facility. Erik's senses were on alert for more altered humans. To his surprise, every person in the building was human. There was no sense of ethereal or demonic presence within anyone. "Regular folk, Counselor."

Denton visibly relaxed. "Thank God!"

Erik nodded. "I'll take whatever help we can get at this point."

Erik strolled into the spacious office suite. He asked a clerk to point out the office of Paul McMahon. The young girl pointed down the large foyer toward an imposing doorway. The detective walked the short distance. Martin followed quietly behind, his hand hovering near his Colt .45 auto pistol.

Erik spotted the bold lettering on the heavy double doors. "Well, Counselor, this is the place."

McMahon's office suite was palatial—more so than even the nearby senate majority leader's office. It was clear to both men that McMahon was the real power broker of the senate. Erik walked up to another stunningly attractive young woman. "Good afternoon." He flashed his CIA credentials. "I'm here to see Senator McMahon. I have a feeling I'm expected."

Denton flashed his credentials while nervously looking for guards or demonic reinforcements.

"Yes, the senator is expecting you, Mr. Knight, Mr. Denton." She smiled, almost seductively. "I'll be ordering a late lunch for the senator. May I get something for the two of you?"

Erik raised an eyebrow, then glanced over at Martin who shook his head. "Thank you but we're fine."

The administrative assistant tapped her intercom, "Senator, your three o'clock appointment is here."

"Send them in," a disembodied voice answered.

"This isn't what I expected," Denton whispered, following Erik toward the large doors.

"I don't think they want another violent display featuring Esper or demonic power. This war is supposed to be low key. The more we slug it out in public, the harder it is to keep the conflict private."

Erik opened the door, stepping into the spacious office.

McMahon stood up from behind his desk.

"Gentlemen, come in, please be seated." He gestured toward a large, plush sofa. "We have a great deal that needs to be discussed."

Erik studied the room carefully, scanning each corner, looking for a random energy signature or heat source. He found nothing.

"Relax, Mr. Knight, there're no hidden entities or boogeymen hiding in the corners or closets."

Erik tilted his head slightly to one side. "Trust but verify, Senator. You'll forgive me if I don't trust you."

The senator laughed as he took a seat across from them. He leaned back crossing his legs. "You're picking a fight with the wrong people, gentlemen. We didn't put a price on your kid, and we were hoodwinked into stealing Light's precious little trinket."

The detective shrugged his shoulders. "But you want him just the same. I got the story from Speaker Collins, at least as much as he felt he'd give me and keep his head firmly on his shoulders and his soul from the burning pit of your employer."

McMahon laughed. "If only it was that simple, but I won't waste time trying to convince you. Your mind is firmly made up and your allegiance to Light is already established for better or worse."

The condescension in the politician's voice was unmistakable. Erik sighed. They didn't have time for more verbal sparring or philosophical debate. "Senator, I'm going to be very brief. I want to know where you hid the Ruby Crucifix. I want to study the area myself. If I have to beat the location from you I can do that or you can keep your ribs and legs intact and simply tell me what I want to know."

McMahon raised an eyebrow. "Are you threatening me? I'm a senator senator! I have connections you can't even comprehend..." He picked up a nearby phone, "With one call, Special Agent Knight, one call and I can..."

The detective's arm struck cobra fast, snaring the arrogant politician, tossing him across the palatial office suite. He landed in a crumpled heap crushing the coffee table under his backside. Before McMahon could gather his senses, Erik's fist slammed into his jaw. His eyes crossed. Erik studied him. As his eyes aligned on him, he grabbed the senator by his thousand-dollar suit jacket.

Erik waited until he was certain the arrogant politician focused on him. McMahon stirred and looked down at the agent with terror in his eyes. "I'm going to ask you again, Senator. Where did you stash the cross?"

McMahon kept quiet. Erik's eyes began to burn. He probed the outermost layers of the politician's mind, peeling through piles of useless information and an increasing miasma of mounting fear, which clouded his thoughts. The senator thrashed about, desperately attempting to free himself.

"Stop that!" The diaphanous miasma became solid walls as McMahon struggled to erect some type of defense against the psychic probing. Erik tore through each mental barrier, inexorably pushing deeper into McMahon's thoughts. "I can rip the information from your mind, McMahon or you can simply give me what I want."

The senator fell limp as a wet washcloth. "Fine, you win! I'll take you to the vault. Just get out of my head!"

Erik tossed the senator several feet back to his large chair. "NOW Senator, I don't have time to fence words with your anymore. I'm trying to do you a favor, you arrogant bastard by finding the object you had stolen from under your very nose. The least you could do is help me out."

McMahon rubbed his temples. "You're a Light soldier. You claim you don't trust us. We feel the same way about you. I don't trust you for a second. You're not even human anymore. They took that from you and you're too damn blind to see it. You're all wrapped up in your holier-than-thou self-righteousness." McMahon spat blood from his ruined lip. "The world is more than just your harlot wife and child, Special Agent Knight, bigger than your puny life and desires."

"I just got that lecture from your cohort. I'm not concerned with the rest of the world right now and I didn't ask to get involved. You sent Bartholomew and the Quints for my son. Molec sent other assassins to kill him. So now I'm involved and whether you or your boss like it or not, I'm going to clean up this mess and go back to my little corner of the world." Erik held up a burning fist. "And if you get in my way...."

McMahon flinched. "Save the sideshow, you freak. I'll take you to the vault. But you won't find anything. The agent of Light that was there didn't find anything. What makes you better equipped than an Ethereal soldier?"

Erik lowered his arm. "I'm a detective, Senator. I don't think there are many detectives floating around the heavenly clouds."

McMahon shrugged his shoulders. "I don't know." He frowned, clearly frustrated. "Let's just get this over with. I have other matters that need my attention."

Denton pointed toward the door. "After you, Senator."

The limousine ride to the vault was silent. The large car pulled up alongside a remote storage facility. McMahon flashed his credentials to the four large, heavily armed guards. The men nodded curtly waving them through. The car pulled up to an innocuous warehouse.

"We're here." The driver opened the door. McMahon got out of the car, Erik and Martin right behind him. The senator walked toward a dilapidated doorway. He pressed a series of buttons on a keypad. The doorway opened revealing an elevator. McMahon stepped in, looking back at Erik and Martin. "Well?"

Erik scanned the area intently,

"What's wrong?" Denton nudged his friend's arm.

"There's no one else here, Counselor. If this is supposed to be some hidden treasure trove, I'd expect to see more guards, more patrols either human or non-human."

Denton nodded. "I suspect this is the senator's private collection of goodies, perhaps some that he acquired by less than appropriate means. More security usually draws more attention." The agents entered the elevator.

"It's a long way down." McMahon pressed a blue button and the elevator began to descend.

"How far down?" Denton watched blank level indicator.

"Over 300 feet. The vault is composed of hi-tensile steel and duraplast concrete with reinforced rebar."

"Does every one of the DC elite have a private storage

vault?" Erik placed his hand against the elevator wall sensing the slight vibrations.

McMahon shook his head. "Not everyone, Agent Knight. I've acquired several unique items during my tenure as a senator and I'd rather keep them out of the public eye and off the tax records."

Before Erik could reply, the elevator stopped and the door opened. He stared down an impossibly long, lit hallway. "Good lord, just how big is this place?"

McMahon actually laughed. "The hallway is nearly two hundred feet. The vault itself is a fifty-foot cube, impregnable to even the heaviest bunker bombs."

As Erik approached the vault, his Esper senses detected the trace presence of supernatural energies. McMahon was telling the truth. Supernatural beings had been here, both demonic and divine. McMahon punched several keys into a large control panel, then slid a card through a reader. He approached the door and endured a retinal scan. A computerized voice confirmed his identity and the door creaked as a heavy bolt slid free unlocking the massive alloy door.

The senior senator opened the doorway and both agents followed him inside. Erik exhaled in disbelief at the number of gold bars neatly stacked in a corner. He spotted several paintings. One looked familiar and he recognized it from a news story. "The Isabella Stewart Gardner Museum theft. You have the paintings!"

McMahon's shark-like grin spoke volumes. "I wouldn't have figured you for an art buff, Agent Knight."

Denton examined the paintings. "This is a huge mystery, Senator. How in the Hell did you get these? The FBI and the Boston PD have been looking for these for twenty-six years."

"And they'll keep looking, gentlemen." McMahon added with an iron tone in his voice.

"I'm not here for artwork, just point out where the relic was stored."

McMahon pointed toward the far end of the vault by an open safe. "There."

Erik walked over and could sense a powerful impression. The closer he got to the open safe, the more powerful the feeling became. The detective had to step back from the intense sensations. "Damn!"

"What is it?"

"The residual psychic feedback is incredible. I have to erect a mental shield just to get close to the safe."

Denton shrugged. "I don't feel anything. I'm glad I'm just a mere human." Denton studied his friend. "Are you sure you're okay? Your face looks pale."

Erik approached the safe, keeping his mental shield in place. He examined the safe. It had been ripped open like the one under St. Martha's Chapel. Sadly the detective had no suspect since Lazarus had been dusted after his theft. "Your thief is definitely demonic, Senator, and I can only guess that he found a way to further contain the relic. The sensations here are powerful but they seem muted, like a residual echo." Erik looked over at Martin. "I don't understand this, Counselor. How could a creature of darkness make off with this thing and not get vaporized? The relic had to be expelled from the Talithum containment to give off such a powerful residual echo. This is dozens of times more powerful than what I felt at Vatican City."

Denton frowned. "So we have another mystery to figure out."

"No, there are only a few beings capable of generating a vessel strong enough to temporarily trap the Ruby Crucifix. Lucifer is one such being. God and the archangels could..." McMahon shuddered. "And possibly Molec."

Denton turned toward the senator. "So Molec is our thief."

McMahon nodded, studying his private treasures. "It would appear that way." The senator looked annoyed.

"Out with it," Erik barked.

McMahon shook his head. "It doesn't concern you, Agent Knight."

"If it relates to this theft, then it concerns me, Senator."

McMahon frowned, rubbing his hand across his jaw. "How did he know? I have a spy in my organization and that's not good for my business or my mortality. If my employer finds out the theft is due to negligence on my part, I've outlived my usefulness."

Denton rolled his eyes. "Forgive me if I'm not all heartbroken."

McMahon smirked, clearly not appreciating the sarcasm.

Erik walked out of the vault, following the traces of the cross and the demonic echo. The echoes didn't dissipate as he expected. Instead, they suddenly stopped. Erik reached an open hand through the empty space that was devoid of any psychic presence. "It ends here rather abruptly."

Denton tilted his head. "Not at the elevator?"

Erik shook his head. "It just stops cold, like it was snuffed out..." Erik felt a pins and needles sensation crawling up his arm. "Sonovabitch, a portal! Whoever took the relic created a Netherspace portal and popped out of this space to make good their escape. I can sense a slight trace of it."

McMahon looked on, watching the detective.

Erik spun around to face the senator. "Was that the answer you were looking for McMahon? You're playing me, but I'm not such an easy mark. You already knew Molec took the damn thing. You just didn't know how he took it, and we just provided you that tidbit." A plasma ball formed in Erik's right hand. "I swear to God I will burn a hole right through you if you keep playing games!"

McMahon stepped back, studying both men. His eyes turned black as coals and his flesh reddened like an angry sunburn—it was a visage of pure evil. "You're too smart for your own good detective. You should have given us your bastard child when we asked. I knew it was Molec as soon as that bone-headed warrior of Light sensed the presence down here. I admit he was easier to fool, a dimwitted soldier angel not tarnished by the human characteristics of suspicion and mistrust. Your side is pathetically naïve, Detective. It makes winning this war much easier. But yes, using your Esper bloodhound senses was Collins' idea. I figured I'd play along with you and see if we could get the last piece of the puzzle, and you didn't disappoint. Netherspace, something rarely used by higher demons but an adequate, if rarely used, travel tool for the more mundane among us. Molec was stripped of his teleportation powers, so he's mastered the old pathways."

Erik's eyes narrowed to angry slits. "That still doesn't get you any closer to finding him."

The demon that was Senator McMahon laughed a hideous chuckle. No, but it gives us a roadmap to search. There are only a handful of places Molec can go using spatial portals. We now know where to look, thanks to you." The demon frowned momentarily. "How did you know? How did you know I was playing you?"

Erik took a step back. "When I started scanning your mind, I felt the non-human brain waves. You masked your presence perfectly, but you can't mask how you think or how your brain works."

MARTIN… WHEN I MAKE MY MOVE, HIT THE FLOOR! He projected into his friend's mind.

Erik shielded Martin. He forced more energy into his fist. The orb radiated its fiery blue essence, lighting up the entire corridor. "What's your game, McMahon, if that's even your name. Give me a reason not to burn you to a cinder."

The demon laughed. "I can't die, hybrid, at least not by mortal means. You can burn me with your Esper weapon but I'll just come back again."

The hybrid nodded, his face an icy glacier. "I'm not gonna kill you, but I will make you pay for the attack at my gym. Give my regards to Bartholomew when you see him in Hell!"

NOW MARTIN HIT THE FLOOR!

Erik spun and launched the powerful plasma blast down the hallway. The burning sphere sped into the vault erupting in a violent blue inferno. Gold, paintings, marble statues and other countless treasures were vaporized instantly as the vault itself dissolved.

McMahon shrieked in utter agony racing toward the evaporating chamber. "You half-breed bastard! Do you know what you've done? You've destroyed billions of dollars in treasure! Priceless artifacts and wealth that can never be replaced" The demon spun toward them, its black eyeballs burning with fiery red flame.

"What I've done is hurt you, Senator. I've caused you pain like you and yours have caused me and my wife. Maybe I can't kill you, but I can hurt you. Payback is a bitch and I've only just begun!" Erik launched another blast striking the demon in the chest, vaporizing it within a heartbeat. McMahon didn't even have time to scream as his flesh evaporated into nothingness. The empty space that housed the vault rumbled as thousands of tons of earth began to collapse and fill the void. The tunnel supports buckled and the sounds of tortured metal dominated the air.

Denton pointed to the elevator. "We need to go, now, before this place falls in on us!"

They sprinted into the elevator. Erik watched somewhat detached as the hallway imploded. The doors closed and they began to ascend. The cramped compartment jerking every so often.

"Let's hope this thing holds together and we don't get stuck mid-way." Denton looked around nervously as the lights flickered.

"There's not as much pressure against the elevator tube, Counselor. It runs vertical not horizontal. There isn't the immense weight sitting on it." Erik tapped the wall. "And the generator and motors are above ground."

Denton nodded. "I hope for our sake you're right."

The elevator chimed and the doors opened revealing the sunlit surface. Erik looked over at his friend and gestured toward the outside. "After you."

The ground above the vault and long passageway collapsed into a large sinkhole. The aftershocks and tremors still reverberated throughout the grounds. The elevator shook. Groaning metal twisted and collapsed as the weakened structure sank into the ground swallowed by earth.

Erik looked over at Denton sheepishly as they walked away. He tilted his head. "Or I could be wrong."

Both men continued toward the awaiting limousine. The driver was finishing off a cigar. He looked puzzled as a dust cloud rose into the sky. The guards arrived to investigate the sounds caused by the destroyed vault and passageway.

"What the Hell is going on?"

Erik stared at the driver. "The senator's been unavoidably detained. He won't be needing a ride back to the capital." Erik pointed toward Martin, "We, however, do." Both men flashed their credentials. The guards' hands fell toward their weapons.

Denton drew his .45. Erik made a gesture toward his friend. "Put the gun down, Counselor, let me handle this." He looked toward the guards raising a burning fist. "You don't need to get mixed up in this. Let's just pretend like none of this happened. We'll leave. You'll get to live another day and everyone will be happy."

The guards stared at his burning fist. Each man nodded slowly and backed away. "I don't get paid enough for this shit," a guard mumbled as they walked back to the front gate.

Erik looked at the driver. "We need a lift back to DC."

"What about the senator?"

Denton looked back at the collapsed landscape. "Senator McMahon won't need much of anything anymore—for a while at least, if he's to be believed."

The driver shook his head. "I don't want to know. The less I know, the happier I'm gonna be."

"Wise decision," Erik mumbled entering the car.

The ride back to DC was quiet. Erik could sense his friend's uneasiness. "What's eating you Counselor?"

"You were reckless back there. You almost got us killed!" Denton pointed an accusatory finger. "I can't leap tall buildings in a single bound or punch through corrugated steel. If a mountain falls on me, I'll get crushed like an ant under a boot. You're on a vengeance vendetta, like with The Observers. Only the stakes are much higher." Denton's voice dropped. "You're playing with powers we simply don't understand. Do you want Lucifer putting a bull's-eye on your back? You vaporized a United States senator! How do we explain that away?"

Erik folded his arms. "I vaporized a demonic entity masquerading as a human, who will undoubtedly be reformed or reanimated rather quickly, I assume, if we're to take the good senator at his word."

Denton sighed heavily, his displeasure still obvious in tone and body language. "If you're going to wreak havoc, give me some advance warning and for the love of God keep me out of the firing line!"

Erik nodded, considering Denton's claim. "I'm sorry, Martin. I should have found a way to tip you off when I realized what McMahon really was. As far as the cave in goes, I honestly believed the elevator shaft wouldn't be impacted."

"Are you a geologist now?"

Erik's face flushed. "No, I'm not."

Several uncomfortable moments of silence passed.

Erik turned to face his friend. "Martin, we have to take the offensive. We have to push back and make them feel some pressure, force them to react out of panic and to make a mistake or a rash move. We're behind here, by a great deal. I don't understand all that's going on between Dark and Light, and as McMahon and Collins both indicated, we're not getting the whole story, just one perspective." Erik shifted in the seat. "You know the game, Counselor, and you know the strategy I'm employing. I admit the stakes are higher, but the cost to me is my son. I didn't choose this and I didn't want it. I got dragged into it just like every other conflict. We need to shake the trees and see what falls out. That's always been the firm's strategy when we've needed leads or needed to flush out a rat or two. The same approach applies here. I know these beings are powerful, but they have to operate in stealth. No one in Washington wants to upset the balance. I believe humans, and the forces of evil and light just want the status quo. If we're going to find any leads on Molec we're going to get them from Lucifer's agents. And they're used to operating with near impunity at this point."

Denton nodded. "I know what you're saying, and I agree to a certain point. But the wrecking ball approach may need to be dialed back just a few notches. Remember what our Vatican friends said about upsetting the balance?"

"I remember, but keep in mind these are the same people that have been losing ground for the last four decades. They're holy men and women unprepared and unfit to engage in the kind of war being waged right now. They're not the folks I'd be taking strategic advice from."

Denton frowned. "Touché. But they have more knowledge about what we're dealing with than we do. We can't just dismiss that either."

Erik watched his friend as they sat in silence. The detective realized Martin was a late sixty-something year old man soon to retire. He had no business squaring off against superhuman entities let alone combating demonic forces. Erik's impulsive actions put his friend at risk and that was something he truly hadn't considered until this very moment. The realization ate at him like acid. "I do owe you an apology, Martin. I put you at risk. You're my best friend and I carelessly gambled with your safety. I am truly sorry, Counselor. It won't happen again."

Denton smiled, easing the tension. "We're almost back to DC. What's our next move?"

Erik returned the smile. Martin gave him the usual 'All is forgiven' treatment brushing the incident away while changing the subject back to work. "We know Molec went through Netherspace." Erik tapped the Sentient Staff hidden inside his jacket. "My little silver friend here has the ability to travel through that dark matter. I'm almost tempted to open a portal and see if I can pick up a trail."

Denton frowned. "You told me Netherspace was a Seelak invention. Do you really want to tempt fate by getting sucked up in a dark void?"

Erik sighed. "What I thought was some high-tech portal is just a demonic highway adopted by the Seelak for their own purposes during the war on their home world and here on Earth. But the staff can navigate it. As long as I have the staff I should be reasonably safe."

"I suggest we stop by and see Congressman Anderson and let him know what's going on. Senator McMahon's absence won't go unnoticed for long. Perhaps he can shed some more light and point us in an Earthly direction in order to sniff out some other leads." Denton grinned wickedly. "And see just how much we've upset the applecart today."

* * *

Congressional Offices. Washington DC

Erik and Martin walked down the narrow basement hallway barely avoiding the mad rush of congressional aides and reporters. This area was far different from the lavish offices of the house speaker and the senate majority leader. Erik casually scanned the mass of scrambling bodies.

"They all appear to be human. But then so did McMahon.

There's no sense of any ethereal presence here."

Denton nodded as they approached the end of the hall-way. "These are small-time players, freshman representatives and some research staff and a page or two. I wouldn't expect much interest in these low level bureaucrats."

Erik nodded. "Maybe, but these are the trenches. I'd want eyes and ears down here. I suspect there's more than meets the eye." The detective pointed. "There's Anderson's office. Let's see what else we can find out."

Congressman Anderson shook his head in disbelief and frustration. "You can't just vaporize a United States senator, Agent Knight. Even if he is crooked and demonic, you've sent a shockwave through the other side and no one knows how they'll react."

Erik shook his head, having already covered the ground earlier. The detective sighed heavily and steeled himself for another argument. "Congressman, it's up to you and your allies in Washington to keep up the pressure. A force that has to play defense doesn't have time to go on the offensive and act out. You and yours have been asleep at the helm for decades and have been run roughshod by your opponents. If both dark sides are preparing for war, and it appears that way, you better get your shit together and start planning for the same."

Anderson shook his head stubbornly. "It's not that simple!" The congressman tossed a report toward Erik. "We're outgunned here. Humanity is already well on the way to corrupting itself without Molec's interference. The archdemon is frustrating Lucifer as much as he's frustrating us."

Erik slammed his fist on the heavy desktop. "Then I would strongly suggest you get some reinforcements and get in the game or else all will be lost."

"Your son and the cross were the keys to keeping evil at bay. We must have the cross back and the light bearer protected. Your escalation of hostilities only makes it harder for us to do our work."

Denton tilted his head. "And what would that be? We're looking for the cross and trying to unearth the trail."

Anderson rolled his eyes and walked over to a small panel. He pressed a series of buttons and the room seemed to brighten, reminding Erik of the White Room at Vatican City. "We're looking for the cross as well gentlemen. You're not the only forces we have scouring the planet and we're monitoring the politicians under Lucifer's control and trying to establish a dossier on who may be working for Molec in the capital. Your attempt to force our opponents on the defensive counters our overall strategy."

Denton held out his hands. "What strategy? You seem to be sitting on you backsides letting us do the legwork." He coughed uncomfortably. "No offense."

Anderson nodded. "That's the whole idea, Mr. Denton. We have all the movements and patterns of known and suspected servants of Lucifer. They all have similar habits and traits as well as attend similar work and social functions. We're looking for breaks in these known patterns, or people who start adopting them. We are watching and looking, I assure you." Anderson paused, sipping from a water glass. "You kicking over the ant hill will force our opponent to act differently, change behaviors and ruin years of surveillance and study. We know how Lucifer reacts when kicked. We know how his puppets here respond to the dark lord's saber rattling and whims. Though you may find it hard to believe, more can be gained by watching and listening than by attacking outright. You've taken out a major player on that side and we don't know how they'll respond to that loss and we don't know if they'll attempt to retaliate in kind. Molec instigated the conflict, Agent Knight. Your pouring gasoline atop a burning pyre of flame escalates the problem rather than solves it."

"So what should we do? Sit back while you keep watch and make notes? Has that recovered your relic? Has it gained you any footing in the overall battle for humanity? You know," Erik's voice dripped with sarcasm, "the war you're losing badly."

Anderson stiffened at the rebuke "How God chooses to fight this war isn't your concern."

Erik made a fist and took a step forward. "When God got my son involved, and nearly got my wife killed, it became my concern, Congressman. If God isn't happy then let Him come down off his cloud and fill me in."

Anderson smirked. "Blasphemy doesn't help our impasse."

"If I may be so bold," Denton interrupted. "What does God want us to do then? I thought we were doing His will by looking for the cross and trying to root out Molec? We identified where the cross was held. We identified who stole it and we know that the strange Netherspace portals were used to transport the item after the theft from Senator McMahon. It's a bit unusual to ask us to solve a problem you created then complain about the methodology employed when we are, in fact, producing results."

Anderson flinched, involuntarily tensing his neck. "No one is questioning your results or your capabilities." He sighed heavily. "We..." He stopped himself. "Excuse me, *they* would rather you not totally disrupt our network inside the capital in your zeal to uncover the culprits and recover the artifact."

Erik sensed there was another presence in the room. He couldn't see it or hear it but Anderson was being spoon fed his reply. The congressman became nervous and uncomfortable.

"Tell our mutual allies I apologize profusely. Going forward, Martin and I will tread more carefully and avoid upsetting the anthills." The detective extended his hand and Anderson shook it gratefully. The detective could read the confusion on Martin's face. He nodded subtly toward his friend and mouthed *later*. "And if I'm to believe Senator McMahon, he'll turn back up before he's missed too much. If he's so important that Lucifer puts all his pieces back together again, you'll know he's worth paying extra special attention."

"A solid point, Agent Knight." Anderson looked relieved and the color returned to his ashen face. The powerful presence that dominated the room vanished. "There's a bistro on the outskirts of DC called The Starlight. Many of the Beltway players loiter there. We've never had the inclination or need to investigate the establishment." Anderson cleared his throat, "Until now. I would suggest you go there and try to remain as inconspicuous as possible and see if your hyper attuned Esper senses can winnow out some type of lead." Anderson scribbled on a notepad tearing off the top sheet handing it to Erik. "I suggest hailing a cab and remaining as inconspicuous as possible. Rolling up in a limousine or unmarked government sedan would mark you a key player." Anderson rolled his eyes. "Just try not to maim or kill anybody of any great importance. The booze flows like water at the Starlight and secrets are traded like Pokémon cards." Anderson exhaled. "One more thing, Agent Knight, a message of a personal nature I've been asked to relay." Anderson took another breath. "There are divine eyes on Brianna Knight and those closest to you."

Erik nodded. "Relay my sincerest thanks, please."

Denton looked confused.

"I'll explain it in the cab, Counselor." Erik headed toward the doorway into the busy hallway with Martin barely a step behind him.

Anderson called out behind them. "Be careful, gentlemen. The Starlight is not friendly territory."

Denton walked beside his young friend and whispered, "Why the sudden change of tune regarding our tactics?"

"There was something else in there, some ethereal presence spoon feeding Anderson his speech. I gather the white light is the same kind of filter we encountered in Vatican City. I didn't want to get into another philosophical discussion anyway. Anderson looked nervous enough and I don't have the patience for it. It was easier to just go along to get along." Erik kept walking briskly toward the stairwell. "Washington stinks of ethereal interference from all sides. We have to find out how Molec is playing the game here and root out a few of his stooges." Erik pointed toward the exit sign. "We can catch a cab and be across town at this place in just under an hour."

Denton nodded as the two men left the small DC office complex.

* * *

The Starlight Bistro

Erik and Martin sat on a large bench across the street from the Starlight. Erik hid behind a large newspaper, telepathically scanning people as they wandered in and out. "Anderson was right. There are a lot of heavy ethereal players here. The psychic essences I'm picking up are massive." The detective sighed. "And have the telltale mark of darkness."

Denton folded his paper down, glancing across the street quickly. "Not to mention the human heavy hitters as well. I've seen five senior senators, and three members of the President's Advisory Council walking in during the last half hour. You were right. Washington is a cesspool of supernatural politics.

Erik chuckled. "Well it's comforting in a weird way to know they're just as corrupt as we are."

Denton shook his head. "Is it weird to say I'm somewhat disillusioned by all of this?"

Erik smirked. "Why Martin, losing your faith already?"

Denton laughed, lifting his paper back up. "I guess I'd make a poor disciple."

Erik folded his paper and tossed in a nearby barrel. "I'm suddenly hungry. Let's go over and grab a bite to eat. Hopefully the food is good."

Denton discarded his section of the DC *Times* and followed.

It was obvious that both men were underdressed. The large bouncer scrutinized them as they got closer to the doorway, then blocked their path.

"You need a tie and a decent dress shirt here, gentlemen. This isn't a McDonalds or Wendy's burger joint."

Erik was about to bully his way past the bouncer when Martin stepped between them. "I completely understand, but we were rushed and our luggage is in the belly of some airplane due to arrive later tomorrow because of some trans-Atlantic screw up. Senator McMahon recommended this place to us personally. I was hoping you might have a few spare dinner jackets in the coat room that we could liberate for the evening. We've been stuck eating airport food and drinking crappy coffee since we left Paris. To top it all off, the senator got delayed and had to postpone our meeting this afternoon. He suggested we dine here and he'd try and come by later on."

The bouncer took a step back whispering into a small microphone on his lapel. "I apologize for the inconvenience. I'll have some jackets delivered to you at Senator McMahon's personal table."

Denton smiled warmly as they were escorted inside by two stunning hostesses.

"Well done, Counselor."

"I don't think the senator is in much of a position to care if we use his table or not. And if anyone here knows he's dead, they'll understand why we got the bum's rush. It's better than trying to bully our way in."

They were seated at a large corner booth. A young waitress immediately walked over. "Welcome to the Starlight, gentlemen. How can I serve you today?"

Denton smiled and asked for a table wine and some bread. The waitress complimented their choice and walked off.

Several people at other tables eyed them with looks ranging from mildly amused to openly hostile.

"They must know who we are."

Denton shook his head slightly. "More likely they don't and that's what's causing the uproar ... Anderson was right. This place is reserved for a darker, more evil clientele."

A man dressed in an expensive suit approached their table. "Gentlemen, may I join you for a drink?"

The man didn't wait for an answer before sliding into a chair. He waived a waitress over and ordered an expensive glass of brandy. "I didn't know the senator was expecting dinner guests." The stranger waited for Erik or Martin to offer some insight.

"I don't believe we've had the pleasure," Denton whispered as he studied their uninvited guest.

"I'm a very close friend of the senator. I'm usually informed when he's expecting guests."

Erik's eyes grew hard. "Well, apparently you didn't get the memo. My friend and I prefer to dine alone this evening. Now if you don't mind, we'd like to be left in peace."

The waitress returned with Martin's bread and table wine. She also placed a large platter of expensive cheeses, grapes and butters on the table. She slid a glass of brandy in front of their unwanted guest. The man ignored Erik's request to leave and instead reached for his glass. He held it up toward Erik. "To the long lost Esper race and their twenty thousand year war." The man drained his glass with one gulp and reached for a slice of bread.

Erik's hand lashed out like a serpent, grabbing the man's wrist. "You made your point. You know who I am. Since you know, I'm gonna assume you know why I'm here." The detective increased his grip on the stranger's wrist. The bones creaked and the man winced in silent agony.

Denton leaned over to Erik. "Ease up. We're attracting attention." The elder agent turned to face their guest. "The senator won't be coming for dinner tonight and maybe for several nights to come. We're not here for trouble. We just want information."

The man rubbed his wrist, eyes narrowed. "You don't belong, Special Agent Knight, nor do you, Bureau Chief Denton. Yes, I know who you are. As for your reasons to be here, I'm not interested in aiding you, nor is anyone else here. This isn't a place for people with your affiliation."

"What about people affiliated with Molec? Do they frequent this place?"

The man's face hardened. "We don't discuss the archdemon. I ask that you finish your drinks and be on your way. Your kind isn't welcome here."

The man stood and turned to leave.

Erik shot out of his seat. He grabbed the stranger's shoulder and spun him back around. Several men stood from their booths as hands reached for concealed weapons.

"Do you know what's going on? There's a war brewing. Battle lines are being drawn while you sit here in Washington playing your little games. Molec is playing with fire looking to instigate a war of mutual destruction. If he succeeds, your little slice of neutrality will be eviscerated and no one knows what kind of Hell on Earth will be unleashed on humanity. If you're human or partially human that has to frighten you. Your boss will lose. Light will lose." He released his grip on the man's shoulder. "We'll all lose." Erik gave the man's shoulder a light, easy tap. "I just want to find Molec and stop him. I promise you, I just want to stop Molec."

The man studied Erik carefully. "Trust is a commodity in short supply, Special Agent Knight. The forces of Light are just as likely to deceive as we are and just as inclined to bend the rules by allowing the unauthorized conception of the Light Bearer, thereby accelerating the conflict."

Erik sighed. "My son."

The man nodded. "Yes, your son. So you see, hybrid, your motivations aren't as pure as you claim. There is a self-service core to your desire to find Molec and to stop this war. You wish to save your son, a child created to end all of darkness and herald in the second coming of your savior." The man took a slow step back. "To help you would bring about the end of mankind. Armageddon's Son should not have been allowed to come into being and the Ruby Crucifix should never have been stolen. I fear the war will come no matter what you or we do. We have crossed the point of no return." The man's face softened. "You think being Dark means being without feeling. Well you're very wrong. We live, we love and we have family just as you do. We're all pawns, hybrid. In this cosmic game of chess played by the lords of Light and Dark we are the disposable soldiers."

Erik felt his eyes water. "You're wrong. I can stop this war. I just have to find Molec. Help me and I promise you the war can be avoided."

The man shook his head sadly. "I believe your intent, Agent Knight, but you cannot change the course of destiny. You cannot stop what your God has decreed will pass. The war will come as long as your son is alive. I have no wish to kill your child, nor does Lucifer. We would rather the child simply go back to the ethereal realm. Molec, however, has no such civility or decency."

The man turned and walked away, disappearing into a different room. The remaining patrons turned back to their private affairs and Erik sat back down.

"We're not going to get anything here, Erik. Maybe this was a bad idea. We were made the moment we sat down." Denton took another sip of his wine.

Erik frowned. "My gut's telling me there's more going on here than just a simple holiday spa for the dark side."

Denton nodded. "Maybe so, but there's nothing we can do about it now. Nobody here is going to lift a finger to help us. Our guest was pretty much spot on. Why should they do anything to help us when it could ultimately lead to their destruction?"

Their waitress brought over another basket of bread. She

leaned in close to Erik. "I can help you. Meet me in the park across the street in ten minutes. My shift is over and we can talk away from all these ears and eyes."

Erik nodded slightly, aware that other eyes were still watching. The waitress grunted softly, picking up his cue. She made a small fuss over Martin and then quickly walked away.

"And the plot thickens," Denton whispered, tearing into another slice of warm bread while shielding his mouth with a napkin.

Erik raised an eyebrow as he peeled the foil off a butter pad. "Or it could just be bait for a dead end."

Denton took another sip from his wine glass. "Pessimist."

The detective nodded. "That way I'm never disappointed, only pleasantly surprised."

Martin drained his wine and sighed. "This may be Lucifer's café, but the wine is heavenly."

Erik snorted, laid out two twenty dollar bills and stood. "Let's move Counselor, unless you want another bottle for the road."

Both men shed their borrowed jackets and headed out, acutely aware of the eyes following them.

*　*　*

Erik and Martin sat partially concealed in the park across from the bistro.

"Are we being watched?" Martin adjusted his light jacket scanning the passersby.

"No, I don't think so. If anyone was taking an interest in us I'd feel it, human or otherwise. The sensation is identical." Erik tilted his head. "On our three o'clock."

Denton strained his peripheral vision and spotted a young woman approaching them cautiously. "That's her."

The waitress walked by and the two men stood, following her for several hundred yards. She stopped by a massive fountain, sitting on a large bench. She motioned for them to join her. Erik sat on her left in silence while Martin took a casual stroll around the fountain before joining them.

"No tails and nobody watching."

Erik nodded. "I'm still reading the all clear too." He glanced down at the young woman. "I'm not one to question the motives of anyone willing to offer me information but," he looked directly into her eyes, "you're risking a world of hurt and possibly your very life by talking to us."

The waitress closed her eyes. "I don't care anymore. I'm not going back to that place after we speak. I'm leaving, getting as far away from this hell infested cesspool as I can get."

Erik wondered where one could hide from evil. "Fair enough. What do you know about Molec and where can I find him—or is 'it' more correct?"

The waitress folded her arms. "My sister fell in with Molec last year. She was infatuated with him for some bizarre reason. The idiots inside the Bistro have no idea that Molec has acolytes in there, watching and listening to every word being said. That's how he keeps himself two steps ahead. He recruits from both sides and then uses them as information couriers. Molec is far from stupid and the Lords of Dark and Light have become far too lazy and complacent in their tedious conflict to even comprehend the idea of stealth."

Martin leaned toward her. "If Molec is so lethal, why would you risk crossing him and earning his wrath? Who or what force can protect you?"

"I don't care about protection anymore and Molec has already taken everything from me. He raped and brutalized my sister and bartered her soul as it still shrieked in agony from what was done to her body and her mind."

Erik tilted his head. "He bartered her soul? I'm afraid I'm not too clear on that concept beyond what the words themselves literally imply."

She looked up, fire in her eyes. "That's just what I mean. He snatched up her soul as it left her dead body and sold it like a yard sale trinket."

Martin gasped. "Dear God! Is that even possible?"

"For lords of the Ethereal Realm many things are possible. Even the most grotesque concepts you could imagine are mere entertainment for some breeds of demon and even some of the lesser lords of light."

Martin shuddered. "That's awful."

"Lucifer established a soul market several centuries ago during an age when men experimented in sorcery and worshiped false gods and idols. Human Sorcerers sacrificed their souls willingly for the power to summon the forces of darkness. As men's greed grew and the lust for power increased, more and more humans bartered their souls for power. At some point Lucifer made a pact with other major demons in other realms for non-human souls from other places and other worlds." The young woman shuddered. "These things were not meant to mix with humanity and the soul market has become a place for predators and cold-hearted demons looking for souls as food for nosferatu or whatever other creatures of the damned that devour such things. Souls are a source of great energy and can be used to power all kinds of divine and non-divine objects." She looked up at Erik. "Alien species, demonic entities from across the universe all come to this one point to sell, trade, and acquire souls, Agent Knight. And in all the known universe of all the sentient species, nothing is more valuable than the soul of an innocent human. The pure energy of an unbound human soul is a commodity of the highest value."

Erik's flesh crawled. "And you think Molec is hiding in this place. How do we find it?"

The waitress shook her head. "I don't know where the market is. That's a tightly kept secret, but Molec isn't there. Lucifer's agents would recognize him eventually and get word back. Molec is no match for the fallen Lord of Light, only the current champion can face the fallen angel. As for the location, the market inhabits some dimensional pocket on Earth. I don't know where, but I know Molec has been there, only briefly, and his acolytes go there and make purchases to feed their hordes. But if he needs to hide briefly, the soul market would be a temporary reprieve and a gateway to other realms that use the market for barter. If you don't find Molec in his stronghold, the Soul Market, though it be dangerous, would be a good place to start looking for leads."

Erik shook his head in disbelief. "I think I'm gonna be sick. This shit can't be real. There's a whole sick underworld existing right under our nose and we had absolutely no idea."

Erik glanced over at Martin. The counselor's face was

deathly pale, his eyes wide with shock and dismay. "Ma'am…"

"Carla, my name is Carla."

Erik nodded. "Carla, do you know where Molec is now?"

Carla's face turned to stone, her eyes burning agates of hate. "Yes. He's hiding out in a puny suburban wasteland in Massachusetts. A town called Hopedale in a condemned mill. No one uses the building and the security guards that keep out trespassers are all on Molec's payroll." She looked directly into Erik's eyes. "Use your powers, Agent Knight. I've heard the talk about how strong you are. Promise me you'll kill that demon, avenge the death of my sister and free her soul. I know Molec took it to the market for trade. If her soul was devoured I'd have felt it."

Erik wiped away the tears from her cheek. "I promise you I'll do everything I can. I wish I could give you some guarantee, but that'd be a lie and I won't lie to you."

Carla stood, looking around carefully. "You have the mark of Light, Agent Knight. It's in your aura and your essence. I believe you. As for me, I'm leaving DC to find a tiny corner of the world and seek refuge in an oasis. I'm through with all of this."

Martin and Erik watched as the young girl vanished into the sea of people.

"Good luck, Carla, and thank you." Erik stared at the ground lost in thought.

They sat in stunned silence for ten minutes, Erik's mind reeling at the revelation. "Hopedale, the sonovabitch is in my freaking backyard under my very nose and I didn't catch wind of it."

"How would you know? We weren't looking for evil. We weren't aware of any of this shit until a few short weeks ago." Denton's hands ran though his iron gray hair.

Erik nodded. "We need to get to Hopedale and do some recon. I know that building. It's an abandoned hulk in the middle of town." The detective shook his head and chuckled.

"I think I missed the joke."

"Molec is hiding in plain sight. There's nothing better than hiding right out in the open. In a million years I'd have never considered that place some sort of evil hideout." Erik frowned. "This demon is always one step ahead. Carla was right." Erik looked toward his friend. "Molec appears to have eyes and ears everywhere."

Erik stood, stretched and flexed his left arm. "Counselor we need to catch a flight to Logan Airport and stake out the old mill to see exactly what we're getting into. Cars and people go by that structure constantly so we can't just barge in. Plus that place is a powder keg of dry, oil-saturated wood. One errant plasma blast and the whole place goes up like a roman candle."

Denton feigned a heart attack. "Be still my beating heart. Agent Knight is suggesting caution."

Erik grinned. "Wise ass." He laughed anyway. "C'mon let's exercise our agency travel cards and hop a flight. I think we've worn out our welcome in DC anyway. We can stop by Anderson's office and let him know what we've learned. I'm sure our Ethereal friends would love to pluck Molec from his little warehouse fortress."

Chapter 6: A Deal with the Devil

Hopedale, MA

E rik adjusted his grip on the tree branch as the limb swayed with the heavy fall breeze. The tall tree gave him the perfect vantage point to observe the back of the abandoned factory. The darkness provided an additional sense of concealment behind the drying oak leaves. He pressed the red stud on his radio. "I see three men in the back and something larger and most definitely not human giving orders."

"It looks black and dead from back here." Martin's voice echoed over the tinny speaker.

Erik focused his enhanced vision around the facility. Powerful alien eyes climbed the upper ultraviolet frequencies. He spotted a dark translucent blister surrounding the entire abandoned facility. The high-powered floodlight's luminance was absorbed by the intangible barrier. "There's some sort of screen blocking out the lights. Can you see anything?"

"I see the outline of the building, barely. The lights in the building are very dim. It's too dark to make out anything else."

Erik followed the dome's outline. "The barrier ends at the very edge of the fence line. No wonder no one's complained. To every nearby house, it looks dead and uninhabited. I know they have a few guards patrolling to keep out the high school party crowd, but I imagine the neighbors probably welcome that. I wonder what they'd say if they knew what lived inside this structure." Erik took one last look, scanning the grounds from his perch. "I'm heading back to you. We need to form some kind of plan."

Erik leapt from his perch, dropping fifty feet. After a brief walk he was back by his truck. Martin parked the vehicle by Bancroft Park, a neighboring roadway that bordered the large structure. The detective looked back, shocked. From that vantage, the warehouse looked completely abandoned. There was no evidence of any activity or sound. He opened the cab door and slid in. "Incredible"

"What is?"

Erik looked over as Martin took a sip from his coffee cup. "There's some kind of protective blip shielding the entire facility. It's absorbing most of the ambient light and sound. I can't imagine how it works during the daylight."

"But you saw people and activity?"

Erik nodded. "Yeah and a rather large 'un-person' that seemed to be supervising."

"Molec?" Martin's voice jumped two octaves.

Erik shook his head. "I don't think so. I don't think Molec is the type who wants to sully his hands. If there's one demon, I'm assuming, like roaches, there are more I didn't see inside. Carla's intel was spot on."

"I don't know why our allies couldn't just come here and do this. Anderson could have passed what we learned along rather than sending us." Denton slurped the dregs of his coffee and crushed the empty cup.

"Like he said, demons were angels once, a long time ago. They can sense each other, as soon as one of the Ethereal soldiers of light popped in, I imagine all sorts of alarms would go off. Also, the kind of power unleashed during an all-out assault would level that building. If this building goes up, a lot of innocent lives are gonna go with it. It's smack dab in the middle of town, not to mention the water source that runs underneath could be tainted by the fire and destruction. We're going to have to get real close before we summon our friends and pray that we get the jump on them before a bolt of fire or any other type of energy is unleashed inside that giant tinderbox."

Denton sighed. "I can't climb a tree, I don't know how I'm gonna clear that twelve foot fence."

Erik turned toward Martin. "I don't want you in this fight, Counselor. There's a chance this could go totally FUBAR and the farther you're away from this place, the safer."

"I can't. I need to do this, Erik. I need the closure. I need to be there. If it goes bad, it goes bad. I'm willing to take that chance." There was steel in Denton's voice.

Erik frowned increasing his grip on the truck's steering

wheel. He didn't want Martin in this fight. "I understand, but just remember what you said about reckless."

"I know Erik, but I can't walk away from this, not now."

"Okay, I have an idea that will get us close, then we can call in the cavalry. I have no doubt somebody somewhere on a puffy cloud is watching us anyway."

Denton opened the truck door. "Let's go. It's getting cold out and my blood is too thin to be out in these elements for a long period of time."

Erik tilted his head, bewildered. "Let just hope we don't wind up in a place that's really warm and requires lots of sunscreen and lip balm."

"Amen," Denton whispered as they moved toward the foreboding structure.

Erik and Martin crept toward the fence, using the thin tree line as concealment.

"Okay, now how do I get over the fence?"

Erik didn't answer. He scooped up his friend and leapt over the barrier, landing lightly on the other side. He carefully placed a stunned Martin back on the ground.

Denton took a breath to recapture his dignity. "We tell no one about that!"

Erik studied the warehouse. The lights were clearly visible again and he could see even more people and demons busily moving among the crumbling dock. "Mum's the word, Counselor, but we have bigger fish to fry at this point." He gestured toward the dock as they took cover behind a large dumpster."

Denton watched cautiously. "Incredible. None of this is visible from the street and we drove right by this!"

Erik nodded. "Right now I'm going to take some safety precautions. I hope you don't mind getting wet."

Denton squinted and shrugged his shoulders. "I don't follow you."

"There's a heavy cloud layer over head. I'm gonna help things along." Erik's eyes radiated a blue energy and his hands gestured toward the clouds. "ARAHKANA SOLOTH KANA ALAYU." The hybrid chanted the same verse three times and the heavens unleashed a downpour of chilling rain.

Denton looked over at his friend. "What now?"

"Now we wait until the clouds finish their work. The building will be soaked and so will the timbers. There won't be as much chance of a fire now. I'm not taking any chances. Plus the rain keeps our scent down and will hopefully buy us a few more minutes. I'm wondering how long it's gonna be before something sniffs us out. We can't get any closer. There's nothing to use for cover."

Both men crouched patiently, counting the minutes. After ten minutes had passed, the rain tapered off to a drizzle, then stopped altogether.

"I think it's time to call in the shock troops and get this over with. There isn't going to be a better time. They're all back inside." Erik reached inside his jacket and freed his sentient staff. Blue lightning danced up and down the powerful silver cylinder as it expanded. The weapon growled fiercely, anticipating combat. Erik closed his eyes and looked to the stars. "Now would be a good time to clean up the garbage."

A flash of white light illuminated the darkness and six powerful Soldiers of Light materialized. Erik recognized the leader. It was the being he'd spoken to in his office earlier.

"Let the battle commence." The blond warrior looked over at Martin. "Stay hidden, human. These demons will take your soul, or worse."

Denton shook his head. He freed a massive glowing pistol from his holster. "Not this time. I came prepared for this!"

The Ethereal shook his head. "As you wish, human!"

*　*　*

Molec studied his captured prize. He could detect minute fractures forming in the ectoplasmic sphere. No matter how much dark power he applied, the demon couldn't boost the vessel's containment power. It was already causing him and his companions discomfort to be in the same room with the object. "Even this safe cannot contain the cursed thing." Molec covered the sphere with Talithim cloth and pushed the cart holding the sphere back into the large safe.

A nosferatu's eyes popped open. Dead, black pupils dilated in fear, the creature looked toward its master and shrieked a banshee like warning call. Molec's flesh tingled and he knew. "How?" The archdemon looked through several cameras to see six soldiers accompanied by the human hybrid soldier and his elder companion. "No!! Curse you, Erik Knight and all that you are! I will have your still-beating hybrid heart on a skewer!" The enraged demon turned to his forces. "Kill them all but bring me the hybrid, alive! Barely alive! I want to suck his soul from his still living body so he can watch in horror!"

* * *

They approached the warehouse and Erik spotted the cameras. "They know we're here."

"They knew the second we materialized. Be ready."

Erik's staff crackled with raw power. The weapon's angry roar pierced the quiet. *EASY, WE'RE GONNA FIGHT, BUT WE'RE GONNA BE SMART!* The staff settled a bit.

"There!" Martin shouted, pointing the large weapon's barrel at large scalloped doors which opened. Several humans and inhumans raced toward them. Before anyone could react, Martin fired eight shots. A flash of blinding white light followed each blast. Erik watched as five charging demons were consumed in a purple fire while the three human soldiers evaporated in amber flame.

The tall, blond ethereal soldier looked back at the old man, impressed. Denton nodded slightly, his face set in stone as he changed glowing ammunition clips. "I made a few contacts in the firm that are familiar with divine weaponry. I borrowed this for a few days."

There was no more time for talk. Molec's other forces fell upon them.

"The nosferatu are taking flight!" Erik shouted as he engaged a snarling eight-foot monstrosity. The beast snapped at him with razor sharp tusks and claws. Erik raised his staff deflecting a powerful slash with the edge of his weapon. He tilted his head backward as massive jaws snapped for his throat. Thigh and calf muscles exploded propelling him forward, driving the tip of his staff through the creature's throat. The weapon exploded out the back of its neck amidst a sea of bloody ichor. Erik jerked the weapon back, swung the staff in a figure eight pattern, then slammed the alien metal down on the beast's skull. The creature dropped as purple ichor hemorrhaged from its ears.

Another demon lunged for him. There was no time to think, he could only react. This one was smaller but had a whip-like tail that reminded him of the original Seelak warrior he'd fought years earlier. This demon was fast, and it took all his power to block the dizzying array of attacks, which forced him backward step-by-step. A sharp lance of pain tore through his back as the creature's tail skewered his torso. Warm blood flowed from the wound staining his clothing and pooling on the filthy soil. He fought on, desperately executing an endless array of defensive maneuvers, never able to launch a proper counterstrike. His body absorbed more punishment as he blocked super powered fists and hoofed feet. The demon got careless and Erik lunged forward, snapping out three trip hammer jabs. Each blow landed solid with a resounding thump. The demon's eyes narrowed, becoming slits of burning rage. It charged, skeletal thin arms flailing wildly. Erik spun his torso, unleashing a spinning back kick. His foot slammed into the creature. He swung his staff in a horizontal arc, timing the weapon's impact perfectly with his kick. The combined force of both blows stunned the creature, knocking it back ten feet.

Erik took a moment to refocus. These beings were powerful, unlike human opponents. The creature he felled leapt back up, charging forward and hissing angrily. Razor sharp claws readied to rend his flesh from bone. The tail whistled forward like a cobra to pierce him again. The hybrid twisted his body and snapped his hand forward, grabbing the prehensile appendage. Erik gathered his strength and yanked on the tail as hard as he could while launching a powerful sidekick into the creature's lower back. A sick crackling sound accompanied the impact of his kick. A shriek of pain and agony broke through the haze of combat as the limp tail now hung lifeless in his grasp, the other end ripped from the demonic torso by the opposing forces. The crippled demon fled, leaving a trail of greenish blood back into the warehouse.

HOW BAD ARE YOU INJURED? A voice echoed I his head.

I'LL BE FINE, I'M ALREADY HEALING, he projected back. Several gunshots caused him to turn. Two creatures beset Martin. The demons didn't appear to be affected by his special rounds. Erik raised his staff and focused his will, unleashing a searing blast of high-energy plasma. The blue energy slammed into one demon burning a gaping hole through its large torso. The second one turned to face Erik. Another gunshot rang out. The second demon's head split like a melon, its body falling forward, limbs shaking violently as it was consumed by purple fire. Martin gave him a thumbs-up gesture as he reloaded another clip into his weapon. Erik heard another scream.

A winged angel slammed into the cement with a skeletal nosferatu clamped onto it. The demon's claws had pierced the soldier's white armor and the creature was sucking away on the ethereal life force, feeding like a hungry leech. The angel struggled, pummeling the gaunt yet powerful demon, but was weakening quickly. Erik looked up at the dark sky pointing toward the demon, *AH EXOTAR ANAHK!!*

A jagged bolt of lightning raced from the sky, slamming into the demon, unleashing hundreds of thousands of volts. The creature shrieked and exploded into tiny smoking shards of ash. The accompanying thunderclap shattered all the window panes in the warehouse. The winged ethereal soldier stood and nodded a wordless thanks before engaging another of Molec's creatures.

WE'RE OUTNUMBERED, THE LONGER WE SPEND FIGHTING THESE FORCES THE MORE TIME MOLEC HAS TO ESCAPE!

Erik ducked a searing fireball and cartwheeled away from a bolt of amber flame. *I HAVE AN IDEA. PULL OUR FORCES BACK AND PROTECT MARTIN!* Erik projected to the ethereal forces. The hybrid stared up at the night sky shouting in his alien tongue. Another searing bolt of lightning plunged to Earth. The bolt struck his staff and he redirected the force through seven separate arcs of energy, each one impacting a demonic foe. Five of the demons vaporized while the other two stumbled back into the warehouse, smoking from charcoaled flesh. The four remaining human servants dropped their weapons and fled, running toward the opposite end of the warehouse looking to escape the forces of light. "We need to move now." He looked over at Martin. "How are you doing, Counselor?"

Sweat streamed from Denton's forehead and he panted, but the old man gave a thumbs-up gesture, then snapped another clip of glowing ammunition into his weapon. "I'm ready for more."

The forces of Light rushed forward, smashing through the feeble wood and cast iron doorway. The noxious smell released from the dark corridor caused Erik and Martin to gag. Denton bent over and vomited violently, each breath making him gag even more.

"For the love of God, what is that wretched smell?" Denton placed a handkerchief over his nose and mouth.

The blond leader looked over at the old man. "It is the scent of Hell." The being pointed down the corridor. "Molec has been here for a while, making his minions at home in this place." The divine soldier spun around, heading deeper into the corridor. The being raised his massive ivory and silver blade, his grip tightening on the fearsome sword. *WE CANNOT WAIT, WE MUST MOVE FORWARD QUICKLY!* His words echoed in their minds.

Erik focused on his staff. He needed a different weapon for such close quarter combat. *KATANA!* The six foot Sentient Staff transformed into a sleek, lethal samurai sword which could be wielded more effectively in the tighter space. He moved forward, hybrid senses on full alert, doing his best to ignore the foul odor that saturated the area.

The corridor emptied into a large open space, easily a hundred feet long and half as wide. The dry, rotted wood floor was covered in layers of black filth. Several alien-looking barrels dripped their contents, forming a toxic ash-colored paste. The scent of oil and alcohol hung in the air.

"No energy blasts of any kind in here!" Erik warned. "Those weird demonic barrels are leaking some kind of flammable distillate, and these timbers are bone dry and saturated with God knows what kind of chemicals. This whole place is a toxic bon fire just waiting to happen." Erik's senses detected the distinct pattern of the Ruby Crucifix. He looked over at the ethereal soldier. "I can sense the cross." He pointed toward the adjoining doorway. "The presence is strongest that way, but I can't sense any other energies." The agitated detective cursed violently. "That bastard got away again!"

The blond soldier nodded. "He did, but his trail is heavy and easily followed." They walked across the large space toward the ornate door. The soldier gestured toward the barrier and it simply flew open. The door tore from its hinges, slamming against the far wall. Erik and the leader rushed into the room, weapons raised.

"Nothing." Erik studied the massive and opulent office area, a stark contrast to the rough, unfinished space they passed through. He looked down another carpeted corridor observing several other doors. The hybrid detective raised an eyebrow. "You're right. He's made himself quite the elaborate nest here." He pointed toward the doorway at the end of the hall. "The strongest emanations are coming from there. I'm guessing that's where the relic was stored." Erik heard Martin and the other soldiers form up behind them as they walked the long corridor. They quickly examined each room. It was evident that the occupants all fled in a hurry. The unearthly scents and colors in some of the rooms were disturbing to his senses.

Martin studied one of the rooms intently. The group paused.

"What is it, Counselor?"

Denton's eyes were locked on a small orb trapped in a glass. The ball of energy dimmed slightly, then flickered back to life. "What is that?"

One of the ethereal soldiers placed a hand on the old man's shoulders. "A feeding soul. A nosferatu dwelt in this space. The very air stinks of the vile creature."

"Can we free it?"

"The soul is dying, human. Its essence has been drained. The spark will fade out in a short time. The containment vessel is very powerful and not easily shattered. The main essence that made this soul has been consumed."

Erik's ears picked up a tiny whimper, the unmistakable cry of a child. His skin crawled. "It was a child. That hellspawn was feeding on the soul of a child."

The ethereal soldier nodded with sorrow. "Yes, they are

the sweetest meats for nosferatu. The innocence of a child provides them a perverse satisfaction, like a human enjoying a particularly tender cut of veal."

Erik watched his friend carefully. Martin's shoulders sagged as his eyes locked on the flickering soul. The light grew dimmer and dimmer inside the transparent container. Erik heard the whimper fade away in a dying gasp. The light flickered one last time and faded into oblivion. Martin wept momentarily then composed himself. Erik felt his stomach churn and struggled to keep his emotions in check.

"Come hybrid, there is little that can be done here. Let us continue the search." The soldier placed a gentle hand on Denton, urging the old man to move on as well.

Erik moved down the corridor toward the far door. He noticed several drops of green blood on the carpet hallway leading directly to the closed door at the far end.

"The one you wounded made it this far. It should be bled out by now." The blond leader approached the door carefully. "On my word, hybrid, we move in!"

Erik raised his weapon. He glanced back at Martin and the others. They were set as well. He looked back and nodded. The blond warrior kicked in the door and they rushed in. The demon Erik had wounded was sprawled on the floor, its head craned in an unnatural direction. Erik lowered his weapon and poked the demon's head. It flopped limply aside. "Its neck is broken. Molec didn't want any wounded baggage left behind."

Amazingly, the beast moved. It hissed weakly and Erik took a sudden shocked step back. "Holy shit! It's still alive!"

"These creatures are not as frail as a human construct."

"Good, then we can interrogate our broken friend here and finally get some answers."

The blond leader stepped in front of Erik blocking his path. "No. We will interrogate the creature ourselves."

Before Erik could protest, one of the ethereal soldiers knelt over the fallen demon. Both vanished. There was no flash of light, glimmer or sound to signify the departure. They simply vanished."

Erik saw Martin tilt his head. The counselor was about to protest. Erik shook his head, warning the old man off. Denton nodded, but it was clear to Erik his friend was disturbed.

The detective took a step back, increasing the grip on his weapon. The staff sensed his change in mental posture. The weapon began to hum its familiar battle drone. The warning sound threatening and ominous. "I thought we were a team. That last move wasn't very team friendly. It tells me you have something to hide and I don't like being played for anyone's lackey." Erik looked up toward the ceiling, "Not anyone's!"

The blond warrior was silent. "I'm not accustomed to being challenged or questioned. I have my instructions by the Father and I follow them. I suggest you do the same without the impertinence."

Blue fire crackled around the hybrid's body and the staff's whining became a loud growl. Jagged arcs of raw power danced up the weapon's lethal edge. Erik's skin began to change, his body swelling larger as the seams in his jersey began to split. "Or you'll do what, exactly?"

The two warriors squared off, each taking his measure of the other.

"I have no desire to fight you, hybrid. There will be time enough for us to practice our martial skill upon the real enemy." The leader retreated two steps. "The demon will need to be rejuvenated before it can be properly interrogated. There is a great deal of discomfort involved, and in its current state, it would likely expire before we could glean any pertinent revelations." The divine being waved its arm in a large semi-circle. "Do you know of a facility here that will treat such a creature?"

Erik's body slowly changed back to normal. His eyes became more human and he took a step back, lowering his weapon. The tension in the area rapidly dissipated and Martin could be heard releasing a long held breath. The other ethereal soldiers also visibly relaxed and appeared relieved.

Denton pointed toward the opposite wall. "An open safe. Can either of you get any mojo or vibes from it?"

The blond warrior looked at Martin, brow raised.

Erik hid a smirk. "I'll check." He focused his senses on the vault. The relic had been there, its echo was noticeably stronger. "It was here. Whatever they're using to shield its presence seems to be deteriorating. At the vault in DC, I could sense the object but not nearly this strong. Erik also detected the fading essence of the archdemon. "Molec took his prize…" The detective walked toward the far wall. "And the trail ends right here. Erik placed his open hand in front of him. "A Netherspace portal. They made a jump. They could be anywhere on Earth or in the linked dimensions tied to Earth." The hybrid detective's hand glowed light blue as he continued to study the remnants of the portal. "There's residual energy from two portals, not one. They're close in frequency and were opened practically on top of each other." The luminescence on Erik's hand increased. "Molec bailed out with his prize and it seems as if his forces fled shortly afterwards. Judging by the proximity in the portal frequencies they all went to the same general area."

"He left his forces for cannon fodder buying time for his escape. Look…" Denton gestured toward the far wall. Several large display units contained various electronic images of the factory grounds. "He knew when we got the upper hand and made good his escape before we even entered the damn building!"

Erik frowned. He pulled his hand back and turned toward the ethereal soldiers. "We're going to have to search each area for a lead." He turned toward the blond leader. "I'm assuming you have assets that can be deployed to search the adjoining realms."

The blond warrior nodded. "As long as Molec has the relic, he is bound to earthly domains. We do have that working for us." The warrior hedged.

"But…" Erik motioned for the being to continue.

"But the places Molec would hide are not welcoming to our kind. There are mutual pacts in place preventing us from invading certain realms. Molec knows this and will hide there. The archdemon is more afraid of us now than he is of Lucifer. He will risk taking temporary respite in one of the darker realms hoping to further shield his prize. Eventually, he will have to come back to Earth… Lucifer's allies will sniff him out, Molec knows that. His victory is temporary." The being looked back at Erik, his face revealed mild annoyance. "We will have to gain permission to violate these agreements. Bargains will have to be struck with the proprietors of each realm."

Erik tilted his head. "A heavenly and demonic bureaucracy? Oh you must be shitting me! No wonder you're losing this war."

The Ethereal flinched. "I do not make the rules, but I must follow them. We all can't run through life bulldozing through problems and bullying as you would prefer." There was a definite edge to ethereal's voice.

Martin jumped in. "So where do we start? We need to get a bead on where he went." The elder agent rummaged through several papers on the large mahogany desk. He picked up a business card, studying the logo and typeface. The old man held it up to Erik. "The Starlight Bistro—it appears Molec does have eyes there."

Erik smacked his fist into his open palm. "We go back there and get some answers. This demon is cagey, like a weasel. He hasn't been caught and seems to know his way around this corner of the universe better than any of us do. We're going to have to get savvy pretty damn fast. This bastard is always one or two moves ahead of us. We need to get some hard data, and The Starlight Bistro is our only lead at this point."

Denton thumbed through more papers. "Every human guard that worked here was loyal to Molec and they made a small fortune looking the other way."

"The archdemon is no feeble human or alien quarry, Agent Knight. Your allies don't give the dark under lord his due." A whisper came from the shadows accompanied by the smell of brimstone.

Erik spun, raising his katana. He recognized the raspy voice in the shadows. "Have you come for a second round, Bartholomew?"

The pale demon walked out of the shadows his hands open and raised partially. The soldiers of Light surrounded Lucifer's aide but the demon appeared relaxed and aloof. "I have no weapon and bear only a message."

The blond warrior stepped forward. His hand whipped forward faster than even Erik could follow, grasping Bartholomew and lifting the skeletal demon off the ground. "You bear only lies and deceit like your master! Now go meet him!" The soldier's hand flexed and a large ivory colored knife materialized in his hand.

Bartholomew shrieked in terror. "I know where Molec went. I have been given permission to bargain his location with you!"

Erik approached. "As much as I'd love to see you filet this bastard, maybe we should hear him out."

The soldier tossed the demon onto the ground. Bartholomew stood slowly brushing himself off. "We know where Molec and his acolytes are. As much as my master wants his head on a trophy shelf, he is willing to bargain. We engage Molec directly and all Hell will literally break loose. Your precious relic has been found as well. I will give you the location of both." Bartholomew paused, nodding his head slightly.

Erik felt something and knew the demon was being fed instructions.

"For a small request granted later."

The blond soldier tilted his regal head. "I have no authority to bargain with the devil, nor do I trust Lucifer to keep his word."

The ethereal soldier paused, looking up, lips moving imperceptibly. The presence Erik sensed was overwhelming and his whole body tingled with warning. His legs buckled, then powerful hands grabbed and steadied him.

"You hear the voice?" A soldier whispered.

"No, but the sensation is flooding my senses! There is a presence here. The last one was extremely powerful and I know who it was, I've encountered the devil earlier," Erik turned pale and his stomach twisted, the realization struck him. He looked toward the soldier, eyes wide, "No! not..."

The soldier nodded slightly pointing back to his leader.

The powerful ethereal seemed somewhat agitated. He looked over at Bartholomew. "Your terms are agreeable provided the demand does not exceed the value of your information. HE will make that determination at the time. Agreed?"

Bartholomew considered that for a moment. "Agreed."

"Where is Molec?"

Bartholomew grinned. "He is at the Soul Market, hiding at an alien soul merchant's interdimensional craft, and he has the relic with him. The moment he materialized through a portal, every creature felt the relic's presence. It contaminates everything with its holiness. Molec is desperately seeking a more powerful containment vessel, but none exists. The relic's presence is more than we can tolerate and demons are fleeing. As you humans would say; it's bad for business."

The ethereal frowned. "We cannot traverse the portals, they will not transport us and we are not allowed in the adjoining realms per the original agreements laid out in the Beginning. Lucifer knows this."

Bartholomew pointed toward Erik. "No, but the hybrid can go. He is a non-ethereal force in your army and now bears the mark of Light though he doesn't wish it. The hybrid can pass through into the Soul Market through a temporal portal nearby. I will provide you the temporary location of the portal and teach him the password which will grant him passage. He can confront Molec. His presence alone will push Molec back to Earth where we can deal with him and then repair the damage he's caused." Bartholomew paused, looking over at Erik. "You want to preserve your offspring, and avert an all-out Ethereal War? Go to the market and confront the archdemon. Drive him out and back to Earth. Take the cross and give us Molec." The demon studied him. "In your true form you should be able to hold the relic for a short time before obliteration, long enough to get it out of our realm and back here where the forces of Light can remove it. Things go back to normal and a centuries' old pain in both our proverbial backsides is eliminated."

Erik looked toward the blond warrior. "Is what he says true? Could I wield the relic? Maybe my son doesn't have to be involved in this."

The Ethereal nodded. "The relic is semi-sentient like your weapon. It would sense your biological relation to your son, but you could not wield the power. I honestly don't know. None of this is supposed to have occurred."

Denton stepped forward, coming between Erik and the ethereal leader. "Before you go making deals and plans shouldn't you be sure? The only person putting himself at risk here is you!" Erik flinched as his friend pointed. "What if this demon is wrong? What if you touch this thing and you go poof too? You're taking the word of a thing that tried to kidnap your son and kill you just days ago."

"I never implied there wasn't risk, human." Bartholomew spat the words with contempt. "I have no need to justify my actions to one who's barely a notch above a primate on the evolutionary scale." The demon pointed toward Erik. "Yes there is risk. The Soul Market is dangerous, and your own soul would be a valuable commodity ripe for the plucking. There aren't many places Molec can hide. We finally have a chance to capture him. The demon lord has overextended himself and is vulnerable. He cannot hide and protect his prize forever. The clock is ticking and we have to move quickly."

"He's done a good job of giving all of you the slip for how long now? What makes this time any different? You haven't exactly been bloodhounds when it comes to finding this guy" Denton looked over at Erik. "Think about this. I know how you love to rush into things but this proposal has 'Catastrophe' written all over it. You're going to a Hell realm where you have no support to confront a demon that wants both you and your son killed. Molec put a bounty on your child," Denton pointed toward Bartholomew. "And his boss did the same! Now we're crawling into bed with them?"

"You will be silent, ape! Or I'll carve out your tongue!" Bartholomew hissed. The demon took two aggressive steps toward Denton. The man had his gun drawn and pointed at the demon's head.

"Let's see if these bullets work as well on you!"

"ENOUGH BICKERING!" the blond warrior screamed. His voice rang loud in their heads. "Put your gun away, Mr. Denton. And you, Bartholomew, step back!" He pointed a pale finger towards Erik. "The bargain is struck, hybrid. Will you go or won't you? You alone must decide."

The silence hung over the area like a heavy fog. All eyes fell upon him. Erik took a few breaths, then stared at his friend and nodded. "Yeah, I'll go."

Erik could see his friend's disappointment. "I'm sorry, Martin. I don't see any way around it. If there's a chance to end this and save my son, I have to do it."

Denton nodded sadly. "I understand. So, hopefully you'll understand when I say I'm going with you."

Erik shook his head. "I can't ask you to do that. I don't know what I'm getting into. There's no need for you to take a risk I signed up for."

Denton grasped Erik's arm. "You said yourself earlier, we're family. You, Shanda and that sweet little boy are all I have left in the world. You don't turn your back on family. I turned my back on William and the price I paid was his life. If this goes wrong, we'll sink together."

"Martin, I can't." Erik struggled to control his emotions. "I can't ask you to do this."

Denton smiled, wiping away a tear. "You're not asking, son. I'm telling you, I'm going with you."

"Are you going to hug now?" Bartholomew's acidic voice broke the moment.

"Your presence is no longer required, demon. He has given me what we need to know to access the Soul Market."

Bartholomew's face took on a perceptible red tinge. "Impossible. No ethereal can know. It's the tightest secret."

The blond warrior laughed. "You have Lucifer's pride. The Father knows all and sees all. There are no secrets from Him.

The demon nodded, clearly annoyed. He looked over at Martin and Erik. "Be warned, human. You have no special powers to protect you. You go to the market and you will be a lamb among wolves hungry to snatch your soul from your living flesh and leave you a walking, soulless zombie."

Denton patted the large pistol inside his jacket. "I'll take my chances."

"You unleash violence there, you assure yourself an eternal death. The forces that keep the peace don't tolerate interference. Get Molec to flee and get out quickly before you draw any undue attention to yourselves. You just being there will be enough commotion." The demon waived his hand and a portal opened. He stepped through, half his body in and half still planted in the earthly plane. "Take it for what it's worth, I wish you luck, hybrid. We would all be well rid of Molec." The portal swallowed the demon and closed quickly.

The forces of light stood in silence, staring at each other. Erik felt the blond warrior's gaze weighing on him. "So where's this market?"

"The portal migrates from place to place. Its next location is an abandoned farmhouse in Connecticut. I will teach you password, though it's more of a physical gesture as well as a phrase. You must be exact or you cannot gain entrance. Go there, find Molec if he hasn't already fled and force him back to Earth. If he has minions there, he won't hesitate to unleash them on you. Bartholomew was correct; there are powerful forces there that keep the peace. They are formidable opponents from distant, alien worlds. If Molec unleashes forces, withdraw. The enforcers of the market will deal with any aggression."

"Can you give me any more information about this market?"

The soldier looked over at Erik and smiled wryly. "As you humans are fond of saying, Google it."

In a flash of light, the ethereal forces vanished leaving the two stunned men behind. Erik's head tingled. The information and password had been placed in his mind.

*   *   *

Erik and Martin sat in the small booth at the Uber Café in Mendon both trying to grasp the events that occurred just minutes earlier.

"We can sleep at the house and head out first thing in the morning. It's about a two hour drive to get to the farmhouse." Erik's finger traced a small road on a map. "The last leg of the trip is all farm roads so we'll have to take my truck instead of your Lincoln. I hope you don't mind the rougher ride."

Martin didn't respond. The old man just sipped his iced coffee watching the beautiful young women at the counter laugh with the customers.

Erik tapped his hand. "Counselor, are you in there?"

Denton flinched, coming back to reality. "Sorry, my mind was wandering." He gazed back at the girls. "So young and innocent. They have no idea what's going on around them, how close they are to oblivion. What we do or don't do will impact their lives."

Erik turned his gaze and took a moment to consider his friend's observation. "You're right. Let's hope we can fix this mess. Not just for their sake but for all our sakes."

Denton took another sip of his coffee. "How did you find this place? This stuff is really good."

Erik took a large sip from his coffee and nodded. "Shanda found it. We've been here a few times and the atmosphere just seemed right." Erik sighed. "It feels tranquil. I can't put it into words, so I come here and think, drink coffee and have lunch when I need to get away."

The old man smiled and nodded. "Anderson knew you'd find it."

Erik shrugged. "I'm not following you."

"Remember back at Madame's in DC? What Anderson told us? I was so busy eating that I really didn't pay it all that much heed. He said there would be another oasis to replace Jeff's, I think you found it, or Shanda did."

Erik looked around. "Maybe. But right now we need to focus on tomorrow."

Denton hesitated for a moment. Erik saw his friend balk. "What's the problem, Counselor?"

Denton scowled. "We'll talk at your place. Too many ears here and voices carry."

* * *

Erik spent several minutes on the phone talking with Shanda and EJ. The detective was relieved that both were relaxing and enjoying Vatican hospitality. The Ethereals were keeping their promise regarding his family. Erik said a final goodbye to Shanda as he tossed Martin a cold beer and grabbed an RC Cola for himself. Denton took a large swig from the bottle as his eyes focused on his laptop's screen.

"Good Lord! There are actual websites discussing the Soul Market and the kinds of demon merchants that go there."

Erik leaned over, studying the screen. "Being buried within a Dungeons and Dragons forum takes it off anyone's radar screen. Again, the forces of Dark are clearly the more clever. They're using technology and fantasy lore to their advantage." Erik took a deep drink from his bottle. "Our friends don't seem to be as steeped into human culture."

Denton scrolled through several images of hideous demonic entities, reading description and power capabilities. "I wonder how real this is."

"My gut tells me it's a veritable guide to the marketplace." Erik pointed toward a map icon. "Click on that gif. Let's get a lay of the land."

The gif map provided a detailed listing of merchants, the types of products sold, and the costs in gold bars or credit. Erik pointed toward the map's far corner. "There. This area seems to be a sort of alien space ship parking lot. If Molec is taking refuge in a craft, he'd be here, somewhere."

Denton slid his mouse cursor over the area and clicked. More detailed data about the "Parking Area" filled the screen. "These ships can only stay berthed for two cycles—whatever a cycle is. So if Molec has limited time and the fact that his little trophy is sending out some really toxic holy radiation only serves to shorten the amount of time our dark friend has to hide in the shadows. We may not have enough time. He may have to leave before we can get there to force him out. Maybe the relic will do our job for us?"

Erik frowned. "I don't think Molec will be driven out unless he's forced. He's looking for a containment vessel, and I believe he'll acquire something to house his prize. Maybe it won't be the perfect thing but our demonic friend isn't going to walk away and leave his prize. He's gonna find something. If the Ruby Crucifix is exposed and freed, his advantage is over. He can't touch it. He can't be near it. He'll have lost his only advantage." Erik went back and sat on the sofa.

Denton studied the scale on the lower corner of the map. "Good God this place is huge. It's nearly the size of Manhattan. There's no way we can cover all that ground in one day."

Erik rubbed the stubble on his cheek. "I can feel the relic, Martin. We'll have to hope that wherever we happen to pop into this happy little Hell hole, we'll be reasonably close and I can get some kind of a fix. We're going to need some luck, of that I have no doubt."

Erik felt the weight of Denton's gaze as the old man shut down his computer. "You have something on your mind. Fire away."

Denton nodded. "I just have to ask, did you fully intend to take on that ethereal earlier or was that just a bluff?"

Erik smiled. "I had no intention of starting a fight there. I was pissed off a bit at the way they just took our prisoner and I wanted to remind our friends that they're not the only beings capable of inhuman feats. We need to be taken seriously and I don't think they have a whole lot of respect or regard for you, me, or any human possibly with the exception of EJ." Erik drained his bottle and placed it on the coffee table. "If I launched a plasma bolt, that whole place goes up like a roman candle, and Hopedale is off the map, literally. I won't have that on my conscience. Our ethereal friend wasn't sure, but I could feel him poking and probing my mind. I was able to block him, and the fact that I wasn't letting him feel my anger pretty much let him know it was a show."

"Well you scared the shit outta me and our other allies."

"Sorry about that. It was a strategic bluff. Sadly, I don't think it bought us any respect or credibility with these beings. I don't think they're capable of feeling intimidation or fear. I wonder if they simply aren't capable of those emotions."

Denton frowned. "We're pawns, Erik. That's the impression I get. As far as emotions, your blond friend seemed pretty pissed off about having to cut a deal back there. He didn't like the orders he had to follow. That much was clear." Denton leaned forward. "We're dealing with beings that can pop in and out of our reality in an instant—no portal, no technology of any kind—just seemingly by sheer force of will. They're as far above us on the evolutionary ladder as we are above a tree frog or toad. It's a wonder they're dealing with us at all. I don't think they have a need to be intimidated or respect us. Use us like pawns, yes, appreciate anything we do, no."

"They're only dealing with us for one reason: EJ." Erik picked up the empty bottle. Walking toward the kitchen, he raised his voice. "The other thing I found disturbing. They're going to heal that creature so they can begin an interrogation process. I wonder what's involved in a divine interrogation. I can't imagine it would be pleasant for a being of demonic nature."

"Does it make me a bad person for not really feeling any pity?"

Erik chuckled as he tossed the empty bottle. "I'm not losing any sleep over it either. But we should probably turn in ourselves. I have the feeling tomorrow is going to be a day full of surprises."

Chapter 7: The Soul Market

Erik followed the dirt road over four miles. The maze of turns seemed endless as they drove around a sea of corn stalks. "There! That farm house. It's just like the image in my head. We're here."

Martin nodded. "Finally! I don't think my backside could take any more of this bumpy pathway."

Erik parked and both men approached the farmhouse. An old man sat by a bench with a wheelbarrow full of freshly picked corn.

"Whose gonna come all the way out here to buy corn?" Martin grumbled.

"Are you fellas lost? Or are you looking for some sweet corn?"

Erik smiled as they approached the farmer. "Good morning. We have another kind of business in a different kind of market."

The farmer's eyes grew shrewd and narrowed. "You're in the wrong place. I sell corn."

Erik's left hand performed a slow series of complicated gestures and he pronounced the phrase as best he could. The farmer tilted his head and pointed toward the dilapidated farmhouse.

"Through those doors, gentlemen. Everything is up for sale at the Soul Market, including your lives. Hold on to your souls. You two are like sheep going to a wolf's farmer's market."

Erik nodded as they walked toward the barn. Both men paused. The barn seemed abandoned and perfectly harmless. Erik looked over at his friend. "Here goes nothing." He pushed the door open and there was a slight sensation of stumbling forward.

"My God!" Martin gasped.

Erik felt his jaw drop as he studied the endless sea of alien beings walking up and down titanic streets with large merchant shops on either side. The sky fluctuated between a dull purple and blood red. Erik studied the skyline looking for the source of the light but there was no sun or other celestial object providing the illumination.

"Remember where this spot is, Counselor. It's our only ticket home."

Denton nodded absently as his eyes strained to take in the hideous wonder. "Remember that *Star Wars* bar scene? Now I know where they go the idea."

Erik chuckled as they moved warily toward the nearest street. Outdoor vendors had carts filled with glass globes similar to the one they'd seen at the abandoned factory. The souls were all different shapes, sizes and colors. Erik recognized some English and a few phrases in Latin, but the other languages were unknown and undoubtedly not of his world.

"The map and this place don't tie together." The detective stopped and spun his head back and forth. The map showed roads in parallel, almost grid like. These venues are haphazardly scattered about intersecting every which way." He shook his head, frustrated. "It's like driving through Boston after some major construction. Everything is ass backwards."

"You there!" A voice cried out in broken English. A large being with crooked teeth and purple flesh placed his seven-fingered hand on Erik's chest. "It is! A cross bred soul! I could smell it across the street!" The being took a step back producing an electronic tablet from the very air. "I'll write you a credit voucher right now if I can have your soul upon the moment of your death. I'm willing to offer you two million in credit. Three million if you sell me your soul right now. You can live like a king for the rest of your natural life."

Erik gently but firmly took the man's hand off his chest. "I appreciate the generous offer but I'm rather fond of my soul and prefer to keep it where it is."

The being spun toward Martin. "And you! An old human soul, not worth nearly as much, say twenty five thousand now for your soul upon your death?"

Martin took a step back shaking his head. "Uhm, no, no thank you." The being took another step closer, its hand glowing red. "Come human, give me your soul." Its voice had a cold edge as it placed its hand back on Martin's chest.

Erik saw his friend's eyes blank and kicked the legs of the being out from under him. The being fell to the ground with a heavy thud. Before it could recover, Erik had his hands around its throat and he squeezed just enough to block the windpipe. "That's not very friendly. We have a saying on Earth. 'NO means NO!' Maybe I'll rip your throat out and see what kind of nasty thing will come for your soul. Better yet, I'll kill you in front of a nosferatu. I'm sure a warped soul like yours will tantalize such a creature's demented appetites."

The being struggled but Erik held it firm.

"Erik, remember we can't raise a ruckus here. Dial it down."

"Please, my friends," it croaked gasping for air. "This was all just a misunderstanding."

Erik hefted the creature over his head and held it up with one arm. "I'm gonna put you down now, but you pull that hocus pocus crap, I'll tear you head off, am I clear?"

The terrified being nodded and Erik roughly tossed it on the alien pavement.

"Before you slink back under your rock," Denton hissed, "we're looking for a demon—a very annoying demon named Molec. We know he's here and we know he's very desperate to buy some protective materials to shield an object he's stolen."

The being studied Erik carefully and looked down at his hand. "Hybrid, the tales are true. You do exist and you do serve the Lords of Light. I gather no one has claimed the bounty on your bastard child?"

Erik took a step forward and the being flinched. "Violence isn't allowed here and you shouldn't even be here. How did you come to be here Esper Warrior?"

"Violence is forbidden but soul leeching is perfectly acceptable?" Erik folded his arms, growing impatient. "Answer the question or I'll break your leg this time and still feed you to the soul suckers."

The purple being flinched. "Molec is here. He brought the cursed relic with him. It burnt and scarred the flesh of thousands before he made it to the place where the outsiders keep their interdimensional craft. If he's still here, he's hiding in one of those vessels trying to find a new ectoplasmic sphere."

"If you'd be so kind as to point the way, we'll part company now." Erik took a menacing step forward.

The purple being shuddered, pointing toward a dark structure at the horizon's edge, "The port is at the edge of the market. Follow that large monolith. The ships are all parked in that area." It stood slowly pointing toward Erik. "Molec won't leave willingly. You bring the Ethereal War here, you'll involve not just your planet, but hundreds of inhabited worlds across not only this Universe but all the ones lying tangent to this one. Walk softly here, Esper Warrior. There are things here that even one as powerful as you need to tread around carefully." Erik stood close to Martin, guiding the old man away from the being and toward their goal.

Erik and Martin walked silently for several minutes, each man studying the dizzying array of life forms. Erik gently nudged his friend. "How you doing, Counselor?"

Denton cleared his throat. "Aside from nearly having my soul sucked out of my body, I'm okay."

Erik tilted his head. "Yeah, aside from that and this demon and alien nightmare we're walking through. I confess my mind is shrieking right now. Let's just keep pushing to the monolith and do our best to stay out of trouble."

Denton chuckled. "Now I know we're in deep shit when you suggest staying out of trouble." The old man moved cautiously, never straying more than a few steps away from his companion.

"I can feel the relic. We're on the right track." Erik pointed up another street. "The trail goes this way, right towards the area our purple goon pointed out." Erik grinned. "Maybe we'll catch our archdemon friend with his pants down this time. I'd like to wrap this up in a nice little bow and rub it in our smug allies' face."

Erik placed his arm forcefully in front of Martin, stopping the old man cold. There was a commotion ahead. Both men slowly crossed the wide street. Three large demons were in an argument with two squid-like beings. Tentacles and claws were waving back and forth in some dramatic disagreement. Trapped in between both parties was a beautiful young woman with silver flesh, and a slender ridge running from the top of her head down her bare back and dark blue glowing eyes. She was locked in heavy chains that glowed red and orange. Erik's skin tingled and something in his mind shouted. The prisoner was an Esper female! She was being tossed back and forth between the groups while the gathering crowd laughed and hissed with amusement.

"My God, Erik! She looks like you when you change."

Erik nodded. "I know. An Esper female. She may be the only one left. They didn't all perish on Earth!" Erik took two steps toward the crowd.

Martin grabbed his shoulder. "What are you doing?"

"I'm gonna free her! I can't let her be harmed!"

"You interfere and who knows what kind of forces you'll bring down upon us!"

Erik spun around. "What are you saying, Martin? I just leave her to be bartered like cattle or a side of beef? She could be the only Esper alive anywhere! I could learn more about my past and my heritage and maybe there's another Esper out there, looking for her. Maybe there's more like me in the galaxy."

Martin nodded. "Maybe. But is it worth bringing down the wrath of whatever keeps the peace here, and possibly letting Molec escape. We're here to help save our planet and your son!" Denton took his hand off Erik's shoulder.

Erik felt his stomach knot, his fists clenched with anger. His eyes burned fiery blue as energy crackled around his body. "I know. But..." his voice had a painful longing.

"I know, son. I'm not heartless. But you can't engage all these beings without putting our mission and ourselves at risk. Bartholomew said there were powerful beings here. Do you want to have to fight your way back to the portal? Remember what you faced at the gym parking lot? What if there are worse things here?"

Erik felt helpless. "You're right. Damn it to Hell but you're right."

Denton pointed. "Look. The squid things are taking her in the direction we want to go. I'm going out on a limb and guessing that these creatures have a ship parked and are taking their purchase there. Let's tag along at a safe distance. We're going in that direction anyway."

Erik and Martin followed the two beings and their captive. The chains had some mystical quality. They continually glowed reddish orange and had a debilitating effect on the female. She could barely walk and at times her captors dragged her limp body behind them. Erik struggled to suppress his rage and burning desire to attack the creatures and avenge the indignation suffered by one of the Esper race.

"They're turning off the road, away from the ships."

Martin nodded. "And into that shop."

Erik stared for a long minute watching the tentacled beings as they hovered over their prize. The Esper female struggled but was too weak. She was fitted with some type of device and then led deeper into the shop out of view. Erik looked over at Martin his eyes, hard. "Let's get to the ships but we're coming back this way, Counselor. I'm not done here yet."

Martin nodded silently as they followed the trail of the Ruby Crucifix.

The two men walked an hour in silence. Erik would periodically pause, reach out into the air and then walk down a different winding road. The market was a maze of streets with no rhyme or reason as to how they connected. Martin walked silently behind.

"Erik, I'm hopelessly lost."

Erik paused, and turned toward his friend. "We've covered about four miles. Do you need to stop for a bit?" Erik looked around. "I'm not sure we could buy a cup of coffee here and I don't think they take Visa, MasterCard or human currency."

Denton nodded then pointed toward a small area that had tables filled with a variety of occupants eating and drinking. "We could ask. Maybe pick up some intel so we're not going in blind. Molec shook this place up. Somebody has to know something and people eating and drinking are more likely to chat."

Erik nodded. "That's actually not a bad idea. And I need to get my head screwed back on. I was ready to come to blows for that girl. An Esper. I think she was a cleric, I could feel her presence inside my mind. She was terrified, Martin. She was absolutely terrified. I knew she could feel my presence. Maybe she was hoping I'd do something."

"Erik, I don't know what to say. I can't imagine what you went through or what seeing that woman triggered. I know you're an Esper Warrior. I know you could probably lay waste to this entire realm if you put your mind to it, but we can't come in here guns blazing." Denton walked toward the crowd. "I see an empty table. I'll see if I can buy us a drink so we can take a break and try and gather some intel."

Erik nodded. "We can't linger. We'll ask a few questions then move on. Our friends say Molec is on a very tight time table here and we don't want to miss him."

They sat at the small table drawing several stares. Erik could hear hushed whispers but the language was unknown. The feelings, however, were quite clear. They were unwelcome.

"We're not wanted, Martin. Maybe this wasn't such a good idea."

A small orange woman approached them. "Humans. She inhaled deeply and stared at Erik. Her eyes widened and she took a step backward. "Not so much human but a warrior of Light. You really don't belong here. The Ocherons will come for you both eventually." Her face grew sly. "Are you here to buy souls? For twenty credits I'll tell you the best merchants with the sweetest treasures from all the known galaxies. Most vendors carry alien souls, but only a rare few have the souls of human children or those that have passed tragically."

"What about Esper souls?"

She laughed. "There aren't enough Espers left and their souls are practically worthless—no depravity or immorality. A few have gone to feed the nosferatu. They thrive on devouring purity, but others like a soul seasoned with debauchery and corruption."

"So there are Espers alive? I thought they all perished during the Great War."

The woman laughed aloud. "Yes the two warring species. God and Lucifer using more puppet races. The Seelak didn't kill all their Esper prisoners. Some were brought here and sold as slaves. We just had one purchased earlier. It is a rarity but there are a few of them around functioning as servants."

Denton took a fifty dollar bill from his wallet. "Will this

work here?"

She nodded. "Human currency is discounted at twenty percent."

"Will this buy us two drinks and a few answers to some questions?" Denton pulled another fifty from his wallet.

The woman frowned. "Two glasses of amber meade and two questions. Meade is about the only thing here you humans could stomach. Do we have an arrangement?" She reached for the two bills, her hand pausing slightly.

Denton nodded. "Done."

The woman pocketed the currency and shouted her order across the courtyard as she took a chair from the nearby table. "Two questions."

Martin leaned over the table so his voice wouldn't carry. "We're looking for a being called Molec. We know he came through here not too long ago and caused some damage in his passing. We were told he's hiding inside an interdimensional craft." Denton pointed toward the dark monolith. "Can you give us any idea where to start looking once we get there?"

The woman shook her head. "Molec, that accursed idiot. He brought a holy object here." She pointed toward a nearby demon. Its skin was horribly scarred. "That one was close by when he materialized. He was lucky. Many in the vicinity were simply vaporized and others have scars covering their entire body. Such a thing cannot be here. It contaminates us all." She pointed toward the monolith. "The more advanced races with better ships are berthed closer to the main port. Molec would be there. Lesser beings would be too fearful to have any dealings with such a being or would even comprehend the value and danger of what the archdemon has in his possession. There are rarely more than a handful of highly advanced craft with beings willing to associate with higher demonic forces or possessing the type of technology needed to assist him." She smiled. "That's one."

Denton looked toward Erik. "Your turn."

"Are any more of Molec's forces here? When he fled, many of his underlings were right behind him. If we're forced to engage Molec, will he have aid? Does he have allies here that will fight on his behalf?"

She grinned wickedly. "Any alliances he made here were forfeit when he brought that cursed thing among us. His minions came here and are dispersed throughout the market, hiding and hoping Lucifer's agents won't bother to track them down. Keep in mind, hybrid ... yes I know who and what you are. Your aura stinks of it. The only reason I'm helping you is because you're the lesser of the two plagues right now. Be warned. Lucifer also has agents hunting Molec. You may encounter them or our own enforcers. I strongly suggest you tread lightly, or as light as possible for you. The market is strictly for barter and commerce. Though we are considered evil, we have become more interested in commerce over conflict. Keep your wars in your own plane and leave us to our business."

Erik nodded. "You steal souls and sell them in a market place, you sell slaves and who knows what else, and your little enterprise was set up by the leader of one of the primary warring factions. How can you not be involved?"

The woman's smile turned deathly cold. "You didn't pay for three questions."

The drinks arrived and their host stood abruptly. "Enjoy your drinks, gentlemen, it was a pleasure doing business with you."

Martin raised his glass and nodded. He looked at Erik. "Well that was somewhat useful, at least we know where to look when we get there."

Denton took a cautious sip from his tall mug. His eyes popped open. "Well now! This is delicious."

After five minutes they began their walk toward the dark monolith. Erik did his best to ignore the surreal environment and to keep his mind focused. The desperate plea from the Esper female echoed in the back of his mind. The sensation of the Ruby Crucifix was stronger now, and he could sense the lingering presence of Molec. "We're getting close, Martin." Erik pointed ahead. The towering black monolith loomed over them, casting a dark shadow over nearby buildings. Several beings moved back and forth between the structure. Small vehicles wended their way among the assorted alien craft.

"Reminds me of an airport." Denton stood beside him as they studied the area.

Erik focused his senses, trying to pinpoint the strongest essence of Molec and the cross. "This way. The lady at the bar was correct. The general direction is toward those three large vessels berthed directly under the structure. Let's hope we can get there without causing a ruckus. I have no idea what comprises security in this place."

"Maybe I should have bought more questions."

Erik looked over at his friend. "Counselor, we could spend a million dollars asking questions and never figure this place out. We stick out like weeds in a rose garden here. These things can smell us like bloodhounds the same way I can sense Molec and the cross. We'll just have to do the best we can and hope the forces here are as against Molec as we're led to believe."

Erik took point and moved quickly toward the three ships, his Esper senses guiding him forward. The trail led directly to a 'U' shaped craft with an odd asymmetrical bulge on the far side. "There's the ship. The trail ends here." They approached, slowly walking by a large craft, ignored by its crew and the beings tending to the ship.

Erik's senses buzzed a warning. He dove toward Martin, tackling him, as a red lance of energy grazed his shoulder. Erik continued to roll, knowing the burning lance of power was still chasing them. "Dome!"

The Sentient Staff flowed from its concealment, covering both men in a silver cocoon. The beam's energy washed over the staff but had no effect on the Esper weapon.

"Martin, are you okay?"

Denton groaned. 'What the hell just happened?"

"We were attacked. We're inside a protective blister right now, but we're going to have to move." Another blast of energy struck the protective dome. The staff moaned slightly as the alien energy sizzled against its metallic shell.

"Molec?"

Erik shook his head as another blast hit. "I think he made some friends. We have to move. We can't let ourselves be pinned down like this. They're buying time for that bastard." A second, longer blast hit emphasizing his point.

"I assume you have a plan?"

Erik nodded. "Yeah I'm going to form a large round shield,

big enough to allow you to retreat, then I'm going to move in. If I can rush them, maybe they'll panic. At least I'll buy you enough time to get out of harm's way." Erik placed a hand on his staff projecting his wishes directly to the weapon. "Okay Martin, the staff knows what I want. When I form the shield, you run like a bat outta hell and find cover."

Denton nodded, terror etched in the old man's face.

"Now! Shield!"

The dome warped and morphed into a flattened disc four feet in diameter. Erik held the makeshift barrier high, providing ample cover for Martin's retreat. Denton fled in a perfect line behind the shield, finding cover against a nearby alien craft. Alarms blared and beings shrieked in various tones and languages. The cacophony of noise was deafening. Erik pushed forward as more red beams impacted against his shield.

"I can play offense too!" Agitated photons formed a burning plasma surrounding his arm. Erik lifted his left arm raising the shield and fired a searing blast of energy with his other arm. The blast ate through the alien hull, burning clean through the entire vessel. The ship shrieked in agony, a wailing scream of pain that echoed off walls and other ships. A hatch flowed open and several frail looking gray creatures fled on flying devices. The alien vessel sagged, then fell over. Its collapse shook the entire hangar. Red ichor hemorrhaged from the gaping hole Erik made. The area around the craft was awash in a pool of alien blood. Erik walked toward the crippled ship and placed a hand on the alien hull. It wasn't metal. His stomach churned. It was a hard shell covering flesh. The ship was alive!

"No, no, no, no!" Erik swore. "Oh God, I didn't know."

The ship began to shift and change. The craft became more like a gigantic armored whale with massive fins and antennae easily forty feet in length. The beast moaned softly, slowly writhing in pain.

Martin came up behind, staring at the creature in disbelief. "This was the ship that fired on us?"

Erik turned. "Yeah, the pilots took off in some smaller craft. They're gone. I can only assume Molec got what he wanted and is gone as well."

Several aliens approached. Erik readied his staff.

"We don't want any trouble. We can help the Space Mariner."

Erik took a step back, letting the strange beings work.

Several minutes had passed and the creature was attached to several glowing pods with filaments touching its flesh. The workers had placed some type of organic bandage over the gaping wound. Erik watched helplessly as the creature moaned, sounding exactly like a whale in distress. Only this whale was easily ten times the size of an Earth mammal.

"The creature needs energy. I fear we don't have enough to revitalize it. The crew that captured it had depleted most if its organic reserves. Forcing it to attack, exhausted it." The being looked up at Erik. "And your blast will likely finish it off."

Erik shook his head. "How much energy can this thing absorb?"

The tiny alien shrugged. "A great deal more than we can provide. I fear its internal systems will shut down soon and parts of the creature will begin dying."

"Is this a naturally evolved creature? I mean it was a ship when it attacked us." Martin looked at the beast with awe.

"They are a combination of natural and synthetic evolution—a process planned by their species over a million and a half years. Its heart is an organic thermal reactor. Arteries and veins have become synthetic power conduits. The brain and other tissues are still organic but enhanced by nanotechnology. This creature is a marvel of the known universe. Sadly this one was captured, tortured, and enslaved while still young."

Erik was silent, staring at the sky. His hands reached outward fingers tensed. "There's enough ambient energy in the air to feed our friend." A bolt of orange energy stuck his outstretched arm from the purple sky. Erik gently lay his other hand upon the wounded being, slowly passing the energy along. The Space Mariner's large tail shuddered as its body hungrily absorbed the power.

MORE, PLEASE, I HAVE BEEN WITHOUT FOOD FOR SO LONG. PLEASE NO MORE PAIN.

The voice in Erik's mind was soft and haunting. The sound of a being terrified of being hurt again.

I WON'T HURT YOU ANYMORE, I PROMISE, I DIDN'T

KNOW, I SWEAR TO YOU I DIDN'T KNOW. Erik gently pushed more energy into the creature.

The massive entity stood upright on powerful fins and began to hover several feet above the ground, antenna gently swaying back and forth. Erik stopped drawing the power and took several steps backward. The massive being looked down at him.

YOU HAVE MADE ME WHOLE. AFTER THOUSANDS OF YEARS I AM RID OF MY CAPTORS! WHAT IS YOUR PRICE FOR MY HEALTH AND FREEDOM?

Erik and Martin looked up at the massive being. Its skin was almost translucent radiating the full spectrum of color. Its eyes sparkled, brilliant white orbs burning with a wisdom that transcended any being in the galaxy.

"I ask only that you accept my apology for wounding you." Erik looked up totally transfixed on the massive creature, too much in awe to project his thoughts. Its intellect and presence was almost too much to bear.

YOU ARE FREELY FORGIVEN. The massive creature studied him. *YOU ARE A BEING OF LIGHT, A SERVANT OF THE FATHER. I MUST GIVE THANKS ONCE I AM BACK IN SPACE. HE HAS HEARD MY CALL AFTER SO MANY CEN-TURIES.*

"The beings that held you captive, they were meeting with a demon—an archdemon—it is he who I'm hunting. Do you happen to know if the demon fled?"

The massive whale's mouth tensed, opening partially and revealing a row of foot-long sharp teeth. *YOU ARE THE HY-BRID MOLEC SPOKE OF. I HEAR ALL THAT ENTER. TAKE HEART, THE DEMON DID NOT GET WHAT HE WANTED, A SECTION OF MY ARMOR. MOLEC WAS BARGAINING WHEN YOUR PRESENSE WAS DETECTED. YOU PREVENT-ED HIM FROM ACQUIRING AN OBJECT THAT COULD TEMPORARILY SHIELD HIS STOLEN PRIZE, MY FLESH. HE DID HOWEVER ACQUIRE MORE TALITHUM SO HE COULD CONTINUE HOLDING HIS PRIZE. MY CAPTORS WERE ABLE TO PARTIALLY REVITALIZE HIS ECTOPLASMIC PRIS-ON, BUT THE BARRIER STILL CRUMBLES AND WILL SOON WITHER. THE HOLY RELIC CANNOT BE CONTAINED.*

"Did Molec say where was going before he teleported out?"

HE IS BOUND TO EARTH AS LONG AS HE HOLDS THE RELIC. THE SACRED CROSS IS TIED TO EARTHLY REALMS. HIS DEMON PRIDE REFUSES TO PART WITH HIS TROPHY, SO HE TOO IS TIED TO THAT TINY WORLD AND THE REALMS LINKED TO IT. THE DEMON HAS FLED BACK TO EARTH TO HIDE AGAIN AND SEARCH ANEW FOR A WAY TO KEEP THAT WHICH CANNOT BE KEPT. The massive being's face appeared to frown. *A HIGHLY IRRATIONAL ACTION.*

The great being looked around the market and its eyes hardened with disapproval. *I HAVE NO LIKING FOR THIS SAVAGE PLACE. IT IS TIME FOR ME TO GO HOME. I WISH TO SWIM IN THE GREAT ABYSS THAT SWALLOWS LIGHT, TIME AND SPACE. I LONG TO TRAVEL THROUGH THE SPATIAL SEAS OF MY ANCESTORS, ACROSS THE COSMOS.* Colored flesh changed to bright luminescent white as it rose higher into the sky. Its massive body turned and, like a whale speeding through the ocean depths, the great being swam off into the sky, vanishing in a stream of colored light.

Erik stared at the purple sky. Martin cleared his throat. "Well, there's something you don't see every day—a gigantic, talking, flying whale."

Erik tilted his head. "Just another mystery, Counselor." Erik turned toward his friend, clearly frustrated. "We missed our window. That bastard always manages to be one step ahead of us."

Martin placed a hand on Erik's shoulder. "My friend, this demon has hid from the forces of Light and Dark for how many centuries? I didn't think we'd just come in and grab him on our second try. But we're following our usual game plan. We're forcing the demon to move quickly and jump before he's ready. Right now he's making mistakes." Martin gestured back toward the marketplace. "Look at how many beings he's killed and maimed here. He's burnt this bridge completely. How quickly will word spread about this little episode? Molec's made enemies here today. We're pushing him. We forced him out of his warehouse stronghold and we forced him to flee the soul market empty handed. I don't think this prick has felt any pressure for eons and he's not used to it. Our demonic friend is desperate right about now. He's got a hot potato he can't carry and each time he tries to find a way to secure it, we're right there to counter his action. He's either gonna have to give up the relic or make a stand. Either way he loses. He won't show himself because both sides will drop on him like a boat anchor and if he flees, he loses his precious trinket and his grand scheme implodes. And for a creature like that, I'd imagine his ego is sizable and the aggravation you're causing must be driving him insane. Our objective was to push him back to Earth." Denton smiled raising his hand. "Mission accomplished."

Erik nodded. "But he scored more of that mystical black fabric. It's going to make tracking him that much more difficult."

"My friend, you are a glass half empty kind of guy. Let's take the win and get the hell out of here. We're starting to draw attention to ourselves." Denton motioned his head toward a gathering crowd of assorted aliens. "I'm assuming they're the crew of the ship we just liberated. I can't imagine they're too happy with us, considering we've stranded them here."

Erik glanced over. Martin's assessment was spot on, several aliens had gathered and they were all in similar attire. They were the crew of the massive Space Mariner. "I think it's time to make a strategic retreat. Most of them saw the battle and know I'm no pushover. I don't think they're going to try anything, but let's not tempt fate by sticking around." Both men walked rapidly away from the hangar.

"Can you find our way back to the portal that brought us here?"

Erik nodded. "Yeah, that shouldn't be too hard. I pretty much have an idea where it is. Martin, I'm sorely tempted to go back for that Esper. I can't leave her here. I can't leave knowing she's a slave or worse."

"I know how you feel, believe me I do. But you go in guns blazing and you'll trigger gawd only knows what kind of response. Your son needs you and your wife needs you. Fighting here doesn't help them. Yes, you'll be righting a wrong, but at what cost? One war at a time son, one war at time. Right now we're up to our eyeballs in angels and demons. That should be enough to keep anyone gainfully occupied. Let's not provoke another realm full of entities we don't understand. I'm guessing we've earned some good graces now that we drove Molec out. Let's not burn that bridge."

Martin and Erik walked back toward the merchant area in silence. Erik did his best to shield his mind and ignore the events occurring around him. He felt a slight tap on his shoulder.

"Erik, I'm sorry. But I need to rest. My leg is killing me."

Erik paused. Martin looked peaked. Sweat poured down his forehead. He realized they'd covered nearly eight miles of ground walking back and forth. "Martin, let's get you seated somewhere, maybe we can buy another one of those drinks and rest." The detective cursed himself. He'd disregarded the needs of his old friend. Erik spotted several large comfortable chairs and tables outside a shop. He pointed in their direction and guided his tired friend toward a chair. "Have a seat, and relax. I'll see what I can do about getting us some water or anything edible to eat and drink."

Before Erik could walk out, a pale man with gnarled fingers on each hand approached them. "If you're not going to buy the chair, then don't sit in it."

"I'm sorry, I thought perhaps this was a place where we could get some food and water." Erik kept his tone soothing and non-confrontational. "My friend is exhausted and just needs a few moments to rest." Erik reached for his wallet. He pulled out two twenty dollar bills. "I know human currency is discounted twenty percent. Will this buy a few minutes rest and a glass of meade for my friend. Do we have a deal?"

The man frowned. It'll cost me another five percent to convert that paper trash into viable money. I'll give you a bottle of my best meade for your friend and five minutes rest.

"Ten minutes, please. He's exhausted. I'll even buy something from your store."

The man frowned as Erik took out two additional twenty dollar bills. The last of his cash. "Do we have a deal?"

The man nodded as he reached forward and took the money. I have some cheap trinkets you can peruse, but forty dollars won't even buy you a goat's soul."

Erik shook his head. "I don't want anybody's soul."

The man gestured Erik inside. "Well, come along. We've stuck a bargain and I'll get your friend his drink and you can shop per our arrangement. Ten minutes, no more."

Erik placed a hand on his friend's shoulder. "He'll be back in a second with your drink. Get some rest, Martin... I'm gonna snoop a bit. My senses are going off for some reason and I want to nose around."

Denton nodded. Erik could see the fatigue etched on his face. "This isn't a place I'd want a memento from. Just be careful."

Erik nodded as the man came out with a large frosted bottle. He popped it open and handed it to Martin.

"Drink up. The additional herbs will restore some of your vitality."

Denton took the bottle and drank deeply. His eyes bulged. "This is delicious, thank you." The counselor leaned back in the chair and closed his eyes, taking another sip from his drink. "I wish I could buy this chair. It's amazingly comfortable."

Seeing that Martin was well tended, Erik entered the store, his senses tingling stronger as he approached several glass globes. There were hundreds of souls trapped inside the vessels. Two fine wires attached to two golden dots on the globe's surface impaled the glowing orbs within. The signs were in a language he couldn't understand. "What are these?"

The clerk looked at him nervously. "They're special souls for sale. You needn't concern yourself. You can't afford them. The crystals and onyx trinkets are on a shelf over there. Those are in your price range. I suggest you shop quickly. Your time is almost expired." The shop keeper was visibly nervous and the detective picked up on the discomfort.

Erik felt compelled to study the containers. As he walked down the aisle, examining each one, the feeling grew stronger. He bent over to a lower shelf. A delicate pink orb of incredible beauty was the source of the feeling. Something inside himself urged him to pick up the globe. He held it up to his eyes, studying the trapped orb. The delicate pink glow grew in intensity then shrank back as something in the thin fibers activated. Erik heard a gasp of pain. It was a delicate female whisper.

"Put that down! Now! You cannot touch what you cannot afford to buy, human. Your time has expired. You and your friend must be on your way now. Our business is concluded."

Something about the trapped soul tugged on Erik's emotions. The merchant looked on nervously as he continued to study the imprisoned orb.

"She's in pain. I heard her cry out."

The merchant took a step back, clearly concerned. "That's impossible..." he stammered. "You'd have to be a descendant of a soul to make any psychic connection."

Erik studied the glass and projected his thoughts at the orb, hoping it could communicate with him. "Hello, my name is Erik Knight. I sensed your presence. Who are you?" he whispered and projected the question.

Erik Knight, it can't be. My son? My baby boy?

Erik choked. Tears rolled down his face. "Mom! Mom is that you! God no, please! It can't be!"

Erik! My son! Are you dead too? Please no, please tell me you're not trapped like me.

Erik turned toward the shop keeper, his eyes slits of burning rage and anger. The sentient staff growled, hidden beneath his jersey, sensing his sudden change of mood. Blue bioelectric energy crackled in an aura of power surrounding his body. "This is my mother. How the hell did you get her soul?!"

The shop keeper took another nervous step back, retreating outside his store. Martin heard the commotion and stood from his chair.

Erik stepped out, holding the globe gently. His eyes blazed like angry twin, blue stars. "My mother died thirty-three years ago in a car accident. How did she wind up here and where is my father?" Erik took one hand and crushed a nearby metal storage container. "I'll do the same to your skull if I don't get an answer."

The merchant withdrew another step. "You can't threaten violence here. It is forbidden. The enforcers will eradicate you."

"Maybe so, but you won't be here to see it if you don't answer my question."

"The market employs several soul leeches that wander the Earth. They wait for tragedies to happen and scoop up the most innocent of souls that perished in terrible ways. Those souls know suffering and are sweet meat for several species of alien and demon alike. I can only assume your mother's soul was captured as it left her body. I was told that soul perished in a tragic accident. The needles in the glass are leeching probes. Touch both probes and the soul's essence is partially diminished, but each soul has the ability to regenerate over time. A soul of this nature can be fed upon for decades before its energy sours. I have..."

The enraged detective cut him off. "Free her! Now!"

"I can't. No one can. She's trapped in there. It would take an ethereal being of extreme power to destroy a soul sphere. The energy binding the clear crystalline glass is immense. Unleashing that kind of power would be devastating."

"Erik, are saying that thing contains your mother's soul?" Martin walked over to his friend, studying the pulsing orb.

"It's her, Martin. I spoke with her. I sensed her soul. That was the impression I was getting earlier."

Denton looked over at the now terrified merchant. "And this soul died in a car accident on Earth, thirty-three years ago." Denton looked over at his friend. "Good God, it could really be her!" The counselor looked ill. He smashed the empty meade bottle against the street and his hand went for his gun. "Jesus H Christ and you sell these souls for profit? What kind of sick, twisted being are you?"

The clerk took a step back. "I'm a merchant at the soul market. It's what we all do, human. Don't judge by your paltry standards old man. The universe has more complexity and mystery than your feeble mind can comprehend." He pointed toward the glass vessel. "The soul is mine. I acquired it and have possession of it. You cannot commit theft in this place. It is forbidden."

"You stole my mother's soul. You've kept her prisoner and tortured her. Don't give me a lecture. She's leaving with me. You wanna call your police go ahead. I'm freeing her! And God help anyone or anything that gets in my way." Erik squeezed the glass globe with desperate superhuman strength. His powerful arms trembled as more and more pressure was applied against the unyielding surface."

The merchant mocked him. "You don't have the strength to shatter that vessel, human. It would take a being of incredible power, an ethereal, perhaps. An army of humans couldn't break that barrier."

Erik took a breath and looked over at Martin. The old man nodded. "It's your call, Erik. I'll back you either way."

"Take a few steps back. I'm calling up the big gun!" He looked up into the heavens and shouted, "I am the Warrior!"

Erik's body began to glow as he changed from human to Esper Warrior. His clothes split and his body grew in size and mass. Heavy chrome armor plate replaced pink flesh and a massive, muscled figure replaced the athletic human. The aura of agitated energy surrounding his body increased as the hybrid applied more physical pressure on the crystalline prison. Erik's Esper body radiated heat and energy setting his tattered clothes ablaze. His Esper vocal cords hissed and roared as more and more physical and bioelectrical power was applied against the supernatural prison. The fabric and tapestries around him ignited in flames. The expanding heat forced Martin back.

"Your friend is no mere human! If that orb breaks, the energy released will cause untold damage. He's going to set the entire market ablaze! I'm getting the enforcers!" The merchant fled, running up the street. Martin had to step back further as aqua blue jagged arcs of energy surrounded the massive silver warrior.

"Erik hurry! Our friend went to call the demonic enforcers. We need to get out of here, now!"

More waves of radiant heat rose from the energy nimbus. The merchant's chairs and canopy covering were ablaze and, inside the fire, the massive hybrid stood, still applying more power against the globe, ignoring the flames surrounding him.

Martin heard a creaking sound that echoed throughout the marketplace. The sound of shattered glass and thunder reverberated, blowing out windows and knocking over displays as a powerful shockwave radiated out among the marketplace. In the center of the destruction stood the massive silver warrior, gently embracing a svelte semi-transparent woman.

Martin peeked out from behind the large metallic crate. His jaw dropped as he watched the mother and son embrace.

"My God, he did it."

A droning alarm broke the eerie silence.

"You fools!" The merchant cried out, coming back down the street. "A soul can't leave the market. It's a closed domain. All you've done is trap her in a bigger prison. She'll be caught again and you'll be killed. Even as strong as you are, you'll both be killed. Lucifer will not tolerate even the theft of one soul! His forces will hunt you down forever!"

Martin we need to get out of here now. Let's make a beeline to the portal. Erik projected to his friend.

Mom, you need to come with me. I can't leave you here. I can save you.

The essence that was Erik's mother nodded and followed.

"Stop thief! He's stealing a soul! Somebody stop him," the merchant shouted.

Erik spun toward the clerk. His arm tensed and he fired a plasma blast toward him. The burning ball of energy roared through several shelves, sending wood, metal and glass in all directions, causing fabric awnings to burn angrily. The heat from Erik's radiant energy drove the angered merchant back, forcing him to flee into the remains of his shop.

The ground shook and the buildings vibrated. Wares fell off shelves and the tremors increased. The hybrid's danger sense shrieked out a warning and he turned, shielding his friend with his body. A beam of energy three feet in diameter slammed into him, enveloping him in a painful emerald plasma. The force knocked him to the ground, pushing his powerful body into the dirt. The hybrid flexed and pushed against the powerful force beam. Inch by inch the silver warrior was able to stand upright and continue to shield his friend. The weapon had no effect on the wispy pink shade.

The beam ceased and the ground continued to shake. Erik recognized the pattern of footfalls.

"Look!" Martin pointed terrified. "My God, they're gargantuan."

The hybrid turned. Three towering creatures, each one easily sixty feet or more in height, the faces featureless save for a gigantic green eye that moved back and forth, approached. Two of the green eyes focused on them again and fired simultaneously. The hybrid spun and covered Martin again. The beams were many times more powerful and Erik's mind shrieked in agony as burning green energy threatened to dissolve even his powerful Esper-armored flesh.

Son, leave me here. Save yourself. Maybe if you leave me, they won't attack anymore.

Erik's flesh was smoking. The silver armor was charred and burnt on his back and shoulder. He spun around, facing the approaching titans. The Sentient Staff growled with rage and anger as its master hissed angrily. The hybrid glanced over at his mother. *No! I won't let you be taken again.*

Blue radiance danced up and down the staff as a powerful charge built up in the weapon. Erik's body continued to glow and burn aqua blue as more and more bioelectric energy was harnessed and gathered. The warrior pointed his staff toward the approaching titans and unleashed a searing beam of destructive power. The surrounding air superheated and thunder cracked as the beam struck the first titan. The burning blue lance slammed into the lead sentinel, burning a large hole in the creature. The massive eye winked twice then went dark. The titan fell over crushing three stores under its bulk.

He fired again. Another searing lance of radiant blue slammed into a translucent barrier shielding the second giant. The beam pieced the barrier but was diminished. The giant stumbled as the weakened beam tore into its flesh but it didn't fall. Erik paused, flexing massive Esper muscle, gathering more energy from the surrounding environment and from within his own reserves. The sky rumbled as he launched another searing blast of power. The thunderclap shattered the few remaining windows. The burning energy lance pierced the giant's shielding and vaporized the sentinel. The third creature advanced, heedless of its allies' deaths.

Behind the sixty foot monster something moved. A flash of red lighting lit up the skies. Erik looked over at his mother, then at Martin,

Run, now! Take cover!

Staff! Shield!!

Erik held his shield and braced his powerful legs. A five-foot thick beam of angry red energy slammed into the makeshift silver barrier engulfing his entire body. The force of the beam buckled his powerful legs but he kept his shield raised, deflecting a portion of the beam away from his body. The overwhelming power of the blood-red energy forced him back inch by inch. His mind reeled in agony as the demonic power tore into his armored flesh. The beam halted and Erik stood upright. The staff moaned, its metallic shell smoking and charred. Erik's silver body was also blackened and burnt. The buildings surrounding him had been vaporized, the entire area reduced to a black carbonized landscape.

"YOU HAVE VIOLATED THE LAWS OF THE SOUL MARKET. YOU MUST BE DESTROYED!" The voice echoed throughout entire area. The creature behind the sentinel moved forward, towering over the sixty foot sentry. The being was easily one hundred feet tall, its flesh a rutted brown and red color. Angry arcs of red energy surrounded the creature as dark winged gargoyles circled its massive head. Five slanted eyes adorned its wedge-shaped head and one massive unicorn horn sat on the top of the creature's massive skull. The sky over the creature seemed to swirl like an airborne tornado. The ground shook as both beings advanced. The hybrid stepped away from Martin and his mother, praying that the creatures would follow him. A whole section of the Soul Market was a smoking ruin. The creatures' weapons had done more damage than his freeing his mother from her prison. The behemoths carelessly crushed buildings and shops as they made their slow yet steady approach. The shockwave from freeing his mother had broken some glass and overturned several tables and collapsed a few walls, but the guardian's weapons decimated anything in their path.

The silver warrior's body was enveloped in an aura of blue. The staff moaned an eerie harmonic as it fed hungrily on the power. Carbonized flesh healed and scorched metal was reformed. Erik raised his arm and gestured toward the sky, harnessing the ambient energy that flowed free throughout the sub dimension. The two beings continued to advance, ruby and emerald eyes glowing. He deactivated his shield and the staff flowed into his forearm, taking the shape of a heavy bracelet.

The silver warrior shouted, ANA KOLAR!!!! At his command, the alien reddish purple sky unleashed a continuous searing lance of energy. The stream of power impacted his outstretched hand, bathing his whole body in the glowing purple radiance. The warrior harnessed the power and redirected the force through his other hand and pointed, open palm, toward the approaching behemoths. The purple energy combined with his own aqua bioelectric force and a beam generated by the sentient staff's myriad power. The triple lances of energy braided together and sped toward the lumbering giants. The sound created by the superheated air was deafening. The braided beams of energy slammed into the emerald giant, penetrating it's shielding, burning a hole clear through its body. The searing energy impacted the titanic red creature, sizzling and charring its rutted hide. The beam washed over the creature's chest and throat, then worked up to its sensitive blood-red eyeballs exploding three of them, vaporizing the ruby organs on contact and incinerating several bat-winged flying creatures. The creature shrieked in agony and raised its hands, swatting at the painful lances of energy.

The hybrid didn't waver. He kept pushing more and more power at the massive entity. The braided lance dropped lower, impacting the creature's neck, boring a hole clean through. Glowing ichor sprayed from severed arteries, flowing down the massive creature like a raging waterfall. The beam moved slightly left, vaporizing the rest of the neck tissue, severing the massive head. The severed head dropped and rolled several feet before the horn impaled itself into the ground. Blood and ichor erupted like a geyser from the headless torso. The great body teetered back and forth, stumbling forward, a titanic marching corpse. The headless entity took one last step, then fell like a massive oak cut by a chainsaw. The headless body flattened another section of the marketplace. The concussion from its impact shook the very ground like an earthquake. The dust and debris from the ruined buildings settled into a wide concentric debris field.

The silver warrior dropped to one knee, pausing to survey the destruction. The soul market was decimated. In the distance dozens of ships were airborne and launching. Several craft disappeared, jumping through multicolored portals escaping the destruction. Erik looked over to where Martin and his mother were hidden. *Martin, are you both okay?*

Martin walked out from behind a massive boulder, followed by the wispy pink apparition that was his mother. She floated toward him, her hand gently caressing his silver face. "My baby boy, what happened to you?"

Erik changed, becoming human. He reached over to hug her, his hands passing through her ghostly form. "It's a long story, but now we have to leave before they can conjure up more creepies." He pointed. "The portal is this way."

"Erik," Martin whispered, blushing slightly. "Do you want my jacket to tie around your waist?"

Erik suddenly realized he was naked. "Oh shit! Staff, body covering, please."

The sentient staff flowed around his torso and limbs. The weapon's color changed to a dark coal black with a silver stripe. Erik was covered in a form-fitting body suit with skin tight shoes. He looked over at Martin and smiled. "Thanks, Counselor. Now let's get moving."

Martin shook his head. "Metal underwear. Just when I thought I've seen everything."

They walked in silence. The sound of distant alarms and voices carried. Erik looked back and scanned the red horizon for any signs of trouble. In the distance, he saw something, something big—even bigger than the reddish demon. The being towered over the alien spaceport control center, the tallest structure in the soul market. Erik estimated the being was easily over a two hundred and fifty yards tall and still growing, as if it arose from the very ground. Its roar reverberated throughout miles of open space.

"Oh boy, we've got more company coming. They called in their 'Godzilla.'" Erik waved his hand over the space in front of him. "Thank God we've reached the portal."

The ground began to shake worse than before. They heard screams of panic. Erik made a gesture and the portal flowed open. They passed through, leaving behind whatever terror had been conjured to attack them next.

Erik stepped into the corn field and knew they were back.

Martin and his mother were already through. The feeling of disorientation passed quickly. The old farmer turned to regard them. The look on his face was one of pure rage. His face split, and spiny barbs protruded from his face and limbs. "You stole a soul! You must die!"

Erik prepared for an attack. The sound of a gunshot rang out and the demon's skull split. It fell to the ground, writhing in agony as purple fire consumed it. Erik looked over at his friend. "I'd like some of those bullets."

Denton shook his head. "Sorry, this is my last clip."

Erik turned to his mother, tears flowing. "You're free, mom. I don't know how to help you now, but I have some new allies that can."

The pink specter became corporeal. Erik slowly reached forward and touched his mother's cheek. He burst into tears. "Mom!" he embraced her as he cried. "Oh God, Mom, you're alive!"

"No son, I've just been given a moment to say goodbye. Look at me, Erik." She held his tear-stained face in her hands. "Your father and I loved you and still love you, always. I am so proud of you, my son. You've become such a fine young man. You saved me. I don't know how you found me, but I'll tell your father you saved me. Take care of yourself, and live a full happy life." Mother and son embraced one last time as, bit by bit, Andrea Knight dissipated and made her final journey home. Erik fell to his knees weeping, heartbroken, as he endured the loss of his mother.

Chapter 8: Power Play

Mendon MA. Uber Café & Music House

Erik absently stirred his iced coffee and picked at his turkey rollup. Martin sipped his tea and was staring at the musician performing on the corner stage. The three-hour ride back from Connecticut had been in absolute silence. They spoke briefly at an outlet store when the embattled detective purchased some clothing. Martin reached out to Vatican City informing them that they had driven Molec back to Earth. The counselor avoided going into more detail regarding their terrifying escapades, but judging from the frosty tone, he'd assumed they already knew of the calamity. Both men were lost inside themselves, processing the mind numbing events of the day. Erik would occasionally let a sob escape as his eyes stayed locked on the road.

"Hi. Is everything okay? You haven't touched your food? You both look like you've seen a ghost or something." The young girl smiled.

Martin looked up, doing his best to be pleasant. "My dear, you don't know the half of it. But seeing someone as pretty and pleasant as you certainly takes the edge off an incredibly bad day."

The girl blushed perfectly and smiled. "Do you need anything else? How about a song? Jimmy can play and sing just about anything."

Denton smiled. "A song would be perfect. Surprise us with something upbeat and light, please."

Erik took a sip of his coffee and finally spoke. "Counselor, I thought I'd seen everything, but today … today just dwarfs it all. I met my mother, Martin. Her soul was abducted and held in a glass globe for sale to some soul-sucking wretch to feed upon like a leech." Erik took another sip of his coffee. "How do you process that?" A tear rolled down his cheek. "I saw an

Esper … an honest to god Esper being sold into slavery and I couldn't save her. What if she died during that onslaught? Now I'll never know. I can never go back there again—if there's even a market to go back to after what those creatures did."

"Son, I don't know. I can't imagine what you're feeling right now, but let me say this. You had an opportunity nobody else in the world will ever have. You got to say goodbye to your mother after you believed the opportunity was long gone. You saved her. She's in a better place because of you and your actions. That's something no one can take away from you. Not too many people get to say a final goodbye at all." Denton paused, "And we both got something else positive from this nightmare."

Erik tilted his head. "Enlighten me."

The old man sniffed and a tear leaked from his eye soon followed by another. "Comfort. We know our loved ones are there waiting for us. William, my wife Edna, your parents…" he wiped away a tear. "They're all waiting for us."

Erik nodded. "Yeah, that's true." He tensed, and his hand formed a fist. "Martin, I just don't understand something. When I broke that orb, I knocked over some shelves, overturned some chairs and caused a few canopy fires and fractured a few walls."

Denton's lips turned up in a sardonic grin. "Yeah, not to mention several windows."

Erik leaned forward and tapped the table. "Okay, so we caused a bit of wreckage, but look what their guards did. My God, they leveled miles of stores and carts. I mean those things vaporized buildings and God only knows how many beings just to get us." Erik sighed. "That final sentinel. Cripes! It was a monster! The caretakers of the marketplace did all that to keep us from taking a single soul? That's a hell of a high price to pay. I don't understand the cost benefit of having that kind of security."

Denton rubbed his chin. "I don't know, Erik, I honestly don't understand that kind of threat response. Would you call the police if you were being robbed, knowing they'd burn down your house in the process of capturing the thief?"

Erik shook his head. "No. I think Molec's disastrous arrival had already pissed off some powerful entities. Freeing my mom was the straw that broke the camel's back though." Erik took a deep sip of his iced coffee, relishing the sensation as the cool beverage slid down his throat. "We pissed off that first purple guy that tried to steal your soul. We had a firefight and freed the Space Mariner stranding an alien crew for who knows how long, and I freed my mother. I guess we were like the annoying mosquito that keeps buzzing around your ear finally forcing a swat." Erik's eyes squinted and he frowned. "A hell of a big swat. How many other flies, gnats, and bugs got squashed in that smackdown? That's a hefty price for justice."

"There are different sets of rules and we have no idea what they are," Denton took a small bite of his sandwich. "All I know is I don't ever want to go back there again."

Erik grinned. "Yeah, I'm with you. I think maybe Congressman Anderson was right. We really don't know what we're up against, what kind of power they can bring to bear." Erik flexed his arm. The burn scars were still visible but had faded considerably. "I was hurt, Martin. Even in my warrior form, I was hurt. With all this Esper power, I still felt the pain." The detective grimaced. "Those beams were devastating." Erik leaned back. "I don't think I could have taken much more of a pummeling. I unleashed more focused energy on that reddish creature than I even unloaded on the Observer battle drones several years back. That thing took those blasts full on and kept coming forward despite the beating it took. I couldn't get a sense of intellect, just a desire to mindlessly kill..." Erik took another sip of his coffee. "Not just us, but everything that got in its way. That thing was just a mindless killing drone. Why would the keepers, whether it be Molec, Lucifer, or whatever force runs this place, trash all of it?" The detective looked up. "Or did we cause it by our actions." Erik considered that. "Correction, my actions. You were just a bystander."

Denton shook his head. "We're in this together. I snuffed out the gate guard, so my hands aren't lily white. We're in the middle of a brewing war, Erik. Molec can't keep a grip on his prize for much longer if we're to believe our large whale friend and that both scares and concerns me."

Erik nodded. "Yeah, the classic next step for somebody pushed too far is..." He let his words hang unfinished.

"The last act of desperation that usually unleashes chaos," Martin took another sip of his tea. "For all parties involved— and I'm not fond of mutually assured destruction. I'm trying not to imagine a similar cast of horrors unleashed on our world that was let loose at the soul market."

Erik took a large bite of his rollup, studying the people laughing, enjoying their food and the music. "I envy them, Martin. I envy their ignorance. I'd rather be blissfully numb to all this drama. I just want to hug my boy, and hold my wife in my arms for a while and live a quiet, boring life." He leaned back sighing heavily. "The vastness of all of this blows my mind. I feel insignificant, irrelevant even, knowing all of this. Maybe it's all just a game played by higher beings and we are pieces to be moved about for someone else's amusement. Maybe our world is just a microcosm of the larger struggle happening the universe." Erik shrugged. "That's how it appears to me."

"Oh Lord thy sea is so vast and my vessel so small," Martin whispered.

Erik tilted his head. "The Breton Fisherman's prayer. It seems appropriate."

Martin frowned. "What did you make of the merchant's last warning, regarding the theft of your mother's soul, saying Lucifer would never let that stand? I don't much welcome the king of the underworld putting a mark out on me."

Erik lifted his eyebrows. "I think our pitchfork carrying, pointy tailed opponent has bigger fish to fry than an old man avenging his son's murder or even a half-alien agent running amok. I admit we've tipped over some apple carts and maybe kicked him in the balls a bit, but we're small potatoes compared to Molec. Lucifer wants the archdemon's head on his trophy case. I don't blame him. I want to get my hands on him too for the soul bounty on my son. But I get the feeling we're just small players on one world in a game occurring across an entire universe with millions of galaxies and billions of planets. All controlled by these Ethereals." Erik took another sip of his coffee. "Does that make you feel any better?"

"Not really. Just more insignificant in the cosmos."

"My point, exactly." Erik nodded with a smirk. The detective seemed to loosen a bit.

"So what's our next move?"

Erik leaned back in his chair. "We go back to the last place we encountered Molec. I want to do a full search of that building. Our creepy friend has been hiding right under my nose for a while and he left in a hurry. There has to be some clues where he'd be. We didn't do a thorough search while our heavenly allies were here. I want to do one tomorrow." Erik pulled out his cell phone. "I need to check in with Shanda and see how things are going with her and EJ, then I'm going to sit here for an hour or so and soak up these positive vibes. After that, I suggest we crash at my place and search that mill from top to bottom first thing in the morning."

Denton nodded as he gestured toward a curvy waitress. "Can I get another tea and some more coffee for my friend here?"

* * *

Molec's Stronghold

"Three emerald sentinels were destroyed, one completely vaporized, the other two have gaping holes through their corpses. Kannaro the giant had his head severed by some beam of incredible power." The voice on the monitor paused. "And the hybrid freed the Space Mariner. The Kenecian crew has to wait ten years for another craft to pick them up from their galaxy. All the cargo and souls inside the mariner's body are a complete loss. The Kenecians hold you responsible Lord Molec and they are demanding compensation. They claim had you not forced the crew to attack the hybrid, they would still have their ship and cargo."

"Damn him. How did he know I'd be there? The forces of Light are using him like a blunt instrument. They cannot go to the marketplace so they send their alien half-breed puppet after me."

"The amount of damage caused when the sentinels fell was substantial. Hundreds of human souls were freed when their containment vessels shattered. Merchants and customers alike were crushed, trapped inside their ruined stores. Our sources say Lucifer is most put out with both you and this Erik Knight being."

Molec leaned back in his chair, stretching his arms, shaking his massive horned head. "I was told he found his mother's soul and managed to free her."

"Yes. That was the lynch pin that set forth the sentinel forces. Many things are tolerated in the Soul Market but theft of any kind unleashes the sentinels and they live only to destroy. Out of fear, no one steals from another knowing the price for such an act is the ruin of all. Erik Knight wasn't aware of that and many merchants paid the price for his ignorance. Now four of the most powerful sentinel guards in the galaxy are terminated and the market will be sealed until all can be restored. This hybrid warrior is fast becoming a nuisance we can no longer afford. If the forces of light discover the Soul Market had been abducting and selling Heaven-bound human souls, they would wage such a fit no place in the galaxy, let alone the known worlds, would be safe. We fear that Erik Knight will inform his allies. If his mother's soul passed through to the next realm, all will be revealed."

Molec frowned. "That's Lucifer's problem, not mine. If Heaven decides to snuff him out, I certainly won't weep over the loss. My problem is the damned hybrid. I can't keep looking over my shoulder having the Esper half breed pop up. He's proving to be more of an inconvenience than I anticipated."

The being on the screen snickered. "What did you expect? You put a soul bounty on his child, sent a demon to rape and slaughter his bride and kill the child. You act stunned when he hunts you without mercy? The hybrid is tenacious, and now his family is out of our reach. Lucifer, for all his prattle, is lazy and content—a fat poodle happy to lay in the sun while others do his bidding. Erik Knight is a wolf—hungry, lean and quick to anger. This wolf has sharp fangs as you've seen, and that wolf is looking to sink those teeth into your backside."

"Don't mock me! I'm in no mood! Knight just needs to have his attention diverted."

"My apologies, Lord Molec, Washington shares your concern about the hybrid, but his family hides under the umbrella of the Vatican. Powerful forces of Light protect his other offspring and those dear to him. We cannot get to his family and thus, he is free to hunt you and us at will."

Molec laughed and flames shot from his nostrils. "I've got it. We can't get into the Vatican, true. But we can make it so that no one else can either. We can prevent people from going in or out by blockading the holy city with our forces. We could erect a demonic barrier around the city and starve the humans out. The soft, pampered priests would beg for a compromise and gladly turn over the child to free themselves." Molec grinned. "We could sack all of Rome and force Knight and the armies of Light and Dark to engage in a war of mutual extinction. All we need is a catalyst and the forces to make it happen."

"Lord Molec, we don't have the demonpower to sustain a blockade of such magnitude. The forces of Light will overrun us for attempting to sack a sacred shrine of God."

Molec steepled his massive onyx fingers. "No but Lucifer does. Perhaps I can reach an arrangement with my nemesis, by offering him Rome as a prize."

The face on the large display frowned. "Lord Molec, Lucifer has sworn oaths to kill you on sight. I implore you not to reveal yourself to him. All we have worked for will be lost."

Molec nodded his massive head. "Wise council. It was merely a muse, I will not tarnish my victory by aligning with him. Perhaps there is another way. Bartholomew is his puppet. Erik Knight throttled him awhile back. Perhaps I can use his pride and vanity for my purposes. He has significant resources at his disposal. I believe we can cut a deal that will benefit both of us. The demon's ego is vast and an opportunity to crush Knight may be enough to garner his support and his forces."

"Bartholomew will not be easily swayed. He has served Lucifer for eons. How do you know he will not simply report your contact to his master and set you up for a fall?"

The archdemon frowned. "Bartholomew serves out of fear, not loyalty. He is a mercenary at best and an opportunist. I will, as the human movie exclaimed, make him an offer he can't refuse." Molec turned directly toward the large screen. "We'll raise havoc on Vatican City and Knight will come running to save his family. Lucifer will take note and move in as will the forces of Light. The final battle will play out and both sides will fight a war of mutual extinction. And when Rome lies in ruin, forces on both sides battle worn and depleted, I will intervene and crush Erik Knight with my bare hands and take this world as my own. Then I'll ransom it back to God for a high price. I will be the lord of the underworld and I will control the forces of darkness. I will fight the eternal war as a new General and begin taking worlds one by one and establishing my rule over Light." Molec slammed his fist on the nearby table smashing it to kindling. "Find Bartholomew and arrange a meeting. Make sure there are at least six bottles of Armand De Brignac champagne and plenty of caviar on hand. The demon is fond of those human luxuries. Perhaps he'll be more amenable to a joint venture after he's plied with enough alcohol."

* * *

Vatican City

Shanda sat on the wooden bench watching EJ play with several young clerics. The courtyard was alive with the sound of innocent laughter as the boy chased a large red ball, throwing it back to his much older companions.

"The child is full of joy, a blessing of God to be sure."

Shanda jumped slightly,

"I apologize. I didn't mean to give you a fright." An elder nun handed her a steaming mug. "Fresh ground French roast coffee with heavy cream and a touch of vanilla and cinnamon. One of my few guilty pleasures and vices."

Shanda took a sip, her brow rose. "Oh my! This is amazing!"

"You look like you have the weight of the world upon you, child. Sometimes it helps to vent and let it out. I have been told that listening is what I do best."

Shanda blushed. "Thanks." She looked back over at her son. "'I'm wondering if he really knows what's going on, what his destiny is, and the level of danger he's in. With all this divine attention and circumstance, will he still need his mother?"

The old woman laughed and gently embraced her. "A boy always will need his mother. Jesus needed Mary throughout his life and EJ will need you."

Shanda sipped her coffee. "It didn't end well for Jesus. He was nailed to cross and betrayed by those he trusted most."

The nun gave a wistful sigh as she sat back, keeping her arm around Shanda's shoulder. "But Child, that was not the end. He rose again, conquered death, and is now eternal. The Son of God gave his life so we could all be eternal. I don't think God is expecting that from EJ."

Shanda's voice broke. "Then what? What does HE want from my baby boy? Why would he do this to my family?"

The nun gently tightened her grip on her shoulder. "Because He knows you're a lioness and your husband a warrior. God trusted you with a great gift above all others. Listen to your heart Shanda and you won't go wrong. Your son is a very lucky boy and we are blessed to have you here among us."

Shanda smiled. "Thank you. I feel safe here. I'm glad we decided to come." Shanda frowned, looked over at her host. "I spoke to Erik a few hours ago. He was less than forthcoming about the progress he was making. I know something's wrong. Something's upset him. I can feel it through our link. I don't like secrets. Sometimes my dear husband decides it's better to keep me in the dark for my own safety." Shanda looked at the nun. "Do you know what's going on? I suspect you're connected with most things that happen inside these walls. I gather that's why they have you here babysitting me."

The nun blushed. "You are intuitive. I'm here to see to your comfort, yes. But you don't need a babysitter." The old woman wrinkled her nose. "I overheard some of the talk after Mr. Denton checked in. There was an incident in a place called the Soul Market." She took a deep breath. "Your husband engaged several forces there. He eradicated beings of immense power and upset the keepers of that realm as well as the Prince of Darkness. We have learned from your husband and Mr. Denton that innocent human souls bound for Eternity were intercepted and abducted. These souls were trapped and sold for profit to aliens and demons alike. This is a strict violation of the Rules and the forces of Light are enraged. The Soul Market will be invaded and the human souls released."

Shanda nodded. "Well, that's a good thing. Why would Erik be upset?"

The nun took a deep breath. "These actions escalate an already tense situation. Lucifer is enraged at the damage caused to his market. We are enraged at the abductions of innocent souls harvested for sustenance. Each side claims violations of the Rules laid out in the beginning. Both grievances have merit and are enough to escalate into an Ethereal War. Tensions are high enough without this new discovery to add fuel to an already raging inferno. It would have been better served if your husband had not interfered, but as it stands, that was beyond anyone's control. His reason for action was pure and even the Father understood."

"My God. Pardon the expression. What happened?"

The old woman leaned forward. "I must swear you to secrecy. You must say nothing if I tell you. Do you promise? I only say this because he will need your comfort."

Shanda nodded. "I promise. Whatever you say goes no further."

"Your husband stumbled upon his mother's soul trapped by a merchant. He freed her soul and in doing so unleashed the wrath of the security sentinels. He destroyed four sentinels and freed his mother's soul. His heart relives old wounds and now he grieves for that which he lost so long ago."

Shanda fought back her own tears. "Oh my God! Poor Erik. This is just beyond crazy! Why didn't he tell me?"

The nun smiled. "My child, he is a man. He grieves, childlike, for his mother. He does not want to appear weak in your eyes. You look to him for strength and he strives to be that pillar for you at this time."

Shanda wept. "I don't want him to have to carry that burden alone. He knows he can lean on me too. How can anyone carry that kind of pain?"

"When this is passed—and I believe God will prevail—you can give him comfort. Until then, this is our secret."

Shanda took a deep breath, composed herself, and nodded. "Agreed."

A loud burst of laughter broke the somber mood.

"EJ looks quite content and there are four guards keeping watch." The nun pointed to the nearby Vatican Police. "Why don't you and I take a quick stroll? There's a bakery by the chapel that makes muffins that are sinfully delicious. I know Brother Brian always has something delectable at this time of day."

Shanda nodded. "That sounds heavenly." She blushed as they both laughed.

* * *

The abandoned mill. Hopedale MA

"The Hopedale PD was pretty miffed we raided this place without checking in," Martin mumbled as he rifled through a file cabinet.

"They should be used to the brush off by now. I can picture me going to the chief. Uhm, yes, a demon is living in an abandoned mill in the middle of your town. I'm going to summon a few angels and we're gonna raid the joint... Want in?"

Denton burst out laughing and Erik joined in. It was the first time in days either man cracked a smile. Erik walked down the carpeted foyer still amazed at the elegant carpentry hidden inside the run down structure. "I'm gonna go through this desk. It seems abnormally large as does the chair. Just how big is this thing anyway?"

"Molec is a category 5 demon, onyx armored shell with overlapping scale plates. The demon breathes a fire capable of igniting wood, paper, or any other flammable substance on contact. The archdemon is said to be between seven and a half to nine feet tall with two eighteen-inch ram-like horns on its head." Denton never looked up from the file he was reading.

Erik's brow raised. "Well, someone's read up on their demonology."

"Know thy enemy," Martin recited, digging through the file cabinet. The old man held up a ledger. "Demons keep records. Go figure." The old man leafed through the pages while Erik examined the large safe carefully.

"They also appear to like currency. There's easily ten grand in large bills here." The detective partially closed the heavy safe door. "Not to mention diamonds and some gold jewelry. I didn't realize these beings placed value on material things. Perhaps they're not as far above us as we're supposed to believe."

Denton frowned. "Let's check the other rooms."

Erik and Martin entered a nearby chamber. The room had several empty glass globes identical to the one that imprisoned his mother. Martin picked up one of the objects and studied it. He looked over at all the other empty ones. "Dear Lord in Heaven. Did each one of these contain a human soul?"

Erik's jaw clenched. "Yes. They did. Look at that symbol stamped into the golden plate holding the filament. It's the same as the globe that held my mother." Erik picked up two more empty vessels. "They all have the same mark and come from the same merchant. We inadvertently stumbled into Molec's supplier. I suspect these were all human souls that fed his nosferatu forces."

Martin studied the purple goo that filled a shallow pool. "I'm guessing this is some sort of resting pool or bed."

"Possibly. Let's keep moving, Counselor. This room is disturbing my calm."

Martin nodded. "Truly."

They moved through five other chambers, each one furnished to the needs of a particular strain of demon. The two men made their way back to Molec's large office, Erik examined the safe again. The residual energy was fading and there was nothing more to be learned. Another Starlight Bistro business card sat on Molec's desk.

"Molec seems to like chess."

Erik turned. Martin studied an intricate chess board with large mahogany and ivory pieces. Erik again marveled at the human qualities these creatures possessed. "All the black pawns are on the white king. I don't think our friend understands the game too well."

"I wonder if our ethereal friend was able to get any intel from the creature we found here?"

Erik shrugged his shoulders. "I hope so. We're not getting any leads here. We may have to head back to DC and snoop some more. I don't know how we'll be able to get back into the Starlight though. We were made the instant we went inside. After the Soul Market incident I can't imagine our presence will be tolerated there." Erik frowned. "I don't get it, this place was a psychic hurricane less than forty-eight hours ago and now there's barely a trace of anything here. It's almost as if the place was wiped clean of residual energies." Erik pointed toward the safe. "But why leave behind the cash and jewelry? If someone came in here to wipe the place, why leave valuables still in the safe?"

"Not all dark forces value human commodity, hybrid."

Martin jumped a foot and Erik turned toward the voice he recognized. The blond warrior stood, as if he'd been there all along.

"You're like a genie," the elder man grumbled. "We mention you and poof! There you are." Denton picked up an ivory chess piece, studied it for a moment, then tossed it back on the large playing surface.

Erik nodded toward the being. "I take it you have news."

The being nodded. "And none of it good. The demon we captured knew very little of Molec's plan. Despite our robust interrogation, we could only glean that Molec had fled to the Soul Market with the intent to acquire another containment vessel. We also learned that human souls were illegally harvested and trafficked across the galaxy."

Martin cleared his throat uncomfortably and rolled his eyes. The ethereal frowned.

"Yes human, we are aware of the discovery you made and are taking action. Raphael is leading his forces into the market now to shut it down and confiscate the remaining souls trapped in that realm."

"I don't understand, just confiscate and not free?"

"Not all the captured souls and the ones freed during your ruckus are human. Some are quite alien and quite evil. We will examine each soul and determine which are worthy of Light and which," the angel sighed, "are not so worthy. Souls of savage alien beings, trapped entities and poltergeists from across the universe were caged in that tiny realm. Fortunately the majority of the souls freed during the battle with the security demons were benign. Raphael will recover and capture the less desirable and imprison them anew." The being gave him a hard look. "Had you freed all the souls as your heart desired, you would have unleashed a calamity upon the universe. Some of the captured souls would have been able to escape the realm aboard ships and wreak untold havoc on several populated worlds." The angel's tone dropped to a gentle whisper. "You did a noble thing freeing your mother. I cannot fault your reasoning or your actions, but I implore you to tread carefully going forward. You do not fully comprehend the dangers and the ramifications of your actions. It is imperative that you tread lightly."

"I am sorry, Michael." Erik waited to see if he guessed right. The ethereal being's eyes widened.

"You know my earthly name?"

Erik nodded. "I've suspected. You resemble the pictures in the Vatican chapels and in many of the churches I went to as a child. I wasn't completely sure until you mentioned Raphael. You're one of the three archangels, the third trinity of ethereal power. The Father, the Son, and the Holy Spirit, then Jesus, Mary and Joseph, then you, Gabriel and Raphael. Three threes according to the Scroll of Parinthia."

Michael tilted his head. "That scroll is secret. How is it that you know of the writings of Parinthia?"

Erik shrugged. "I didn't but Jakor did. It was his Esper knowledge I tapped for that tidbit."

Michael approached, his face set in stone. "Jakor! You house the memory and knowledge of the Esper warrior, Jakor?" For the first time the ethereal seemed excited.

Erik nodded. "I also bear his weapon, though now it's bonded to me."

"May I please see it?"

Erik held out his hand and the weapon materialized.

"It is! I felt it earlier but wasn't sure. It is Jakor's Sentient Staff. You carry his genetics." Michael reached out and touched Erik's temple, probing his mind. Erik didn't resist and allowed Jakor's essence to come to the surface.

It was an odd sensation having the archangel engage the genetically added Esper intellect while he was just a sidelined observer. The angel broke contact and took a step back, appraising him anew. "That was odd, I don't want to do that again." Erik rubbed his temple.

"You are truly an Esper Warrior. I had thought you were just altered but you truly have his genetics and his persona locked inside your subconscious. The essence is Jakor."

Erik nodded. "I gather you know him."

Michael looked nostalgic. "We fought side by side on the

Esper home world thousands of years ago." The archangel frowned. "Too many were lost when the world expired." The divine being sighed. "Another casualty of our conflict."

"There's an Esper trapped in the Soul Market. Maybe you could have your forces track her down and free her. It looks like she was sold into slavery."

Michael raised an eyebrow. "I will inform Raphael. But right now our focus must return to the problems we are facing here, in this realm."

"Agreed." Denton nodded as he studied some papers on the desk. "This whole place was cleaned. I can't find a print or anything else that would be of use."

Erik turned toward Michael. "What about Lucifer? He must have eyes all over the place. Can't his people get a lead on Molec? This archdemon is a huge threat to him and his control over..." Erik frowned. "Whatever evil empire he controls."

The archangel managed a smile. "Lucifer is most vexed right now. You are high on his hate list and he still has desires upon your child. He had hoped to keep his little black market operation a secret. Our forced alliance has been strained. I don't think my renegade brother will offer us anything in the way of assistance with Molec. In fact, I fear we have only driven the wedge further toward war. Lucifer is not one to forget those who cross him."

Erik winced uncomfortably. As Michael said, his actions did have consequences. The detective flexed his forearm. Agitated ions of bioenergy surged and burned around his powerful flesh. "Neither do I."

Michael studied Erik's glowing arm. "You are powerful, hybrid; strong beyond any mortal being He has created. But you are mortal and not invincible. Lucifer is not without power. You have already earned his wrath. I implore you not to cause him more angst or he will lash out blindly at you and those around you he can reach."

Denton looked over, his face pale. "Yes, hybrid, please don't piss off Satan any further. I always seem to be in the line of fire when you aggravate someone." The old man imitated Michael's voice and manner perfectly.

The angel glanced over raising an eyebrow. "Humor.

Another human concept I do not understand." He looked back over at Erik. "I fear Molec has gone into hiding again, and we will have to wait until the Holy Relic makes its presence known. There is no more trail to follow."

Martin shook his head. "Molec is here, on Earth. He has to be getting information regarding our activities from somewhere." He pointed toward the card in Erik's hand. "Everything points back to Washington DC and the Starlight Bistro. All the rats appear to live in DC and I'll wager my retirement pension Molec is somewhere in that vicinity. We just have to sniff him out. If he's arrived in the beltway, I promise you somebody there knows."

Erik nodded. "We can chase down property leases and look for recent activity in the DC warehouses." Erik gestured around him, "He has a penchant for hiding in abandoned areas and making himself a luxurious nest. We can have the firm's resources sniff around these areas. If there's been a lot of unusual activity in an area around DC, we can focus our search there."

"Anderson can be of service in the search. He is our eyes and ears." Michael looked over at the detective. "Look but please, for all our sakes, tread lightly and be cautious. We cannot have the kind of destruction wrought at the Soul Market unleashed upon this realm. That type of calamity would be devastating."

"Understood," said Erik. "Simply recon. If we find his lair I'll call out and we'll let your forces take point."

Michael nodded and simply vanished. There was no flash of light, no appearance of a portal. The powerful ethereal being simply winked out of reality.

"That irritates me to no end." Denton flopped heavily on a nearby crate, staring into the once-occupied empty space.

"What? The vanishing act?" Erik frowned. "Yeah it's a bit unnerving. I was just thinking back to some old scriptures. God is everywhere and sees everything. We're never really alone. I don't know if I find comfort in that or feel like my privacy is being violated."

Denton groaned. "Please, let's not debate theology. It gives me a headache. I don't want to have to picture a divinity watching over me the next time I use the bathroom."

Erik laughed. "You seem to be in a somber mood, Counselor. God knows, pardon the pun, we both have reason to be in less than happy spirits."

Denton shifted his weight on the wooden crate and it creaked. "This thing sounds like my back feels." The old man stared at the floor silent for several moments. He looked up. "Michael is right." Denton shuddered. "Cripes I've been talking with an angel. This has to be a dream."

Erik shook his head. "I know. Every once in a while the reality of this all creeps in and it threatens to eradicate my sanity."

"Look, Erik, we're dealing with forces we can't even begin to comprehend. The fact that the Prince of Darkness has you on his personal hit list doesn't scare you? I'm one step away from needing a change of underwear. A month ago I didn't buy any of this shit. Now, I'm talking with angels, shooting demons with divine bullets, pissing off the devil, and traveling to interdimensional soul markets." Martin's face was wrought with fear. "There's a price, my young friend, a price to pay for treading where mortals shouldn't. I fear the price will be something neither of us are willing to pay."

Erik walked over and placed a hand on Martin's shoulder. "We didn't ask for this dance, Counselor. We got dragged onto the floor. Look, you've more than avenged your son's death. Lazarus is dust and there are already powerful forces scouring the planet for Molec. His time is rapidly running out. No one would blame you if you sat out the rest of this. You've more than done your part."

Denton placed a weathered hand on Erik's. "I can't, not while that sweet little boy is in danger. You're my family. I won't turn my back on you, Shanda or EJ. I failed my son. I won't fail you."

Erik's eyes grew moist. "You're a part of our family, Martin, and I'm proud to have you as a friend." The detective's eyes turned solemn. "But you're right, for all of my bluster, we're over our heads in some pretty deep water."

Denton's face turned to stone. "Then we'd better swim a bit harder and keep watch for the sharks." The old man stood up. "Let's stop by your gym and see how the repairs are progressing, then we can catch a flight back to DC tomorrow. We can meet up with Representative Anderson and fill him in, unless our divine ally has already done so. Either way we need to get to DC."

Erik nodded, then turned to the safe and emptied the abandoned valuables into a nearby cloth sack.

Martin raised an eyebrow as Erik carried out the cash and valuables. "Stealing from Molec?"

Erik shrugged. "There's a local shelter and food pantry run by Sacred Heart Church right down the road. This can do a lot of good for a lot of needy people. I can't just let it sit there. The gold jewelry alone is worth at least another ten grand." Erik grinned. "I'm doing the Lord's work by helping the poor and needy. If it drains Molec's coffers a bit, all the better."

Denton laughed as they left.

Chapter 9: Blockade of Evil

Starlight Bistro. VIP Room

Molec finished his second glass of wine. Hard eyes stared at the ornamental clock decorating the far wall. Bartholomew was late. "The bastard isn't going to show." The archdemon's fingers tapped an angry beat on the large dining table. The wine rippled with the rhythmic vibrations.

A slender, buxom waitress escorted a tall, gaunt man wearing a long dark jacket. The garment whirled like a cape as he walked toward the table. The man's skin was almond colored and his hair an obnoxious carrot orange. Molec tilted his massive head as the man tossed his jacket over a nearby chair. The waitress left quickly. As soon as they were alone, the almond pigment vanished, revealing pale, milky white skin with black, pulsing veins. A river of black raced from the man's scalp, saturating the loud color with a dull, flat inky dark matching the pulsing veins easily seen beneath the being's pale flesh.

Molec reached into an ice-filled bucket, freeing a bottle of chilled champagne. He popped the cork and handed the bottle to his guest. "You're late."

"DC traffic is a bitch." He tilted the open bottle, nodding toward his host then drank deeply. Bartholomew drained half the bottle before sitting. The pale demon placed the bottle down, wiped his lips with his hand and reached toward the full basket of bread. "Okay Molec, this is your dime, but tell me why I shouldn't summon my boss to vaporize you right this instant? You upset the very cosmic balance when you stole that damned relic. Raphael, Michael, and Gabriel are scouring the planet. The forces of Light are preparing for war, and as much as my boss loves war and sees this planet as a potential prize, prophecy says this is one we are destined to lose." The demon tore into a large hot roll savoring the delicacy. "Not to mention your theft led to that accursed Esper half breed sticking his nose into our affairs." The demon dipped part of his roll in a bowl if warm, spiced oil. "Thanks to Erik Knight, the Soul Market has been gutted and Raphael has reclaimed several hundred souls destined for trade." He leaned forward. "Lucifer lost a great deal of capital thanks to Erik Knight and he blames you for forcing the hybrid into an offensive mode." The demon popped the rest of the roll into his mouth then smiled revealing jagged, uneven teeth. "And your accursed soul bounty has demonic hoards scouring the Earth looking for a way to kill Heaven's child. The Creator will never let that happen."

Molec nodded. "Are you done repeating the obvious?"

Bartholomew took another deep drink. "Yes, but I'm still waiting for a reason."

"I want to rule not just Hell, but other worlds existing throughout the Multiverse. Lucifer has no grand design. He accepts his punishment and grows lazy, content to merely steal souls and simply be a thorn in the side of divinity. I want to rule Hell and extend its influence through several worlds in this universe and others. The rules do allow it, but Lucifer seems unwilling to push forth and conquer. He has won nothing since the Beginning. The forces of Light are lazy and naïve. We can conquer worlds and build an empire."

Bartholomew drained his bottle and devoured another roll as he considered Molec's words. "What do you need and more importantly what do I get for this yet to be named assistance?"

Molec smiled, sliding another bottle of champagne toward Bartholomew. "Knight's child is protected inside Vatican City. I can't get to him there due to the abundance of Light's forces. I still have some human forces inside. Most are locked up but a few are still free to move about. We can create a diversion, draw away their forces and I can have my allies freed. They will hunt down and kill the child ending the possibility of Armageddon's Son ushering in the new age of man. We will have Earth as our first trophy and we can begin conquering new worlds. The forces of Light will be stunned and worlds will fall like dominos before us."

Bartholomew frowned. He ran a pale, bony hand through flaxen hair. "How do you propose we engage the forces of

Light? If we attack the Holy City, all hell will break loose, pardon the pun. You'll unleash all the Hosts of Heaven upon us."

"We don't have to ransack the city. We can block it off from the outside world. I have one of the last remaining mystical barricade stones. I'll have one of my agents detonate it outside Vatican City. The demonic energy will surround the city, choking it off from the outside world. We may not be able to enter but no one will be able to leave either. My human forces can hunt the child with impunity inside the city while the forces of Light are busy defending our incursion into Rome. If we attack quick enough, and with the element of surprise, Vatican City will be blockaded like a castle under siege and its defenders turned back. Once the hybrid child is killed, the Ruby Crucifix will be useless on this world."

Bartholomew nodded, flexing bone white fingers. "The energy from the stone will repulse angelic forces and I can marshal up enough demons to patrol the outskirts of the city." He looked over at Molec. "We'll be making our presence blatantly known to the humans, in direct violation of the rules. God will not sit idly back while we make this attack."

"We won't be attacking, just isolating. Humans inside the city will be doing our work. They do it of their own free will. They have chosen. The rules will be followed. We will not kill the child. Humanity will … just as they killed Christ. They will kill the bearer of their own salvation yet again. Free will, Bartholomew—they will do it of their own free will. I admit we are adding fear and motivation but the actual knife that will slit the child's throat will be wielded by a human. God has allowed war, the starvation of millions and the genocide of millions more, all by the hands of humans with free will. This death will be one of the same, just a savage human killing another human. Some humans will die during the siege but the forces of Light will be powerless to do anything about it." Molec laughed. Fire spewed from his nostrils scorching the table and singing the expensive tablecloth.

Bartholomew nodded once. "I agree the plan has merit but you still haven't told me what I get from this arrangement."

"I'll give you free reign in Hell and I'll give you half the Earth and the entire next world I conquer. I'll give you power beyond your imagining." The archdemon leaned forward, his hand balled in a fist, fiery red eyes burning. "I will give you the broken husk of Erik Knight to do with as you please and his slut bride to rape and plunder for all eternity if you desire it. Knight will come running once the blockade is up in a desperate attempt to rescue his wife and child. Once there, I will confront him and break the Esper warrior's back and spirit. You can have his broken remains to do with as you please afterwards. I want the pleasure of bloodying my fists on his face for the problems he's caused me."

Bartholomew drained the second bottle of champagne as he considered the offer. "Very generous, Molec." He leaned forward extending a pale hand. "I accept."

Molec shook the arm of his new ally and laughed, fiery exhales threatening to burn the fabric table cloth and chairs as the archdemon bellowed in joy.

Bartholomew joined in, adding his evil hiss as he slapped his new employer on the back jovially. He held up the empty bottle. "To the death of Erik Knight and the conquest of this world!"

* * *

Dawkens' Gym. Milford, MA

Erik sipped from his Styrofoam coffee cup studying the refinished walls of his business. The construction crews worked at a feverish pitch throughout the mall adding plumbing improvements and higher quality glass to replace what had broken during his earlier battles.

"I went with a lighter color in here. The grey was too depressing." Alissa pointed toward the freshly painted back wall separating the dojo from the main gym facility. "I think it brightens up the place. The workers rewired the old outlets and threw in a new breaker box. We won't have to keep changing fuses every two or three weeks so the treadmills and ellipticals can run without constantly blowing a damn fuse."

Erik nodded. "The place looks amazing. It looks like the entire mall is getting a face lift. I imagine the shop owners aren't too upset about the upgrades."

Alissa laughed. "Nobody's complained, that's for sure. A couple of managers have come by snooping, asking me what kinds of connections you have to make all of this happen."

Erik shook his head. "Everybody's a busybody."

The young woman frowned. "And I think we've had some of your divine friends poking around. I catch the essence of that tall blond being that was here earlier but to a lesser degree. We're being watched, but at a distance. Every time I try and get a lock on the presence, it shifts and evades my senses. I don't mind admitting it's got me frazzled."

Erik turned. "Alissa, this has gotten way out of control. I've seen things and fought things I couldn't conceive of even in my worst nightmares. We're just a microcosm in a massive struggle that transcends our planet, our solar system, and even our damn galaxy. These beings don't just traverse space, they traverse universes. The power is beyond anything we could ever imagine or comprehend. Our human theology doesn't even begin to explain the eternal struggle occurring all around us." Erik pointed to the ceiling. "It's terrifying. I understand why humans don't know the full scope of reality and why theology is limited and vague. The truth would turn a man's mind to jello. God's Multiverse is in a constant state of flux with good and evil constantly fighting for possession of worlds and souls."

Alissa took a step back, stunned. Her lips pursed into a tight oval. "I've read some books about the cosmic struggle. They were written by philosophers centuries ago but I never paid them much heed. I always assumed they were fairy tales like the gods and goddesses of old. But it's all real."

The somber detective blew out a long, thoughtful breath. "It's more than I care to know. If the forces of Light are watching over this place, so much the better. That means the other side won't be poking around." He frowned. "It also means the firm is involved deeply in ethereal matters. They have an interest in this place and I'd like to know exactly what that interest is and why. There's a reason they bankrolled our business loan and acted as a silent partner. I aim to get to the truth once things get back to normal." He sipped his coffee. "If they ever get back to normal."

"Maybe it's just a courtesy? I think you may be a bit para-noid."

Erik snorted. "Just because you're paranoid doesn't mean they're *not* out to get you."

She shook her head and rolled her eyes. "That's a lame comeback and you know it."

"Yes it is," admitted Erik, "but right now it's the best I have." He glanced at his watch, "Martin will be here in about an hour then we're heading back to DC to chase down a possi-ble lead. After that it's back to Vatican City."

Alissa stepped up to the desk. "Mr. Denton made all this possible, Erik. If you have a question regarding the firm's in-volvement here he'd be the logical person to approach."

The detective frowned, rubbing the stubble on his cheek and chin. "Good point. Martin and I have enough on our plate right now, and I don't want to press him on something he may not want to talk about just yet. Like I said, one mystery at time."

"Since you're here, you may as well be useful. The workers need to have the larger pieces of equipment moved so they can bring in ladders to fix some ceiling panels and clean the venti-lation ducts. We can rent a hydraulic lift or you can move them yourself before we open. Put those Esper muscles to some good use while you're here."

Erik laughed. "Yes Ma'am."

* * *

Washington DC

Congressman Anderson studied the business card. "It's not a Starlight business card, Erik." He tossed it on his desk and opened the top desk drawer. "This is a Starlight Bistro card. There are dozens of them floating around the building. This specific card grants access to a very exclusive Bistro outside of DC run by the same shell corporation. Only the super elite power brokers in Washington are admitted here. I'm surprised Molec left this behind."

"Our demonic friend had to make a rather abrupt exit." Denton picked up the card carefully examining edges. "There's a chip in here. The card's been laminated back together but this corner edge is thicker and not pliable like the rest of the bonded paper." He handed the card to Erik.

The detective studied it carefully, running his finger over the surface. "Nice catch, Counselor. I'll bet you Molec is holed up somewhere close, right under our very noses. The key to finding him is this establishment!" Erik shook his head, cursing under his breath. "Martin we were made the moment we stepped into the Starlight. Odds are the security is even tighter here. We'd be made the second we walked in. We may have to watch this place from a distance, or go in and hope we can catch wind of Molec or the relic before someone or something confronts us. If I can get a sense of the relic, we'll know that bastard is close by too. He won't leave his 'Precious' out of arm's reach."

Martin laughed at the movie reference. "Let's keep a distance at first. If you can get a read on the relic, we promised Michael we'd let him take point! I'm not one to piss off our divine allies."

Erik smacked his fist against his open palm. The sound cracked like a whip. "Damn it! You're right. I did make a promise to our angelic ally. It's probably better if they handle the capture and recovery. I won't deny I want a piece of that bastard though."

Anderson nodded. "Since you're actually exercising common sense, I have something for you both, provided you promise me you'll only do reconnaissance work."

Erik nodded and extended his hand. "You have my word."

Anderson clasped his hand, then reached into a lower desk drawer. He placed two green amulets on the desktop. "These amulets mask your aura. You, my hybrid friend, have been branded with the mark of a warrior of Light, whether you like it or not Divinity has marked you." Anderson looked over at Denton. "You too have been marked as a guardian. The link between you two has been sealed: Warrior and Spirit Guide if I were to fall back on Native American folk lore." Anderson slid the amulets across his desk. "The energy from these stones will mask your essence and make you appear as a Greylord, completely neutral and non-partisan in the Eternal Conflict."

Denton frowned. "Greylord? There's yet another layer we

don't know about?"

Anderson laughed. "Mr. Denton, there are layers of mystery and ethereal beings that even I don't know about, nor do I wish to. Greylords existed before this universe was formed. They inhabited the cosmic vacancy that this space and time supplanted. These beings come and go as they please in and out of space and time, and have no interest or stake in the battle we fight. They simply exist and wait for this universe to come to an end so they can inhabit the void once again. Neither side sees them as ally or enemy so they're paid no heed."

Erik's jaw dropped. "They existed before our universe was formed. Holy shit, and I felt insignificant before."

"They are but one of many old powers, Agent Knight," Anderson replied. "Earth has appeal to many diverse beings. The bounty of life energy on this planet knows no rival. It is a beacon for many. As you saw at the Soul Market, that bounty can be harvested for malicious purpose." Anderson sighed. "But let's get back to the matter at hand. Keep those amulets on your person and you will be read by all as a Greylord. No ethereal will approach you and you can observe and gather information freely. Without their cover you would be identified immediately and the proprietors would do everything within their power to eject you both." The Congressman pointed toward the detective. "Your exploits at the Soul Market have spread throughout the Multiverse." Anderson chuckled. "Never in my life have I seen one individual piss off and annoy such a wide variety of organic and divine life forms. You are certainly a vortex of mayhem. Tread lightly and carefully in this establishment, you will have no friends there. This version of the Starlight is a cesspool of evil and corruption. Any human there has sold his or her soul to darkness and has surrendered any claim to humanity. Even the wait staff is pledged to darkness." Anderson leaned forward, eyes intent, "You will be alone. If you find Molec there or you find the relic, leave the place and summon aid outside. You will be unable to contact the forces of Light once you enter."

The detective studied the amulet before slipping it in his pants pocket. "Understood. Can you arrange a ride for us?"

Anderson nodded. "You'll need a change of clothes, too."

He snapped his fingers. "Do you have your Esper weapon? If so, you'll have to leave it behind. You cannot carry it there. It too will be sensed. Even the gemstone cannot shield a weapon so powerful."

"I sent the staff back to Vatican City to protect EJ and Shanda. I trust our allies, but I feel better having the weapon there if needed." Erik and Martin displayed their standard agency pistols. "Will these cause a ruckus?"

"Greylords don't carry guns. If you must be armed, keep them out of sight. But bullets will be of little use to you."

Denton flashed a wicked grin. "We have special rounds just for these ethereal types, I liberated another batch from the firm before we flew up here."

Anderson shook his head. "Gentlemen, I implore you *not* to embark on your pattern of rampage. Get the needed intelligence and withdraw. We cannot afford a Soul Market incident here."

"There won't be one," Erik assured. "We're not looking for trouble. I'm saving my rage for Molec."

Anderson nodded. "I'll have the proper attire delivered to your hotel room, I know someone who can make a reservation for you. One does not simply walk into this place. Even a Greylord would need a reservation. That access card will verify your credentials.

* * *

The Starlight Exclusive Club. Lower Washington, DC

"This suit itches and I look like a damn thunder cloud." Denton shifted uncomfortably in their spacious booth adjusting his heavy suitcoat.

Erik nodded and tilted his black sunglasses down the bridge of his nose, gesturing at his own charcoal grey sleeve. "They take the grey in Greylord to an extreme." He sipped his water quickly slipping his dark glasses back up as a waitress approached. Blood red eyes studied each man. Erik felt a telekinetic power probing him. The jewel in his suit coat pulsed and the women shuddered as if something slapped her.

"I don't like people poking where they're not invited." Erik turned toward her doing his best to project hostility.

"My apologies. I've never encountered a Greylord in this establishment. I needed to be sure." She took a deliberate step back.

"Is there a problem?" A tall gangly man in an impeccable suit approached.

Denton looked up. "There was a question regarding our identity. I believe the matter has been settled." His voice was frosty.

"We are honored to have Greylords in our establishment. I'll have your drinks brought over immediately." He grabbed the waitress, dragging her away. Erik could hear the man scolding her under his breath.

"These jewels are as good as Anderson claimed." The detective focused his Esper powers. "Time to go mind fishing." Erik took a deep breath and opened the telekinetic receptors he normally kept shielded. Hundreds of random thoughts avalanched into his head.

We can't sneak these funds through.

Where can I bury the body?

If my wife finds out about my affair, she'll take me for every penny.

How can I get rid of my husband?

I just wanna take you home and screw you.

That waitress has a great ass!

I'd sell my soul to get out of this mess!

I need the vote on this bill to fail. I'll have to bribe everyone on the subcommittee.

We can't possibly move ten million without anybody knowing.

If this came out we'd all be ruined!

"Anything?"

Erik frowned. "Just random thoughts, none of them pertinent to our situation. I'm still winnowing though all the clutter."

The waitress came back and placed two tall, slim glasses filled with ice and lime green bubbling liquid. "Mr. Potts, the owner of this establishment sends you his regards. He knows Greylords are fond of this concoction. It's on the house."

"Thank you."

Denton stared at the glass. "We're being watched. I think we're expected to drink this concoction."

Erik picked up the glass and cautiously took a sip of the liquid. "It's lime Gatorade, vodka and soda water." Erik frowned, "and some other type of flavored liquor. Greylords have unusual drink preferences."

Denton took a deep swig and nodded. "It really isn't bad. I may have to keep this in mind."

Erik raised his glass and took another sip. "Cheers."

When do they attack Vatican City?

Erik flinched as the thought registered. He focused his senses on that particular thought and concentrated, filtering out everything else but that singular mental pattern.

Molec's forces are massing. We have to move our assets out quickly!

We have to get our money out of Rome! That idiot is going to unleash chaos!

Erik turned slightly, locking down the source. Two men were frantically whispering in a corner, neither one happy. "Something's going down, Counselor, Vatican City is in danger!" Erik hissed. "We need more details." He pointed to the men. "Let's gather up the gnats and have a conversation."

More thoughts registered. *Must blockade the city and kill the hybrid child.*

Erik stood, his eyes burning fires of aqua energy that even the dark glasses couldn't shield. "They're gonna kill my son!"

"Erik, no! You can't go off like a cannon here. If they're planning an attack, we have to pass on the intelligence. You promised not to go rogue!" Martin gestured toward the seat. "Sit down. Let's finish our drink, leave a fat tip, and get out of here. We now know what Molec is planning so let's get the information to Anderson so we can prevent the disaster."

Erik sat slowly, ignoring the few curious stares. He drained his glass with one gulp, slammed it back down on the table. The frustrated detective took a crisp twenty from his wallet and slipped the bill under some silverware. "I know. I'm sorry. We act out here, we give away our advantage to Molec and he knows we're on to his plan. I get it, but my son and my wife are in Vatican City and I'm not there to protect them." Erik flexed his arms and the suit coat fabric strained under the pressure of bulging muscle. "I'm done. Let's get out of here. The sooner we pass this along, the better for all concerned."

Denton took two more sips and nodded. "I understand, believe me I do. But your staff is there and it vaporized the last threat. I'm sure it'll do the same to any other. Plus there's no way Molec could successfully attack such a holy place without a devastating response from Light's army." He placed his empty glass on a napkin and nodded. "Let's go pass along the intel."

Erik nodded as he stood. "What you're saying makes perfect sense, but I'm getting that buzzing in the back of my head, even in here. Something's wrong, Martin, terribly wrong."

No one approached them. In fact, the crowd seemed to part as they moved toward the door. Erik wondered just how powerful these beings were that existed outside of the known universe.

As they approached their limousine, Erik's Esper senses fully engaged. His telepathic link to Shanda and EJ was severed. He stumbled and grabbed his head, struggling to cope with the sudden loss of their presence.

Martin helped his friend into the car. "Are you okay now? You scared the bejeezus out of me back there!"

Erik nodded. "Sorry. I'm okay. I think the attack is already under way." Erik closed his eyes, attempting to summon Michael as he'd done before. "Nothing! My direct line to the Ethereals seems to be closed. Can you get Anderson on your cell?"

"I'm trying but I keep getting dumped straight to voice mail." Denton dialed another number. "The firm's Washington line is jammed too." The old man slipped the phone in his pocket. "I don't have Esper senses but something feels wrong in my gut. The firm's lines are never jammed and we have Anderson's direct office line. I don't like this. Denton leaned forward. "Driver, we need to get back to DC as soon as possible."

* * *

Washington, DC

Martin and Erik were escorted into Anderson's office. The man was frantic, pacing back and forth, talking heatedly into his phone. He looked over at Erik and shook his head. Erik's gut tightened. Anderson hung up the phone cursing, his body shaking.

"How bad is it?"

Anderson activated his flat screen television. CNN was reporting live from Rome. Vatican City was hidden under a massive plume of black. A gigantic onyx dome covered the city. Audible screams and wails of agony sounded from the speakers and intermittent brilliant white light appeared and arcs of energy flashed above and around the darkness. A reporter shrieked in terror as hideous malformed creatures ran amok in the streets chasing humans. Something huge and scaly approached the reporter. Her shrieks silenced abruptly and static filled the screen. The image jumped back to a local newsroom and a terrified news anchor. Anderson flipped through several other channels to see variations of the same scenario.

A white phone on the congressman's desk rang. He picked up the receiver. His face paled as he nodded several times. "I understand. God help us all." Anderson collapsed in his chair.

"What is it?"

"Vatican City is blockaded. We cannot get through. The forces protecting her have been overwhelmed by this unprecedented attack. We've lost all communication with the holy city. The forces of Light are gathering for war and we can only assume the same is being done on the other side." Anderson's voice trembled. He looked up, color drained from his face. "The Ethereal War has begun. Evil is running amok all over Rome and innocent people are being slaughtered."

"I need to get there. My wife and my son are trapped!"

Anderson pointed toward the white phone. "Light knows you're here." A tear rolled down his cheek. "Will you fight? Will you take up the cause for humanity? This isn't just about your family, Agent Knight, it's about saving all of us. Molec has triggered the end. Demons are running amok contrary to God's law. If Heaven's army is unleashed, Lucifer will also unleash his forces and this planet will be destroyed in the conflict. You have to be the stop gap. You have to aid the remaining forces still battling for Vatican City before they all fall."

Erik gave a firm nod. "I'm going to personally break Molec

in half with my bare hands."

"Will you fight, hybrid? Will you fight for the survival of humanity?"

The detective clenched his fists. "Yes. Given the circumstances, I have no choice anymore."

Martin placed a hand on his friend's shoulder. "I'm in too."

"No, Counselor. This is a fight I'm going into in full Esper mode. I'm going to harness all of Jakor's power and skill. He's fought this type of battle before and I'm going to use his experience along with my power to unleash my own brand of Hell on Molec's army. I don't want you anywhere near when this goes down."

Denton ignored his friend. "I can lead some forces in Rome to deal with the overflow of demonic activity. The firm has weapons for this kind of problem." He opened his suit coat, displaying his specially modified guns. "I know we're involved in this. Maybe I can't fight like my friend here but I can clean up the demonic trash killing innocent civilians and I can lead some forces to keep the threat contained."

"Agreed," said Anderson. "I'll call the firm and we'll have a special team readied and a cargo bird prepped to take you all to Rome."

Erik slammed his fist on the desk. "Damn it! That'll take hours. If I had my staff I could open a portal and get there in an instant."

"No." Anderson disagreed vehemently. "You open a portal, every demon will know the second you arrive and be on you like flies on horse poop. Netherspace is a demonic highway and right now it's full of evil traffic. Besides, this is a special bird. She can move eighty tons of cargo at Mach 4 plus she has plenty of teeth. Call it a byproduct of our Area 51 research. We'll get you there quickly. The remaining Ethereal forces we have on Earth are already rallying. If we fail, Michael and Raphael will intercede, and Lucifer will engage them in an effort to take this world. We'll all perish if that happens."

Martin narrowed his gaze. The old man looked flummoxed. "Why won't God intercede? If he wants humanity to survive and keep his 'Son' safe why not just snap his fingers and end all this?"

Anderson met Martin's gaze. "Look at the world Mr. Denton. Everywhere we look God is being expunged on our planet. We've dropped the very mention of God in our schools, in our courts, and in our hearts. Look at the music and movies that dominate our culture. They are a cesspool of depravity. Man has come to serve money and secular humanism. We've been given free will and we've chosen poorly. God will not directly intercede, but He will act through His forces if the rules governing his worlds are violated. These actions violate those rules, if we cannot correct them, war will follow and God's legions will unleash His fury just as Lucifer's legions will battle to take this world. If God were honored and respected, perhaps He would intercede as you suggest. Sadly that isn't the case for this planet." Anderson pointed toward the old man. "You yourself were a devout Atheist just weeks ago, were you not? Yet now you ask for God's intervention. Even your powerful hybrid friend had little to do with God prior to the incidents that brought him into this war." Anderson pointed at Erik. "And you, Erik, would you fight so hard if your wife and child were not endangered? If God sought you out on your own for such sacrifice would you have made it freely and willingly?"

Erik looked away, uncomfortable at the accusation. "Based on my harsh prior experience with the church and the molestation of my step brother, I would have said no if a man asked me. If approached by God or Michael, I would have fought." Erik looked back at Anderson. "If God wasn't happy with the way shit played out, he should have hired a better PR firm than the corrupted Catholic Church. You guys aren't doing yourself any favors with all the bad PR over the last few decades." The detective spun. "And don't lecture me, Congressman. I'm in no mood. If God wanted things to be different maybe 'He' should have played a more active role. If God knows all, He should have seen this coming. I'm sick of rules and I'm sick of being pushed around on your blasted chess board. My patience is at an end. I trusted you to keep my wife and child safe and all I get in return for my assistance in chasing down your wayward demon is my family in cosmic jeopardy smack dab in the middle of your holy war! You've carped at how I do my job and the way I do my job and frankly I'm sick of all of it." Erik jabbed his finger at the congressman. "To be blunt, Martin and I have had more success hunting down Molec than all of your heavenly hosts put together! I admit we've caused some carnage but then again you knew that was gonna happen and since we're being honest, lets lay all the fucking cards on the table." Erik slammed his fist on a table, crushing the top into splinters. "That's exactly what you wanted us to do despite all your protests to the contrary. You wanted us to come in and shake shit up! You wanted us to push Molec and keep him off balance. You wanted to rattle the evil cages in DC and send a shockwave to Lucifer's Washington contacts." The detective took a step toward the congressman. "And the Soul Market? Did you really think I'd just accept that I'd find my mother's soul at random and not be suspicious? You must have known if I went there, I'd find her and what I'd do, which means someone on your side knew she was already a captive there! You and Michael knew exactly what I'd do once I found her soul. You knew I'd free her and you knew the place would be scrapped by those security forces. I gave you the excuse to go in there and bust it up. You knew what was going on but you needed proof and a reason to intercede. Sending us there was a twofold gesture. We pushed Molec, yes, but we ultimately gave you an excuse to shut the place down and gather an advantage you wouldn't have had without human interference based on your bizarre rules of engagement." The detective paced back and forth. Anderson appeared more uncomfortable as the detective tied more events together. "If you were so concerned about neutrality, you wouldn't have given up your Washington opposition so willingly. You wanted me to rattle the House Speaker. You knew I'd find Senator McMahon's cache and you probably knew I'd make the bastard pay for what was done to me earlier." Erik looked over at Martin. The old man was stunned.

"This whole thing was a set up?"

Erik nodded. "Martin, I'm getting that vibe and the more I think about it, the more the pieces are coming together that way. They needed a way to get me involved. What better way than to give me a child with divine province?" Erik spun back toward Anderson. "Then you took advantage of William Denton's death, already knowing my relationship with Martin. You knew once the powder puffs at Vatican City couldn't solve his son's murder, he'd come to me and eventually I'd come here. You knew that was the way in." Erik's voice dropped to a deadly baritone. "You played us like a couple of chumps. We were the bullets in your loaded gun, and you just pointed in the direction you wanted and squeezed the trigger letting us unleash the havoc your ethereal overlords were forbidden to do under the cover of solving a murder and protecting my family."

Martin stumbled forward in shock. "No, no that can't be right." He looked at Anderson, desperate. "Tell me you didn't play on my grief like that." Denton's right hand reached for his pistol.

"Tell me!"

The Congressman barely flinched. "Take your hand away from your gun. You're not going to kill me." Anderson's tone was gruff, nails on a chalk board. The mild demeanor vanished. "Of course we used you, both of you. But that doesn't make the danger you were in any less real, Special Agent Knight. Your son was brought forward to draw Molec out and end his threat forever. We had to up the timeline for Armageddon's Son and we needed someone with enough power and courage to bear the burden and keep the child safe while at the same time combat the forces both at Molec's and Lucifer's command. Once the child was revealed, we knew all literal Hell would break loose. Who better than a genetic mutant human with the DNA of an Esper soldier to serve as guardian?" Anderson sat down, ignoring the ringing phones on his desk. "You were the right man at the right place at the right time for our forces, Agent Knight."

"He's my son. You deliberately put my son in danger, and my wife. She was nearly killed and brutalized by some godforsaken ghoul. Was that part of your divine plan, too?"

Anderson steepled his hands. "Nobody predicted the attack on your wife or your son. We had assigned them protection as you well know. Molec was a few steps ahead of us and we grossly underestimated his audacity and cunning." The congressman took a deep breath. "Since you're fond of honesty, let me tell you something else; the boy isn't solely your biological son."

Erik shook his head. "You're wrong. He's an Esper, Shanda

saw it. I felt it during the battle in the parking lot. They said he was my son."

"Yes, genetically he has your markers because he was willed to be your offspring, but EJ is so much more than you imagine. He's not just your son. He's divinely engineered from many sources. Yes, you were picked to nurture him. Yes, your genes are part of him, the biological organic building blocks, but to say you are his father oversimplifies his cosmic significance. Biologically you are his father. But in the cosmic sense, Erik, you're not. You are more than human, and your son is so much more than you, me or any being alive in this universe. You were the perfect anomaly as I stated earlier, and we used you to further our purposes and lay a scheme to rid this plane of a great evil." Anderson's face softened slightly. "I'm sorry for the subterfuge, really. But I was given my instructions to follow." He gestured toward the ringing white phone on his desk. "Agent Knight, I can't explain all of this to you, nor do I have the time or patience to justify the actions taken to save this world. You're far too clever for your own good. We figured if you were kept busy enough, you wouldn't see through the ruse." Anderson glanced over at another phone, "Right now you two have a choice to make. Refuse to fight and sacrifice your family or get on the Mach 4 transport with the tactical team I'll be assembling and prevent Molec's forces from taking Vatican City and hopefully avert the inevitable war about to happen."

Martin and Erik were silent. Erik glanced over at his old friend. Denton's hands shook, his face blood red to match the fire in his amber eyes. One hand clenched, knuckles white. The other slipped inside his jacket, smoothly freeing the large demon slayer pistol. The man was deliberately holding back tears. Before Erik could react, Denton squeezed the pistol's trigger and fired. The bullet grazed Anderson's right arm. Blood flowed from the torn flesh. "You knew my son was going to die, didn't you? You needed that death to set this complex play in motion." Denton locked the barrel of his gun on Anderson's forehead. The congressman held his other hand against his wounded arm, his eyes locked on the weapon.

"We knew your son was snooping where he wasn't supposed to be. We didn't know how he felt the presence of the relic. He was an anomaly we wished to study. We knew someone was contracted to steal the relic, but we didn't anticipate the use of mystical garbs and the undead in the process. Our priests were woefully unprepared for such a clandestine attack. Molec's theft of the relic and your son's death were not part of our original plan, but we decided to use the events to our advantage."

Denton's aim wavered as a sob wracked his body. A flood of tears broke free. "We're just pawns to you." Denton holstered his weapon. "We have no free will. That's an illusion. We're puppets in some awful cosmic play."

Anderson shook his head. "Some men and women are not free to choose. Some are called to action and destined to be a part of something greater than themselves, Mr. Denton." Anderson looked from Denton to Erik. "You and Agent Knight are two of those people destined to be a part of the eternal struggle as have been so many more before you and so many that will come after you." Anderson moved his hand. The bloody wound was healed and the sleeve of his jacket magically repaired. "Gentlemen, you need to get to Vatican City. We have no more time to discuss the Cosmic Truths. The battle for this planet is at hand. If we survive this calamity, you're more than welcome to return here and we can pick up this conversation." Anderson pointed toward the door. "My driver will take you to the hangar. I'll have some special weapons and body armor loaded for you, Denton. As for you, Agent Knight, your Esper flesh can provide more protection than any armor in our arsenal."

* * *

Vatican City

The Vatican Guard formed a defensive wedge around Shanda and EJ, shielding them from the attackers. Shanda tried to reach out with her mind through the endless void as she was forced through several corridors leading to the White Room. *Erik, we're in trouble! The entire city is under attack!*

"Please, Mrs. Knight, we must keep moving!" A guard urged her forward as she clutched her terrified son.

Shanda nodded and increased her pace. The next attack came from behind a large pillar. Seven men with spears and swords charged, chanting and screaming. The guards were hard pressed to keep the attackers back.

"We can't hold them off much longer. I'm sorry!"

A deep snarl overwhelmed the battle cries. A guard cried out as a blade pierced his chest. Blood sprayed over the defenders, covering Shanda and EJ in a layer of warm crimson. The Sentient Staff flowed like liquid chrome from EJ's arm, buzzing and growling as it took shape, hovering over the defenders. The attackers paused, studying the object with momentary confusion. Angry jagged arcs of energy blasted them, vaporizing three men on contact. The four others retreated behind heavy marble pillars, cursing and promising death to the child. Lances of raw power tore into the columns, blasting away large chunks with each impact. The stressed load bearing pillars collapsed, burying the four men under tons of marble and stone ceiling debris.

"God is watching over us."

Shanda shook her head as they continued. "I'll take any help I can get right now."

"Where's Daddy?"

"I'm sure Daddy's on his way, hun. We just have to hold on for a little while longer." She held EJ tighter.

"We need to keep moving, Mrs. Knight. The weapon's discharge has crippled the entire structure over our heads. The roof could collapse burying us as well."

Shanda nodded. "I hear more footsteps coming. I thought you cleaned out all the rats?"

The burly guard clenched his ceremonial blade tighter. "As did I. Obviously we missed a few and they've freed their cohorts in the dungeon." The guard gestured overhead. "I've read about these blockades in the library of scrolls. I fear our forces will have their hands full. I suspect the Prince of Darkness will make his move during this chaos."

"I'm not giving up!"

"Nor are we, Mrs. Knight. We are sworn to protect you at all costs and we will follow our holy orders."

The staff reformed around EJ's forearm. The weapon

buzzed and gently hummed. The child answered, conversing with the weapon in a series of hums and whistles.

"Though it appears the child has the best protector God can provide on this world."

Shanda sighed. "It appears that way."

The sound of a massive tree falling echoed throughout the open space. They all flinched, startled, looking up. Chunks of plaster fell. Pearl colored raindrops of various shapes and sizes plinked against the marble floor tiles. The ceiling sagged, over-burdened, weakened beams bowed under their tremendous load. A large stress fracture appeared and spawned a network of tributary cracks sending down a stream of fine powder. Powder and plaster fell like winter snow covering the already pale floor with a coating of white.

"Run!"

They fled from the large chamber as larger blocks of concrete, plaster, and wood imploded into the chamber.

Shanda knelt down, breathing heavy. EJ fidgeted. "At least we won't be followed."

The guard pointed down the adjacent hallway. "Through there. The sacred room is not much farther."

Gunfire erupted and two guards fell. Bullets chipped marble and granite pillars. Shanda heard the dull thud of lead piercing human flesh. The large guard fell over dead, eyes open in shock.

"The bitch and her offspring are here. Take them out!"

EJ broke free from her grip. He pointed toward one of the gunmen. A searing ball of aqua plasma burned through the stunned man. He fell forward, with a six-inch cauterized hole in his torso. The staff formed a shield as dozens of bullets filled the air. The tiny boy unleashed a firestorm of energy at the hapless assassins.

A machine gun erupted. Muzzle flash and flame lit up the foyer as dozens of armor-piercing bullets bit into walls and deflected off EJ's shield. Shanda watched the battle behind a large statue. Stray bullets ricocheted off the walls and EJ's shield, forcing her to duck. The gunfire intensified and she screamed in terror. "EJ!!!" All she could do was scream out her son's name. Thunder echoed from the walls and the smell of burnt flesh and ozone stung her nostrils. Flashes of blue light continued to accompany the thunder until the gunfire finally ceased and silence reigned.

The cry of innocence lost shattered the silence. "Mommy? Mommy where are you?"

Shanda peeked around the large statue's base. Her son stood alone in a sea of charred, smoking bodies, burnt by her son's bio organic weapons. EJ held the staff loosely in his hand, weeping as he studied the mayhem surrounding him.

"Oh my baby boy!" Shanda raced to her son and held him tight. "It's okay baby. Mommy has you now. It's okay!"

EJ broke down. "I couldn't make it stop! I tried to but it just kept coming out of me! I didn't mean to hurt anybody. It was an accident!"

"I know honey, I know." She scooped him up with one arm and picked up a loaded assault rifle in her free hand. "We need to get to the White Room. I should be protecting you, lil man, not the other way around."

Shanda glanced back at the bodies of the Vatican guards that gave their life for her. "I'm so sorry." She turned and walked down the long hallway adjusting her grip on the heavy weapon. Shanda walked down the long corridor, her finger resting on the trigger guard, ready to unleash hell upon the next wave of assailants. The hallway curved and she recognized the pillars and chairs outside the chamber known as the White Room. Three guards greeted her.

"Mrs. Knight, thank heaven! Where is your escort?"

"They were all killed protecting us."

The man bowed his head. "Regrettable. They were good men, all of them. I am sorry you and your son had to witness such savagery—but come." He gestured toward the heavy white door that opened on its own. "We can take sanctuary in the protection of the White Room. We will be safe in here from all external forces."

Shanda followed the three men. "Erik, where are you?" she wondered as the heavy door closed behind her.

* * *

Erik studied the team of heavily armed men sorting through gear and parachutes. "Counselor, you're really hell bent on jumping out of this aircraft and parachuting into Rome?"

"I was hoping we'd be landing." Denton frowned. "Praying actually, but God seems preoccupied at the moment. What about you? You have that look about you."

"Look?"

"Yeah, you get that look right before you're about to unleash a hellstorm. Your brow furrows and you keep making a fist with your right hand." Denton managed a smile. "What's your plan?"

Erik sighed. He really didn't have one. "Drop in and kill everything that needs killing, find my wife and son, then go home."

The old man rolled his eyes. "Okay, well that's a good strawman, but maybe you can provide me a bit more detail?"

The detective shrugged his shoulders. "Martin, I wish I could. Truth be told, I have no idea what we're dropping into. It's literally a Hell on Earth in Rome right now and it's spreading like a cancer. You need to stop the spreading and I need to kill the source." Erik flexed powerful muscles. "I'm gonna start by shattering that dome any way possible. I'm going to unload everything I have into one massive blast. If I can break the shell, I'll draw Molec out, then I can finish this once and for all. Michael can get the relic back and we can go home and do our best to put this shit behind us." Erik shook his head, frustrated. "To be honest though, I'm never gonna be the same again. No one on this world will be. How many millions saw the news broadcasts until the local channels were wiped out and the reporters eaten or worse?" Erik sighed. "Nothing will ever be the same again. Our entire world is tainted by this."

"I guess you're right," mused Martin. "Maybe people will start being nicer to each other when they realize Hell and demons exist." Denton rubbed his nose. "If we survive." Martin glanced over his shoulder. "I need to go check my gear and inspect my chute. Captain Tilson is about to give me a crash course in jumping out of a Mach 4 transport. It's been forty-two years since I did a combat jump."

Erik chuckled. "Good luck." He watched Martin leave.

"I need to talk to a friend and get some strategic advice. Erik closed his eyes and focused his concentration inward to the deeper recesses of his brain to a portion inhabited by something else.

* * *

Welcome back Erik, it is good to see you. Would it be presumptuous of me to say I know why you are here?

Erik smiled. *I figured you would. I'm about to engage a demonic legion of great power and possibly square off against an archdemon named Molec. The archangel, Michael, claimed to have fought with you in the Esper War on your home world.*

Jakor looked up to the sky and nodded briefly. He called aloud and several great flying beasts circled overhead. *Yes. I know of the battle angel. We spoke briefly earlier. He is a great and powerful warrior. We fought many battles together but it wasn't enough to save my world, and now Earth is in danger of becoming extinct as well. I am aware of what is going on.*

Erik nodded. *Good, I need your guidance on how to fight Molec. I have no practical experience with demonic combat. I could use your skill set when the time comes. I have your native powers and the like, but your internal experience isn't part of the package, I can't access that directly. If you know how to transfer those skills to me, I could certainly use them. We're closing in on the focal point of the disturbance and I need every advantage I can get to save my wife and son.*

Jakor placed his hand on Erik's shoulder. *You've fought well so far against many demons, but yes, I will give you the knowledge I possess.* Jakor stood, rising several inches above Erik. *Demons like Molec thrive on attacking. You prefer a defensive mode of combat. This will be your downfall. To defeat a being as powerful as Molec, you must attack and keep attacking. Don't allow the demon to formulate any strategy. Use your enhanced powers to keep him on the defensive and off balance. Molec will grow frustrated and lose his composure once the fight does not go his way. He is powerful but easily sidetracked. His power has made him arrogant over the eons. Don't become overconfident even if it appears you are winning. Fight aggressively but with purpose and caution. You have many powers and gifts. Now is the time to bring all that power to bear on this adversary.*

When you need my skills, you will have them.

Erik lowered his head. *Thank you again. I promise once this is over we'll have a social visit. Perhaps we can even link in my bride and she can meet you.*

Jakor smiled. *I would welcome that. Good luck, hybrid. Fight well and bring honor to our race.*

A voice sounded all around them. "We're approaching the drop point and going subsonic. There'll be a jolt as the braking thrust fires, so hold onto something."

* * *

Erik opened his eyes and gripped a nearby handhold. He heard the drone of engines firing and his stomach went queasy as the large sleek aircraft began to decelerate. After two minutes, the pilot announced they were subsonic. The sound of Velcro snaps and boot laces dominated the aircraft cargo hold. Erik watched as large clips of glowing green and orange ammunition were loaded into several assault weapons. Martin was helped into his parachute and then began issuing commands to the soldiers. Erik remembered his friend would be in charge of the defensive perimeter and in full command. He watched silently as Martin gave directives and devised strategy to effectively bottleneck Vatican City and the rest of Rome. Sixty armed soldiers would scarcely be a sufficient force against what was infesting the streets of Rome. The detective wished his friend had stayed back in DC. He was fighting a losing battle.

"We're fifteen seconds from the drop. We're laying down a field of suppression fire." The plane shuddered slightly as several 125mm explosive rounds erupted from the craft's five heavy gun ports. Erik heard the distinct whine of a 30mm Vulcan Cannon dispensing hundreds of rounds a minute into the drop area. The plane shook violently. "We've taken a hit from some sort of beam! We lost an engine! You need to jump now!"

Several more heavy cannon rounds fired in response. Erik looked through the tiny view plates and saw ordnance detonating. "My God, I hope there aren't any people there!"

"From what we were told in our initial briefing, Agent Knight, no one is left alive in Rome. Those who survived the initial assault have already been evacuated." Erik looked up at the young soldier preparing to deploy.

"I hope you're right." Erik extended his hand. "Good luck, soldier."

"Thanks and good luck to you as well. From what little we were told, you've got the heavy lifting on this job."

Erik looked back. Martin was busy issuing directions and prepping for departure. The old man looked back at his friend and smiled. He held back a tear, fearing for his friend's safety. "Take care of yourself, Counselor. EJ needs a Grandpa!"

Denton gave a curt nod. "I will. Be careful, son. I'll be praying for your success and your family's safe return." The old man turned and headed toward the rear door and attached his jump line. Two large soldiers formed up around him to make sure he'd make the drop safely.

A red light flashed and an alarm sounded. One by one they leapt into the darkness. Erik watched helpless. His gut tightened. "God, please keep him alive."

"Agent Knight, we need you up front."

Erik turned and headed toward the cockpit as the jump door closed behind him. He studied the terrifying scene outside. "My God it's a dome of complete blackness covering Vatican City!" The aircraft's surveillance cameras showed several winged creatures circling the dome.

Vatican City was totally encapsulated. Fires raged outside the city and dark clouds circled in a vortex directly overhead. Erik could see bursts of light but they were sporadic.

"There's some crazy ass creatures flying around the dome, and the occasional flash of lightning. There's definitely some kind of conflict, but nothing like I've ever seen in my thirty years of service. We can't get too close without drawing more fire."

"Can you unload a few 125's at that blister? Maybe we can break it open."

The pilot studied a scope. "It reads solid. We can try and punch a hole through but we can't get in close with just three engines. If one of those beams hits a fuel tank or our munitions store, we're gonna go off like a firework."

"I gotcha. Take us as close as you dare and then unleash a

volley and let's see what happens. Maybe we can actually crack this nut."

The large plane banked, spilling altitude. Erik heard vibrations beneath the cockpit as the transport's large main guns locked onto the demonic dome. With a shudder, twelve high yield explosive rounds with phosphorous tracers sped toward their target. The men watched as the projectiles impacted and exploded on the dark surface. After several seconds, the pilot looked back at Erik. "Nothing. Not even a scratch."

Several beams of energy raced toward the plane and the pilot had to bank hard to avoid the incoming fire. "They know we're here, Agent Knight. We're a sitting duck at this speed. I need to get some more forward velocity." The plane's Vulcan Cannon fired as several winged creatures approached. The dark sky lit up with yellow tracers and depleted uranium rounds. "Our automated defensive systems can knock down the smaller bogeys, but that big blip is too much."

Another beam collided with the aircraft, violently shaking the frame. Panels sparked as energy surged through delicate circuitry and the aircraft's carbon fiber skin melted.

"We're not designed to take this kind of punishment. We gotta get outta here, sir. If you're gonna do something, it needs to be now!"

"Climb," Erik ordered. "Take us higher up out of range, then circle the area. It's time to make my presence felt. If this bird has EM surge protection, I suggest you engage it now!" The engines whined and rocket-assisted motors pushed the large craft higher and higher, Erik felt the g-force pushing against him. "What's our altitude?"

"Fifteen thousand feet. We're circling the disturbance. Nothing's climbing up to attack us." The pilot studied another scope. "Correction, I've got a blip climbing up. Our automated systems are tracking..." The dull whine and vibration of multiple cannons sounded as thousands of rounds descended upon the intruding blip. "The contact is falling, but I'm picking up something larger on an ascent path. We need to get out of here!" The plane's automated defenses fired again. This time several larger cannons activated and a dull thud shook the plane as dozens of rocket-assisted shells sped toward the new threat. "Agent Knight, we need to bug out! Our fuel is low and our munitions are nearly expended."

Erik looked out the window. "Are the EMP systems activated?"

The pilot nodded. "She's built to resist an EMP pulse and the other circuits are shielded."

Erik closed his eyes, focusing on the ambient energy outside the aircraft. Not only could he draw on the agitated energy in the atmosphere, the demonic disturbance was a massive source of power he could tap The hybrid's hands reached skyward, summoning more and more power, expanding his sphere of influence and control. Hail battered the damaged aircraft as turbo jet motors strained to keep the craft on a true course. Still he reached out, gathering more and more power, compressing it, summoning the elemental energies of the planet to serve his wishes. Titanic arcs of aqua lit up the skies above Italy. The entire landmass along with Sicily, Austria, and Croatia were covered by roiling clouds arcing with electricity.

"Knight, we can't hold course. Whatever you're doing out there, you're gonna bring us down too if you keep it up!"

Erik nodded briefly and looked toward the sky. He whispered, "Michael, tell your remaining forces to withdraw. I'm about to rain down some hurt!" The hybrid waited five seconds, compressing aggravated ions and ambient energy into one massive blast.

ANARAH KONNAR ANKOLAH!!!

The sky erupted. A jagged plume of unfettered energy raced down from the heavens slamming into the demonic barrier, vaporizing hundreds of winged demons and gargoyles. The lance of power continued to batter the onyx shield fracturing the powerful membrane in dozens of areas. When the static discharge dissipated, the dark blister still stood, but the forces around it had been wiped out along with several nearby buildings. The area around Vatican City had been flattened and reduced to rubble. The dome seemed to fluctuate, winking in and out of existence. Large cracks were visible and parts of Vatican City could be seen through the inky darkness.

Sparks shot throughout the cabin as ambient static electricity tore through the battered airframe. Erik opened his eyes.

The copilot had a fire extinguisher and frantically sprayed multiple wall panels. The detective looked out the cockpit windshield. The sky was blue and clear as far as the eye could see. The pilot shook his head in disbelief. "Sonovabitch, that scared ten years off my life." He glanced down at the fuel gauge. "We can't stay here anymore. We need to set bird down. Our tanks are bone dry."

Erik nodded. "The dome? Did we get it?"

The pilot tilted his head. "We? Brother that was all YOU! According to the scope, you damaged it. It's fading in and out, but still holding. Our camera can actually see Vatican City through some sections of the blip. Your little pyrotechnic display vaporized a great deal of the opposition. Our guys have a perimeter about five miles back and have been killing anything that moves." The pilot paused to listen to a voice in his headset. The smile faded from his face. "Denton just checked in again. Something's happening underground! He says it feels like an earthquake."

Erik's senses triggered a warning, unlike anything he'd ever felt. "Tell them to pull back, now! Something's coming and it isn't good."

"The sky!"

Erik turned back toward the cockpit windshield. A sea of inky black spilled onto the clear blue skies, blocking out the sun. Rome was once again immersed in darkness. The damaged aircraft buckled as wind turbulence battered the stricken plane.

"I'm getting out of here, now!" The pilot banked the plane hard over away from the spreading disturbance. The airframe creaked in protest. "Agent Knight, we're not gonna make it to our landing point. I have to set this tub down, now. We've done all we can. Whatever's going on here is beyond our ability to cope. If they can bounce back from that lightning bolt you just unleashed, we don't have a prayer, so to speak." The pilot looked toward his second. "Take the controls."

Erik gritted his teeth. "I'm not done yet. My family is still down there." He walked toward the jump door, the pilot behind him. The detective slammed his palm against the large red button. "Get to safety and thanks for getting me here." Erik paused and extended his hand. "And for sticking around longer than you should have. I appreciate it."

The pilot clasped his outstretched hand. "You're welcome, and good luck." He coughed uncomfortably. "Uhm, Agent Knight, you don't have a parachute and were 15,000 feet up. That's a long way down for a man with no wings."

Erik's eyes burned as the jump door opened. "I don't need one!" He spun and leapt from the speeding plane. "I AM THE WARRIOR!" Within several heartbeats Erik fully transformed. He fell into the dark abyss, plummeting like a laser-guided bomb toward the damaged blister surrounding Vatican City. As the hybrid fell, he gathered agitated photons of energy, pulling more and more static power around his body. He plummeted toward the flickering dome like a burning meteorite slamming into the blister at terminal velocity. The concussive blast sent shockwaves rippling over several miles. Rubble and debris from ruined buildings were swept up in a flowing cascade.

The demonic blister ruptured, shattering like overstressed glass. A high-pitched evil shrill of agony pierced the silence as bits of fractured demonic energy vaporized. Smoke, debris and heavy dust covered the battle-torn city. Inside the darkness, two aqua eyes burned like raging infernos. A powerful silver being flexed large muscles. The hybrid raised his arms and shouted a battle cry easily heard for dozens of miles. *MOLEC! I'm calling you out, you son of a bitch. Let's settle this just you and me, one on one, winner take all!* The hybrid tensed, massive leg muscles contracted then exploded with superhuman force. His leap carried him over the Vatican protective wall a hundred meters outside Vatican City. Several dozen demons erupted from beneath the ground gathering and circling, preparing for an all-out assault against the helpless holy oasis. The hybrid took a step in front of the large gates. He picked up a fallen lamp pole and dragged a heavy line in front of the holy city. *Don't cross this line!*

A massive creature hissed mockingly and rushed forward. The hybrid hurled the lamp pole like a javelin, impaling the charging beast. The lamp post bore through the creature as it mindlessly rushed forward. The beast stumbled and fell forward, sliding in the dirt. Its body stopped inches before the line, dead. *Anyone else?*

The demonic army moved forward as a unit. More dark acolytes materialized to join the advance. Erik gestured toward the sky. Thunder cracked and angry jagged arcs of lightning danced in the heavens.

NOW for some payback!

* * *

Vatican City. White Room

Shanda held EJ tight. The child trembled in abject terror. Molec's human forces had decimated the last of the Vatican defenses. The incessant pounding on the large 'White Room' doors grew louder and louder. A veritable increasing drumbeat of doom. The vile shouts and screams permeated through the heavy walls, each voice threatening death or something worse if they did not surrender EJ.

"Will the door hold?" Shanda's grip on her stolen assault weapon tightened.

The Archbishop's pasty face, shaking, and wide-eyed terror broadcast her answer.

The heavy door groaned in duress as more and more powerful concussions slammed against the blessed barrier. Cracks and splinters formed along the stressed frame and timbers. It wouldn't be long. Evil would come. They meant nothing. Her life meant nothing. Darkness only wanted the child, the bearer of the Ruby Crucifix, Armageddon's Son. For evil to hold sway on Earth, EJ Knight had to die and the archdemon was determined to possess Earth no matter the cost.

"What about the outside shield you said was supposed to keep out the darkness? Will the shield stop the demon army?" The terrified mother held her son close.

The Archbishop shrugged as the lights flickered. "I don't know. The barrier was designed to thwart demonic forces. We didn't believe Molec would have so many human accomplices working for him, let alone have more forces already hidden within the city." The old man shook his head. "Nor could we anticipate that we would be attacked by such a powerful demonic weapon, here, in holy Rome, of all places! The fiery hosts of Hell have fallen upon us."

"What about the sisters and the other priests? Are there places for them to hide?" Shanda's thoughts were of the kind nun who shared coffee, pastry and pleasant conversation earlier. She had taken an instant liking toward the woman.

"The Holy Father has a private shelter and there are a few hidden places away but I don't know if anyone had time to flee. This attack was pre-planned and well orchestrated. I wonder where our divine forces could be. They must know what's going on here." Bishop O'Malley studied the heavy door as it shuddered under the constant barrage. "God cannot let this place fall."

The voices and the incessant pounding stopped. For a single heartbeat, silence reigned. A shockwave shook the entire city. Overhead lighting exploded sending shards of glass and angry sparks cascading to the ivory marble floor. Three heavy wall supports cracked under the massive blast. Several more concussive impacts shook the holy city.

"My God, was that a bomb or an Earthquake?!" The Archbishop hid under a large table as ceiling pieces of the supposedly impregnable White Room rained down upon them.

Bishop O'Malley struggled to stand upright. Blood trickled down his forehead in large drops. "Is everyone okay?" The bishop stared up at the damaged ceiling. "What power could do this? We can't endure another blast like that."

Shanda screamed as another massive shockwave blasted Vatican City shaking the blessed steel and timbers of the fortified safe room. A main support beam buckled, raining down more debris, forcing them to retreat under the slight protection of the conference table. EJ looked at his mother, youthful, innocent eyes burning like blue suns.

"It's Daddy! He broke through Molec's blockade." The three-year-old child stood bathed in an aura of pure white energy. Marble and plaster chunks fell toward the child, evaporating as they touched the burning aura. The aura expanded vaporizing large chunks of falling debris. EJ gestured toward the door and an unseen force blew the weakened barrier off its hinges. "The hybrid has taken his role as Earth's champion and issued a challenge. The forces of Light are gathering, The Ethereal War has begun." The men attacking the White Room turned and fled.

The words came from EJ, but the voice and cadence were that of a much older child. Shanda looked down at her son, stunned. She felt her connection with Erik restore and immediately knew he was engaged in some type of combat. A gentle hand tugged on her sleeve.

"C'mon, Mommy. Daddy's gonna fight the bully bad guy!" EJ's voice was his own again. The young boy was determined to get to his father. EJ held up his tiny left arm. The staff moaned and whined as it sensed the upcoming battle and wanted to be with its rightful master. "I don't know if you can hear me, but go help Daddy, please!"

The staff flowed off his arm, adopting its standard foot-long cylindrical shape. The weapon flew off, crashing through the overhead ceiling. The low pitched moan faded as the staff sought out its master. EJ tugged Shanda's hand gently guiding her. "We're safe now. Daddy's friend the angel is here too and he brought lots of help. Daddy is very angry and wants to hurt the bad guy."

Shanda nodded, still stunned by her son. "Okay, lead the way, little man."

Chapter 10: War!

Vatican City

Jagged arcs of power decimated the charging demonic forces. The hybrid launched salvo after salvo of burning plasma orbs, pitching spherical blasts of energy into the advancing army like a desperate ambidextrous baseball pitcher. Through sheer force of will, he commanded the elements to rain down lightning bolts into the advancing demonic forces. At some unseen command the army halted its advance. The line Erik had drawn in the dirt hadn't been crossed. From behind the sea of evil, a stream of scalding fire raced toward Erik. He dove to one side, barely avoiding the stream. He could feel the ambient heat as the fiery weapon streaked past. The fire stream slammed against an unseen barrier, spreading and dissipating before it could damage the wall of the holy city. Erik took quick note of the holy barrier. His wife and son were still relatively safe—he hoped.

The sea of demonic entities parted and a large onyx black figure approached. Erik's flesh crawled. The large being exhaled streams of fire vaporizing both dead and wounded alike as it approached. It carried a large curved saber of some unknown material. The weapon hissed and glowed with an evil energy. The hybrid's danger senses flared and instinctively he knew this was his nemesis: the archdemon, Molec. Angry growling filled the air as Erik's own Sentient Staff streaked toward its master's hand. Erik sensed the weapon, extended his hand, and felt the powerful staff settle in his grip. Once held, the weapon expanded. A lethal edged blade formed on one end and a savage barbed hook on the other. Aqua lightning danced up and down the weapon seemingly as a challenge to Molec's demonic blade. The staff had taken the customary shape of an Esper heavy weapon, the Ahn-so-lak.

I'm glad you're back. I assume my son is safe?

The weapon buzzed softly and Erik knew Shanda and EJ were fine.

Jakor, now would be a good time for the brain boost we discussed. Neural impulses inside his mind fired, transmitting reams of knowledge and skill acquired by the alien intellect. Erik marveled at the incredible martial tactics and skill possessed by Jakor, capability he'd never be able to gather in his own lifetime. The staff sensed the link and responded to the telekinetic signature of its former master. More powerful ambient energy coursed through the weapon. *Yes, Jakor is here. We need him in this fight.*

The nine-foot towering onyx-colored archdemon paused, stopping several feet away from his smaller silver opponent. The two combatants faced each other, each warrior a drastic contrast to the other.

"You have been a thorn in my side for too long, hybrid. I plan on killing you! You have the audacity to challenge me!" Amber flames seared the ground as Molec spoke, accentuating each word with a flaming exclamation point.

Erik focused his will. *MOLEC, you finally stopped running. This is it? This is your grand play? Attacking a city defended by all the forces of Light? Do you want to bring down all the Heavenly powers to destroy you?* He looked back at the still standing city and then back at his opponent. *Bad news, asshole, it's still there!*

Molec tapped the side of his head and laughed. "Ah I'd forgotten, Esper soldiers have no real vocal chords beyond a primitive hissing language. It's been centuries since I've killed an Esper. I look forward to breaking your spine with my bare hands. And after I kill you, I'll wait until I'm invited inside the city by terrified, cowardly clergymen. Once invited, the barrier will fall and that'll signal the end of your bastard divine offspring," The demon raised a hand gesturing his army forward.

You failed again. My son is still alive. The hybrid crouched adopting an Esper battle stance, allowing the alien warrior skill to dominate his essence.

Molec shook his massive head. "All in due time. The battle is not yet over. But your role soon will be once I kill you.

Are you gonna talk me to death? Put up or shut up! I'm gonna snap your neck like a stale breadstick, demon, and then slice your head

clean off and let the Pope mount it on a pole high on the city walls.
Any other evil sick bastard with bright ideas toward violence will sim-
ply have to look up at your withered skull and instantly know what a
foolish endeavor attacking here would be and the price to be paid for
such folly.

Erik raised his weapon, ready to unleash all the power at his command. The sky overhead crackled with thunder and his mind willed the agitated electrons in the upper atmosphere. Erik's skin tingled and he felt a powerful presence materialize behind him. Molec stopped his advance and his forces cautiously retreated.

"You have no cause to interfere, angel. This is not an ethereal affair!" Molec took another cautious step back.

Erik turned to see Michael and several dozen ethereal soldiers garbed in white armor with ivory white weapons. He nodded once and turned back to face the archdemon.

Michael's laugh was a silvery, mocking cascade dominating the battlefield. The voice came from behind him, above him and even seemed to emanate behind the enemy army. "After so many centuries, you finally crawl out from under your rock. In your haste to kill the child, you have brought us into the conflict by attacking this oasis."

Molec laughed. "I didn't attack. A human established the blockade. The forces here simply enforced it. No demonic entity entered the city uninvited and no demon hunts the child. Mere humans are doing all the dirty work. As it was with the Son so it shall be with the child. He will die by free human hands."

The archangel crossed his arms. With two wing beats he was beside Erik. "You initiated the Soul Bounty on the chosen vessel. You brought forth an army to attack the child. You brought forth a wraith inside the holy city to attack and kill. You're the cause of many human deaths and you stole the Ruby Crucifix." Michael pointed his lethal ivory sword toward Molec. The weapon glowed white hot. "Plus you've decimated the entire city of Rome and slaughtered hundreds with this rampant attack! Your guilt has already been determined, archdemon of Hell. You're stained with the blood of innocents. As for your ludicrous analogy of humans with free will acting on their own volition, need I remind you that the humans you refer to are under your direct control with no free will? They carry out your orders and desires as mere automatons. That is a violation and you do know it." The powerful archangel gestured out toward the ruined city littered with corpses. "Killing innocents and letting demonic forces run rampant is also in violation of the original pact between Heaven and Hell after the great war." Michael stood silent, but the rage in his voice shook the earth with its powerful tenor.

"Save your outrage, angel. Mankind has slaughtered and shed more blood than I ever could here. Your pathetic tirade is laughable." He pointed toward the hybrid. "You unleashed your own weapon of destruction upon me and upon Lucifer. This silver puppet and his aging ape meddled in affairs forbidden to humans. The fact that you allowed the vessel to be born is also contrary to the original laws set down by your boss. The Soul Market: destroyed. The leader of the Space Mariners, a hostage for ten thousand years: freed by your puppet. You know the species will spread throughout the cosmos again, spreading His word to other space faring life forms." Molec pointed back toward Michael, flames spewing out his nostrils. "The Mariners lost their war and you had no right to set this half breed abomination upon the space port, let alone have him free the leader of a defeated army."

The archangel shook his head. "Had Lucifer not acquired human souls illegally the interference would not have been necessary. Had you not used the Mariner to attack the hybrid, he would not have had to defend himself." Powerful biceps flexed on the archangel's arms. "I grow weary of talk. I've come to dispose of you once and for all."

Molec laughed. "I have the relic and I will have it sent to oblivion where you will never find it. Do we fight with armies, or will you allow me to crush this half breed, silver plated minion?"

Michael stepped back. "You may engage the Esper in combat." The angel glanced over at the angered hybrid. "Though you may regret it." He gestured toward his forces. "Stand down for now. Let the hybrid and the archdemon settle their differences."

The two combatants circled, weapons whistling through the air. Molec lunged forward, the burning blade rushing toward the hybrid's head. The silver warrior easily ducked the blow and thrust under the demon's attack. The Esper blade bit into black stony flesh. The silver warrior charged, swinging the weapon up in a circular motion, smashing the lethal edge down to decapitate his foe. Molec shifted slightly and the weapon's blade missed the neck, slicing clean through one of the demon's heavy horns.

The archdemon glanced at the severed horn, eyes burning with fury. The demon charged, roaring and breathing fire. He raised the great burning scimitar over his and swung the weapon down, lumberjack fashion, to cleave his opponent's skull. The weapon shrieked, hissing through the air. The hybrid retreated, catching the falling blade with the hooked edge of his alien weapon. Demonic and ethereal metals clashed, multicolored sparks bathed both combatants as each weapon shrieked in anger and protest. The staff growled, vibrating angrily in its master's hand. Erik twisted the hook, stressing the captured blade and forced the weapon down. He spun his body launching a hard kick into Molec's unprotected face. The sheer power of the blow forced the demon lord back several feet falling flat on his back.

Erik pointed his weapon and tensed powerful muscles. Bioelectric power raced through this body into the staff, blasting forward in a beam of burning plasma. The radiant energy tore into the fallen demon, scorching and searing his armored stone flesh. Erik increased the blast intensity as he charged forward. He leapt the last few feet, raised his weapon and swung down on Molec hoping to disembowel the demon with one strike. Molec raised his blade in a dual handed grip, forming a desperate last-second defense. The demonic weapon and the alien metal crashed again, blocking the attack. The Sentient Staff whined, angered. It generated more internal power. Heavy jagged arcs of energy leapt from the heavy Esper weapon as it pushed harder against the demonic steel. Molec pushed up harder, desperately, to keep the Esper weapon at bay. Erik added more of his own strength leaning forward and pushing down with powerful muscles. Slowly the heavy devil blade fell, inch by inch. Aqua blue arcs of energy struck the archdemon, causing him to gasp in pain. Erik rapidly pulled the weapon back. The staff screamed in protest. Molec's sword, now free of the down force, arced into the ground, driven by Molec's own strength and momentum. Erik spun the Ahn-so-lak in a fluid motion overhead and slammed the shrieking blade down on Molec's now unprotected shoulder. The blade sliced cleanly through the demonic flesh, shattering bone and severing muscle tissue. Greenish yellow blood sprayed from the gaping wound. Erik forced the blade edge back, sawing deeper into the soft inner flesh severing more heavy bone and tendon. Molec's blade shrieked as it sliced across the hybrid's unprotected left quadriceps carving a deep six-inch cut. Blood spilled from the wound, cascading down his leg. Erik felt a bout of nausea and weakness but it passed quickly.

He took a step back out of the scimitar's reach. The demon blade could react and attack on its own volition, guiding its wielder's hand. *I'll need to watch that.* He blasted the fallen archdemon with another energy blast. Molec rose to his feet, his stony flesh smoking. Ichor still flowed from the gaping wound. Erik could see the exposed shattered bone move as the archdemon forced his crippled arm to function despite the pain. The remaining horn on top of his head glowed bright red. A searing beam slammed into Erik, knocking him off his feet. Armored chrome flesh on his left pectoral muscle was blackened and blistered. His mind reeled from searing pain. Another lance of ruby energy hit him square in the stomach, burning and scalding his flesh.

Erik focused his will and launched a plasma salvo, striking his adversary in the chest. Ebony flesh smoked and the air smelled like burnt sulfur and brimstone.

You cannot win a battle trading blows at a distance. You must attack! Jakor's voice echoed inside Erik's mind. *Attack! Use the skills I've given you. The archdemon's blood beam will keep burning away your flesh while his wraith blade leeches away your power! Soon you'll have no reserves left to heal.*

Erik took a deep breath, lifted his weapon, and surrendered to the skills of his Esper counterpart, allowing the Esper warrior to fully dominate his essence. His body crackled with more ambient energy. The wound on his leg healed. Overhead, the elements gathered as agitated electrons collected inside gathering thunderclouds. A blue nimbus of power surrounded him. He made a slight gesture toward Molec. A searing bolt of lightning crackled from outstretched fingertips. Thunder exploded as the jagged lances slammed into Molec's body. The hybrid rushed forward, swinging his Esper weapon with blinding speed. The sharp edge sliced several deep gashes through Molec's chest and stomach. The burning scimitar retaliated in Molec's grip, thrusting forward, slicing through the air. Erik caught Molec's sword arm. He dropped his staff, taking the bulky arm in both hands smashing the demon's elbow joint against his thigh. The crack of shattered bone dominated the air. Molec screamed in agony, spewing demonic fire thirty feet into the sky. The blade dropped from his grip, clanging on a heavy blood-coated cement slab. Erik smashed his foot down upon the weapon, snapping the blade in half, crushing the concrete. A banshee wail rose up and a cloud of emerald vapor swirled, dissipating in the wind.

Erik unleashed an Esper combination of strikes. His blows sparked against the demon's hide, each impact drove it farther back. Esper combat movements mimicked reptiles and serpents, blinding open hand strikes and rapid slashing combinations quickly followed by a single power blow. The alien combat tactics were brutal and savage—far more lethal than any human martial art. Molec dropped to one knee, arms dangling useless by his side. *Now I do this my way!!* Erik unleashed a powerful uppercut, his fist smashing under the demon's chin. The force of the blow launched the stunned archdemon fifty feet into the air, landing a hundred feet away. Molec's impact caved in the surrounding asphalt, swallowing him in a deep crater. Erik pointed skyward, a heavy lightning bolt thicker than a tree trunk struck the crater, blasting flaming chunks of asphalt into air and surrounding battlefield. The accompanying thunderclap shook all of Rome and caused combatants on both sides to flinch momentarily.

I'm gonna make you wish you stayed in Hell!!! The battle-enraged hybrid leapt into the crater. His feet slammed against the stunned demon's chest shattering its ribcage. Molec's body tensed as he cried out in pain. A fountain of gore and fire erupted from his mouth. The silver warrior perched upon his larger foe, raining down super-powered punches. Each strike shattered the stony demonic flesh. The hybrid raised both fists over his head. He hissed savagely into the dark sky. Thunder shook the entire city as both fists slammed down upon the archdemon. The shockwave from the titanic blow created a large dust cloud, lifting chunks of brick, asphalt and other debris. The stunned demon coughed great fountains of yellow blood and gore. A pool of greenish ichor flowed from its caved-in chest and open shoulder wound. Erik gathered all of his physical power and swung down on the demon lord with a vicious left hook. The punch shattered Molec's jaw sending several large teeth airborne. The demon lay completely still, broken and bloodied. Its once burning eyes now black and lifeless. They hybrid raised his hand for another punch ... *You wouldn't even feel it at this point and you're not worth another punch.*

Erik leapt from the large depression and picked up his staff. The broken saber had vanished. He looked over at the stunned demon army. He took an aggressive step forward and they all retreated. *That's what I thought, cowards, all of you.* He walked back toward the ethereal soldiers. Erik glanced back and saw several creatures dragging Molec out from the burning crater. To his shock, the archdemon still lived. A multi-legged creature tended to his wounds.

"Molec is immortal. You cannot kill him, but you have brought him as close to death as I've ever seen." Michael watched as their enemy was partially revitalized.

Is this the Ethereal War?

Michael laughed. "This is but a mild skirmish, foothills of a massive mountain. Raphael's and Gabriel's forces are gathered in wait. My soldiers are here, hidden awaiting my word to strike should the time come." The archangel placed a hand on Erik's chrome shoulder. "I sense Lucifer is close by with his army ready to do battle at a moment's notice. He watches in the Netherspace, waiting to see how this exquisite ballet unfolds." Michael smiled. "You fought well, hybrid. Worthy of the power bestowed upon you." He gestured back to the holy city. "This battle liberated the holy city and freed the chosen vessel and his mother. Your son is at the gates watching you. Your bride is there too."

Erik hissed. *They should be back in the White Room, hiding.*

Again, Michael laughed. "Your attacks on the dome have severely damaged several structures, the White Room included. I have an army of eyes on the chosen vessel. They are safe. Other forces are gathering the last of Molec's human army. The boy is more than able to protect himself and his mother now. We must focus on the matter at hand." Michael pointed at Molec's forces. "Our enemy comes to parlay."

Molec's fire dimmed. The flaming aura surrounding the large demon seemed to sputter. The archdemon's wounds had been healed, but not completely. His regenerated flesh was off color and he walked with a decided limp. He held a large burning emerald long sword similar in nature to the weapon Erik destroyed earlier.

"Let's go talk to our foe." Michael advanced.

Erik followed close behind. His powerful staff ready to unload a titanic blast of energy at the slightest hint of aggression.

Michael stopped several paces from Molec. The archdemon had to step back, and his army retreated several steps. The angel's aura was so powerful that even his mere presence was disturbing and uncomfortable. "Speak your mind, Molec, quickly."

"I am willing to bargain, angel. This battle gains us nothing."

Michael glanced toward the sky, his nod almost imperceptible. "Especially after the beating you endured."

Molec frowned, glaring toward Erik. "The hybrid is full of surprises. Yet I still stand."

Michael shook his head. "You fought, were defeated, and now wish to bargain? You have gall, demon. I grant you that. But it has been agreed upon. What is your proposition?"

"I will give you the holy relic and I will spare the child's life if you give me sovereignty over Hell. Otherwise I'll see that the Ruby Crucifix disappears forever, lost in the Multiverse where it will take, even you, thousands of years to find it. There are no more Esper bloodhounds in the Multiverse, just the one here, and you've used him up." Molec pointed toward

Erik, laughing. "You're a stooge, hybrid, blinded by some false sense of loyalty to 'Good'. But you're wrong, Esper. There is no Good or Evil. There is only the war and the battle for worlds in the Multiverse. You believe you fight for a cause but you're no more than a puppet, a plaything." Molec pointed toward Michael. "In the end, you will be betrayed and regret your choice."

"Silence, hell spawn!" Michael snapped, clearly annoyed at the accusation.

The relic is still here, on this world, burning through his containment orb. Martin and I have been close to it. EJ is safe behind those walls and I can sense my wife is safe, too. We can recover the relic once the sphere dissolves. They can't touch it. We take him out now and his own forces will betray him. If you let him go, he'll keep plaguing this world and others in his quest to rule Hell. Erik forced the thoughts toward Michael.

It is a fool's bargain. Molec is buying time for something, stalling and trying to build discourse. The angel dipped his head slightly.

Erik's danger sense triggered. He studied the army facing them. Ten huge demons joined hands at the back of their army. Twenty massive horns burned a purple so hot it was almost white. Erik's mind shrieked out a warning. *They're gonna attack, take cover!* He dove, tackling Michael to the ground. Twenty lances of burning power tore through the space where they stood heartbeats earlier. Erik and the archangel came to their feet. The Ethereal soldier was enraged. He gestured toward the attacking forces and three of the massive creatures vaporized. "I owe you one. Take the archdemon. I will personally tear the location of our relic from his mind!"

Molec launched a savage blast of demonic fire. Erik avoided the blast but it struck Michael dead on. The archangel stumbled back, screaming in anger more than agony. Erik tensed his arm and launched a bio electric blast toward the attacking demon. The burning blue orb exploded against dark onyx flesh, charring and incinerating the demon's freshly healed, rock hard skin. Molec was forced to retreat. Erik unleashed a second burning salvo that caught the demon square in the chest. Molec shouted in rage and pain. Fire shot from his mouth and nostrils as his chest smoked from the burning plasma.

Erik hefted his Esper weapon as all around him, demonic and ethereal forces collided. The sounds weren't human, more like an orchestra of stringed instruments playing badly out of tune. He had to block out the eerie noise of ethereal combat. Molec stood in the center of the battle directing his army, unchallenged. Erik looked up to the sky. *ANARAH KONNAR ANKOLAH!!!*

A jagged arc of power rained down from the sky, striking the archdemon dead on. Molec shrieked as millions of volts of energy charred and seared his flesh. The hybrid charged, swinging his Esper weapon in rapid arcs. He leapt twenty feet and slammed the edged blade down upon the stunned, smoking nine-foot demon. Edged metal bit through onyx flesh, slicing a deep nine inch wound. A river of chartreuse ichor hemorrhaged from the open gash.

Molec turned and made a feeble thrust with his straight blade. Erik easily avoided the blow and kicked the demon hard in the ribcage. Chrome-armored flesh crushed the weaker stone, fracturing several bones beneath. Erik was wary of the demon sword and reacted when it attacked of its own volition. He slammed the blade into the ground and kicked it forcefully from Molec's grip. The archdemon cried out for help and three twenty-foot monstrosities fired their own beam weapons. Erik was hard-pressed to avoid all the incoming fire and winced as one beam seared his upper back and shoulder. He executed several one-armed cartwheels, avoiding the follow up blasts, then returned fire with a volley of burning plasma from the staff's organic power reserves. Two of the attacking demons fell while the third turned to flee. As the demon spun, it was eviscerated by a slender ivory weapon. An ethereal soldier covered in greenish and yellow ichor pulled the weapon free and with a precise slice, decapitated the wounded giant. "Take down the leader again and the rest will fall. Molec is your responsibility, Esper." The soldier held up its bloodied weapon and flew off to engage more demonic forces.

Erik felt a searing burst of pain. Something struck his back, pushing him forward. He stumbled, falling face first into the ground. A burning agony tore through his body as something pierced his shoulder and erupted through his chest. His eyelids fluttered, limbs went numb as his very life force flowed toward the blade and away from his body.

"Die!" Molec shrieked as he slammed his large foot down, driving Erik's head deep into the ground. Molec stomped down with massive, hoofed cloven feet again and again, smashing Erik's back and partially exposed skull. The archdemon drove his sword deeper into the wound, twisting the demonic blade, opening up a larger hole. He rained blow upon blow against his stunned opponent.

The intense pain kept Erik from totally blacking out! *YOU MUST ATTACK!* Jakor's voice rang in his head over the pain and agony. *Take out his shins and kneecaps, do it now!* Jakor urged. *While you still retain some strength. The sword is sapping your life force. You are not immortal. You will die if this continues!*

Erik gathered his remaining strength, ignoring the agony of his wound. He forced himself to turn his head, and look up. Molec was ready to pierce his heart with the next blow. The hybrid brought his leg back and extended it with all of his remaining strength. His foot slammed into the demon's knee, crushing it and shattering the surrounding bones. The large leg folded in half. Heavy flesh tore as severed, fractured bone pierced the softer inner tissue. Molec toppled over, flailing in abject agony. The green battle blade dropped to the bloody pavement. The hybrid stood, blood spilling from the gaping hole in his chest and shoulder. He extended his hand and once again, his staff was in his possession. The hybrid's eyes burned. Blue fire radiated an aura around chrome flesh. *Club!* The staff took the shape of a massive, spiked club. With his good arm, he swung down upon the demon's head, fracturing the skull and breaking off the other massive horn. *This is for my son who you wanted to kill!* The club smashed down again with a sickening crunch. *And my wife because you sent that ghoul to rape and slaughter her!* Another blow impacted, breaking the archdemon's arm and crushing a shoulder socket. The sword tried to counterattack, but he stomped the weapon into the ground, pinning it immobile with his foot. *This is for Martin's son!* The club smashed Molec's face, popping an eyeball and crushing the socket. Erik paused, looked up to the sky. *And this, this is from me! ANKO-LAH!!!!!* Thunder shook the landscape and a bolt of power slammed into the archdemon. Erik was in an angered frenzy as he unleashed another titanic blast that shook the Earth. The sky blackened overhead as bolt after bolt rained down upon the helpless demon. Molec's flesh glow red, nearly melting from the intense bombardment. The ground around the combatants morphed to an inferno of yellow flame and liquefied asphalt. The angered Esper warrior picked up his near-dead adversary, gripping the helpless giant in his wounded arm. The fingers on his good arm tensed. Three-inch razor sharp claws extended. *I was told you're immortal and can't die. Let's see how close to death I can get you.* He slashed four deep lacerations down the demon's entire torso. The superheated armor was soft and pliable, easily cut by the sharp claws. Miraculously, Molec still lived. The demon's one good eye opened wide as his burning flesh was filleted. He flailed wildly in a desperate attempt to escape. The battle-raged warrior slammed his adversary face-first into the molten muck. Before he could unleash another blow, the crippled demon vanished.

It's over. There is no more need for vengeance of further bloodshed. Molec is vanquished. His army defeated and Rome is safe.

Michael's soothing voice echoed inside his head.

Erik turned. Three fearsome looking warriors, each twelve feet tall, lifted Molec from the ground. Erik allowed himself to relax momentarily. The demon army fell back. Three ethereal soldiers lay broken on the battlefield. Dozens of demonic corpses lay in a soup of dirt, dust, and greenish yellow blood. Erik sensed danger. He spun. There was no time to react. Molec's discarded demonic sword flew through the air under its own mystical force. The weapon cut clean through his chest and right lung, exploding out his back. Muffled hisses escaped his throat. Unbearable waves of agony tore through his body as the blade drank his essence. He desperately grasped the blade with both hands, pulling at the embedded weapon lodged in his torso. The razor sharp edge bit into his fingers as the blade sucked away his life.

Erik pulled with all his remaining strength, forcing the blade out of his body. Hungrily the sword continued to drink his power, growing stronger while he grew weaker. The hybrid stumbled, dizzy and weak. The world seemed to spin and go dark. The demonic sword struggled in his grip, a writhing angry serpent. The blade was enveloped in white. It shrieked in agony, vaporized into a harmless mist. Erik coughed. A fountain of blood vomited from his mouth, covering his chest, as he struggled to breathe.

Two strong hands held him. "Easy hybrid. The blade is gone, focus your remaining energy. Heal your wound as best you can."

Erik focused on healing. He closed his eyes, willing the last fragments of energy to seal the damaged blood vessels in his lungs. He felt his body change, shrinking back to human form as the last of his reserves failed. He fell to his knees, coughing up great chunks of dried blood and mucus. He took a large breath through the pain of multiple battle wounds. He stood, wearing only a black spandex undergarment. His body was littered with deep purple scars and open wounds. Blood still flowed from his back and shoulder, and continued to leak from his nose, but he was alive.

"How bad?" Michael reached out an arm for support.

Erik shivered. The cold was unbearable. "I'll live, I think, but I'm done. It'll take time to heal now. I'm freezing, I can't stop shivering. This cold is unlike anything I've ever felt before."

Michael held out his hand. A white blanket materialized. He gently draped it over Erik's battered body. "This will help. The chill you feel will subside. It's the side effect of a demonic attack. You will recover in time." His angelic face grew solemn. "Wraith blades are nasty weapons. How Molec could acquire such things will need to be investigated."

Erik pulled the blanket around himself to ward off the chill. The cold, however, wasn't elemental. It was spiritual, internal in nature. Erik heard a soft whimper. He held out his hand and his staff settled into his grip. The weapon morphed into a heavy walking cane, sensing its master's immediate need.

Michael pointed. "You have visitors."

"Daddy!"

Erik's heart leapt. "EJ!" His son approached with Shanda one step behind. EJ ran into his father's arms and Erik held his son, weeping tears of joy. "Oh my son, thank God you're okay." Ignoring the pain, he hefted the child up and held him close. Shanda stopped mid stride, she gaped at her husband's bloodied and battered body.

She broke into tears. "Oh my God. What happened to you baby?"

Erik reached for her. She ran into his outstretched arm crying. "It's okay, angel. I'll be fine. The ugliness is almost over now." Erik held his family in silence for several seconds, not wanting the moment to end. "I've missed you both so much."

"Erik?"

He looked up. Michael approached. The archangel nodded toward Shanda and EJ. "Molec's army has surrendered and I will personally pry the location of the Crucifix from his mind." The powerful angel looked over at EJ. "Your father is a great warrior and you, child, are brave beyond words, as are you, mother." He reached over and gently stroked Shanda's tear-stained cheek. "I am hoping further bloodshed can be avoided but I sense this isn't over yet."

Erik nodded. "Let me talk to Molec. Maybe I can wring it out of him. He tends to bluster a great deal. Maybe I can give you something you can use." He looked down at Shanda and EJ. "You guys wait here…"

"No!" Shanda's voice cracked. "I want to see that sonovabitch. I want to see the thing that wanted to hurt my son and give him a piece of my mind."

"Oh angel, no you don't."

Shanda shook her head. "Yes, Erik. I do."

"Molec is in shackles. The beatings you gave him broke his spirit. She will be in no danger. Our forces are in clear control here." *Confronting the source of her fear and anger may give her some closure and peace.* Michael softly projected. *I believe she will go whether you accompany her or not.* Michael grinned. *She is more fierce than Molec.*

"Don't brain banter behind my back! I know you two are chatting!"

The archangel laughed aloud and raised his hands in surrender. "This way, mother."

* * *

EJ's arms tightened around Erik's neck as they studied the imprisoned archdemon. Molec was bound in heavy white chains and manacles. The three burly guards never took their eyes off the prisoner. Whatever power had healed his wounds, faded. Broken bones protruded from his leg and shoulder again. The deep cuts he received during his combat with the hybrid covered his ruined body. The creature's one good eye studied them with little interest.

"Have you come to gloat, hybrid?"

Shanda jumped back, startled.

Erik took a painful step forward, placing EJ in his mother's arms. "I'm not here to gloat. I'm actually here to help you. The archangel is going to tear through your head to get the location of the relic. He'll turn your brain into a bowl of lime jello to get what he wants. You lost. Do the right thing and help set events back to normal and give him the location of the artifact. It's here on Earth burning through its ectoplasmic prison. We'll be able to track it soon without your help." He took another painful step forward. "Maybe God will have mercy on you if you show some contrition and actually help."

Molec laughed. He moved his arm straining against the shackles. "I see my blade got a good piece of you. They can all rot as far as I'm concerned. I have nothing to say."

Erik shook his head, then turned, leaning heavily on his staff. He looked toward Shanda, her eyes were riveted on the battered demon. She took two steps forward, looking up at the creature.

"I hope you burn in the deepest, foulest pit of Hell for what you've done. You'll never hurt my son, ever!" She spat on the ground by the demon's feet and turned away. "Let's get out of here. I want to go home and forget this ugly ordeal. She put her arm around Erik, holding him tight."

The sensation hit Erik as they walked back toward the ethereal force. His staff buzzed with alarm. Erik placed his family behind him and willed the staff to change back into the Ahn-so-lak. The ethereal soldiers sensed the presence and prepared for a confrontation.

The space several hundred yards from them opened. A large blood red portal deposited a tall lean man in a tuxedo amidst the bloodied battlefield. A large glowing orb hovered above his outstretched hand. He wore a wicked, self-satisfied smile, visible even at the distance separating him from Michael's forces.

"Molec can't give you the location of the relic, hybrid, because he no longer has it. I do." The silky dark voice echoed everywhere. Erik felt his stomach churn. It was the same voice he'd heard earlier in the parking lot after his battle against several demonic forces. That was the first time he'd encountered Michael. The staff cracked with raw energy, feeding a portion of the power into its master. Erik's body was still weak. He tried to transform but knew he needed more time to heal and regenerate. He'd have to rely solely on the staff and Michael to protect his family.

"Erik, my flesh is crawling. Who is that?"

Erik turned toward her. "Lucifer."

Shanda's face went pale and her jaw dropped. EJ clung to his mother tighter, trembling.

"Have you come for battle, brother. If so I stand ready to beat you again." Michael's voice trumpeted.

Lucifer laughed, casually strolling across the ruined roads and collapsed buildings that were once Rome. "Oh no, brother. Ethereal swords, fisticuffs, particle beams and the like I leave to the harsh, unsophisticated brutes. I choose to get what I want through wits, intellect, and cunning." He stopped several yards distant. "As I plan to demonstrate this very moment."

Molec shrieked in anger and outrage, struggling against the divine chains keeping him prisoner. "How? How did you get the relic?"

A puff of black smoke materialized by Molec's shoulder. Bartholomew appeared, perched upon the helpless prisoner. "I told him!" He gushed, mocking the captive. "I told him we were meeting and I acquired a human tracer to plant on you. It was easy enough to play you along, then get close enough to pat you on the back and stick the tracer in your thick ugly hide. The slender demon disappeared in a puff of smoke and reappeared perched on his other broad shoulder. Molec winced as the slender, pale demon ground his foot into the open shoulder wound. The sound of grinding bone permeated the air as did Molec's shrieks of pain. "I played upon your massive ego and you were so eager and stupid to make this move that you didn't think it through all the way. Now you pay the ultimate price."

One of the guards swatted the gloating demon and he sailed through the air, slamming into the ground several yards away. The pale demon disappeared in a puff of smoke, reappearing directly behind his employer. Molec hung his head, totally defeated.

Michael sighed, frustrated. "Give me one reason not to send you both back to Hell right now!"

Lucifer waved his other hand over the flaming orb. Inside was the Ruby Crucifix. "Congratulate me, brother, for I alone have created a trinary ectoplasmic sphere. Oh I know your little trinket will burn it away in a week or two, but for now your little Esper dog can't sense it and none of you can either. It is totally isolated." Lucifer's eyes fell upon the wounded hybrid. "You're not much of a threat to anyone right now are you? But you did beat Molec, I will give you that credit." The Prince of Darkness looked back toward the archangel. "Unlike your prisoner, I actually have the power to send this orb anywhere in the Multiverse. Perhaps I'll send it a trillion light years away to another dimension totally dominated by evil. You would need to wage war against an entire universe of horrors to recover your little trinket." Lucifer's eyes burned red and his tone became cold. "Or give me what I want."

Michael's grip on his ivory blade tightened and he walked toward the dark prince. "Why don't I just kill you now and take the orb. I can shatter it easily with one blow of my sword!" Michael raised the powerful weapon. The blade burned with white hot fire.

"I'll unleash my troops! We'll have the Ethereal War you so much wish to avoid!" Lucifer was visibly nervous. Blood red eyes never left the edge of the Michael's flaming ivory blade. "Remember the other planet that orbited this star, we fought there and the planet fell apart. God favors this blue rock among the other chunks of life in this universe. I don't think He wants it destroyed." Lucifer retreated a step. "My demands are few and most reasonable. Hear me out, brother."

Michael looked up to the sky, responding to some unseen voice. Erik's senses picked up on the mind-numbingly powerful sensation. His knees buckled.

"What's going on?" Shanda trembled.

"Michael is talking to the Father of all of us, Mommy." EJ looked at his father. "Can you hear him?"

"No son. I can sense His presence. Can you hear him?"

EJ nodded. "Yes, he wants Michael to listen to the terms. Michael will do as is told but he is upset."

Shanda shook her head. "I think I'm going to pass out. This is too unreal!"

Erik placed his arm around her. "We'll get through it. All the players have checked in now. Let's hope we can avoid an all-out war."

Michael lowered his weapon. "He will hear your petition."

Lucifer smiled a wicked grin, adjusted the bow tie on his white shirt, and paced back and forth through the filth and rubble. "Molec is mine. He's mine to torture and needle through all eternity."

Michael nodded. "I'd rather not have to deal with his filth. So be it."

"And..." Lucifer turned toward Erik. "You must pay for your insolence. You and your hairless baboon counterpart." Lucifer turned toward Michael. "Summon his partner."

Martin Denton materialized out of thin air. The agent was holding a radio and an assault rifle. He spoke into a headset. The old man paused, glanced around confused and nearly fell over with shock.

"What the Hell...." Denton studied the legion of ethereal soldiers. Michael and the large archdemon chained against a heavy white wall, under heavy guard. His jaw dropped and his radio fell from his grip. "Oh shit. Now what did I do?"

"Stand with your accomplice." Lucifer pointed towards Erik.

Martin raised his weapon. The glowing clip of ethereal rounds was visible. "You don't zap me somewhere unannounced and expect to just comply meekly." Denton's finger fell on the weapon's trigger. "Nice tux, but who the hell are you?"

"Stand by the hybrid, Agent Denton. Do as Lucifer requests."

The color drained from Martin's face and he slowly lowered his weapon. His head tilted as he regarded the human-looking male, then Michael, and back toward Erik.

"Welcome to the party, Counselor. It appears the devil's pissed off at us."

"Ya think? Who isn't pissed off at us right now?" Denton cautiously walked over to his friend. He studied Erik's battered and broken body. "Jesus Christ!" he gasped, "Ooops, sorry!" He glanced over at the archangel blushing, then back toward his friend. "What happened to you?"

Erik tilted his head, gesturing toward the onyx colored prisoner. "That's Molec. We exchanged pleasantries."

Denton looked over at the battered archdemon. "He's responsible for William's death and all the abject misery we've endured?"

Erik nodded slightly.

Denton took two steps forward, shocking everyone. "You bastard!" Thirty rounds of blessed trinuim bullets tore through Molec's weakened hide. He roared in agony as the alien holy metal burned through his tissue. The old man's hand still pulled the trigger as he wept openly and emptied the magazine.

Erik reached up and took the weapon. "It's okay, Counselor. Things aren't going to end well for our archdemon friend."

Martin turned, defiant, to face Michael, Lucifer, and the rest of the Ethereal forces.

Lucifer regarded the old man, rubbing his chin. "You are impudent, just like your half breed partner."

"Get on with it." Michael commanded.

"Armageddon's Son must return to the Ethereal Realm. Molec's interference caused his premature creation. Now that the nuisance is disposed of, there is no need for him." The devil pointed directly toward Erik. Fire danced around his fingertips. "And the hybrid shall be alone and walk this world alone as long as he lives. He shall never know happiness or fulfillment. When God erases all this from the memories of man, I want him to remember. I want him to feel the pain of loss, alone. I want him to suffer with an endless black hole in his heart, forever unfulfilled and unquenched. I want him to remember his wife and his son and his prior life and know all that he's lost and will never have again." Lucifer looked over at Michael, his eyes burning and face vindictive. "I want to drink of his misery, like a fine wine, and enjoy the taste of his agony as it slides down my gullet. I want him to dread and loathe each day so I can savor his torment." He pointed again toward Erik. "You've caused me undue pain, Esper warrior, and it's my intention to make you live a Hell on Earth. To show you I'm not completely without heart, your accomplice can share in your misery. He too will know the truth and carry the burden of the truth of his son's death. There will be no peace for you, Martin Denton. You will carry the burden of your lost child and never know a light heart as long as you live." Lucifer turned toward Michel. "That's the price for avoiding the Ethereal War and getting your precious trinket back."

Lucifer waved his hand and a massive portal opened several hundred yards distant. Michael responded and a white vortex split the sky and bathed the ground in a blinding white light. Forces on both sides were gathering. Erik clenched his staff, readying himself for combat, though deep inside he knew there was little he could do in his current physical state. *Staff, when I fall, protect EJ and Shanda ... do not let them come to harm.*

Michael pointed his blade toward Lucifer. "I will run you through before your army can get here and this time I'll see you're caged in Hell forever!"

Lucifer opened his hands and a flaming trident materialized. "Can you back up your words, brother? Let the battle for Earth commence. This time I will win."

NO!

The voice echoed from every surface louder than a thousand blaring trumpets. Young EJ Knight leapt from his mother's arms and bravely approached Lucifer. The child was bathed in an intense aura of white energy, his voice and demeanor not belonging to a child but to a young adult. "Put down your weapons! Call off your armies! I will leave freely, dark one. This vessel can be returned to the Father. The bonding of two souls can be undone. The pain caused by an unwilling break is torment enough for them to carry. You need not pleasure yourself in his misery, nor will you condemn him to solitude. He will, in all probability, walk the Earth alone going forward because his heart will be empty—not because you decree it but because he knew and lost his true love. The Father above agrees to these terms and will reset the conditions of this planet to a state prior to Molec's intrusion."

Lucifer nodded. "I was winning here. I will have my advantage back?"

Michael shook his head, angrily sheathing his blade. "It will be done as the Father decrees."

EJ made a slight hand gesture and the burning sphere broke from Lucifer's grasp and floated above his tiny hands. With a simple touch, the ectoplasmic barrier melted. The child held the Ruby Crucifix. He pointed toward Lucifer. "Go back to Hell and take your prize with you." Armageddon's Son looked up at the captured archdemon. "You have much to pay for, Molec. Eternal punishment is no less than you deserve. I would punish you myself for harming my mother and father, but I sense you will have enough pain and misery to last you all eternity. The world is well rid of you."

Molec glanced over at Erik. He laughed the laugh of one gone insane. "I go to my punishment, hybrid, but I'll laugh knowing you were sold out by your own allies. You followed all the rules, did all the right things, and you still got burned in the end. In my darkest hours as I'm filled with unbearable agony, that one thought will give me comfort—knowing you got screwed by your own forces." Molec laughed. "Your own son, the child you fought with your life to protect, just sold you out! I am redeemed. Light is just as corrupt as Dark and just as disloyal." Molec laughed as he was drawn toward a glowing red vortex and to the first hours of his eternal torment.

Shanda fell to her knees weeping. "EJ, my son, why? What are you doing?"

The young boy walked over and gently hugged her. "Please don't cry, Mommy. I had to say it. I didn't have a choice. If I didn't, you and Daddy would have died in the war. Everyone would have died. God told me so." EJ's voice was his own again. Shanda held her son, weeping uncontrollably.

"I can't let you go. You can't leave me and your father.

We're a family." She stared over at Erik, desperate. "Erik! Do something. Please, stop this! Don't let them rip us apart!"

Erik stumbled forward, leaning against his staff. He focused his internal power, forcing his body to change. The staff fed him energy but it wasn't enough. His internal cellular structure was too weak from the prior battles and the leeching sword's wounds. His body couldn't withstand the strain of a genetic transformation. Erik willed the staff to expand and he stood guard over his bride and son. He swung the weapon, shaking as he fought to keep his balance. "Stay back, don't touch her!" Erik looked down at his son. "EJ, don't do this. You're our child, please don't go back. We're your parents! You can stay here, son. I won't let them take you. I'll fight till my last breath."

Seven warriors approached, weapons raised. Erik lifted his staff, his body trembling with weakness. The staff crackled angrily. Arcs of power danced up and down the weapon's surface. "Don't make me attack you!" Erik leveled the weapon, struggling to hold it steady. "I will unload everything I have left. I'm not done yet! Don't come any closer! I'll kill to keep my son!"

Michael approached, his hands were raised. "You cannot stop what must be, hybrid."

"You wanna place money on that?"

Erik felt a gentle touch on his leg. "I have to leave, Daddy, and we have to honor our bargain. You can't fight this. I don't want to see you hurt anyone or get hurt. You can't fight God." EJ hugged his father, "I have to go now." The child's voice echoed everywhere, again the voice of a young adult.

Erik looked down at his son. The child's eyes were wet with tears. He lay down his weapon, knelt down, and hugged his son. "You're my son. How can I just let you go?"

EJ wiped away a tear. "Because you have to. In order to save everything and everybody, you have to let me go home."

Erik knew he couldn't fight. The deal was struck and he was too weak to do anything about it. Even in full warrior mode, he wasn't a match for the ethereal army. He lost. There was no working through it or finding a way around it. He was going to lose his wife and his son. "I'm going to miss you, son. You brought me nothing but happiness." He pointed toward

Shanda. She was weeping uncontrollably. "Your mom, too."

EJ touched Erik's cheek. His eyes glowed and the aura of white surrounded him. "Always be a superhero, father. It's not just your bravery and strength that make you special. It's your compassion. Never let that go. No matter how hard the road may get, never lose your compassion."

Shanda knelt down, struggling to control her tears. She wrapped her arms around them. "My special men, how am I supposed to go on? How can I just forget my life and my loves?" She looked at Erik. "I love you. I can't believe this is happening. I don't want a life without you. I don't want to forget us." She touched her chest. "My heart's breaking, hun. Why us?"

Erik wept. "I don't know. I'm so sorry. It wasn't supposed to end like this. I swear to you it wasn't. I started this to protect our family, not destroy it." Erik held her tight and she clung to him, desperate. "I love you so much, angel. I don't know how I'm going to go on."

"I'm sorry. But it's time for Mom to go home now."

EJ touched her head. "You won't remember any of this, mother. You'll be spared the pain. You were the best, and I will never forget you." Shanda's eyes fluttered and she fell into Erik unconscious. EJ touched her again and she vanished.

Erik screamed her name. He fell over on his knees, mourning the loss of his wife and the life they'd struggled to build.

EJ walked toward Michael. "I'm ready to go now." The child grew taller. Gossamer wings erupted from his back. A blinding white light radiated out from his body and he held the Ruby Crucifix close to his chest. The child transformed into an angel. "Goodbye father. I do love you. You will always be with me." EJ Knight disappeared inside a blinding flash of light.

Erik buckled over, weeping as his heart tore open. He looked over at Michael, eyes filled with anger and hurt. "You betrayed me!" Heaven's army stood around him, silent, as he began to pay the price for Earth avoiding an Ethereal War.

Martin walked to his friend's side, placing a comforting arm on his shoulder helping him to his feet. "Oh Erik, I don't know what to say. I'm so sorry. If I didn't push you to investigate William's murder..."

Erik's wounds had reopened. Blood flowed from the gashes in his chest and back. The hybrid placed a hand on his old friend's shoulder. "It's not your fault." His voice was a soft longing whisper. "I picked this fight and I was out of my league. Now I have to pay the price. I knew there'd be a cost, Martin. But I never imagined this … I can't go on without them. I have nothing now. The pain … it hurts so much."

Denton turned toward the Ethereals. "Is this God's justice?" He looked up to Heaven. "Is this your idea of rewarding someone for taking up your cause?" Tears flowed down the old man's face. "Take my life. Punish me if you need blood to balance the ledger, but not him." He pointed toward his friend. "I'm begging you, he's had enough hurt, enough loss already." Denton broke down. "His father, his mother; gone. He grew up in orphanages, passed off like some bad luggage. Don't take away the only source of love in his life. Don't take away his happiness!" Denton fell to his knees. "I'm begging you, God, don't hurt my friend like this. I love him like a father loves a son. Please don't do this."

"God is not without compassion, Martin Denton. He feels the pain of the hybrid's loss and he knows of your love for him. But there had to be a price to pay. Every soul on Earth or one man suffering for a lifetime. It wasn't a difficult choice to make. Even you must see that."

Denton frowned. "Not so easy if you're the one paying the price."

Michael looked over Denton's shoulder. Erik stared out into space, lost and desolate. A whimper escaped him. His staff seemed to be wailing a song of loss, reflecting his master's empty melancholy. "Sadly it is the strong that are chosen to carry the heaviest cross." Michael studied the powerfully muscled human. "And the hybrid is indeed strong. He has survived multiple demonic attacks, unholy weapons of all types, and still he lives. He stood up to the sentinels in the Soul Market and that is no small feat."

Martin nodded. "Yes, he's strong. But every man, no matter how strong, has a breaking point. You're pushing him to that end." Denton sighed, uneasy with the conversation, doing his best to keep his temper in check. A philosophical debate with an archangel required one to tread cautiously. "With all due respect to your kind, it seems like you made a bargain with the devil and someone else is paying the price. I don't see the justice. I don't see the goodness or the righteousness nor dare I say, holiness in this bargain." Denton shook his head sadly. "I know I'm just a mere human, but I'm calling a foul here. I am allowed to do that right? Free will and all?"

Michael glanced back at Erik. "Some men are born to suffer, old man, just as some are born to greatness. The hybrid was born and allowed to acquire great power to help keep order in this world and play his role in this crisis." Michael turned back to Denton. "Some men don't have free will." Michael's voice turned melancholy. "Molec changed the rules and upset the balance. Balance is now restored. Armageddon's Son is home and need not be born for several more centuries. Order is established and Molec has been abolished. The feelings of one human, even a hybrid human, are of no consequence in such cosmic affairs. Earth continues and humanity is allowed to go on." The powerful entity crossed his arms and it was clear he wearied of the conversation.

Denton read the tell but kept pushing, hoping to change the outcome. "You heard Molec's final words. You don't think he'll be hearing those same words for the rest of his life, that he won't be haunted by it. You sentenced him to a lifetime of torment. My life is almost over, but his isn't. He'll be carrying these scars for decades. His own son betrayed him, Michael. A father doesn't ever get over that hurt. You betrayed him!" Denton raised his voice and Michael's powerful back stiffened. He knew he'd finally struck a nerve.

The angel pointed, his face lined with fury and his eyes slits of anger. "Out of respect for the hybrid, I've tolerated your nuisance. I grieve that your son has passed but know he is in a better place." Michael took a step forward. "You use puny human standards to judge events of titanic consequence. You know little of the universe, so don't presume to judge what you cannot even begin to fathom with your limited knowledge." Michael waved his hand in a shooing gesture. "Go home human, your part in this is done!"

* * *

Martin saw a flash of light and he found himself standing in his living room. His military gear had vanished and he wore a robe and slippers. Next to him was a large cup of coffee and a bagel. Denton sat down and took a sip from the mug. He sighed heavily. "My God, what have we done? What folly did we bring for that young man to deserve such a fate? At least I'm home and don't have to endure another transatlantic flight. My backside's already screaming in agony." Denton shook his head. "Erik, I hope you can pull off a miracle because I don't see a win here for either one of us." Denton looked up. "Have mercy on him, please. I know I have no right to ask it but I am. I'm begging you, have mercy on him."

* * *

Erik sat on the rubble of a destroyed building. The scope of the damage to Rome was incredible. Michael claimed his initial blast against the demonic dome leveled dozens of city blocks. Erik was thankful that the people fled prior to his attack. His lightning strikes had caused craters the size of football fields and the road where he had battled Molec was now a solidified puddle of molten goo fifty feet across.

The damage caused by the skirmish between ethereal forces had decimated even more of the great city. Rome was a post-apocalyptic wasteland. Michael approached. The battered detective looked up. "May I approach? I understand your anger and your hurt, hybrid. I do not wish to fight with you or fence words as I did with your partner earlier."

Erik nodded. "My anger, my hurt, and my pain are all one numb mess. I can barely hold my staff let alone pick a fight right now." Erik looked around at the ruined cityscape. "Speaking of messes, we made a big one here. How are you ever going to fix all this?"

Michael smiled. "He created the universe and all the matter therein, so fixing Rome won't be much of a challenge." The archangel turned serious. "Adjusting the timeline is a delicate task only done three times in the annals of cosmic history."

"I'm sure God will get it right." Erik sighed. "I just said that like it was mundane, God's going to fix it." Erik looked over at the angel. He placed his hands on his head. "I don't want this. I don't want these memories. I don't want this knowledge. I just want Shanda and my son." A tear rolled down his face. "Tell me, truthfully. Was he ever really my son?"

They watched in silence as ethereal troops were busy exorcizing Molec's demon army back to the underworld. Hisses, shrieks and unholy sounds filled the air as each hell soldier was consumed in a sea of purple flame. The archangel turned to face the human he'd betrayed. "I owe you the truth, Erik. It will hurt you more, but I owe you the truth." The archangel paused. "Or I can tell you a lie which will make you feel somewhat better and give you some false illusion of comfort. The punishment decrees you must remember what happened here and your role in it, even after we repair the timeline. I feel you deserve to know the total truth. But are you prepared to carry that awful burden?"

Erik wrapped the heavy white blanket tighter around his shoulder. Michael pointed to a large rock outcropping several yards away. "Let's sit over there, away from this unpleasantness." The two soldiers of Light paused, the sounds of shrieking demons still audible in between intermittent flashes of fire and eerie light.

"I hope it hurts."

Michael looked over. "Being banished back to Hell? Oh yes, it is a most painful experience. No sane demon or any sentient entity wants to go there. But there are parts that aren't the biblical seas of burning fire and agony. Lucifer, for all his evil and bluster, does serve a purpose. The Father doesn't like losing souls, but there are some entities in the universe that have souls unfit for anything but Hell. Therefore Lucifer serves a greater purpose and his hijinks are tolerated to some degree. But his punishment for starting the first war and ruining mankind is eternal damnation."

Erik raised an eyebrow. "A big price for making someone eat an apple."

Michael managed a smile and nodded. "There is a bit more to the story than is written."

The battered detective sighed. "There always is. Lucifer was correct though, the human race is going to hell on a rail. He doesn't have to do anything. We're doing it ourselves."

Michael nodded. "The game continues, Erik. All hope is not lost. There is still good in the world. Men like you and your stodgy, impudent friend, Mr. Denton, and women like Shanda give hope to the Father." The angel stiffened. "Now I must answer your question truthfully."

Erik tensed. "Your words portend unpleasantness."

Michael folded his hands. "He was never intended to be your son. We had planned this conception after you had been transformed, battling the Seelak. You had become powerful, and we needed a being with your kind of power to father and protect the essence of the holy vessel as it developed. The genetics in your human/Esper DNA was the perfect defense mechanism. The vessel would be able to defend itself if, for some reason, you fell. We needed your unique genetics and the choice was made to allow the vessel to come into being through the act of conception between you and your wife."

Erik sighed. "But that personality, the child I held in my arms, the little boy we had before all this happened, that was EJ."

Michael nodded. "Yes, the soul of a child existed within the vessel and developed as the physical body grew. That was your son, a byproduct of the vessel's creation, existing to keep you and your wife fulfilled as the vessel grew in strength. That part of the being grew and developed more and more and became the entity you called EJ."

Erik felt his stomach twist. "My God. His soul was just a byproduct. An unwanted side effect of some holy biological experiment." The detective wept. "You used us both, like a cuckoo bird drops its own chick in another bird's nest. Shanda and I were the birds in the nest. The vessel was your chick."

Michael pursed his lips. "An uncomfortable analogy, but accurate. You must understand, Erik. Your son's soul exists now, in a better place. The vessel is home and Molec's tampering has been stopped. I must also tell you that this wasn't the first attempt on the vessel."

Erik raised an eyebrow. "What?"

Michael shifted his position. "The Observers."

"The Observers wanted my son?"

Michael shook his head. "No, Molec had managed to control Colonel Ross. The demon used his powers and influence to push Ross through the ranks faster than normal progression and landed him the plum position at Area 51. Molec knew the vessel had been born and used Ross' position to gain access to the child. Molec also wanted to wreak havoc on this planet by instigating an interstellar conflict, which is forbidden."

Erik narrowed his gaze, remembering. "Ross wanted to study EJ, to clone him and make an army."

"That was what Ross intended," said Michael. "Molec used him and had he been able to get the child into his labs, he would have had the child butchered, but your Esper genetics gave EJ the means to defend himself even as an infant. The child called out to you, his father. He called out to you and you heard. You protected the vessel as God ordained and followed through with your destiny. After you defeated the Observer drones and recovered your son, Molec fled and abandoned Ross. The human officer once again had control of his faculties. He couldn't bear the guilt nor even comprehend what was done to him or why. In the end, he took his life. Without Molec's influence, he was simply an empty shell, corrupted and tainted by evil."

Erik shook his head sadly. "Did you know my mother's soul was there? Anderson didn't come right out and say it, but I got the feeling you knew she was there."

"We knew her soul was missing. We suspected Lucifer had it in the Soul Market but we had no jurisdiction there. Having you and your colleague there to chase Molec and push him gave us the wedge and the excuse to snoop. We knew if your mother was there, you would sense her presence. A child will always know when his parents are near." Michael placed a hand on Erik's shoulder. "But I assure you, we had no idea what was being done to the souls. Had we known, I would have personally led my forces to overturn the marketplace. He would have suspended the rules to free the innocents."

Erik ran his fingers through his hair. "My entire life, I've been a puppet. The only real thing I had was Shanda, and now she's gone. I'd rather be dead than have to carry all this with me."

Michael sighed. "The exact intent of Lucifer's punishment. He knew exactly how to torture you. Physical pain and normal human weakness wouldn't impact you, but the loss of your life and what you hold dear would cause you great agony." The archangel shook his head. "My fallen brother is a vindictive bastard as much as he is twisted and evil. I confess, I didn't anticipate Lucifer's interference nor did I expect to have you bear the brunt of our campaign to clean up Molec's and Lucifer's long-standing feud."

Erik turned to face Michael. "But you had no problem using me like a pawn these past years and now destroying my life."

Michael winced. "Again, we did what needed to be done for the greater good and the salvation of this world. For what it's worth I do regret that you, alone, have to bear the burden. I did not want that. I cannot apologize for you fulfilling God's destiny. These were unusual and dangerous times and drastic measures had to be taken. In the end, Earth is safe and despite my brother's meddling and mankind's slipping into the sewer of depravity, there is still hope. Where there is hope, there is God. Light will triumph as is foretold in scriptures." Michael stood up. "I have given you the truth, hybrid. There is nothing more to be said. I must now send you to your life so this timeline can be reset. The holy men inside Vatican City will also know the truth of what happened. You are one of Light's greatest warriors and will be heralded as such. It has been an honor battling by your side." The archangel extended his hand. Erik reached forward knowing what was about to happen.

"Good luck, Michael. Look after my son and please tell him his father will never forget him."

Michael nodded. "You have my word."

They clasped hands and Erik vanished.

Chapter 11: The Hollow Man

Dawkens' Gym. Milford, MA

Martin Denton was nervous as he walked into the facility. He'd been here dozens of times before but this was the first time since the Ethereals "fixed" things. He'd reached out to his young friend several times but Erik never responded. Two months had gone by; dozens of phone calls and e-mails unanswered. Martin realized he needed to visit his friend in person.

"Mr. Denton!"

Martin turned. "Alissa, how are you?"

The young woman ran over and gave Martin a warm embrace. "I was going to call you this evening. I'm so glad you're here."

Martin smiled as the young woman escorted him to a table at the juice bar. "I've been trying to get a hold of Erik for weeks and he's been excellent at avoiding my calls."

Her face grew solemn. "He's like a hollow man, Mr. Denton. He comes to work, teaches his classes, then hides in his office till well past closing and then lifts enormous amounts of weights and exercises like a madman until well past midnight. I don't think he's been back to his apartment since you both returned from investigating your son's murder. I can only sense that he's in great turmoil. The pain is intense but he won't talk about it. I confronted him last week, asked him what happened and that I could sense his hurt. He told me I wouldn't be able to help and I could never understand and he hoped I never would."

His apartment? Denton remembered the work being done on Erik's house. The old man wondered what kind of changes his young friend discovered upon his forced alternate reality. "Is he back in his office now?"

Alissa nodded. "Yes, he hides back there between appointments and classes. Mr. Denton, I listened by his door a few times and I heard him crying. He kept saying the words 'Shanda' and 'EJ' over and over again and how much he misses them. When he left to teach a class I found a small picture of a woman with wild purple hair holding a small child on his desk. The picture was worn and creased, like he'd been carrying it on his person for some time. Do you know who they are? I've known Erik for years and I've never heard the names before."

Denton sighed. "I don't know," he lied smoothly, "but I promise I will go talk to him and see what I can do to break him out of his funk."

"Please do," she pleaded. "I'm really worried about him. He's been in moods, but never this bad or this long."

Martin walked down the narrow hallway toward Erik's office. He was nervous and felt a pit form in his stomach. He wondered what he'd find behind the door. He gently knocked. "Erik, it's me, Martin. Can I come in, please?"

"The door's open, Counselor, come on in."

Martin opened the door and was shocked by his friend's appearance. "A beard and moustache, well that's different."

Erik pointed toward the chair on the other side of his desk. "Have a seat. A lot of things are different." Erik reached behind to a small table. "Can I pour you a cup of coffee?"

Martin nodded. "Please."

Erik poured. "I'm sorry, Counselor, I should have returned your calls. I've been in brooding and self-pity mode for several weeks now. There are some drastic changes, starting with my home ... well, not actually having my home anymore." Erik sat back down and raised his mug in a toast. "To the one friend who I can talk to about this crazy shit." They clinked their mugs and sipped the hot beverage.

"What happened after I got zapped back here?"

Erik laughed. "I got the whole truth about me. This was a preplanned setup dating back to the Observer invasion, which, by the way, was caused by Molec."

Denton nearly choked. "Good Lord, how deep in bed are we with these ethereals and demons?"

"The relationship runs deep, Counselor, deep enough that they feel free to mess with my life, Shanda's life, and give us a phantom son to raise for their own purposes. Beyond that, I really don't want to think about it anymore. I've been pondering the universe, the multiverse, Heaven, Hell and whatever may lay in between for six weeks now and I'm no closer to understanding any of it, so I choose to just leave it be."

Dentin nodded. "Amen. And yes that was meant to be sarcastic." He leaned forward. "Erik, what exactly has changed in your life besides the obvious we both already know?"

Erik's eyes widened and he sighed deeply. "I still live in my apartment in back of what was once Madame's Restaurant. I'm loaded with cash. Apparently I haven't spent much of my sign on bonus or the bonus I got for ending the Observer conflict. I still drive my black coupe and deposited most of my firm paychecks for the last four years. In this timeline, you guys never laid me off because Shanda and I were never a couple and EJ never existed. The Observer war still happened but was solely about Gray's abduction. As far as the gym goes, Alissa still knows the firm is bankrolling us but nothing there has changed except that you dumped it on me as a training center for new recruits. It's just like Shanda was wiped out of my life and I just went on living like I was single." Erik tilted his head. "Which I am, now."

"Nothing else is different?"

"Counselor, I think it's quite enough as it is, don't you?"

Denton sighed and nodded. "Yeah." He took another sip of his coffee. "Did you follow any of the headlines regarding Rome?"

"Yeah, a massive underground geological disturbance that devastated the city and cost hundreds of lives." Erik frowned. "I read it. He looked up toward Heaven. "Not the most original idea, no offense." The detective took another sip of his coffee. "I gottta level with you though, Martin."

"What?"

"I've been staking out Shanda's shop."

"Oh boy!" Denton cringed. "Did you make contact?"

"No, just watching." Tears streamed down his face. "Every time I see her, I feel it here." He pointed to his heart. "It hurts so much inside. The emptiness is more than I can take. I feel the shattered link in my head. This void won't ever fade. She had a place inside my mind and it was ripped away and now there's nothing." Erik sobbed. "Just a big empty space."

Denton sighed. "Alissa saw a picture of Shanda and EJ on your desk. How did you manage to keep a picture of them?"

"Alissa is too nosy for her own good. I kept a wallet-sized photo inside my staff so I'd always have them with me whenever I traveled. When I placed the weapon in my gun cabinet, the staff pushed the picture out for me, like it knew I needed a memento. I guess that was one detail that fell through the cracks. It's the one thing I have that links me back to my past."

"And keeps the torment fresh in your heart."

Erik nodded. "Yeah, that too."

"So what have you learned about Shanda?"

Erik raised an eyebrow.

Denton laughed. "Come on. I know you. You dug deep. I'm sure you have details of her life somewhere already."

"I do," Erik admitted.

"And…"

Erik stared at the floor. "And she got married back in 2014…to Carla her store manager." Erik took a moment as Martin digested the shocking news. "Carla's pregnant and they're expecting sometime next month."

"Invitro I assume."

Erik nodded. "Yeah. Charlie Gallagher gave me all the details. I'm happy for her. I admit I was a bit surprised, but Carla always was keen on her."

"I'm sorry Erik. I don't know what to say."

Erik drained his coffee cup. "There's not much to say, Counselor. I'm thirty-five years old. I've fought demons, archdemons, aliens, criminals and I've destroyed a fucking Soul Market. I lost my wife. I had a kid that really wasn't mine and I've battled alongside angels." Erik slammed his mug down. "And none it was worth a damn because everything I was fighting for was taken from me. Now I'm alone and miserable." He looked over at his friend. "Just like I'm supposed to be." Erik wiped away a stray tear. "When I first saw her, I figured I could rekindle our romance, show up, knowing her favorite flower, her favorite movie, her favorite food and all her quirks and literally sweep her off her feet. We'd have a whirlwind romance, some great passionate sex and then get remarried. I thought maybe we could start all over again." He looked away. "I didn't think she'd find happiness in the arms of her manager."

"I don't know what to say, Erik. Love transcends gender."

"I don't care about that, Martin. I'm beyond that shit. She doesn't even know I exist. I'm nothing to her! She's happy. I watched them together. They're genuinely happy. They laugh, they dance in the store, they giggle and hug carefree of the world around them. God we struggled so much and so much happened to us. Her life is simple and uncomplicated now and she's with the woman she loves all the time." Erik sobbed. "We barely had four hours a day together and we both worked like dogs to keep things going." Erik stood and paced. "I envy her, her happiness and at the same time I'm relieved that she doesn't remember the pain." Erik spun back. "I guess I'm jealous and my pride is hurt. She found happiness without me."

"Oh my friend, you can't think that way. She loved you. I know that was taken away, but you can't forget how you two felt about each other. I remember your wedding and the reception; how she looked in your eyes and how she melted into your arms while you danced. She loved you, son. She was happy with your life. Don't torture yourself like this."

"I need time, Counselor. I just need time to get my head around this."

"Okay! Take the time, take a trip, have a vacation, God knows you've earned one!"

Erik nodded. "Maybe I'll do that. I've been contemplating something but I'm going to need to reach out to a few people and call in a few favors."

"Well then do it. Let time heal you, or at least start the healing process."

* * *

Milford, MA. St. Michael's Church

Erik forced the lock on the front door of St, Michael's Church. It was one in the morning and darkness claimed the massive open space. A single light lit up a large marble crucifix. In the corner a massive bronze statue of the archangel Michael stood towering ten feet in height. Erik stopped to study the massive statue. It looked nothing at all like the real ethereal being. He bowed slightly toward the cross and nodded toward the statue, feeling ridiculous talking to inanimate objects.

"Hi. I know it's been several weeks, a little over eight weeks now. I'm doing the best I can given the circumstances, but I made a promise awhile back I need to keep. In order to keep that promise I need some help." Erik turned up the collar on his jacket. "I'm not gonna push the issue and say you owe me one but let's lay the cards out on the table. You guys kinda owe me more than one. I'm calling a chip in. I need a favor. Can you guys hear me?"

Erik waited, pacing back and forth, "I'm new to this so I'm not sure what the protocol is here. I know you can hear me." An hour passed, Erik stood stone still staring into the darkness, waiting. "Okay, let me rephrase this." He tensed his arm. A burning ball of blue plasma formed in his hand, lighting up the darkness. "The inside of this place is made of wood, plaster and a great deal of other flammable materials." He added more power to the burning orb. The energy expanded, basketball size, hovering inches above his open palm. "One plasma blast is all it would take to…"

"You have my attention, hybrid. Cease your blustering."

Erik felt the archangel's presence. His Esper powers were even stronger since his combat with Molec. With that power came an increased sense of confidence. Through his binding with Jakor's knowledge, he'd learned to focus his power even tighter and the bioelectric energy surged through his body, enhancing his already superhuman ability. "Glad you could finally make it."

"You spoke of a need." Michael folded his arms. "You have my attention."

Erik outlined his intent, and listed the allies he required to achieve his end. The archangel nodded intently, his eyes narrowing. Michael managed a grin. "It has been approved. I will make the arrangements." Michael vanished, his laughter echoed off the church walls.

Erik looked up at the cross, his body burning with raw unchecked power. "Thank you, God. I don't get hit and not hit back. I intend to make that cocky bastard pay, for everything."

* * *

The Soul Market

Erik felt eyes on him as he left the spaceport. It was rare such a large ship would berth and only a single passenger disembark. The destruction caused by his confrontation with the sentinels was gone. What power could repair such intense damage so quickly? The sky was the same off color and the spaceport still loomed large, towering and casting shadows over the smaller merchant buildings. He walked quietly through the market. The area had a festive quality. His attuned senses picked up on the darkness and he knew evil was still prevalent. Raphael's forces may have cleansed the market, but the roaches returned quickly. Erik walked the dizzying array of streets and narrow alleys. He eventually wound up by the vendor that originally held his mother's soul captive. He saw the merchant inside actively engaged with several customers.

He adjusted the dark glasses concealing his eyes and patted inside his heavy leather jacket, tapping the concealed sentient staff and the two Wilson Combat 45 caliber pistols loaded with divine trinium bullets. His right hand clung to a heavy black case. He could retrace his steps from here and find the store. "It should be up this road and around the next bend. Damn I should have paid better attention!" Erik moved quickly, doing his best to ignore the commotion and the heavy bargaining occurring all around him. Several beings approached him as he walked, offering him otherworldly trinkets. He calmly shook his head, moving constantly forward. He could sense her presence now through the psychic clutter and followed the signal as it grew stronger. Her sense of despair and hopelessness dominated the telekinetic connection.

Erik turned a corner and saw her chained and shackled. She struggled to move several heavy crates constantly under the scrutiny of a large squid-like being that balanced itself on two large tentacles. She dropped a crate and was instantly whipped by the being's hooked tentacle. The blow cracked against her silver flesh, flaying her skin, spilling a river of blood. He walked over in between them and picked up the heavy crate with one hand. The being struck out again. He dropped the box and caught the appendage in an iron grip.

"There's no need for this. I'll gladly move the crate in for you."

The alien gestured inside the shop and Erik carried the heavy crate inside, winking at the Esper female as he walked by. Erik placed the crate down and moved toward the counter area. Another being watched him intently.

"I assume you wish to conduct business. Nobody simply offers to help in the Soul Market." A green necklace glowed, translating a series of clicks into English.

Erik approached the counter. "I do. But I was more than happy to lend a hand." He pointed toward the Esper prisoner. "I'm interested in her."

Both beings laughed. "Our trophy? You cannot afford her. She is ours to torment and torture as we desire. We cannot avenge ourselves upon the Esper race, but we can take comfort making her extended life miserable."

Erik placed the black case on the counter and opened it slowly. Both beings gasped. "The horn of Molec!" They stared at him for a while, then stepped back in shock. "How did you acquire such a rarity? This is of immense value!"

Erik didn't answer. "I'm not interested in your beef with the Espers. I'm not interested in politics. What I am interested in is doing some business." He closed the case and took a step back. "The onyx material in this horn is said to be more valuable than diamonds on Earth. If you don't want it, I'll be on my way."

A third squid barred the door and produced a slave collar from a flesh pouch on its side. "Why buy it when we can take it and take you at the same time?" The squid lobbed the prison collar toward Erik. The object moaned and expanded as it raced toward his neck. Erik caught the object in midflight, stopping it dead. With little effort he crushed the alien metal. It shrieked in agony under the force of his grip. The object ceased shrilling and turned a flat grey color. Erik tossed it under his foot and slammed the ruined slavers necklace into the heavy stone tile with the sole of his boot.

"That wasn't very businesslike." He reached inside his

jacket, freeing a Wilson pistol. He spun and fired four rounds of heavy trinium bullets into the squid. It shrieked in agony and fell over dead. A pool of brown blood spread upon the stone floor. "Erik spun toward the other two. One of the squids had another slaver's collar. "I'll kill you before you can throw it."

The squid slowly placed the collar on the counter. Erik walked over, pistol still locked on its head and smashed the collar, crushing it and collapsing the heavy countertop. "I gave you a chance and a very lucrative offer and instead you chose to cheat. You broke the rules of the Soul Market. Maybe I should call security?"

"No, by all the Gods do not call security. We cannot withstand another mindless attack and bloodletting."

"Then give me the Esper." Erik raised his pistol, finger falling on the trigger, "Or I'll just kill you both and take her for your treachery."

They looked at each other. "Take her, hybrid. She is close to death anyway and of little use as a worker. She's also just a mere biological construct like you."

Erik tilted his head. "You know who I am?"

"Who else would have the horn of Molec but the being that defeated him in combat? You would be a great prize for us, but even you are not worth the trouble it would be to capture and keep you." The being pointed a tentacle toward the door, "You are the victor in this encounter. Take your prize and leave us. But be warned, she is bound here. The forces that control the market will not let her go as long as she has a collar on her. And her collar isn't a mere capture collar like the ones you destroyed."

Erik backed away slowly. "Let me worry about that." He backed out of the shop, holstered his gun and walked toward the frail Esper. She cringed as he approached.

I'm not going to hurt you, he projected to her. Eyes that held only misery looked up with a spark of life and hope.

You will help me? A soft voice caressed his mind.

Erik reached over and gently touched her filthy cheek. *Yes. You need to follow me.*

Erik gripped the manacles holding her captive. A shock went through his body. He ignored the pain and exerted his strength against the mystical bonds. With a groan, he snapped the chains and tore the manacle from her leg. He extended his hand, helping her up. She clung to him as they walked away toward the spaceport. She tensed and whimpered as they passed each merchant. Erik reassured her over and over. *No one will harm you.*

They approached the Spaceport. A massive wedge-shaped ship was surrounded by several aliens and demons brandishing weapons of some kind. Erik immediately sensed trouble. *Stay behind me.*

They know I cannot leave and have come to take me back. She looked at him sadly. *This collar will explode if I leave this place. It cannot be removed and I may never leave.*

They approached the crowd. Several demons pointed weapons at him. "Surrender your slave! She cannot leave and she is not yours to take. Your ship will not leave here until she is in our custody."

"I bargained for her fairly. By the rules of the Soul Market, she is mine." Erik's voice was iron.

"No payment was issued. We were told she was taken by force. Surrender yourself and your ship can leave. The two of you will be held and charged." The demon pointed to Erik. "You with thievery and murder and her for attempted escape."

Erik shook his head, frustrated. "Your squid friends tried to capture me, twice. They failed. In lieu of pressing charges, they gave her to me as payment. Our business was concluded. I'm leaving."

The demons laughed. "You are a delusional pissant. Who are you to defy the Soul Market?"

Erik's face turned to ice. He reached inside his jacket. "It's time." Erik freed his staff. "I AM THE WARRIOR!!!!" He shouted, challenging the devil himself. His cry rose above the sound of the busy port, echoing off hull metal and buildings. In two heartbeats he was no longer human.

The powerful hybrid stood facing the army. The demons and security forces fell back terrified.

"You! The Esper Warrior! You cannot battle all of us by yourself, hybrid. Will you unleash the sentinels again?"

I brought along some friends thus time, and they also have an axe to grind with you. Erik raised his voice to the sky, shouting an Esper war cry. Hundreds of flashes exploded in the reddish purple skyline. Dozens of massive whale-like Space Mariners, each over a hundred meters long, filled the sky, circling over-head like angry buzzards.

A dull whine broke the silence. Powerful weapons emerged from the titanic space cruiser. Angry yellow arcs of energy cracked as each weapon built up a charge. Erik raised his staff. His own aqua blue energy lit up the spaceport. *We will destroy this place or your own sentinels will do so during the ensuing battle. Who wants to die first? I'm in a killing mood right now. I've lost a great deal the last few months and I'm itching to unload my rage on someone. I promise you, I will destroy this place and I don't need their help to do it. They're just here to watch the fireworks and be back up.*

The demons lowered their weapons. "Hybrid, you would kill us all for one slave girl?"

She's my kin and she's not a slave. The hybrid reached over, touching the slavers necklace. With gentle force, two fingers crushed the necklace lock freeing her. The jewel on the shackle began to whine a high pitched harmonic. Everyone flinched, anticipating a massive explosion. He squeezed the gem, trap-ping it in his powerful fist. A dull thud made his hand shake and smoke escaped his grasp. The hybrid opened his hand and tossed the detonated shackle toward his adversaries. *Now she's truly free. You have two choices: face me and this place will be de-stroyed again or save your lives and your market. Let us leave. We'll be on our way and you have my promise I will never return.* Erik tossed the black case with Molec's horn. *Let me sweeten the deal!*

The larger demon approached the case, opened it and its jaw dropped, studying the contents. It looked up at the silver warrior. "The stories were true. You bested Molec in combat and prevented the Ethereal War on Earth." It picked up the case. "I accept your terms, but never return here. This place belongs to Lucifer and with your bargain you have no more sway here."

The hybrid nodded. *Agreed, once I leave, I have no sway here and will not return.*

The demon picked up the case, laughing. "You pay a king's ransom for a pauper." It pointed to the sky. "Go and plague us no more. We will now plunder with impunity. The deal has been struck by the rules of the Soul Market and cannot be broken."

The hybrid placed a protective arm around the frail Esper female. Behind him a ramp extended from the massive ship. A small grey being and a human waited at the entrance. Both Espers retreated into the vessel and the causeway retracted. The great ship's weapons portals closed and it gracefully floated skyward. The Space Mariners formed a protective wedge beside the massive craft as the vessel ascended higher into sky. A large portal formed ahead of the powerful fleet.

Aboard the ship, Erik changed back to his human form, the Esper female embraced him, weeping openly. Erik held her tight.

"*You came back for me. I prayed to the God that you would not forsake me here and He heard my prayer.*"

"I wasn't going to let you rot here. We're Esper. You're my last link to a part of me." Together they walked to the bridge.

The small alien gently patted Erik's back. "It's good to see you again, Agent Knight."

Erik smiled warmly "It's wonderful to see you Gray. You look well and you've grown quite a bit since our last meeting." Erik looked over at Sergeant Phelps. "Space seems to agree with you."

Phelps laughed. "It does, Agent Knight. I couldn't return to Earth after all I'd seen." Phelps raised an eyebrow. "Where's Shanda and your son?"

Erik tensed. "You remember them?"

Phelps nodded. "Yeah, why shouldn't I?"

"Because the timeline where my son existed and I was married was altered. Nobody on Earth except Counselor Denton knows I had a family."

"The Ethereal War." Phelps shook his head sadly. "Wow. We'd heard rumors all across the galaxy about what was going on with Earth. When we received your call we got here as soon as we could. This shit is playing out all over the galaxy and all across our universe."

"All across multiple universes," said Erik. "This was just one tiny battle on one world."

A door opened and the four entered a large comfortable control center. Erik placed an arm around the Esper female, projecting feelings of warmth and comfort. "You're safe now. I promise."

"I know I am. I am forever in your debt. I know now what you are and who you carry inside your mind. I can sense the warrior spirit burning in you."

Erik raised an eyebrow. "You know English and you can speak!"

She smiled. "Yes. I had many years in captivity to study language. Learning standard English occupied my mind."

"We need to talk a great deal later."

"I would welcome that, Erik Knight, Esper Warrior."

A taller being approached. "Hybrid, we are at the departure point, ready to leave this realm. I am repulsed that such a place exists. They are preparing to harvest souls again. Our eavesdropping equipment told us that much."

Erik nodded. "Thank you, Diplomat. I owe you a huge debt." Erik looked back at the view screen. "There are no innocent souls here?"

Diplomat nodded. "Not yet and you took the only remaining slave. The dark one is preparing the space port to receive fresh shipments of slaves and souls. We've monitored the spaceport comm traffic and several ships are en route. Right now barter is limited to low commodity goods and services as determined by the warrior, Raphael. But each merchant here is a slaver and soul trader. When those ships arrive with their cargo..." Diplomat shuddered. "The filth of our galaxy will be back in business." He gestured toward the view screen. "They are preparing, and once established, Light will have no sway here and they will continue abducting and selling souls and slaves for profit."

Erik flexed powerful muscles. "Then let's close it up for good. Signal our Mariner friends we're ending this on my mark!"

"We have seventeen plasma torpedoes prepped for fire." Diplomat stared over at a comm officer. "The Mariners are waiting word to attack."

Erik walked toward the monitor, his body glowing with

aqua fire. "Elahoano Ikatalr Anakar!" His hands gestured commanding the sky. The reddish purple skyline turned charcoal black, agitated lightning lit up the horizon. Erik turned toward Diplomat. "Let's close in on the portal."

The ships advanced slowly as lightning danced throughout the dark skies, thunder shook every corner of the Soul Market."

"Now Diplomat, let's give them our parting gift!" Erik whispered one final command. His voice cold like winter ice. "Keyatah Ankarak! Rain fire down upon them!"

The skies unleashed a torrent of lightning, exploding buildings and chewing up roadways. The Space Mariners fired in unison. Sixty-four thick ruby lances tore through the space station, slicing buildings and boring through several berthed ships. Fuel stores and other combustible liquids exploded, unleashing a sea of fire. The Observer plasma torpedoes detonated in a blinding sheen of ivory brilliance, blotting out the ships sensors. Through the sea of plasma destruction, lightning continued to fall and the Mariners' lethal beams swept over the decimated marketplace.

The Observer craft and the Mariners passed through the portal. The space faring beings continued firing through the portal until the very last possible moment.

"The portal is closed. Our instruments are detecting a violent disturbance. The entire pocket realm that contained the Soul Market is imploding. It appears our attack was enough to destabilize the gravimetric forces holding that realm together." Diplomat turned toward Erik. "We have cleansed the galaxy of a great filth."

Erik nodded, satisfied. "Will you be in any jeopardy for taking part in this?"

Diplomat laughed. "Like your firm on Earth we have weapons and defenses against the darker lords and Light does look upon us with favor." The frail alien smiled. "We will be fine." Diplomat nodded towards the ship's captain. "I thank you for the use of your fine craft. You have done a great service to our race and for the galaxy." The captain nodded once and went back to tending his vessel.

"The Mariners have signaled. They are departing for their home in the abyss of space. Five vessels have emerged into this sector. Do we intercept?"

Erik spun back. "Give the Mariners my thanks and wish them good journey." He reached for the Esper and she melted against him. "The other ships will realize the Soul Market is gone and be on their way. We've had enough destruction for one day."

Diplomat nodded as they left the command center. "Let us talk, I sense much has happened and the implications run deep."

Erik nodded. "Can she get some food and some medical care? She's been treated harshly for a very long time."

"I don't wish to leave your side, Warrior." She clung to his arm.

Erik gave her a reassuring smile. "Okay." He looked at Diplomat. "To be honest, I'm a bit hungry as well."

"I will have sustenance brought to the ship's main observation room. We can talk there over food and she can be tended to in your presence."

* * *

Several hours passed as Erik relayed the tale of the past month to Diplomat. The alien's dark almond eyes focused intently on every word. Medics had busily scanned the female Esper, feeding her healing fluids and medicines.

"So now I'm alone, the timeline of Earth rewritten, and my wife remarried and my son gone to the Ethereal Realm."

Sergeant Phelps sniffed and wiped away a tear. "I'm so sorry, Agent Knight. We'd heard rumblings on other worlds that the war on Earth was coming to a head and I've read several files on Molec in the central databank. I'm glad the Earth is rid of his influence and all is back to normal." He reached out and laid a gentle hand in Erik's shoulder. "However I'm not happy that you alone paid the price for peace."

Diplomat nodded slightly. "Now you know the burden all advance races carry, the ultimate knowledge of the eternal Great War, the struggle that never ends. Your species is not ready for this kind of awakening and awareness. The grief you carry is too much for one man. I hope you find solace in the vengeance taken against the dark enemy."

Erik flashed a wicked smile. "I don't enjoy taking life, any life. But cleansing the universe of that filth and rubbing Lucifer's nose in it does ease the burden a bit."

The medics finished their ministrations and the female Esper walked to the large window and gazed at the sparkling starscape.

Diplomat's tiny hand rubbed the corner of his mouth, a human gesture of contemplation. "The Ethereal beings are very active in the cosmos. I fear battles will take place on other worlds with other champions fighting the same cause. We can only hope with Molec back in Lucifer's custody, things will resume their normal course and both sides will follow the rules laid out in the beginning. The archdemon did his best to, as you say, tip the apple cart."

Erik sighed. "I'll never understand these rules, but Michael seemed hell bent on killing Lucifer. I know battle lust when I see it. My large blond angelic friend wanted blood and had his leash yanked by my son." Erik paused and considered that. "Or the being that was my son." He took another forkful of a something that resembled mashed potatoes but had a very pleasant fruity taste. "For now, Earth is safe. The price is paid and I gave Lucifer a kick in the crotch he won't forget as a thank you." He stared over at the Esper female gazing at the stars. "I don't know what to do with her now. I don't even know if she knows where her home is." Erik dropped his fork, wide eyed, "Holy crap!! I don't even know her name."

Diplomat laughed. "She is a gift to you, a soul mate. Life abhors a vacuum, what was taken has been returned. You just don't see it yet because you're still focused on the loss." Erik was about to respond when Diplomat cut him short. "You freed a being that's only known slavery and hardship for a millennium. You broke those shackles and gave her freedom. She saw what you were and she is bonded to you now. You are an Esper. She is Esper." Diplomat smiled. "She is a Cleric and a Companion. Just what you need right now."

"I'm married, Diplomat. Plus, she's been alive for over a thousand years and she'll be alive probably a thousand more. In less than forty years or so, I'll be dust."

The alien smiled and shook his head. "No. You are not married anymore. You said Lucifer wanted you to wallow in self-pity and loneliness but your son forbids it. He knew what we know. Life and love abhor a vacuum." Diplomat leaned forward. "Also, let me enlighten you regarding your longevity. Your genetics are not fully human. Your lifespan is far longer than you believe. Lucifer knew this, which is why he chose such a unique way to torture you. You age like an Esper Warrior. You will be around for many, many years and I look forward to a long, prosperous friendship. The space in your heart needs to be filled. You cannot go for centuries tormented by the loss of a timeline that can never be recovered. In time, you will realize she is the perfect soul mate for you. Your human bride is no longer yours. She has happiness in a new life and a new family. You need to move forward as well." Diplomat smiled. "You were compelled to free her and risk your very life to save a stranger. You were drawn to her even then as she is drawn to you." Diplomat raised his glass, "To new beginnings. Take the time to explore some of God's universe with us and explore her. You will find all that you're missing is over there looking out a portal at the stars." Diplomat pointed toward her. "Earth is not the center of the universe. We can go there if you like, though it's quite dull. You said Mr. Denton wanted you to take a vacation. I invite you to spend time here, on this ship. Explore new worlds, meet new people..." Diplomat pointed again to the shapely Esper female. "And perhaps find love again with one of your own." Diplomat smiled. "Join her, ask her name and talk. Learn about your other half and open yourself to new possibilities. When the creator allows a door to be closed he opens another one for a very good reason. You need but walk through. Embrace the future. Don't dwell upon a past you can't ever recover."

Erik narrowed his gaze. "How do you know about my lifespan?"

Diplomat tilted his head. Dark almond eyes squinted. "How do you not? When we scanned you years ago we realized your human pathology was not the dominant force in your genetic makeup. You really don't know what you are or the potential you possess. Do you?"

"No. I don't." Erik shrugged and held his hands out to the side. "How could I? I tried to bury that part of me and live as a human for my wife's sake and my daughter's."

"When you changed Erik, your whole life changed. Everything changed. You sacrificed what you were to save your daughter against the Seelak threat. You risked combat with us and the human military to save your wife, and you fought Ethereal powers to protect your son, all the while never knowing who or what you really are. At this point in time, don't you think you need to find about what you've become? I assure you, hybrid, you're far more alien than human. The dark forces have severed most of your Earthly ties. You need to discover yourself. Allow her to guide you along the journey of self-discovery." Diplomat sipped his drink while staring intently at Erik.

Erik squirmed under his scrutiny. "I dunno. I am curious and I should at least try to make her comfortable. I did free her after all and set her on this course."

Diplomat pointed. "Go."

Sergeant Phelps gave him a friendly punch on the shoulder. "The Universe is a great place, I found my wife on a distant world and I've never known such happiness." He pointed, his finger accompanying Diplomat's. "That, my friend, is your future. Embrace it."

Erik walked over to her and gazed out the large window. "I've never seen space up close like this before. It's beautiful, frightening, and mysterious at the same time."

She kept looking forward at the stars. "There is much pain and horror hidden within the beauty."

Erik smiled. "I don't know your name or anything about you."

She turned, looking up at him. "And yet you waged war against an entire realm to save me, risking your own freedom in the process. I have no words to express my gratitude or my amazement at the powers you have at your command."

"I heard your call the first time I was there," Erik's voice caught. "I wanted to free you then but I couldn't without risking..."

She touched his face. "I know. I sensed the conflict within

you. I am humbled beyond words that you would return to rescue a mere slave." She took a step back studying him. "Like you, I'm not a natural born Esper. I'm a genetic construct trained in healing and in the art of companionship. I'm telepathic, like you, and designed to give my owner exactly what he or she desires in a mate or servant. I'm genetically programmed to fulfill the needs of an owner." She reached up and her silver finger brushed his temple. Erik felt a bioelectric surge of excitement course through his body. "I know of your loss and of your pain, your whole aura reeks of it. Your mate had Esper blood. You were bonded. I sense the empty void."

Erik shook his head. "Yes, she did have a touch of Esper blood. As for you, you're free now. Free to make your own choices and answer to no one. You deserve a life and happiness like everyone else."

She smiled a sad smile. "I'm not free. I'm a genetically engineered servant. That is what I am. That is what I do. That is how I was able to survive captivity in the Soul Market for so long. I knew what my captors needed and how to act accordingly."

Erik frowned. "I don't understand. The Espers made you to be a slave?"

She laughed. "They are not the pure race you believe them to be. Overall they are good, but even some good beings can be jaded and twisted. I am the result of that twisting of technology as are you. Your purpose was nobler than mine. You were created to save a race. I was made to be the perfect concubine."

A wave of sympathy swept over him. He reached for her, placing a gentle hand on her cheek, a silver tear leaked from her blue, pupiless eyes. "I'm so sorry."

She reached up and touched his arm. "I know. I feel your compassion. For years, I have longed and desired to hear genuine words and thoughts of compassion focused toward me. Not something I created for the amusement or pleasure of another." She stepped into him. "If I am free to choose my path, I choose to be with you. Will you have me? I will walk behind you and do my best to serve you."

Erik shook his head. "I'm flattered and honored to have your company. But as an equal; you'll never walk behind me but always by my side. I don't want a slave, but I'd welcome a partner." Erik took her hand. "I don't even know your name. I should have asked you back at the spaceport as we walked together."

She squeezed his hand. Erik's heart beat faster. "In my entire life, no one has seen fit to ever ask." Burning Esper sapphire blue eyes found his deep aqua blue human gaze. Her blue light softened. "I was never given a name by those that made me." Her eyes burned brighter. "You may call me Cha'llara." Her voice rose. "My name is Cha'llara. I am a free Esper Cleric."

"Cha'llara," Erik repeated the name. "You know more of the universe than I ever will." He pointed towards the stars. "Let's explore the wonders together for a while and see what the universe has in store."

She embraced him. Erik was reluctant at first but found comfort and solace in her warmth. He wrapped his arms around her, losing himself in her touch, surrendering to her bliss.

Diplomat looked on in approval and Sergreant Phelps wiped a stray tear form his eye. "Our family just got a bit bigger."

Diplomat smiled. "Ah my friend, one can never have too much family. Love is a bounty best grown and spread among many. Let us join our friends and celebrate our good fortune."

* * *

Newton, MA. Townrise Suites

Martin Denton's jaw dropped as Michael appeared in his home. "Please don't do that! You're gonna give me a heart attack." The counselor gestured toward a large chair. "Have a seat. Don't tell me there's another war brewing."

Michael awkwardly sat, his powerful frame swallowed by the soft, overstuffed chair. The archangel leaned forward. "Nothing so dramatic, I have a message for you from your friend."

"Erik!" The old man's eyes widened. "He's dropped off the face of the Earth! Missing for over a month. Please tell me he's okay. He's been a hollow shell for almost three months now and not getting any better."

"The warrior is fine. He's been busy exacting vengeance upon Lucifer and destroying the Soul Market, permanently." The archangel actually laughed. "I heard my brother's wails of agony clear across the Multiverse and it warmed the cockles of my heart." He waved his hand and a stack of papers materialized on Denton's coffee table. "The hybrid has found some happiness with the Observers and the Esper slave girl. His return to Earth is questionable at this point. The one you call Diplomat is taking him to the far corners of this galaxy and beyond."

Denton shook his head. "Take a vacation I said, relax I said." He laughed. "I didn't mean start another freaking war or piss off the devil." He looked over at the divine entity. "I hope he finds happiness out there. I hope my friend comes back because I miss him, Michael. He's like a son to me."

"Read the letter."

Denton opened the large envelope.

Counselor,

Sorry I've been away. I had some business I needed to take care of and didn't think you'd want to revisit the Soul Market. I'm with some old friends and I've made some new ones too. But I miss my old friend and mentor. Diplomat has extended an invitation for you to see the universe and spend the rest of your days exploring the cosmos. All I can say, my friend, is that it's incredible.

Martin looked up. "I'm not going into space. I'm retiring and parking my butt in that chair and then spending three months a year in a beachfront home in the Bahamas."

"Keep reading."

I told Diplomat you'd refuse; I know you have that beach house in the Bahamas you've been waxing about nonstop for years. I just wanted to extend the invitation and let you know I'm okay and I should be home in a few months, or maybe a year, with a special friend. Please look after things until I get back. If, for some reason I don't return, there's a letter here for Brianna explaining things as much as I can and as much as she'd understand. You've been more than a friend, Martin and I hope to see you again and share my experiences.

Your friend always,
Erik

Denton looked over at the archangel. "Do you know if he'll be coming home? Or will he stay out in the cosmos."

Michael frowned as he considered the question. "Beings such as your friend are meant for conflict and war, as I am." The archangel stood up. "Let him enjoy the tranquility and companionship he's found. It will help him in the short term to accept his loss and face the challenges that lay ahead."

Denton nodded. "Yes, but then give him something else to grieve."

Michael shook his head. "You humans are pessimists." The angel vanished as quickly as he appeared.

Denton took a sip of his drink. "And you Ethereals are a pain in the ass." He stood up and walked over to the balcony, opened the glass door to stare up at the stars. "Enjoy your vacation, Erik. I'm glad you found some happiness, son. I look forward to seeing you again." He wiped a tear from his eye and headed back inside. He took one last look toward the stars before calling it a night.

About the Author

Greg Ballan is a graduate of Northeastern University holding bachelor's degrees in Marketing and Management. Greg enjoys several outdoor activities such as hiking, archery and shooting. Greg was an avid MMA fighter but realized after fifty, getting punched hurts … a lot! He discovered the safer hobby, learning the acoustic guitar. When he's not working his full-time job as a financial analyst or exploring some unknown woodlands, he's crunched over his laptop putting his warped imagination into words or penning a column about the outdoors or his latest misadventure avoiding house and yard work.